TRUST NO ONE

TRUST NO ONE
by Laurel Bradley

ISBN-13: 978-0-9898303-0-0

Book Website www.LaurelBradley.com

Give feedback to: Laurel@LaurelBradley.com

TRUST NO ONE is a work of fiction. Apart from the well-known actual people, events and locales that figure in the narative, all names, characters, places and incidents are the product of the author's imagination or are used fictitiously. Any resemblance to current events or locales, or to living persons, is entirely coincidental.

Printed in U.S.A

ACKNOWLEDGMENTS

Thank you:

God, for the countless blessings you've given me: faith, a fabulous husband, health, and talents among the many.

Tom, for your constant love and support.

Benjamin, Adam, Jacob, Emily and Daniel, for being patient when writing got in the way. Each of you kids is a blessing.

Peg, Lorrie, and Janet, for alternately cheering me on, holding my hand, and kicking my butt.

Mom and Dad, for being my personal booster club and selling copies of my books out of the back of their car.

Book club and Central WI Writers, for pointing out the individual trees in the forest. Trees are good.

DEDICATION

To Tom, my personal "happily ever after."

CHAPTER ONE

July 6—Bethesda, Maryland

This was the reason men shouldn't marry for love.

Fuad Accawi's favorite wife, the woman of his heart, skipped through the garden bubbling like the small stream that wound its way between manicured flower beds. His first and second wives would be cowering at his feet, but not Aisha. No, not Aisha. Watching her tugged at his heart. Her motions were graceful yet frenetic; her eyes unnaturally bright. Despite her promises, he'd seen her like this too many times before. Another relapse, but this time he knew who to blame.

"I believe I told you my patience had reached an end," he told her as she passed.

"I know, Fuad," she laughed, too sure of his love. "But I couldn't resist. You'll see why in just a moment." She returned to his side and slid her hand into his, her bones as thin as a bird's.

Accawi looked at his wife's face. His feelings for her had made him weak.

Near the center of the garden, a warm breeze wafted through the ornamental poppies. They followed the flagstone path around a corner to reveal Aisha's surprise.

"We simply must have this sculpture." She opened her arms as if to embrace the beautiful work of art. "Isn't it fabulous?"

His stomach lurched. There it was, The Bedouin Ship, right in front of him instead of in Consul-General Farah's office where it belonged. The three-meter-long bronze *dhow* with its lateen sail sharp as a gull's wing sailed in a sea of decorative grass. The sculpture's enameled finish depicted a Bedouin desert camp on the sail detailed with images of dromedaries and elaborate tented pavilions.

Accawi shook his head. This could not be happening. Already, the police blamed him for the death of the drug agent masquerading as his wives' personal shopper. Her killer had planted the body beside the trash just outside his back gate. Now this. He hadn't wanted to believe his assistant's call. Didn't want to believe the consul-general's missing statue had finally been located—in his own private garden.

This had to be part of the plot to discredit him.

"Isn't it fabulous?" Aisha asked.

It was breathtaking. It was inspiring. It would destroy him and his entire family. And all he'd worked for.

Allah, help me.

"Oh, Aisha. Kahil is a serpent." His heart bled the words.

"Kahil?"

"Yes, Kahil." Betrayal was bitter on his tongue. He had warned her not to have any more dealings with Kahil, her false friend, the blue-eyed Arab. "Your shopping woman was a drug agent. She recognized him. Called to him. But he lowered his head and ducked into the shadows avoiding the cameras once again." But Kahil had misjudged his timing. Accawi arrived before he could sneak out the gate. He was not near enough to hear her words, nor see the man's eyes, but no matter, his image burned in Accawi's mind.

Worse than a viper, Kahil was a demon. He was to blame for everything. Accawi hated what the man now forced him to do. He closed his eyes for a moment, preparing himself before allowing his anger to bubble to the surface, hot and caustic.

"Stupid bitch. He puts eyes and ears in his art. In this." He pointed to the statue. "Even now, he listens and laughs at your weakness, your stupidity. He wants me destroyed, and you have given him the way." He backhanded her beautiful face, knocking the most beloved of his wives to the ground.

"Fuad!" She touched her cheek, staring up at him in disbelief. Tears chased some of the drug-induced sparkle from her eyes.

"That statue belongs to the consul-general." He reached down and ripped the lace *hijab* from her head. "Do you not understand what that means? His cruelty knows no bounds. Your stupidity brings death to the entire Accawi family." He punctuated each word with angry blows of his wingtip shoes to her soft body.

"Fuad, don't." The terrified woman at his feet curled protectively around her slightly rounded abdomen. "Kahil would never—"

"Fool! He already has the police investigating me for the death of that secretary—and now this." He hurled the *hijab* to the ground.

"No." Her left eye swelled, and her black hair stuck to her damp cheeks. "There must be some mistake. Kahil will take it away. He will fix it for me."

"For you? Have you no idea how Kahil uses you?" He spat on the flagstones. She was on her knees before him, defending the bastard. He hit her again, knocking her once more to the ground. "He will do nothing. This was no accident. This is what I warned you about. He brings nothing but death, and you have helped him."

"I...I am sorry. It was a momentary weakness. He gave me a bag. A whole bag. Gave it, asking only that I do this one small favor—store this sculpture in our garden." Sobs overcame her voice. Her eyes widened as he drew a curved blade from the jeweled sheath at his side— the blade and sheath he had worn specifically for this purpose. She had given them to him as an apology for previous weak moments.

"I thought you would like the sculpture," she gasped out between sobs. "He said—"

"He said what you wanted to hear. He played you. Waved drugs before you, and you forgot all else." He shook his head like a maddened bull, embracing the anger.

"I won't do it again," she cried, cowering.

Dear Allah, how he wanted to believe her. His beautiful Aisha.

"I promise. I will be good. Please. Th...the child—"

"—has been poisoned by the drugs you take again and again. He is better dead than with you as his mother." Accawi grabbed a handful of hair and yanked her to her knees, drawing her head back to expose her throat.

He had kissed that neck, caressed those silky locks while taking his pleasure hours earlier. That was before he had received the call, before she'd fed her nose, and before they had taken this walk in the garden to see her surprise. Her beauty and ability to pleasure him made this final betrayal all the harder to take.

"Fuad, that cannot be. He gave me the bag in memory of his mother. He said she used it, and I would honor her memory if I used it as well. The powder is safe. Sons do not hurt their mothers. He said..." She blinked back tears. "I was weak. I am sorry. I promise to be better, Fuad. I promise."

He looked into her glittering, pleading black eyes. His heart hardened, leaving him empty and cold. "You have promised the same before. Your promises mean nothing now."

"B...but I love you."

"You have killed us. Do you not understand?" he shouted. "This time you have killed us all."

The pleading in her eyes turned to fear.

His throat was raw with unshed tears. She was already dead to him. Had been from the moment he had seen the glitter in her eyes fueled by Kahil's drug; from the moment he heard she had another surprise for him. This was just a formality.

"I love you. Allah, help me." He slit her throat with a hand heavy enough to cut bone. Her blood gushed, splattering the waving grass at the base of the ship sculpture.

He wiped his blade on her discarded *hijab* before

sliding it back into the scabbard. Blood seeped into the thirsty ground between the flagstones, rimming them in red. He knelt in the blood to close her eyes. Maybe he could still save his sons.

He pulled a cell phone from his pocket and dialed. His assistant answered, but Accawi cut him off. "You were right. Arrange for its removal. I want it at the consulate this afternoon. And dispose of the...the corpse. Now."

He turned his back on Aisha's cooling body.

§

October 21—Fort Wayne, Indiana

Taylor Wilson always claimed coffee brought her to life, but this morning it saved her.

In the back corner of her deep, perfectly landscaped yard, bundled against the chill breeze, Taylor balanced a particularly warty pumpkin on top of the pile already mounding her wheelbarrow. She had more pumpkins to pick but left the wheelbarrow to take a break. Crouching down, she reached behind a decorative granite boulder to retrieve her precious cup. The coffee had cooled while she'd been working, but it was still good.

She stood, looking at the house. Where was her husband, Phil? They had both been on their way outside when Sean, Phil's art agent, called. Poor Phil. She knew he'd rather pick pumpkins than talk business. She took one last sip and bent low behind the rock to return the mug.

A tremendous boom shattered the air.

In an instant of terror, she saw her wheelbarrow full of pumpkins take flight and slivers of glass slice through surrounding foliage. Flaming chunks of wood and stucco siding flew over the privacy fence into the neighbor's yard. Taylor slammed into the ground, and the world went black.

She came to on a gurney between two paramedics.

Her front yard looked like a war zone from an old newsreel or Hollywood movie. Fire engines pumped water on the smoking crater that had been her beautiful home.

Nearby houses were missing their windows. Her neighbors huddled like refugees while men and women in uniform seemed to be everywhere. Police, firemen, bomb squad...

It took only a moment for her strange new reality to turn into fear. Phil had been inside the house.

"Phil!" She tried to sit up, but a paramedic pressed her back down on the gurney. "But Phil is inside."

"There's no one inside, ma'am."

"But he was. I left him there. In the kitchen." She struggled against newly buckled straps. They'd made love, had breakfast. Bacon and eggs with whole-wheat toast. "Phil!"

She shook as she stared at the remains of the house. There was no kitchen. No bedroom. No house. Breakfast rolled in her stomach.

The paramedic looked into her eyes. "No one was inside."

She clawed at the IV in her hand. "You're wrong. I have to find him." Her head screamed with pain.

A second paramedic put her hand over Taylor's. "Relax, honey. You're going to be okay."

Taylor blinked at the EMT. The woman clearly didn't understand. Phil was inside. They needed to find him. Save him. "Phil..." The world went muzzy. Taylor struggled to gather her thoughts, but the words slipped away unspoken.

§

Six blocks away, the explosion shook Starbucks. Rattled mugs. Cracked the glass door. Sirens wailed.

Seated in a plush chair, Accawi sipped sweetened espresso. It was an insipid version of the *qahwa* Aisha made so well. The flavor was wrong. Too sweet. No cardamom. Unsatisfying, like the flames from the blast and the rising smoke. Six blocks was too distant to feel the heat. He should have been close enough to hear Kahil scream.

The Americans stood with their backs to him; faces pressed against the coffee house windows as they buzzed to each other or reassured loved ones on cell phones. Their fear fueled the air, taking the edge off his disappointment.

Accawi wiped his prints from the phone he'd used as the detonator before submerging it in his drink. He snapped the lid back in place and tossed the mess into the trash.

Gas and the artist's furnace made the perfect bomb, but Kahil's death was too fast for proper revenge. He should have suffered.

Aisha deserved better.

§

Taylor woke in the hospital emergency room with a blood pressure cuff inflating on her arm. A stern looking woman listened to her heart.

"Phil?" She wanted to look around, but a strap on her forehead and pads around her neck prevented her from moving.

"Taylor, can you tell me where it hurts?"

Her eyes strained to scan the room. "Where's my husband?" Please, please, God. He had to be safe.

Nurses poked and prodded her. "Can you feel this?"

"Yes, but my husband. He was at the house with me when... His name is Phil, Philip Wilson."

The woman looked across the room.

Taylor squirmed trying to see who the lady was looking at. "Please, where's Phil?"

The woman patted her arm. "Don't you worry. We'll have someone find him. But right now, they're ready for you in radiology. He'll be here when you come back."

Phil was here. He was fine. That's all that mattered.

§

Still immobilized after the MRI, Taylor was wheeled back to the ER. They lied. Phil wasn't there waiting.

The doctor came in and introduced himself. "I've looked at your images. You are one lucky young lady. You have a concussion and whiplash, which means we'll keep you overnight for observation. But aside from those things and some minor contusions and lacerations, you are remarkably unharmed."

She looked up at him from the stretcher. "Where's my

husband?"

He seemed confused. "Waiting room, I expect. One of the other nurses should know. I'll have them check."

After he'd gone, the attending nurse removed the immobilizer. Taylor whimpered as the woman helped her into a wheelchair. Every muscle in her body screamed in protest. Pain stabbed her neck and radiated to the top of her skull and down her back. The muscles in her shoulders burned. Her body throbbed to the beat of her heart as the nurse wheeled her to her room.

Finally tucked in bed, Taylor couldn't keep the tears from sliding down her cheeks. Where was Phil?

Her heart sped up as the door to her room opened. Finally! But instead of her husband's welcome form, a man in a dark suit filled the doorway. "Taylor Wilson? I'm Zak Peterson with the FBI." He flashed his badge. "I have a few questions for you." He crossed the room until he stood at her bedside.

She didn't give him a chance to start. "Do you know where my husband is?"

"Do you?"

Her heart froze. "Here. In the hospital."

"You saw him?"

"No. The nurse was going to get him from the waiting room, but..."

His voice was grim. "There were no other victims."

Victims or survivors? A sob caught in her throat.

"One of your neighbors saw your Volvo drive off a few minutes before the blast."

She could breathe again. Phil was okay. He didn't know she was hurt. That explained why he wasn't at her bedside. Her relief was short lived.

Before she could find out more, a barrage of questions started. "Where were you when the explosion took place? Where was Phil? Why didn't he go outside with you? Let's start when you woke up..."

She'd survived the explosion and the medical examination only to be questioned to death.

A lifetime later, the agent stepped into the hall. She sighed in relief, but he was back in a moment.

"So, your husband answered the phone, filled your mug, and told you to go outside by yourself. Did he seem different in any way? Agitated? Was this—?"

"Have you reached Phil yet?" she interrupted. They'd been through this already. "I want to see Phil." She'd have insisted they call her parents as well, but they were in Cancun and their contact information was now ash. Her brother would have it. When they let her use the phone, she'd call him.

"In a moment, ma'am. Just a few more questions."

She'd gone through the morning step-by-step. Now he wanted heartbeat-by-heartbeat. She closed her eyes, hoping he would take the hint and go away.

"Why do you think your husband left you?"

Geez! The man was relentless. "I told you before, Phil didn't leave me. He just left." The agent worded his questions to make everything sound worse than it was. "Haven't you been able to reach him, yet?" Phil didn't listen to the radio in the car, so he probably wouldn't find out about the blast until someone called him, or he returned home.

"I don't know, ma'am."

Ma'am? She was twenty-eight and looked much younger. She couldn't go into a bar without being carded, and this bozo was calling her ma'am. "Why don't you know? You are calling his cell, right? The phone at the house is gone." Every inch of her that could hurt did, and it was making her cranky.

"Can you tell me why your husband left this morning?"

"I already told you." Her neck ached so much it burned. "He was on the phone with his agent, Sean O'Hearn. Maybe Sean needed him to meet someone. I don't know. I'm sure Phil left a note on the counter. We always leave each other notes for stuff like that. I just thank God he was called away." This was the first time she'd ever thanked God for Sean. She nearly smiled at the irony.

"Do you think he knew about the bomb?"

"Bomb? Who'd bomb my house? I figured it was a gas leak or something." She rubbed her knotted shoulder. "Bomb?" she snorted. "You watch too much television. Besides, Phil would never leave me if he thought I was in danger."

"If I were in your shoes, I'd find myself wondering why he left right before the house exploded."

Taylor bristled. The nerve of this guy. "If you were in my shoes, you'd know just how stupid that question is. First, I'm a landscape designer and Phil is a sculptor. Who would bomb our house? A crazed art critic? A free-the-plants nut? Second, Phil is one of the real life good guys. He's thoughtful, kind, generous, chivalrous...For heaven's sake, he always walks between me and the road, so I won't get splashed by trucks driving through puddles or hit by some run-away car."

"Did he think someone would try to hit you with a car?"

She closed her eyes and groaned, ignoring her interrogator. It felt good to close her eyes.

"What can you tell us about your husband's family?"

A new voice.

She opened her eyes. Another suit had joined the first. It felt as if she'd blinked and they'd multiplied. Her eyes settled on her new interrogator, a dark-haired man several years younger than Phil. He seemed nicer than the first guy somehow, but maybe that was because he wasn't looking at her like she was either stupid or guilty of something. He was perched on the room's only chair, so she didn't have to strain her neck to meet his eyes while answering his pointless questions.

"His parents died in a car accident when he was in college. He has a sister, Lisa, in Florida, but they don't keep in touch." A sister who wanted to be president of the United States but ended up being an accountant. But what did that matter? She'd never met the woman. She blinked at the new interrogator. "Who are you? Have you found Phil? What does his family have to do with my house blowing up?"

"Special Agent Mark Cochran, FBI." He flashed a badge she didn't have time to read. "We haven't been able to locate your husband yet. He's not answering his cell. Is there another number where we can reach him?"

She shook her head. The movement turned the ache into a throb and sent spikes of pain down her neck and into her back. "No."

"Where was Phil born, Mrs. Wilson?"

"West Allis, Wisconsin."

"Have you ever been there?"

"No."

She fought the urge to shout her answers. "There was no reason to visit, with his parents gone and his sister in Miami."

Taylor sighed and massaged her forehead with her fingertips. Where was Phil? Had he gone somewhere with Sean? Surely, he'd heard about the explosion by now. Nothing made sense.

"I can see you're in pain. Would you like me to get the nurse back in here to get you something?"

He seemed almost nice. Taylor nodded, wincing as she did so. He left her bedside to flag down a nurse.

The more irritating of the two men continued the questioning.

"You said you were in the backyard picking pumpkins when the explosion occurred. Do you have any idea how you came to be in the front yard?"

This was a perfect example of the sort of stupid questions he'd been asking her all morning. She'd been unconscious, for heaven's sake. She took a deep breath and answered as patiently as she could. "I don't know. I'm guessing the paramedics."

"The paramedics claim you were already in the front yard when they arrived."

She held the sides of her head to keep the pieces of her skull from exploding. "I don't know. I was unconscious." Taylor groaned. "Can we be done, now?"

Agent Cochran returned to the chair. "How long has your husband been a professional artist?"

Taylor sighed. "For as long as I've known him."

"What did he do before becoming an artist?"

"Chemical metallurgist."

A long silence followed. Taylor hoped the string of questions had ended.

"Who did he work for?" The other guy's voice badgered.

She didn't answer.

"Taylor?" Agent Cochran's voice was soothing. She opened her eyes a slit. The room was so bright her eyes watered. She closed them again as he asked. "What did he do as a chemical metallurgist?"

"I don't know. Whatever chemical metallurgists do."

"Who did he work for?"

"I don't remember. It was before I met him. I only know about the chemical metallurgist part because he still does some of that with his sculptures." Taylor squinted at the man. "It's too bright in here. Could you dim the lights?"

Papers rustled. Taylor sighed. Surely, they were done now.

"Is your husband now, or has he ever been, a member of the armed forces?"

Taylor opened one eye. "No." Someone had thankfully dimmed the lights.

"Employed by the government?"

She wanted to scream, to cry from the pain. "No. He's an artist."

"Does he have foreign interests?"

Bile rose in her throat again, but she swallowed it down. "He's a sculptor. His art is marketed worldwide."

"What other languages does he speak?"

Tears pricked her eyes. "Can we stop now? My head really hurts."

"The nurse will give you something for it in a moment. What other languages does he speak?"

"None." Phil, where are you?

"That you know of."

"That I know of," she agreed with an exasperated sigh.

"Has he taken any trips to the Middle East lately?"

"I don't think he's ever been to the Middle East. His art goes places. He stays home." Sweat chilled her forehead, and she shivered.

"Has he received any overseas phone calls?"

"I don't know. Maybe. Sometimes collectors like to talk to the artist, but Sean usually handles that sort of thing. Talk to his agent, Sean O'Hearn."

"Do you have a number for Mr. O'Hearn?"

"I don't know it." She wanted to scream. She'd answered this question before as well. "It's in the phonebook."

"Any other number where he can be reached? A cell phone, perhaps?"

"He's Phil's agent, not mine."

"Sounds like you don't like him?"

"He's Phil's friend. My head hurts." She swallowed heavily.

"Do you think he had something to do with the explosion?"

Taylor groaned. Maybe she'd feel better if she vomited.

"No." She pressed her head into the pillows and closed her eyes. Sean was a pest, but that didn't make him responsible for what happened to her house.

Drums banged in her head. Light stabbed her eyes. Why couldn't the men go away and leave her alone? And where was Phil?

Someone came in with medication—a horrible banana-scented liquid. One whiff and she vomited all over the bed.

§

After evening prayers, Accawi turned on the hotel television. He lingered to see the results of his actions. The bombing led the news. Footage showed the destruction was complete. The house was a burning crater of refuse, but the sight gave him no joy and Aisha's soul no rest.

His ears pricked as the newscaster continued.

"Twenty-eight-year-old Taylor Wilson, owner of Landscapes by Design, is being kept overnight for observation at Parkview Hospital in Fort Wayne. At this hour, authorities are still searching for her husband, thirty-five-year-old Philip Wilson, who reportedly left shortly before the blast. Anyone with information regarding the location of Philip Wilson is asked to contact the Fort Wayne FBI at..."

Kahil was not dead. The authorities seemed to believe he was to blame.

"Allaha akbar." God is great. He'd been falsely blamed for the secretary Kahil killed, so it was justice that Kahil be held responsible for this attack.

Accawi laughed.

Now that Kahil knew he was coming for him, the revenge would be all the sweeter. His suffering would grow with his fear after each precious item Accawi took from him. The destruction of his home and art were only the beginning. A judiciously planted word would ensure the Feds continued to believe he was to blame. Stripped of his honor, he would then lose his wife. He would watch her terror and, unable to save her, be stripped of his manhood. His children would die unborn. When his suffering was complete, Accawi would come for him, look him in the eye and see his despair. Then Aisha would be avenged. Praise Allah.

CHAPTER TWO

Lying in her hospital bed, Taylor's pillow grew damp with tears. The agents were gone, but her husband still hadn't come. Hadn't called. Hadn't left a message. Friends had come. Anne. The Piersons. Father Dennison. Every television and newspaper reporter in the area had tried to come. But not Phil.

Each heartbeat brought a pulse of pain that burned through cuts and careened achingly across bruises to gouge her brain. Nothing the nurses gave her did more than take the edge off. Worse still, nothing helped quiet the thoughts. Time paused and stretched. The length between one tick of the clock and the next grew until Taylor was certain time had stopped altogether.

She stared into the darkness and wondered, was Phil dead? She shied away from the thought only to be drawn irresistibly back. No. He had to be alive.

It seemed clear the agents thought Phil was alive, but that's where their agreement with her ended. The agents seemed to think Phil was responsible for the explosion. But he loved her. She knew it like she knew her own name.

So then, where was he? Why hadn't he returned?

Minutes ticked into hours.

Blurry-eyed, Taylor stared at the slivers of light that seeped in around the partially open door. She closed her eyes and tried to summon the sensation of floating that presaged sleep, but it wouldn't come. Instead, scenes from the day played through her head in a continuous loop. Snippets of things. The slick, arousing feel of Phil's hands soaping her breasts in the shower. The sting of bacon fat on her hand as she turned the slices. The scent of breakfast that clung to her clothes as she left the house. The cool breeze after the warmth of the kitchen. The firm, waxy feel of pumpkin skins. Pain everywhere. Banana-scented medicine.

"Why do you think your husband left you?"

§

Sunday morning, Taylor was in the bathroom when she heard the television go on in her room. Phil! Smiling, heart racing, she opened the door. Agent Cochran occupied the chair Phil should have been in. Her smile froze for a second and then evaporated. "Oh."

"Sorry, it's just me."

Taylor looked away so he wouldn't see the disappointment in her eyes. He wasn't a bad guy. He just wasn't Phil.

He turned the television off. "There are some clothes." He pointed to a plastic bag with a red bull's eye on it at the end of her bed.

"Thank you."

"Your friend Anne brought them while you were sleeping."

She couldn't help but smile. Trust Anne to think of what she needed.

"The doctor is making rounds. He should be here soon. Once you're discharged, I'll take you to your office to get your files..."

Taylor blinked at him. What could he possibly want her files for?

"...then you'll need to tell us where you'll be staying."

Her feet rooted to the floor as her mind spun away. That's right. No clothes. No house.

"I'll stay at my office," she whispered.

The doctor rapped on the door and walked in with a nurse.

"I'll give you some privacy." Cochran headed to the door.

Forty minutes later, Taylor was dressed and sitting on the bed working the tangles from her long, damp hair when Agent Cochran returned.

A nurse held the wheelchair, but it was Cochran who spoke.

"Climb aboard and let's move out."

Agent Peterson held open the door.

Twenty minutes later, Agent Cochran and company brought her to the sprawling campus of Landscapes by Design. She was relieved the two greenhouses, small grove of potted trees and bushes, and the building which served as warehouse, showroom, and office looked exactly as she'd left them. When they were out of the car, Cochran handed her a set of keys with the Landscapes by Design logo on the key chain.

She hadn't thought about how she would get inside. Her own keys had met the same fate as the company van which had been blown up in her garage. "Where did you get these?"

"Lance. Your manager has been very helpful."

"Oh." Taylor was unsure if it was a good thing or not. She led the way to the steel employee entrance next to the oversized garage door and unlocked it. It bothered her that they had apparently already searched her office.

"How much of your husband's art have you sold?" Agent Cochran asked as they walked into the building.

"Through Landscapes?" The question gave Taylor pause. She didn't remember telling them she handled any of Phil's sculptures. "I don't know, maybe a dozen pieces."

"Do you have any here now?"

She had the feeling they already knew the answer. "Just one."

"We'd like to see it."

"Of course." She led them into the showroom where the fifteen-foot-tall sculpture stood. At a distance, it looked like an attractive tree with a brown finish, but as the viewer came closer, it became a beautiful woman in a flowing gown. Her arms were raised, and her hair flowed upwards to become branches and twigs. Leaves became butterflies. Close up, the colors were distinct and striking. Like brightly colored reef fish whose contrasting colors and patterns cause them to blend into the reef, so too did the reds and greens, purples and yellows of the sculpture blend, with distance, to a lovely brown patina.

"Wow."

Taylor smiled at Agent Cochran's response. "I know. Phil's work never fails to strike me that way."

"Does the name Maxwell Kennedy mean anything to you?"

Taylor shook her head and winced at the pain. "Should it?"

"You tell me. Your husband's art reminds me of Kennedy's paintings."

"Really?" She kept her tone polite. She'd never seen anyone's work that even came close to Phil's.

"It's uncanny how alike their work is."

Taylor's hackles rose. "That may be, but I've watched Phil work. His designs are original, and every piece is unique. I can't speak for this Kennedy guy."

She turned back to the door that connected the showroom with the warehouse.

"We're going to want to take that sculpture," Agent Peterson said.

"Good luck with that."

Agent Cochran followed her. "What did you say?"

She turned back to him. "I meant it was heavy. If you want to take it, you're going to need to get a forklift and a flatbed truck."

"So, you're saying something like this statue would be hard to steal."

"All of Phil's larger works require special bases. Most require forklifts or are assembled onsite. His smaller pieces are a different story. However, yes, I'd say something like The Dryad would be difficult to steal."

The men followed her through the warehouse asking if she knew a list of foreign-sounding names: Kahil, Aisha, Mustafa... She didn't. She led the agents past the front end loader, bags of fertilizer, and various other landscape materials into the small break room apartment. The kitchenette and lounge area looked the same as always— same Formica table and matching chairs, same castoff hide-a-bed, same pile of magazines, and rack of coffee cups. It was stunning how this could remain unchanged when nothing else in her life had.

"If someone is really trying to hurt Phil and me, will I be safe here?" As familiar and comfortable as her business was, she didn't feel safe. Not anymore.

"We've assigned a patrol."

Somehow his answer did nothing to calm her fears. She pulled a pot of cold, scummy coffee out of the coffee maker and poured the dense, bitter-smelling brew down the drain.

"We don't have time for coffee," Agent Cochran said. "We just need your computer."

"I know. I'm getting the key." Taylor pulled the used grounds out of the machine and banged them into the trash. She rinsed out the empty container before setting it aside and turning the coffee machine upside down. The spare key to her office was taped to the bottom.

The men exchanged glances.

"I lock my key in the office sometimes. No one ever looks here."

Key in hand, Taylor stood outside her office. "I don't understand why you need my computer. It wasn't used in a crime, and I need it for business."

Nasty Agent Peterson answered. "It's part of the investigation, ma'am. We don't need your approval or even your cooperation to take the machine. The only reason we asked was to expedite matters. We can get a warrant."

Every time Peterson spoke, Taylor was awed by his rudeness. Agent Cochran was a prince in comparison.

Inside her office, Agent Cochran asked questions while the jerk unhooked her PC. "What's your password?"

"Forget me not. Here, I'll write it down for you."

He exchanged another glance with his co-agent. "That's okay. I think we can remember that." He shook his head.

"Didn't anyone ever talk to you about weak passwords?"

She picked up a pencil and wrote: 4gEt-me_kn*t.

He looked at it and then looked at her with a shade more interest in his eyes before showing the paper to his partner. Agent Peterson looked at Taylor as if seeing her for the first time. Now, maybe they'd realize she wasn't as stupid as they'd assumed. She wasn't guilty either. And neither was Phil, wherever he was.

A few minutes later, she unlatched the showroom door and held it open while they used her dollies to take out her hard drive and boxes full of her files. It was like she was helping them rob her.

"We'll be back for the statue and to take you by your house."

Cochran and cranky-man had left her a copy of her designs. They'd allowed her to copy next week's schedule onto the dry-erase calendar that hung on the wall by the time clock. She should have been happy they'd left what they had, but she wasn't. She'd lost so much, and they were taking what little she had left. "When can I expect to get my stuff back?"

"We'll get it back to you as quickly as we can."

She locked the door behind them and leaned against the wall.

Why was this happening to her? Friday night when she'd driven home, her life had been normal. She and Phil had eaten pizza and gone to bed. Saturday morning they'd made love, showered and eaten breakfast. What had happened to cause the explosion? And where was Phil?

Could Cochran be right that Phil was somehow involved? Impossible. Phil was one of the truly good guys. He wasn't secretive or sneaky. He was nice. Everyone liked him. Everyone trusted him. Heck, Dr. Davidson let him in the children's zoo during off hours, so he could sketch undisturbed.

She smiled, remembering the first time she and Phil met. She'd just finished pruning the Indonesian Rainforest exhibit under Spencer the spider monkey's close supervision and constant commentary. A leaf hit her arm and stuck to her damp skin. No matter what she wore, she always left this particular exhibit sweat-covered and filthy. "I'm done, Spencer. You can stop throwing things." Dr. Davidson had told her that spider monkeys responded to threat by shaking trees and throwing things. She was lucky Spenser only threw leaves and twigs. Not that she was a threat.

Taylor unhooked the pruning platform and dropped it to the ground. The branches of the trees were moss covered in the understory making even the rough-barked dipterocarp slippery. One false step and...her left foot slipped out from under her.

"Oh!" Before she knew what had happened, she'd slid through the final five feet of twigs and leaves.

"Ook brack! Whoop! Whoop!" Spencer scolded.

She stood at the base of the tree, dusted off her backside, and ran a quick inventory. Nothing hurt. The elastic tie that had held her hair back lay at her feet and half of her hair was above her head, tangled in the branches. But barring a few scratches and shaky nerves, she was fine.

"Oook, ook, brack!"

"It's okay, Spencer."

"Whoop, whoop." The monkey paid no attention to her reassurances.

"Are you all right?"

She turned her head at the sound of a man's voice, further tangling her hair. "I'm fine, just caught." Above her head, a brilliant blue butterfly landed on her arm and uncurled its long tongue.

Phil climbed from the walkway where he'd been sketching to free her. They laughed about it later—Taylor the tree nymph caught fast as opportunistic butterflies sipped perspiration from her arms.

There was nothing then or now that even hinted that Phil was anything other than a talented artist and a nice guy. Her nice guy. Cochran was wrong.

§

A couple of hours later, Cochran picked her up in a dark blue sedan to take her to what had been her home. They turned onto her street—ground zero. Chunks of asphalt and potholes marred what had been a newly resurfaced road.

Another special assessment. Her neighbors were going to be livid.

Cochran parked behind several dark blue sedans and a big, white Bureau of Alcohol, Tobacco and Firearms van. It shouldn't have surprised her that there were other government agencies investigating the site, but it did.

A group of people milled about inside the police tape that surrounded her yard, but she looked past them. It was worse than she thought—an uncovered landfill, just dirt and pieces of things. It didn't smoke, but clear vectors of heat rose shimmering in the sunlight.

Cochran lifted the yellow tape to let her duck under. "The investigation is ongoing and will be for some time, but I'll show you around."

She walked gingerly across the uneven ground toward the crater that had been her house. This wasn't her home. It didn't even look like the shell of a house. She stared at the leaning block wall that was all that remained of the basement. Unbelievable.

Taylor could feel him watching her like a vulture. Her house. Her life. Gone. Tears sparkled in her eyes and worked their way down her cheeks.

She hugged herself, shivering despite the warmth of the sun. She shouldn't be doing this alone. Phil should be here.

Agent Cochran followed as she picked her way over the rough ground. "Did you or your husband have any enemies?"

"That would do this? You've got to be kidding." She shook her head. Pain shot up her neck.

"Who would you say were Phil's enemies?"

"No one. We have friends, not enemies."

"Professional jealousies, maybe?"

She almost shook her head but stopped herself just

in time. "No."

"Were there financial issues? Did you owe anyone money? Anyone owe you?"

"No." She didn't want to answer his questions. They'd gone through it all before. She stared at the hole in the ground. "There had to be a gas leak; something wrong with the forge."

He didn't comment. He didn't need to. The FBI didn't investigate gas leaks.

She walked along the edge of the hole. "This was our home; Phil's studio. There had to be eight or ten finished sculptures down there, and who knows how many partials. Do you know how many months of work that represents? How much money? Who would destroy that?"

Special Agent Mark Cochran remained silent. His eyes followed her every movement as she wandered through the devastation. Taylor recognized the couch—a bit of tweed on a chunk of charred wood. The mangled, blackened shell of what might have been the oven was wrapped around the scorched trunk of her huge sugar maple. Nothing remained of the tree's brilliant leaves. It was hard to reconcile what she was seeing with what had been. Granite countertops, maple flooring, cherry cabinets—gone.

She stumbled through the rubble of the garden. Had Cochran brought her here just to see her reaction?

Chunks of pumpkin rotted in the dented, overturned bucket of the wheelbarrow. She looked at the decorative boulder that had saved her. Remembered the machines needed to move and position it. Now it leaned awkwardly as if shoved by an angry giant.

Her hand shook as she touched the cold rock. At its base, close to where she'd been when the explosion happened, her mug poked out of the dirt and leaves. Taylor snatched it up, turning it over in her hands.

"What's that?" The special agent held out a gloved hand.

"M...my mug." Her voice shook as she pressed it to

her chest.

"Let me see."

She didn't want to show him. She was sure he'd take it from her. Finally, she held it out, but didn't release it even as his hand closed around it. "I want it back."

"You'll get it back."

She watched him examine it, expecting him to slide it into a plastic evidence bag. Of all Phil's marvelous creations, it was her favorite. The mug was formed of a series of Siamese fighting fish entwined in battle. It was delightful to look at, wonderful to hold—all rounded and textured, swirled in shades of azure, emerald, and crimson. She took it everywhere. It was portable, functional and, best of all, made especially for her. She was grateful when he handed it back to her.

"I had it yesterday. I think I'd been reaching for it when..." She and the mug. The sole survivors.

And her husband?

§

Taylor spent the night tossing and turning on the office hide-a-bed. Monday morning. Phil had been missing nearly forty-eight hours. The more she tried not to think about it the more it filled her head. Where had he gone? Why did he stay away? Was he all right? She climbed into the shower and turned on the hot water. Liquid fingers massaged her neck and shoulders easing her cramped muscles. If only the water could work as well on her worries.

An hour later, Taylor met her five-man crew inside the break room.

Sally pulled Taylor into her arms for a hug. "You okay?"

Taylor returned the squeeze for a moment before pulling away. "Not really."

Sally opened her arms to draw Taylor in for another hug. Taylor shook her head. "No more hugs, please. I'll cry. I..." Her voice caught, and she cleared her throat. "If we could just pretend that everything is normal, I'd really appreciate it."

Lance shot her a sympathetic glance before heading to the coffee pot. "Where are you staying?"

"Here." Taylor watched coffee splash into Lance's John Deere mug, glad she had her own now. Her new clothes felt wrong—the straps of her new bra slid down her shoulders, and her jeans were loose in the waist and tight in the thigh—but the mug felt right in her hand.

Fighting back tears, Taylor cleared her throat again. "Can we skip this for now? We've got a busy day ahead of us. We've McCarthy's to finish, so we best get started."

The compassion in Lance's eyes was her undoing. Tears trickled down her face. "Stop it, all of you. I can't do this now. I really, really just want to finish the McCarthy place." She handed out sheets with diagrams and lists of materials.

There was a long minute of awkward silence as Taylor backhanded the tears from her eyes. Her employees were like family. She felt like crap keeping them out this way. But she couldn't talk about the explosion or Phil. Not yet.

"I'm sorry," she said. "I'll talk when I'm ready. I'll probably talk so much you'll want me to shut up, but I can't do it now."

Jeff cleared his throat and held out Taylor's cell phone. "You dropped this in my truck when the battery died, and you used mine Friday."

"I did?" Her hand shook as she took the phone. Phil might have called. Left a message. She turned her back on her crew. "Get started. I'll catch up with you in a bit."

She ran to the office to plug it into the charger.

When the phone beeped announcing missed calls, she jumped.

Twelve missed calls, six voice and a text message that had come in Saturday night. Her hands shook as she scrolled through the calls. Two calls from home. From Friday. Her breath caught in her throat. Ten numbers she didn't recognize. Sure to be business related. She hit the message button, listened for the prompt and keyed in her PIN. Phil's voice. The sound squeezed her heart. He wanted to know if she'd like to go out for dinner Saturday night. Tears spilled down her cheeks.

She saved it and raced through the rest of the messages hoping one would answer her questions.

Four messages were work related. The final message was dated that morning from Agent Cochran telling her to call him when she got this message. He must have amazing resources since she'd never given him the number. She'd thought her phone had disappeared with the company van and her garage.

She called up the text message from a blocked number. No one ever sent her text messages. She hadn't thought her phone even had that feature, so it took her several tries before she was able to make the message appear.

Be smart, Tink. Trust no one. Lose the phone. Run. You know where. I will meet you. Love you always.

She stared at the message in disbelief. Tink. No one called her that but Phil, and he'd only called her that in private.

She sank to the couch and sobbed. Phil was alive. Telling her to run. Telling her she knew where. But she didn't.

Trust no one.

Why?

Nothing made sense. Where was he? Why had he gone? What was he involved in?

She shivered, not knowing what to think. The text said, "Be smart." But she didn't feel smart. She felt scared. The shrill ring of the business phone caused her to jump and drop the cell phone. It clattered to the floor. Stepping over it, she answered the landline.

"Taylor. Special Agent Mark Cochran here. You found your cell phone."

Sweat trickled down her back. It was a statement instead of a question.

"Y...yes, I..." How did he know? Had Jeff told him? Did the phone have GPS? Was the office bugged? Her stomach clenched. Trust no one.

"Did you get my message?"

"Yes, I... uh... I just listened to my messages."

"Good. Was there anything from your husband?"

He seemed to know the answers. Seemed to be testing her. "A message..." her hand shook as she picked the phone up from the floor. "...from Friday." The text message was still there with its blocked originating number.

"I'd like to hear it. Meet me at the shop entrance."

He ended the call before she had a chance to answer. She fumbled the phone into its cradle and looked at the cell phone in her other hand.

Trust no one.

She deleted the text message.

CHAPTER THREE

Her hand was damp with sweat as she handed over the phone with the message from Phil. Special Agent Cochran wrote down her PIN and listened to the messages asking questions about every caller. "Were there any text messages?"

Taylor's heart raced. Did he know? Did he know what it said? She looked at the phone in his hand as if it had betrayed her. "There was one. I was trying to get it to come up, and then it was gone. I think I accidentally erased it. I'm sorry." She gave him a shaky smile. "It was probably a wrong number anyway. Everyone knows I don't do texts." She couldn't tell if he believed her or not.

Would he be able to retrieve the text? Would he think she'd gotten it?

He would if she ran.

Trouble was, she didn't know how to run. Or where. She was supposed to know where. Plus, she didn't have any cash, and the FBI had frozen her accounts. It wasn't as if she could simply drive off. Not with a huge truck with the company logo on its side. Not with Cochran in constant attendance.

Cochran pocketed the phone. "Let's go. We have an errand to run."

She followed him into the parking lot. "So, what's the errand? You've already searched the shop, my parents' house, and interviewed everyone I know. What have you missed?"

He opened the car door for her. "Your safe deposit

box."

Reluctantly, she slid onto the vinyl seat of his navy sedan. "I don't have a key."

"Not a problem." He closed the door and rounded the car to let himself in.

She watched him with narrowed eyes. "So, what do you need me for?"

"It's easier this way. You open the box and show me what's inside, and I'm saved a lot of paperwork." Cooperation would benefit her as well. She could get a new driver's license in an hour with her birth certificate in hand.

"Are you looking for something specific or just fishing?"

"Hoping for fingerprints."

Taylor shrugged. Landscapes' showroom was too public to do them any good, and she couldn't remember the last time Phil had been to the staff lounge or her office. "I don't think that will help. He's never been arrested."

"As far as you know."

"Right." She glared at him. "Well, at least you know what he looks like. I've described him, and my parents and employees have described him. He's handsome, six feet tall, dark hair, dark eyes, well built, muscular arms, long fingers, knobby knees... You have his driver's license." Not that the license photo looked anything like Phil. He wasn't photogenic and not much for having his picture taken. He wasn't obvious about it. He was just always the one with the camera.

"Now, about that safe deposit box, which bank did you say it was in?"

§

Taylor filled out a ream of forms, had her signature compared to those on file, and authorized a fee to drill out the lock. While they waited for the locksmith, Cochran checked bank records.

"According to the log, your husband withdrew five thousand dollars and accessed this box just after your house exploded."

Taylor's heart was lead. The text message was proof he loved her and wanted her safe. But then, why did he go and empty their savings, clear out their safe deposit box, and leave her with a bomb?

He wouldn't, but apparently he had.

Her throat was sore from holding back unshed tears, and her stomach ached when she finally pulled the long box from the metal sleeve. Cochran accompanied her to the closet-sized private viewing room. She set the box on the table and stood back to let Cochran take pictures of it.

"Okay. Open it."

She didn't want to. Didn't want proof Phil knew she was in danger and left her.

She opened the lid. Her heart was in her throat. As she feared, the box was nearly empty. The paper listing the contents, Phil's birth certificate, their marriage certificate, his passport, and other sentimental artifacts were gone. In fact, the box was empty of everything except her birth certificate, a postcard, and a thick envelope with her name on the outside.

The postcard contained a picture of a beach with a single palm tree and the words, "California! Wish you were here." The instant she saw it Phil's text became clear.

A beach vacation in California was a running joke between her and Phil. Her sister-in-law's family, the Bachmans, owned a posh cabin near Huntington, Indiana, at the head of a series of bike/snowmobile trails. She and Phil had spent a week there the first winter they'd been married. The furnace hadn't started, and a raccoon had come in through the dog door in the basement. They'd spent the better part of a day chasing out the raccoon and cleaning up its mess. And the rest of the week in bed. Phil had commented, "Who needs California."

She knew exactly where she needed to go.

The little room in the bank seemed small and hot. She wished she'd driven herself, so she could leave immediately. But she hadn't, and she didn't want to raise Cochran's suspicions. She took a deep breath and held it.

Be smart, Tink.

Cochran photographed the box from several angles and gave her a pair of latex gloves before letting her touch anything.

"Okay, Taylor. Let's see what's in that envelope."

Faking a calm she didn't feel, Taylor picked up the envelope with gloved hands, opened it, and dumped the contents on the table. A note and banded packages of twenties plopped out. Ten packs in all.

Five thousand dollars.

"Oh, my goodness."

All the money he'd withdrawn.

A strangled laugh bubbled from her throat. He hadn't betrayed her. Tears slid down her face, dampening the pile of money as she picked up the note. He loved her. Her hands shook as she unfolded the piece of paper. If she'd only come here yesterday...

She felt Cochran over her shoulder as she read the handwritten note.

Stay safe. I will find you.

Call me.

Phillip

She couldn't help shooting a smug smile at Cochran.

Still, there was something more there. She looked back at the note. The handwriting was Phil's, but the signature was wrong. He never signed anything with his full name. And besides, Philip had only one "l", not two.

"Do you normally keep cash in this box?" Cochran broke into her thoughts.

She shook her head. "This proves it. He knew something was wrong, but when he left, he didn't know I was in danger."

"This proves nothing."

It didn't matter what he thought. She was right.

He picked up the postcard and handed it to her. "Tell me about the postcard."

Afraid her hand would shake, or she'd do something to give everything away; Taylor held her breath as she took it from him.

"Uh...I don't know what to say. We never went to California together."

His eyes bored into her.

Sweat trickled down her back. "I went as a kid, but I don't think he's ever been there."

"Does your husband have family in California? Friends?"

"No." She shook her head. "Not that I know of."

She picked up the pile of cash while Agent Cochran slipped the postcard and note into evidence bags. He held his hand out for the money.

She held tight to the cash. "My house exploded. You've frozen my personal bank accounts, taken my computer, and all my files." Her voice cracked. "I need this money. If you want these bills, you need to provide me with others just like them."

He bagged the money as well. No replacements. She glared at him, silently wishing him ill while he dusted the box for prints.

He swore when the powder stuck to everything. "Damn box has been coated with oil."

She bit her lips to keep from smiling. Served him right.

§

Several hours and a couple of stops later, they returned to Landscapes by Design.

"Thanks for taking me to the grocery store. I've never gone shopping with an FBI agent before. It was... enlightening." Actually, it was nerve wracking. She'd wanted to go alone. Possibly leave for the Bachman's directly afterward, but Cochran had insisted on taking her. She'd wanted to get instant on-the-run food but, because of his presence, had been forced to buy normal food.

As soon as Cochran shifted into park, Taylor opened her door and got out of the car to grab her groceries.

Cochran appeared at her elbow, cell phone in hand. "Jacobs, status." He listened for a second. "Copy that." He snapped the phone shut. "Taylor, let me get those."

"I got it, thanks." She'd had the food bagged in plastic,

so she could carry them all in one trip.

"Don't be ridiculous, Taylor." He reached around her and hooked two bags in his left hand.

Taylor bit her tongue to keep from protesting. Anything she said would make it look as if she were trying to get rid of him. And while that was true, she didn't want him to become suspicious. "Thanks."

At the utility door, he waited while she unlocked it. "I'll lead."

She froze, uncertain whether his vigilance made her feel safe or worried. Everything seemed normal to her, but Cochran looked around as if expecting someone to jump out at them. Her heart pounded. He checked the lock on her office door and poked his nose into the restroom. At least, he hadn't pulled his gun. She followed several feet behind, just in case. She purposely didn't catch up with him until after he'd set down his bags in the break room.

"I thought you said I was safe here."

"You are. Jacobs kept an eye on things while you were out. The place is clear."

"Good." She set down her bags. "What was that all about? Are you trying to scare me?"

"Not at all. Just double checking." He plopped down on the couch. "You're safe. Just stay in tonight. I'll stay with you until after the shift change."

So much for packing up quickly and sneaking off to Bachman's cottage as soon as he left.

Cochran's cell phone rang. "Cochran." He listened. "Copy." When his phone was back in its case, he got up from the couch. "That's it for me then. You have a good night."

She followed him to the door and locked it behind him. She checked the garage. Her truck with the business logo adorning the cab doors beckoned. "Soon," she told it. Tonight she'd pack and work out the details. Tomorrow morning, instead of driving to the work site, she'd drive out of town. It wouldn't be hard to lose the FBI in rush-hour traffic. They wouldn't know she was gone until they arrived at the work site and discovered she'd disappeared.

The following morning, she awakened early and discovered one of her staff had used the last of the coffee beans. She could have sworn she'd seen a bag last night next to the coffee maker. Grumbling, she slid on her new jacket, grabbed her new purse and the truck keys before heading into the dark morning. She hadn't slept more than ten minutes in a stretch last night. If she was going to function at all, she needed coffee.

§

Accawi stood in the silence of Taylor's sales office with her bag of coffee in his hand. He watched her pull out of the garage and onto the dark street. He hadn't expected her to leave this early, but he was ready for this next strike against Kahil's woman. He sniffed the beans. This was the way coffee should smell—rich and spicy. Too bad the brown bag was unlabeled. This was a blend he would have his wives get for when he traveled.

Accawi smiled as a blue sedan accelerated after Taylor's Landscapes by Design truck. Her sudden departure caught the agent unaware. As the car passed beneath the street light, Accawi saw the agent on the phone, probably calling in Taylor's movements and requesting backup that would arrive too late. It was already too late. He'd nearly finished what needed doing.

Accawi tucked the coffee into his left jacket pocket, set the timer and slipped out the door, disappearing into the predawn. The near miss would terrify the woman. Her cries of terror would slap Kahil. Show him he was helpless to protect his own. Perfect.

§

Taylor's truck nearly drove itself to Starbucks out of habit. She grabbed her purse and was pleased to see she'd automatically taken her mug along. Smiling, she picked it up and climbed out of the truck. It wasn't until she saw the blue sedan pull into the lot behind her that she realized she'd also brought along a tail. She was an idiot. If she made the FBI agent think she was a flight risk, her flight would end before it began. She waited for the agent to park before walking to his car.

He rolled down the window.

"I'm sorry. I forgot about you. I woke up, discovered I was out of coffee and..." She was certain she sounded as flustered as she felt. "...I'm really sorry. Can I buy you a coffee?"

In the store, she sat in the overstuffed chair and poured her grande extra hot latte into her mug. The agent stood by the coffee display talking on his cell phone. With her mug in hand, she watched the sun rise. She was pretty certain the agent believed her story. After all, it was true. She was going to have to pay close attention. If whoever was assigned to her for the day seemed reluctant to let her go to work, she might have to change her plans and postpone leaving. Geez, she hoped not.

She heard the boom halfway across town and froze, shaking in her seat, spilling scalding coffee.

Not a bomb. Just a loud noise.

She opened her eyes. Oh, God. A loud noise with billowing smoke in the direction of Landscapes.

She sat in Starbucks, staring out the window.

Her house. Her business. Things like this didn't happen. Not to anyone. Especially not to her.

Her hands cramped around the strap of her purse and the handle of her mug.

She became aware someone was trying to talk to her. Remarkably, Cochran appeared in front of her. He gently steered her to his car, gave her truck to the bomb squad, called her parents at home and took her to a safe house.

§

Phil keyed in the code for Taylor's mug, reaffirming that she, or at least it, was at the safe house before he hacked into her email. Shit. It was full of unopened messages. He knew Cochran and company had taken her computer, but it shouldn't have mattered. Most people would have gone to the library or, in Taylor's case, a coffee shop with computer stations to access their account. But, no, not his Taylor.

He dialed his answering service and then the area code and 744-5547. No messages.

Damn. Why didn't she call?

He'd made the messages cryptic enough to confuse any watchers, but they should have been obvious to Taylor. If she got them. She was smart and resourceful, but she was under Cochran's eye. Maybe she hadn't had the opportunity to act on them. He sighed. Maybe she hadn't even gotten them. To be honest, the text had always been a long shot. She didn't text, and he had no idea where her phone was that morning. Without the phone, would she think to check her messages? Not if her email inbox was any indication. Still, the safe deposit box should have been a sure thing. If Cochran gave her access to its contents.

He rubbed his tired eyes.

This wasn't supposed to happen. The mission was failsafe. He was anonymous. Sean was the front man.

Leaving was supposed to have drawn the danger away. Sean was sure the Volvo was bugged. The information leak made Phil the target, not Taylor. Please God, not Taylor.

Phil glanced again at the artist's sketch of the man who left his cell phone in a cup of sweetened espresso following the first bombing. Fuad Accawi. Iraqi's Consul-General Farah's head of security. The man suspected in DEA agent Carrie Sheffield's murder. The man who'd unsuccessfully targeted Sean. The one who was now after him.

Two bombs. He could easily imagine how frightened Taylor had to be. Man, what he wouldn't give to hold her and tell her she was safe. But there was no way he would risk exposing the safe house and putting her at risk again. No, the best way to protect her was to catch Accawi and plug the leak. Still, he had to let her know she could trust Cochran. If he could. If she would just call. He pressed six and followed the menu directions, keying in his PIN to change the message. The canned voice prompted him to, "Start recording at the beep."

CHAPTER FOUR

Lying atop the roof of an apartment building adjacent to the safe house where Taylor Wilson was hiding, a dark-haired man watched through the scope of a sniper's rifle. He knew she was somewhere inside, but the closed curtains masked her exact location. He needed to flush her out, so Accawi could hunt her down. There'd been too many bombs already. He couldn't allow Accawi to use another.

It was imperative to maintain the wider profile they'd established. The sloppy killing of the low-level operative outside Accawi's estate was a start. A sloppy killing, two non-lethal bombs, and a nice sniper shot. Diversity was important. He couldn't let the man appear too predictable because that's what helped profilers catch killers. Patterns.

He focused on the front door. Should he send a bullet through the picture window in the living room, or the double hung window in the bedroom?

A green pickup truck blocked his view for a second as it turned into the driveway. He shifted a fraction of an inch to look over the scope. Even from a street away, Taylor's truck with the Landscapes by Design logo on the door was clearly recognizable. He smiled. He hadn't expected the truck. He'd used Peterson's voice to order its delivery because Cochran had already refused to return it and risk the security of the safe house. Cochran was a rule follower. Peterson was a jackass. Creating a conflict between them weakened Taylor's protection and made her an easier target. The order had the side benefit of casting doubt on Peterson. When they were forced to move Taylor, their boss, Tim Rogers, was certain to wonder what prompted Peterson to give away a secure location.

The gunman raised binoculars to his eyes in time to watch Peterson explode from the house. The poor driver's ears were going to blister. The shooter grinned. Perhaps he'd take out a person instead of a window.

§

Taylor sat at the safe house kitchen table sipping coffee when she heard the unmistakable growl of a diesel motor. Her truck? She stood, drawn to the living room window. Cochran told her she wouldn't get it back any time soon.

"Get back here." Her present babysitter, Special Agent Peterson, grabbed her arm, stopping her as she tried to walk past him. She shook her arm from his grasp. He hadn't improved with familiarity. He pointed to the chair she'd just vacated. "Wait here. I'll see who it is." She refused to look at him. The jerk waited and watched until she was seated before leaving.

It had to be her truck. She'd recognize the sound of its engine anywhere. As soon as she heard the front door close, she raced into the entry and peered through the glass. It was her truck all right. Her escape plan was back on.

When she'd come up with the idea, she'd worried her disappearance might get someone in trouble, but she didn't mind leaving on Peterson's shift. She spun away from the door and raced to the bathroom. Inside, she turned the shower on, grabbed her bag of personal items from under the sink, locked the door and left, pulling the bathroom door closed behind her.

The plan hinged on her assumption that they'd stash her truck in the garage. She fumbled with the lock on the door between the kitchen and the garage. Inside the garage, she relocked the door and pulled it closed. If Peterson and crew didn't put the truck inside the garage, she'd escape through the people door and get to it in the driveway.

Her heart beat double time as she ducked behind the full garbage cans. The fishy stench of Peterson's discarded sardine cans colored the air. She crouched low and pulled the collar of her shirt over her nose. The spare truck key in her pocket poked her right leg, the discomfort oddly reassuring. The overhead light went on as the garage door opener motor engaged.

Crap. She'd forgotten about the light. She was too obvious where she was, but there wasn't time enough to move or find another hiding place. This wasn't like a normal garage with bicycles, lawn furniture, gardening supplies and a lawnmower. It had two stinky garbage cans just outside the kitchen door and nothing else. She made herself as small as possible, trying to keep to the trash can shadow. How had she possibly thought she'd go unnoticed?

She watched the garage door inch open revealing the tires and then the front bumper of her truck. When the door reached the top, the truck rolled inside. Would the driver kill the engine and then hit the button and wait for the door to close? Or would he leave the truck and close the door as he went into the house?

Diesel exhaust belched in a nauseating stream from the back of the truck. It permeated the fabric of Taylor's shirt and filled her nostrils before the engine died. The agent stepped from the truck onto the concrete floor. Black dress shoes. Gray dress pants. Peterson. The door slammed shut. If Taylor could have merged with the floor or the garbage cans, she would have. She kept her eyes low. Maybe if she didn't look at the driver, he wouldn't look at her.

The soles of his shoes tapped against the floor as he rounded the front of the truck. He was nearly to her when he stopped.

The breath caught in Taylor's throat. She squeezed her eyes shut. Keys jangled. Taylor's ears pricked, but she didn't move a centimeter. More rustling. Taylor's lungs burned with the need to breathe. The knob to the kitchen door rattled. Opened. The garage door opener motor roared back to life as the door began its descent. The utility door slammed shut.

Taylor exhaled. She stood and hit the garage door opener button next to the kitchen door. The overhead door paused in its descent. One more tap and the door was once again on the rise. In an instant, she was in the cab jabbing the key into the ignition.

This shouldn't be working. Peterson should be opening the door, pointing his cursed finger.

She shifted into reverse and pulled out of the garage. The utility door sprang open, and Peterson ran toward her. Several heartbeats later, she was out of the driveway and accelerating down the street. She glanced in the rearview mirror expecting to see Peterson climb into the blue sedan parked in front of the house, but the sedan was missing. One moment Peterson was in the middle of the road waving his hands and running after her. The next, he dropped out of sight. Had he tripped? It didn't matter. Without a car, he didn't have a chance of catching her.

She'd done it.

Taylor's hands shook as she turned off the quiet street onto another equally quiet one. There were no cars in the rearview mirror. No cars driving down the new street. Should she take side roads or main ones? Head directly toward Huntington, Indiana, and the Bachman cabin, or drive in the opposite direction to throw off any pursuers? She imagined Peterson screaming instructions in the safe house phone. How long did she have?

Sweat trickled down her back. She had an irrational urge to giggle. She was fleeing a safe house. Running away from the FBI. It was the only way to find Phil and figure out what was going on. Ha! Her mother was going to have a cow.

§

The sun was low in the sky when Taylor pulled the truck into the Bachman's driveway. The icy breeze surprised her as she hurried to the front door and knocked. She looked through the decorative sidelight hoping to spot Phil. Nothing.

Silly. He wouldn't answer the door if he were hiding, would he?

She left the door and picked her way through the shrubs to the side of the cabin. The last time she'd been there, the key to the back door had been hidden inside the electrical outlet box. She prayed it still was.

She flipped open the lid and felt inside until her finger hit the key. Bingo. She shivered as a gust of wind whirled past carrying a few white flakes. Was that snow? Indiana didn't get snow this early.

The inside of the cabin was warm. "Phil?" She pulled the door closed behind her and called his name a little louder. She was certain he would be here. "Phil?" Despite the truck in the drive, she was afraid to turn on a light and announce her presence to the world. She felt her way to the kitchen utility door.

The garage smelled of old oil and dried leaves. She hit the glowing garage door opener button. The deep rumble of the opener motor and the sudden blaze of light made her flinch. *Déjà vu.* She fought the urge to lift the door to hurry it open. The darn truck with her business's name plastered all over it seemed like a bullhorn announcing her presence. She wouldn't feel safe until it was out of sight.

Outside, a thin layer of snow melted on her windshield. Taylor hugged herself as she rushed to the truck. With the way it was coming down, it looked like she got here just in time. As she rounded the back of the truck, she noticed that the rear passenger side taillight was broken. She skidded to a halt. All that remained was bent chrome and a few shards of broken plastic. Crap. When had that happened?

Back in the darkness of the kitchen, she set her plastic grocery bag of belongings on the table. Where was Phil? The postcard said he would be here.

It was clear he wasn't.

When her eyes adjusted to the dim light, she looked

around. A business card and a stack of cash sat beside her plastic bag in the middle of the table. Her heart thudded as she picked them up. The business card felt slick and plastic coated beneath her fingers. It was too dark to read, but instead of flipping on a light, she carried the card and money into the windowless powder room just off the kitchen. She closed the door and fumbled for the light switch.

What she'd thought was a business card was actually a pocket Notre Dame Football schedule. The stack of cash turned out to be ten twenties. She looked from the money to the card and back again. That's it? She expected Phil, or at the very least, a note from him. Not that she couldn't use the two hundred dollars. She could. But was the money even meant for her? She set it down on the counter next to the sink and focused on the card. Notre Dame Football. There had to be a message somewhere. She flipped it over.

Call Phillip

Again with the two l's. It had to mean something. Phil wouldn't misspell his own name.

Her chest ached. He had to know their home phone was gone. He had to know the FBI was monitoring his cell phone. How could she call him? Her eyes burned with exhaustion. There had to be something else. Another meaning. She stared at the card until it blurred before her eyes. Notre Dame Football. Crap. At least the money was for her. She tucked the two hundred dollars and the schedule in her pocket before flicking off the light and returning to the kitchen.

Now what was she supposed to do?

Wind blasted the windows with snowflakes. The ground and trees were quickly becoming covered in white.

Her stomach growled reminding her she hadn't eaten all day. Taylor lit the burner beneath the teapot on the stove and then worried the gas flame was too bright. Maybe Phil had just stepped out and would be coming back. No. She knew that was a lie. He wasn't coming back. It probably wasn't safe to stay here. But where else was she supposed to go?

The snow swirled around the streetlight like angry bees around a hive. Not good.

At least she could see if he'd left some other sign and make certain she was alone. Armed with a frying pan, she systematically searched the dark house while the water boiled.

There was no sign of Phil or anyone. No one hid in the closets, under the beds, or in the basement. The storm looked equally bad from every room in the house. Back in the kitchen, she pulled a packet of instant soup from her bag and dumped it into her mug.

Taylor pulled an afghan off the back of the couch and wrapped it around herself. She settled in the corner with her cup in hand. As soon as the storm broke, she'd leave for Notre Dame. It was the only thing that made sense. Except it didn't. Where was she supposed to look at Notre Dame?

Call Phillip.

The double 1's looked like eleven. Was it a time? A date? An address? What else could his message mean? Goal posts? Score? He'd directed her to come here. Did that mean she was safe? That she should sit tight until he came back? Darn it, Phil, how was she supposed to know? She wasn't a secret agent. Tears burned her tired eyes.

Outside, the sky glowed and snow fell. Regardless of whether it was the smart thing or not, there was nothing she could do at the moment but sit. No one was going anywhere. She finished her soup and set the mug on the end table. A swirl of white battered the window. Snow on snow. Her eyes drifted closed.

It was still snowing when she woke in the morning.

The road out front was an unbroken sea of white. Out back, it looked as if there were six inches of snow on the roof of the shed. She'd never get her truck out.

She turned on the television and wasn't surprised to hear that the storm had smashed the snow accumulation records hours ago. The meteorologist claimed the blizzard would continue most of the day. She folded the afghan and returned it to its spot before heading to the kitchen with her mug.

She pulled the money and schedule from her pocket and examined them again in the light of day. The money was just money.

Call Phil? Was that safe?

She looked outside at the snow. No one could reach her because of the storm. By the time it cleared, she'd be gone.

She picked up the phone and dialed Phil's cell.

It rang and rang, eventually launching into his recorded message. "You've reached Phil's phone. I can't answer right now, but you know the routine. Leave a message at the beep." Her throat grew thick as she listened to his voice all the way to the beep before hanging up. She called once more just to hear him.

Okay, she told herself, setting the receiver in its cradle. That's enough of that.

Calling Phil wasn't the clue. He had to mean something else. Was it code for something? A Notre Dame hooded sweatshirt was draped on a chair. She picked it up and searched it. There was no message pinned to it, nothing in the pockets, and nothing strange with the cuffs or the seams. Had Phil put it there or had it been left by someone in Marlene's family?

Nothing else was out of place in the entire house. There wasn't even scrap paper by the phone.

She should go. But where? Huge snowflakes swirled outside the window. She'd never seen this much snow this early in the season. If she left now, she'd end up in a ditch. If she could even get her truck out.

Call Phillip.

She looked at the phone. Had he contacted her parents? It didn't seem likely. The message hadn't been call your mother. Still, she couldn't think of another option. At the very least, her parents would be frantic. Their worst nightmare repeated. It might be her last chance to touch base with them. She'd be leaving as soon as the snow stopped, and who knew what would happen next? Heck, she'd already tipped her hand with her call to Phil's phone. She dialed her parents' number.

"Where are you?" Her mother nearly screamed the words as soon as she said hello. "You left the safe house without a word to anybody. We thought you'd been kidnapped..."

"I'm sorry. I know I should have called earlier. I'm fine."

"Where are you?"

"It doesn't matter. I'm not going to be here for long."

"I want you to come home. You need protection."

"I don't seem to be safe anywhere." Outside the kitchen window, everything was white on white. She didn't like the lack of definition. Something could be out there, and she wouldn't be able to see it. "Look, Mom, has anyone called for me? Left a message or anything?"

"Agent Cochran called. You have to let him help you."

"He wasn't much help before."

"Maybe he didn't think you were in real danger. We didn't think you were. You didn't think you were."

"I know." She stared outside the window, and then something caught her attention. Had that drift been there a minute ago? The snow swirled before the window.

"Tell me where you are. Or better yet, call him. Let me give you his number. Do you have a pen and paper?"

"No, Mom. That's okay. I'll be okay."

"No you won't. You're just a gardener."

Taylor winced. Just a gardener. Why didn't anyone but Phil ever see how capable she was? She could move seemingly immovable objects—boulders, trees. It was all about planning and leverage. The right force at the right angle. She would find him, and they'd prove his innocence together.

"Agent Cochran is a professional," her mother continued. "You need to trust him to take care of you."

Phil's text message came back to her. Trust no one. "I don't want Agent Cochran to reach me."

"Why not?"

Taylor didn't know what Phil was involved in or why

he hadn't come to get her, but she knew Agent Cochran would never help her in the way she needed.

She took a deep breath and edged away from the window. She was a sitting duck where she was. If someone was out there. "I was hoping maybe you'd heard something from Phil or someone? Got something in the mail?"

"No." Her mother's voice sounded sad and sympathetic. "I keep hoping, too. Agent Cochran called with more questions. He seems sure Phil is to blame somehow, but I know he is as much a victim as you are in this."

"Thanks, Mom."

"Which is why I'm worried. I'm afraid something happened to him, and I don't want it happening to you. He wouldn't want you hiding God-knows-where. He'd want you to come home where we can keep you safe. You might as well tell me where you are, or I'll just star-six-nine you."

Crap. How did she think she could elude the FBI and find Phil when she forgot something as simple as star-six-nine? She was a landscape architect, not a spy. She was going to need to act a whole lot smarter if she hoped to stay free long enough to find Phil.

"I've got to go, Mom. I love you. Tell Dad I love him." She hung up over her mother's protests and unplugged the phone to keep her mother from calling back.

Now that Taylor had compromised her location, she needed to leave immediately.

There was no time to wait for plows or to dig out the driveway. Besides, if star-six-nine was a giveaway, so was her easily identifiable truck. By now, the FBI would have a trace on it. Good girl. Now you're thinking like a spy. Mentally, she patted herself on the back. She had to get the snowmobile from the shed. With this much snow, a snowmobile could go anywhere.

The feeling that she was being watched began as a tightness in her shoulders, an itchy sensation in her spine. She stepped out of the hall closet where she'd been searching for a snowmobile suit. She looked over her shoulder at the window. Was that a shadow? She had only just called. How could they have found her so quickly? But something had definitely just passed the window.

Oh, God. Somewhere, despite the storm, someone was watching. She should be gone already. Sidling out of view, she raced to collect what she needed. Her mug was wrapped in a hand towel cushioned by clothes in the middle of her borrowed duffel bag. She added two Ziploc bags, one containing instant soup, dried fruit and granola bars; the other a bar of soap, toothbrush and toothpaste. She took the money from her pocket, slipped it into another Ziploc bag along with her newly replaced driver's license and credit card, and then taped the entire package to the inside of her pants. She found someone's old white ski jacket and matching bib snow pants in the hall closet next to another Notre Dame sweatshirt.

Notre Dame. The words jarred her.

Phil's message was on a Notre Dame Football schedule. That had to mean something. The sweatshirt had to mean something. There weren't any other personal items out of place; no shoes by the door, no clothes or papers left about. Nothing. That sealed it. It had to be where Phil had gone. So, that's where she'd go. Notre Dame was only about seventy miles from here. She would go there and find him.

She zipped the jacket with shaking hands, grabbed a pair of sunglasses, and pulled on the heavy thermal snow boots. If someone was outside watching, they'd be focused on the doors. They wouldn't expect her to leave by the dog door.

She pounded down the basement stairs to the doggy door that allowed the resident pet access to the caged run in the backyard.

Outside the pet door, the plastic weather curtain hung stiff with snow. Taylor got down on all fours. Pushing the duffle bag in front of her, she crawled into the snow-choked run. An icy blast had her wishing she could turn around and go back inside, but she had to get out of here while she still could.

She clutched the duffel to her chest and stood, back pressed against the rough concrete-block of the house, as she surveyed the yard through the snow-encrusted chain-link fence. Nothing but white on white. Hopefully, that's all that anyone else would see as well.

Wearing the duffle bag strap across her chest like a purse, she followed the fence to the gate. She fumbled with the latch, but the gate wouldn't move. On the other side of the enclosure, something moved—a shadow raced toward the far gate.

Her heart lurched. No! She threw her body against the door in jarring shoves that rattled the gate but didn't move it. Oh, God, please. Snow stung her face as she kicked along the bottom bar in a vain attempt to wrench it free from the ice. Another series of body slams moved the door a hand's width. The man in white had the other door open.

Taylor threw herself at the gate. Open, dammit. She rammed herself against the door again. This time it flew open. She fell into the yard.

She didn't pause to look over her shoulder.

She scrambled to her feet and ran like hell.

CHAPTER FIVE

Taylor burst into the shed and locked the door. Her hands shook. The swirl of wind and snow was bright. The shed was dark. She yanked the glasses from her face, stumbled to the snowmobiles and whipped the dusty cover from the closest machine. The key was in the ignition. Thank God. She grabbed the helmet from the seat and jammed it on her head.

Damn. The other sled had a key in its ignition, also. Shit, shit, shit. She stripped the second sled and shoved the key into her pocket.

The door rattled.

Hurry, hurry.

She lifted the bar off the double doors at the back of the shed and opened one before leaping astride the machine. Start, start. She pressed the choke and turned the key. Nothing. Not even a click. Her eyes widened at the betrayal. Dead battery.

God, please. She was on the second sled, fumbling the key out of her pocket and into the ignition when the side door broke open.

Please, please, please. Choke. Key. Start, darn it. Two men rushed through the open double doors in front of her as the sled roared to life.

"Move," she yelled, hitting the throttle. The sled hurtled forward.

The men lunged at her. One man hit the front of her machine and bounced off. The other? Taylor didn't look back. Flying out of the shed and across the yard, she raced to the street. A too-sharp turn made her lean and cling. She struggled to keep on top of the sled. Sweating, she recovered her balance on the road and bolted. Nearby was the park, with its biking/snowmobile trails. She knew the trails. She'd biked them with Phil.

Visibility was poor, made worse by the fogging helmet visor. Flipping it open, she lost her protection. Snowflakes and wind blinded her. Still, she didn't slow. No one would be out. No one in their right mind, at any rate.

Once in the park, she used the darker tree line to find the trailhead. She knew three trails converged there. She searched the whiteness. The first trail she spotted swung toward the house. Not that one. The second one looped into town. Crap. Where was the third? She stopped the sled and scoured the tree line. Left. Right. Where was it? One, two... She needed the third trail which headed toward South Bend. Nothing. The sled idled beneath her. Her pursuers would be there any moment. Where the heck was it?

Her eyes snagged on a break in the trees further down. There. That's right. It was separate. Now, she remembered.

She hit the throttle, and the sled leapt forward.

Snow swirled. Minutes ticked by. Her eyes hurt as she struggled to follow the trail in the storm.

Once the trail ended, Taylor made certain she pointed the sled so the dash compass read northwest. More or less. A country lane led her to a farmer's field. She raced cross-country. The Bachman's sled gobbled ground. Barreling toward fence posts she only saw at the last minute, she squeezed the brake lever and jerked to a stop. Blood hammered in her ears. She stared at the barbed wire stretched between the posts. Holy... Running full speed into one of those would stop her flight in a hurry. She rode more slowly, trying to spot a break in the fence through the swirling snowflakes. Traveling as the crow flies was only good for birds.

Back on the road, she roared unrestricted for some

time. For a couple of hours, the minor roads were hers, but as the day progressed more and more fell under the plow blade. Then she rode the ditches going up and down huge drifts at every intersection.

She tried following snowmobile tracks through fields and woods when she saw them, but most of the trails looped back on themselves, and she found herself traveling in circles. The real trails weren't open, a fact she was reminded of when she stopped for gas.

She stood beneath the protective canopy watching the cents turn to dollars when a blue sedan slowed and pulled into the gas station. As it crept past her, she could feel the driver's eyes on her.

Cop. The breath caught in Taylor's throat. Act natural.

She looked at the gallon meter. How much gas did this tank hold? It had to be almost full.

The car pulled to a stop beside her. She turned to ice where she stood with her hand fisted around the pump handle. The driver's window rolled down. Despite the cold, sweat dotted her brow. Any moment now the passenger door would open, and his partner would jump out and grab her. She was done for.

A man in an orange cap leaned his head out the window. "Make sure you stay in the fields. The trails ain't open 'cuz the water ain't frozen. My brother sunk his sled last year."

"Thanks." Taylor nearly sagged in relief. "I'll be careful."

The handle clicked. Her entire body jerked in response. Tank full.

The man beside her raised his window and pulled up to the adjacent pump. Taylor's hand shook as she replaced the nozzle and screwed on the gas cap. She swung her leg to mount and then remembered she hadn't paid. That would get her noticed for sure.

She didn't breathe normally again until long after the station and the road it was on disappeared from her rearview mirror.

As evening approached, the snow trailed off and the wind died. The sun was no more than a glow in the west as she chased it toward the horizon. It was full dark when she reached the outskirts of South Bend. She prayed she would find Phil at Notre Dame.

All day long, she rode toward South Bend focusing on escape. She looked at the dash. The gas gauge had slipped into the red again. She was going to have to abandon the borrowed sled and find another way to the campus. The bad guys knew she was on a snowmobile. She couldn't fill her tank this close to the school.

The country road she was following was unlit. She needed a country tavern or something. She needed a person she could ask for a ride into town. She glanced at the gas gauge hoping she would have enough gas to get her there. A light glowed in the distance. She headed toward it praying it was a bar.

As she neared, the bar turned out to be a farm house. The light she'd hoped illuminated a sign was a yard light on top of a utility pole. She made note of it as she rumbled past. The needle was firmly in the red now. She needed to find a place to stop soon.

The darkness stretched before her. As she mounted a rise, the engine sputtered. Great. Just great. Getting stranded in the middle of nowhere was not the plan. The engine perked up as the sled leveled off. At the bottom of the long hill, a neon sign proclaimed the Eagle's Nest was open for business.

Thank God.

The engine coughed. Too bad snowmobiles didn't coast.

Taylor made it through the parking lot and around back on fumes. The engine died just outside the circle of lights between the backside of the building and a tree trunk.

The snow-covered branches hung low. Taylor ducked beneath them to strip off her helmet and bib-snow pants. They were too big to fit in the sled's storage compartment, so she stuffed the pants in the helmet and left them both on the seat. She exchanged heavy snow boots for tennis shoes and swung her duffle bag over her shoulder. She was as ready as she was going to get.

Outside the door, she stopped to brush off snow, smooth her hair, and rehearse the story in her mind.

The scent of smoke, fried food, and stale beer greeted her in a thick heated blast as she tugged open the door. Quickly scanning the room, she found an empty stool near the end of the bar next to a woman in her mid-thirties. She hoisted herself up and rested the duffle at her feet. Over in the corner, a sitcom flickered on the television. Weather bulletins ran on a banner at the bottom of the screen warning of further snow.

"Damn!" The first line in her act was honest and heartfelt.

The woman to her left glanced over, made curious by the sudden outburst.

"Sorry," Taylor apologized, more for the story she was about to tell than for the curse or the disruption. "My boyfriend and I had a fight, and he dropped me off and drove away." Her voice quavered, and her stomach twisted. She hated lying. Was horrible at it. "How the heck am I going to get back to school?"

"Your boyfriend ditched you here?" The woman turned on her stool to face Taylor.

Taylor nodded. "Ex-boyfriend now, son-of-a..." Sweat trickled down her back.

"Poor thing." The woman nodded with sympathy. "Men suck. My ex was a son-of-a too. My sister Betsy and me were about to head back to town. We could give you a ride."

"Could you really? That would be so great." Her relief wasn't feigned.

"Notre Dame?"

Taylor nodded.

The woman set down her beer and extended a hand. "I'm Peggy."

"Kate," Taylor said, shaking Peggy's hand. "I really appreciate it."

"Not a problem. Betsy lives over by the airport anyway,

so you're kind of on the way." She picked up her glass and drank the last swallow. "We spent the day with an old aunt down the road and just stopped by for dinner and a couple beers on the way home. Aunt Flor has a way of making you need a drink." She grinned. "Or two. Anyway, we're going to head out when Betsy gets back from the bathroom. Wouldn't want to stay too late tonight. There's another storm on the way."

Twenty minutes later, Taylor thanked Peggy and Betsy, closed the Chevy's back door and walked toward the gold-domed building. Cars, it seemed, weren't allowed on campus. Clumps of students walked quickly along freshly shoveled sidewalks.

Where would Phil be? Where would he think she'd look? The art department? She looked at the dark bulk of brick buildings. The art studio, if there was one, would probably be closed for the night. Where else?

The library was sure to be open. She could check the section with the art books. "Could you tell me where the library is?" she asked a group.

"Hesburgh?" A shivering blonde hung back a step as her friends continued. "It's the one with 'Touchdown Jesus' on it."

Confused, she looked the way the girl was pointing. A huge mural with Jesus, arms raised, covered the side of a tall building. Taylor smiled. Touchdown Jesus.

"Thanks."

The girl nodded and hurried to catch up with her friends.

Taylor looked back at the library, and her heart raced. Jesus's raised arms reminded her of an eleven or double "l"s. This had to be what Phil meant. Now, she'd find him. Part of her warned that he probably wouldn't be there waiting for her, but that part was easy to ignore. She picked up her pace.

Despite its outward appearance, inside the Hesburgh Library was a typical multistory university library with two sets of glass doors. Taylor hurried through the library's inner door. A large sign announced the building closed at two a.m. The clock above the checkout counter said it was a few minutes after eight. She had plenty of time.

Smiling, she toured the first floor, checking for Phil in every study desk. He wasn't in the stacks or by the catalogue computers. Her smile stiffened. It wasn't as if she'd really thought he'd be sitting there waiting for her; still a wave of sorrow and disappointment swamped her. Her throat felt thick.

The second floor was the same. And the third. She searched each successive floor with the same diligence as the first. Each chair, each desk. But he wasn't there. She scraped her hope from the carpet. He might not be there at that moment, but he would have left a clue. She pulled Phil's Notre Dame Football schedule from her pocket and reread it. Call Phillip. She was at Notre Dame. Were the double "l"s the Touchdown Jesus Library? The eleventh floor? Would there be an eleventh aisle, an eleventh book case, an eleventh shelf? Please, God, let it be that easy.

Taking a deep breath, she crossed her fingers and headed for the elevator. She took note of where the stairwell door came out on the outside wall before taking the elevator to the eleventh floor. She'd use some of the duct tape securing her money bag to her jeans to defeat the automatically locking mechanism on the stairwell door. That would allow her to leave the floor during the suspected inspection and return.

The ding of the elevator and the swish of its doors were loud in the stillness. Taylor turned down a darkened hall within the stacks only to have the bank of lights overhead spring to life. Some of the floors had the older lighting system with switches at the ends of the stacks instead of motion detectors. She'd hoped that would be the case here, but no such luck. There would be no dashing out of sight to avoid detection. Of course, it also meant no one could sneak up on her once she'd found her hiding spot.

She searched the rows section by section. There wasn't an eleventh section. Dewey decimal classification didn't go into the eleven hundreds. Art was the seven hundreds.

Eleven was computer science. In fact, the eleventh floor housed Desktop Computing and Networking Services—home of the university's geek squad. The eleventh computer yielded nothing by way of clues. She jiggled the mouse, and the screen came awake. Phil could have left her a message on her email. Maybe she should check. She pulled out the chair and sat, fingers poised over the keyboard. Unless accessing her account would flag it, would tell the FBI where she was. She'd tipped that hand at the Bachman's, no way was she going to make the same mistake twice. Fisting her hands, she got out of the chair.

Somewhere else. There was a room eleven on the eleventh floor, but there was no note. There was nothing written on the table and nothing but gum stuck to the underside of the table or chairs. She checked them all. Each disappointment chipped away at her optimism.

She grabbed an art book from the shelf, held it by the spine, and shook it. Nothing. She shoved it back on the shelf and grabbed the next, focusing on metals. Nothing. And the next. Faster and faster. She glanced at the clock. It was getting late. Come on, Phil. Where was the damn clue? Why'd you have to make this so hard? By the time she finished the second floor, she wanted to cry. But she didn't. Crying wouldn't make Phil appear.

She hit the elevator button for the twelfth floor which housed the bibles, religious studies, and church history sections. The deeply tranquil air about the floor attracted her. It was the perfect place to hide for the moment and think about what to do next. Where could she sleep? Finding a sleeping spot wouldn't have been an issue if the library didn't close. Universities were one of the few places a person could find a couch, chair, or cubical and go to sleep without causing speculation. Except this one, apparently.

It was after twelve o'clock when she chose her chair, propped open a few books and shrugged off her coat. She was numb with fatigue and yet wide awake. She pulled the schedule from her pocket and looked at it again. Call

Phillip.

She had to be missing something, but what? Why couldn't she be like Langdon in Dan Brown's books who saw a clue and instantly knew what it meant?

Maybe if she cleared her head for a moment, it would come to her. She closed her eyes, but instead of nothingness, the unwelcome replay of that morning's scene ran inside her head.

Nothing made sense. Exploding buildings. Phil's disappearance. The clues.

She wanted to think the FBI had traced her call, but how did they get there so fast? Had Cochran figured out the postcard clue? Had she been followed from the start? Or had the phone calls revealed her location? How had they gotten there so fast? She hadn't seen cars or tracks, hadn't heard snowmobiles. It was like they'd dropped from the sky like the snow. But no one flew during a blizzard. She wanted to think it was the FBI. But it didn't seem likely. The good guys came to the door and introduced themselves. They didn't hide in the snow and make a grab for you.

She was out of her league. Maybe she should call Cochran. Let him protect her. Phil's words looped through her mind like a mantra. Trust no one.

She pressed the balls of her hands hard against her eyes. Phil sent her here for a reason. There had to be another clue.

But what? And where?

Phil's face flashed before her, making her heart ache. Darn it, Phil. Where did you go? He had to know leaving made him look guilty even when he wasn't. And he wasn't. His messages proved that. He loved her. She believed in that love. Still, why leave clues? Wouldn't it be easier to come back and explain? He'd clearly stumbled into something dangerous.

His absence was an open wound she couldn't bandage.

It burned to remember his kiss, his touch, his arms around her... the cryptic clues.

Tink.

§

She remembered the first time Phil had called her Tink.

She had leaned back against Phil's chest in the bath. His knobby knees poked out of the water on either side of her, framing her. The air was thick with steam and the scent of bayberry candles. An ice-cold bottle of Riesling sweated next to two half-filled wine glasses on the edge of the tub.

He kissed her neck in that sensitive spot just behind the right ear. "You are my everything."

She arched her neck to give him greater access.

"My tinker... tailor... soldier... spy..." he continued, raining kisses between words.

She sighed blissfully. "That's a title of a spy book, you know."

He reached for his glass. "No, it's a nursery rhyme."

She sat up enough to grab her own wine. "No. Le Carre based his title on a nursery rhyme. It goes: Tinker, tailor, soldier, sailor, rich man, poor man, beggar man, thief. No spy."

"I like Le Carre's way better. If we were spies, I'd give you the name Tink."

"Tink?" She looked nothing like Tinker Bell.

"Yeah, after that nursery rhyme. Tinker, Taylor, you know. You'd be Tink."

She smiled, playing with the dark swirls of hair on his legs. "And what would you be?"

He took her glass and set it on the ledge next to his. "You can call me Lover Boy."

"Lover Boy?" she snorted, watching him pick up the bar of soap and work it into a thick lather. "How about just Boy?"

His long-fingered sculptor's hands moved to her breasts, the roughness of his calluses sensitizing her skin. "How about just Lover?"

She'd meant to say something, but before she could think of what, she was facing the other way framing him with her knees. Lover indeed.

§

She blew her nose and tried to remind herself there were details and facts she didn't know which would explain Phil's side of this mess. He hadn't really abandoned her. He'd sent a text message. He'd left money and clues. Clues she didn't completely understand.

Laying her head on folded arms, sleep caught her unaware.

"The library will close in five minutes." The voice coming through the speaker was male.

What?

In her dream, she'd been spooning with Phil; his breath moist and warm on the back of her neck. His hand gently cupped around her breast. Home. She didn't want to let go of the dream, but the words repeated overhead.

Taylor opened one eye. She was in a study cubical with her face pressed against an open book. Drool-dampened pages clung to her cheek. She peeled them away.

She sat up with a groan and rolled her neck to ease the stiffness that came from sleeping hunched over with a book for a pillow. Memory slammed into her. Another heartbeat and she was on her feet, shrugging into her coat. Her heart pounded as she picked up the duffle bag from beneath her seat. Run. Hide.

Taylor looked around, as much to reorient herself as to see if she were alone. Seeing no one, she raised her shirt a few inches to reveal the duct tape that held her bag of cash to her jeans. She pried a corner free with her thumb nail, fighting to free a couple of inches of the top layer. Damned tape was too good.

It let go in a rush, and she ended with a length far longer than she needed. She tore it off. The speaker crackled to life again. "The library is closing. Please check out your items."

She hurried past the stacks to the stairwell. If she was caught and escorted out, where would she sleep? Taylor passed a row of meeting rooms. She noticed something and stumbled to a halt. Was that door ajar? She backtracked to the room, took hold of the handle and pushed. Sure enough, the door swung open to reveal a darkened office.

She stepped in, trying the knob. It didn't turn. Apparently, someone had locked the door but failed to pull it closed. She pushed it shut now and leaned against the door. Safe. A single beam of light angled through the window in the door creating a gray rectangle on the linoleum tile. The rest of the room was deep in shadow.

She stared into the darkness. No need to worry about taping the stairwell lock or hiding between floors while they closed the building. She'd sleep safe behind a locked door.

It was about time something went her way.

CHAPTER SIX

Accawi knelt beside his wife's kerb set. The pale light of early morning eased the darkness of the private garden just enough for him to see and admire the carved ebony that outlined her grave. Even in this light it was beautiful—a work of art.

She would have approved. His fingers caressed the dark wood sculptured in an intricate twist. The foot posts were ball-shaped and smooth, firm and rounded like her abdomen would have been now, swollen with their son. The lacquered wood warmed beneath his hands.

"Aisha, my heart." He rested his forehead against the grave outline as he repeated her name. Aisha, Aisha, Aisha.

Kahil had murdered her as surely as he'd killed the drug agent. He deserved to suffer. This time Accawi's plan was perfect.

The voice on the phone whispered of Kahil's pain. Like a bird trapped in a house, Kahil's wife battered herself against the glass. Terrified, she flew from those who would protect her. Her husband reached for her, crying out when she lit just out of reach. Helpless to do anything as his darling pet turned her frantic eyes his way. Soon, she'd fly. Soon, she'd land too near the cat. Then, Accawi would have her.

He would hold her in his hand and feel the frantic beat of her heart. He'd listen while her Philip, his Kahil, begged for her life. He'd tell her of other pretty birds crushed by her beloved's hand. It was better he kill her than leave her to her husband's tender mercies. A man who killed casually, who poisoned innocents and caused others to seek his ruin, was not a man to cling to. Not a man to trust.

When she realized her husband's true nature, Accawi's vengeance would begin. Perhaps he'd let Kahil plead his innocence. Watch the infidel's words fall on his wife's deaf ears. See him writhe as her love for him withered. Ah, yes, slow vengeance. If the voice on the phone were to be believed, Kahil had many sins to atone for besides Aisha.

But first, he must find where Taylor perched.

He rose to his feet, walked to the headstone and kissed it. "I will not fail you, my heart."

§

As soon as Taylor opened her eyes, she knew where she had to look. The meaning of Phil's text message seemed so obvious this morning. How could she have missed it? She found Le Carre's book in the literary section right where she knew it would be. This had to be it. Still, her hand shook as she reached for Tinker, Tailor, Soldier, Spy. She clutched the book to her chest. Oh, please, let there be a clue.

She held her breath as she fanned the pages. A piece of paper fell to the floor. She snatched it up. It was a Notre Dame Football schedule. Disappointment hit hard. She'd been so sure there'd be a clue, so certain. Disheartened, she turned the card over. Nothing. Someone had simply used the football schedule as a bookmark. But it was last year's schedule. The one at the Bachman's cabin was for this year. She pulled that schedule from her pocket and looked at it again.

Call Phillip.

Nothing had changed. Why couldn't he just write what he wanted her to do? Why couldn't he be clear, just this once. Couldn't he just write meet me at this place at this time? Couldn't he just be there? She crushed the schedule in her hand. "Call Phillip." Where? Our home is gone. She'd called his cell phone. He hadn't answered. Call Philip, where? It had to mean something. But what?

She had to have missed something. She smoothed the card open.

The double "l"s of "call" and "Phillip" each framed an away game. The first highlighted game against the Boston College Eagles had taken place in Chestnut Hill, Massachusetts in early September, nearly a month before any of this mess—while her house was still a home. The second highlighted one was against the Georgia Tech Yellow Jackets this Saturday. Was she supposed to meet Phil there?

It seemed so unlikely. Georgia Tech was a huge place. The stadium would be huge. How could he possibly think she would find him there? The clue had to mean something else.

Phillip had seven letters. Philip, six. Maybe... She left the library and joined the early crowd at the student union. She finally located a pay phone beside the information desk and dialed their area code and P. H. I. L. L. I. P—744-5547

Phil's voice filled her ear. "Taylor, honey. Cochran can't protect you. You need to go see Lisa. She doesn't live in the house she wanted, but it has the same address. Tell her Bob Smith sent you. You know Lisa's address. Think about it. I'll meet you, but there are things I have to do first to make certain you stay safe. I know this sounds crazy, but I promise to explain everything when all of this is over. I love you, Taylor. Leave a message so I know you've received this. Say anything. Please. I will leave a new message after hearing from you. I love you." His voice ended.

She didn't wait for the beep but fumbled the phone into the cradle. Oh, God. Can't protect you? Lisa's address? Bob Smith? She stumbled away from the phone, merging with the stream of people and letting it wash her away. What the hell was Phil messed up in?

When the wave of people dissipated, Taylor found herself in front of a coffee kiosk. She smiled. God was looking out for her after all.

Minutes later, she sat at a table with her hands wrapped around her coffee-warmed mug. Now she could think. First, she reviewed the things she knew. Phil loved her and wanted her safe. He was messed up in something frightening. Then, there were the things Phil supposed. Cochran couldn't keep her safe, but she'd be safe at Lisa's. She knew where Lisa lived.

Except she didn't know where Lisa lived. She had never met Lisa. Never talked to her. Never even seen a picture of Phil's older sister. Yet Phil thought she knew where Lisa lived. Caffeine caressed her nerve endings, urging Taylor's brain synapses to fire. The sum total of what she knew of Phil's estranged sister could be contained in two sentences. Lisa was an accountant who lived in Miami. When she was little she wanted to be the first woman President of the United States.

Phil's words came back to her. "She doesn't live in the house she wanted, but it has the same address." The White House. 1600 Pennsylvania Avenue.

Maybe she did know where to find Lisa. She had two hundred dollars, well...a hundred eighty. She'd spent some of it. She could probably fly to Miami on one-sixty, one-eighty. And then what? Hitch to Lisa's, and hope she hadn't moved? Hope Phil was right that Lisa would take her in and keep her safe? How could an accountant keep her safe when the FBI couldn't?

She shook her head. Flying required identification and her budget didn't allow for many contingencies. There had to be another way to get to Miami.

Taylor finished her coffee and tucked the mug safely in her duffle in time to watch the bookstore clerk unlock the metal security gate and slide it into its pocket in the wall. The bookstore was awash in Fighting Irish clothing of every size and description. The green leprechaun with its orange hair and upraised fists adorned a display of huge banners that lined one wall.

Football.

§

The ride board at the student union was a collection of fringed paper. Each piece of paper listed destination and approximate departure time with tear-away phone numbers on the fringes at the bottom. There was nothing for Florida, but there were rides to Georgia Tech for the game. Once in Atlanta it would be easier to catch a ride to Miami. And it was cheaper. And untraceable. Taylor dropped some coins in the pay phone and dialed the number on the paper with the most intact fringes.

Chaz answered his phone. "It's your lucky day. I've got room for one more rider." Taylor smiled as he chatted on and on about how he and his roommate had decided to go to Atlanta even though they didn't have tickets to the game. "I've got this great Notre Dame van. You can't miss it." Taylor, Missy to Chaz, arranged to meet him Friday morning at 9:15 on the Notre Dame Avenue circle.

She hung up the phone. Her fingers itched to call "Phillip" again and leave a message, but she hesitated. Phil's text message looped through her mind. Trust no one. If Cochran couldn't keep her safe, would leaving a message be safe? Cochran had seen the misspelling of Phil's name in the safe deposit box. He could have figured it out too. Maybe he was monitoring that number as well. Or perhaps the bad guys were. They could already know where she was. She needed to disappear.

She headed back to the bookstore.

Her list was short, but essential—a Notre Dame athletic bag, two greeting cards and stamps, hair ties, eyeliner, mascara, lip gloss and a pocket-sized notebook.

Leaving the store with her overpriced merchandise, she picked up her duffle and stuffed it into the larger Fighting Irish bag.

In a corner of the student union, Taylor found a seat near a window and looked out. The snow banks glistened in the sunlight. Groups of students in jeans and sweatshirts navigated the sidewalks, avoiding the puddles. Inside, students streamed by, chatting about upcoming mid-term projects and papers due before the weekend. She tried to remember what it was like when tests, papers, and class projects were the only things she had to worry about.

She shook her head. She didn't have time to mull over a distant past. There were plans to make and things to do. She pulled the list from her pocket. If she were truly going to disappear, she had to do it right. South Bend was the last place she could leave a trace.

Taylor pulled the two identical greeting cards from the bag. They were appropriate. Each had two large turkeys on the front commenting on how they were going to try to make a run for it.

The first one was easy to write—an apology to the Bachmans for taking the sled and clothes. She gave no reasons, just a detailed description of where to find the snowmobile.

The second was much harder.

How could she say good-bye to her parents? She wanted to pour out her feelings, but she knew whatever she wrote would be inadequate. She settled for: Don't worry that you don't hear from me. Keeping you safe is what matters most to me.

It was all she could do, but she knew it wasn't enough. Her heart was in her throat as she slid the card inside the envelope and addressed it.

She'd put them in the mailbox outside the library. They'd end up with a Notre Dame postmark, but she'd be gone before they arrived. Besides, she was going to let whoever was watching know she was in South Bend, anyway.

She crossed off that item and looked at the next thing on her list. Her direction was clear. Step by step she'd lay a false trail and then, once they were racing down the wrong path, she could slip away in safety, go to Miami, and find Phil.

§

Hundreds of miles away a cell phone vibrated in the agent's front pocket. "Yes."

"My wife's blood cries for vengeance."

He recognized the heavy accent as Accawi's and had

to remind himself not to adopt the same speech patterns. "Kahil betrayed us both." He prayed Accawi still believed that. He must, considering he'd bombed the hell out of Taylor Wilson's office.

"So you say, and so the betrayer shall die." The voice was calm. "But first, he will suffer. His wife's blood will soak the ground and his children will never live to see the sky."

It was disturbing how, as crazy as Accawi was, he had somehow managed to pare the betrayal down to its essential elements—how no matter what man did it was woman who was to blame. Eve and the serpent. "You missed. She ran to her brother's in—"

"It matters not where she was. Where is she now?"

Damn incompetent fool. Did he have to hold the slut down while Accawi cut her? He bit his tongue. What did he expect? Accawi let a DEA agent attend his druggy wife. "Hold on a moment. I'll find out where." He needed to log onto the computer.

Accawi snorted his disdain. "I will not hold for you to trace my call. Do not think to play me for a fool. You forget I know what your man has created. Do not insult me by suggesting he has not marked her—given her a tattoo, perhaps. A rose above the heart that will always call to him? A serpent around her ankle to remind her of Eve? A man with such talents takes care not to mislay that which belongs to him. You must find her quickly, or soon I will be thinking I should punish you as well. I will call again. Have the answer ready."

The agent listened to the dial tone. Accawi had hung up. Idiot. In another moment, he'd have had Taylor's present location. Accawi was a crazy religious fanatic and wonderfully violent, but he was also stupid, condescending and much too sloppy. Perhaps he couldn't be counted on to actually kill the whore after all. Still, he remained the perfect foil. He would take the blame.

The agent slid the phone into his pocket. Once Taylor was dead, he'd kill Accawi. Then, he'd be the savior.

CHAPTER SEVEN

In Indianapolis, Cochran covered the telephone receiver and took a deep breath. It wouldn't do any good to swear. Killing the messenger would not locate Taylor nor keep her safe. What he needed were results. He set his pencil on the desk to stop himself from breaking it.

"Okay, Jacobs," he interrupted the voice on the other end of the line. "Let me get this straight." He willed himself to remain calm. The rookie seemed to understand the magnitude of his mistake, but 'sorry' didn't erase the error. "Not only did you bring an easily recognizable truck to a safe house which allowed Taylor Wilson, a woman under our protection, to drive out of Fort Wayne without permission or protection, but you took Peterson's car so he couldn't follow her." Which might not have been a bad thing considering Peterson had been the one to order the truck's delivery. But he didn't mention that aloud. He was reprimanding Jacobs, not commending him. "Then, after locating the truck and following it to her destination, you and Masters failed to take her into protective custody. Instead, you left her inside the house, vulnerable to attack, while you waited, hoping her estranged husband would arrive. When he didn't, you let her climb out of a dog door in the middle of a blizzard and evade not only you and Masters, but also several other unidentified persons you were not aware of at the time. In a matter of moments, she accessed a snowmobile, leaving you and the unknowns running after her. Since then, you've lost both her and the unknowns. Is that correct?"

"We found where she filled up with gas, questioned the employees and others, who according to sales records, were at the station at the same time. We don't know her direction, but using tank capacity to figure out how far she might have gotten on that gas, we're circulating her picture."

"And," Cochran prompted.

"And nothing so far, but we're still checking."

"Okay. Her accounts are flagged. Make certain you monitor them." This was his team that screwed up. "You have a description of the sled, right?" It was his responsibility to recover Taylor before anything happened to her. "Good. Call me this afternoon with results."

§

Taylor hovered in front of the mirror gently tugging sections of hair out of her up-do. She'd noticed that two out of three girls wore their hair pinned up in an oversized clip with tendrils hanging down. At the end of a day of work, it wasn't uncommon for her ponytail to have achieved the half-up-half-down state, but she had never considered starting out that way. Still, it was the way she needed to style her hair today.

Leaning toward the mirror, she applied dark eyeliner, thick mascara and shiny lip gloss until she looked like eighteen aiming for thirty. She needed to look as if she were trying to disguise herself, but who would have thought being recognizably unrecognizable would be so tough.

Stepping back, she regarded her reflection in the mirror. It was amazing what hair and make-up could do. In her Notre Dame hoodie, she looked like a hundred or so college coeds until she smiled, and then she looked like herself trying to be someone else. Perfect.

Taylor climbed onto a city bus and set her Notre Dame duffle on the seat beside her. Five students boarded the bus right behind her. Good. She would blend in.

She looked out the window feeling like a kid leaving home for the first day of kindergarten, excited and yet frightened to be leaving the security of home and mother.

It was silly. The university wasn't home, but she had a room there with a locked door and a ride that was leaving tomorrow. She turned from the window and faced forward. No looking back. Today was a necessary part of her disappearance.

She opened her notebook to the front page and checked the list. Her first stop was coming up. She was about to raise her hand to pull the bell cord when she heard the telltale bing. Her heart lurched. It's okay. Someone else wanted to get out at her stop. That's all. They couldn't be following her if they rang for the stop first. Still, she quickly took note of the threesome who exited in the rear. Red hair guy, pierced nose dude, and a blonde girl with the same scraggly up-do she had. She hurried to the front for a transfer.

Outside, the others chatted amongst themselves. "You going home for Thanksgiving?"

"I can't think about it. I've got two papers due before we go."

"I've got one after, but it's the same as having it due before, like I'm going to do it over break."

They were just students. It was fine. She was fine.

A mother towing a toddler by the hand joined them. Normal people living normal lives.

She glanced at her wristwatch and then looked down the street. Where was that bus? She shifted weight from one foot to the other and back again. The little boy stuck his thumb in his mouth and stared at her. She shifted back to the first foot, checked her wristwatch, and looked down the street.

By the time the bus finally arrived the transfer slip was damp. The trio boarded first. She waved the mother and child inside and then handed the limp transfer to the driver with an apologetic smile.

She really needed to calm down if she was going to make it through the day.

Her next stop came. She walked past the trio. Stay here, stay here.

When the bus pulled away with them still aboard, she

breathed a sigh.

Outside South Bend International Airport, Taylor stopped. Breathe. Focus. She checked her list, reading the crucial next steps twice before returning the notebook to her pocket. She shouldered her Notre Dame bag. The electronic doors shushed open, and she was inside. The airport was as busy as she'd hoped. It was the only time today when a large flight arrived at nearly the same moment another was scheduled to leave. She checked the board. Right on schedule. She wanted the crowds so she could disappear. But first, she needed to appear.

Anyone looking for her would watch the airports and monitor her bank and credit accounts. She thought of the five thousand dollars Agent Cochran had taken from her. If she had that, it would be so much easier to disappear. The money in her pocket would get her to Georgia Tech, maybe Miami, but that was all. Once she met up with Phil, she'd be fine.

What if he wasn't there? What if she couldn't find him? Not now!

She shoved the negative thoughts aside. Get to the ATM. See if, by some strange chance, the FBI had unfrozen her account.

Someone jostled against her, smashing her bag into her side. The mug bruised her hip. She turned to see who'd hit her, but the man had passed without an apology. A bank of lockers lined a wall under a large sign. "Lockers: Yellow—short term. Blue—long term."

Her beloved mug weighed heavily in her bag. She rubbed her hip as she walked closer to the sign. Long term was up to two months. In two months she and Phil would be together somewhere. In two months, the nightmare she was living would be nothing but a memory. It was the next few days and weeks that were unsettling. Who knew where she'd be holed up? She and Phil could be rushing around the country. She could lose the mug.

Before she even realized she'd decided to leave the mug, she scanned the lockers and found an open box with a number she could easily remember.

It will be safer here, she told herself as she unzipped her bag and drew the wrapped mug from inside. She was doing the right thing. A bit of anxiety eased as she placed it in the small locker, deposited the coins, and removed the key. There was strength and peace in knowing something she cared about would be safe.

Maybe this was how Phil had felt about leaving her. Of course, Phil had been wrong. She was still in danger.

And she still had a mission.

Pocketing the key, she turned and looked for the ATM.

South Bend International was a small airport where arrivals and departures took place in the same area. A general waiting area allowed friends and families to say goodbye, meet travelers, or merely watch the planes take off without passing through the security gates.

Taylor checked the time on her watch against the arrival board. They would announce the departing flight in a couple of minutes. There was just enough time to try to make her withdrawal. She scanned the room for the ATM. There was a line. Her stomach fell.

She joined the queue as number four. Did nobody plan ahead? She'd never gone to the airport without the money necessary for her trip, but apparently she was the exception. She consulted her wristwatch. It was okay. There was time.

Before the first person was done, someone stepped behind her. She shot a quick glance over her shoulder. Her breath caught in her throat. It was pierced nose dude.

No. She forced air into her lungs. Pierced nose dude didn't have a black coat, did he? She turned as if to look at the arrival board, but really to get a better look at the guy behind her. It wasn't the same one. This guy's hair was normal brown, not Goth black. He had a piercing above his left brow. Not the same guy.

"You worried about missing your plane?" he asked.

She smiled. "A little."

The line diminished by one.

"I'm going to Orlando, too. Thought I'd go early and do

some business. Miss the Thanksgiving rush."

"Uh...good idea." She looked at the back of the person in front of her. Hurry up!

There would be a camera at the ATM. She needed to remember to smile with relief when she finally got there. There'd be no smiling after because, of course, her transaction would fail.

Her turn finally came as they announced the first boarding call to Orlando. She barely remembered to smile for the camera. Her hands shook as she slid her card through the reader and keyed in her PIN.

There was usually a pause while the ATM accessed the account and processed the request, but today the delay seemed overlong. Just reject it already and let me get out of here.

The stupid waiting sign blinked the seconds. Come on, come on. She was on the clock now. Across the country computer systems were taking note of her attempted transaction. The FBI would be notified. Come on!

Sweat dotted her brow.

When, at long last, the transaction was denied she wanted to cheer, but that would have been inappropriate. She needed to look worried. Not much of a stretch there. She frowned for the camera and pressed the button to clear the screen.

Free at last, Taylor had to keep herself from running to the restroom. It felt as if a stopwatch had started somewhere. How long did she have until the airport was swarming with feds?

Taylor grabbed a paper towel and ran it under the faucet on the way to a stall. Scrub off make-up. Change hair. Pull off sweatshirt. Swap out bags. Slip on wedding ring. Put on coat and hat. Get out.

The Taylor who left the bathroom looked nothing like the one who'd just hurried in. All signs of Notre Dame insignia were gone. Her hair was under her knit hat and tucked inside her coat. She carried her bag in her right hand rather than her left and took relaxed, measured steps. At least she hoped they looked relaxed. She kept her face angled down as she merged with a group and ended up in the line for the Holiday Inn Express courtesy van.

She'd meant to get on another city bus, but this was better. No one would expect this. Damp with perspiration, she climbed aboard. The vinyl seat sighed as she lowered herself onto one on the side farthest from the terminal. Hurry, hurry. Her knuckles were white around the bag's strap. An eternity passed before the driver finally boarded. Taylor's breath escaped with a shaky sigh that blended with the sound of the door swishing shut. She remained frozen until the bus pulled away from the curb and merged into traffic.

When it was too late to do anything about it, she looked around at faces. Senior couples, one young family and half a dozen business travelers. Had she seen the man in the black dress coat before? No, he'd boarded before she did. Besides, the FBI wasn't that fast.

But they had been alerted. Or would be. Taylor smiled, hoping they would spend hours poring over passenger lists trying to find her.

The Holiday Inn was several blocks off the bus route, which made the trip back to the campus more complicated. But that was okay. Now, she was positive no one followed her. Still, her shoulders remained tight until she exited the last bus and set foot onto the Notre Dame campus. It was as if the sun came out for the first time all day. She was safe. Silly as it seemed, it was as if Notre Dame was that safe base in a childhood game where, as long as you touched it, no one could tag you. It made no sense. But nothing had made sense since the day her house blew up.

Taylor stood in line to enter the dining hall. Students in front of and behind her chatted with their friends, making plans for that night or rehashing the day. The line inched forward. Someone jostled her. Her duffle bag smashed against her.

"I'm sorry. Did I hurt you?"

She shook her head. This boy was so much more polite than the man at the airport. And this time there was nothing hard or heavy inside it to bruise her.

The key. The thought slammed into her. Where had she put the key? She plunged her hand into her pocket and encountered a handful of change. Her heart rate picked up as she shoved the coins back with one hand and reached the other into her other pocket. She couldn't have lost it.

There was nothing in that pocket but a small wad of ones. Oh, no. She had lost it.

The girl behind her tapped her on her shoulder. "You dropped this."

The key, safe and sound, in the girl's hand.

"Thank you." Taylor's throat was thick and tight. Her stomach clenched uncomfortably at the thought of how easily she could have lost it on the street, digging for bus fare. The scent of fried chicken, so appetizing moments ago, was now nauseating.

Though it was nearly her turn at the register, Taylor left the line, mumbling apologies as she wound her way against traffic and out of the vestibule. The geometric pattern on the carpet blurred as she made her way through the lounge to the nearest ladies room. Inside the restroom, she ducked into a stall and leaned against the metal divider. Keeping the mug safe meant nothing if she lost the ability to retrieve it.

Her hands quaked as she took off her shoe and unlaced it halfway before threading the key into her lace. She re-laced her shoe, slipped it on her foot and tied it securely.

It was okay. She would be okay.

Tomorrow she'd be on the first leg of her trip to Miami. To Phil.

She would find him, and he'd be able to tell her what the hell was going on.

§

On the library wall, The Word of Life Mural glowed as if lit from within rather than illuminated by well-placed lights up and down both sides of the mosaic. Taylor admired it briefly before going inside. Phil would have liked the colors, the composition. Inside the building, Taylor headed to the tenth floor. It was busier at night than the twelfth. The quiet buzz of hushed conversations blended with the electric whine of an overhead light ballast to create a white noise which calmed her. That, and the presence of students, gave Taylor the illusion she wasn't as alone as she felt.

She nodded over her book.

Overhead, the chimes rang, and the voice on the intercom announced the end of the library day.

Taylor yawned and stretched as she got out of the chair she'd been sleeping in. A group stood waiting for the elevator. She looked at a girl with long brown hair and a smiling face. Taylor wished she could join the group, walk with them to the dorms—carefree. No explosions. No one tracing her. But that's not the way it was. The elevator dinged and the door slid open, but instead of crowding into the car, she walked away to the restroom. She ducked inside and massaged her forehead to ease the dull ache.

The area in front of the elevator was empty and the stacks dark when she left the restroom. Alone, she headed up the brightly lit, concrete tower of a stairwell. She walked softly, but the concrete stairs still echoed with the sounds of her footsteps. The echo sounded lonely. Wait. She froze. A footstep? Was there someone else on the steps? Her heartbeat thudded loud. She held her breath and listened. Nothing. She took a ragged breath and ran up the remaining steps to the twelfth floor. Panting more from nerves than exertion, she slid her finger tips under the face plate and eased open the fire door.

The hall was empty. Still she froze, visually checking every hiding spot she could see from where she stood. Reassured she was alone, she ripped off the duct tape. The rhythmic shush of the automatic closer was loud. She pulled the door shut behind her, rushing the automatic closer, speeding the darkness. Her eyes adjusted to the comparative dimness. The exit light glowed, casting shadows. An imagined sound made her turn to listen. Nothing. She took several breaths and ordered herself to relax. Quit being silly. No one lurked in the shadows. She was alone.

She inched down the hall. Outside the door to her room, she paused, and forced herself to breathe. The knob didn't turn beneath her palm as she pushed open the door. Removing the tape, she wadded it into a little ball before stepping inside and pressing the door closed behind her. Safe. She sighed with relief.

She was in the middle of the room when the man sitting on the couch flicked on the reading lamp.

"Hello."

Taylor gasped, slapping a hand over her mouth to stifle the scream. She spun on her heels and fumbled for the doorknob.

The man lunged for her. His fingers brushed her sleeve as she yanked open the door. Before her loomed another man. Younger.

Hard hands grabbed her arms.

"No!" She thrashed against him, but he held her tight. Her heart pounded in her chest, and she kicked his shins, desperate to get free.

CHAPTER EIGHT

Taylor sat on the couch in the library room—her room. A fit-yet-graying man in his mid-fifties hovered over her. He was dressed all in black.

How could they have traced her attempted withdrawal and followed her so quickly? It was clear she didn't know who she'd been dealing with. Still didn't.

The man's thinning gray hair and the crinkles at the corners of his eyes showed his age. "Don't be afraid."

She was outnumbered, trapped, doomed, and he said, Don't be afraid. Her heart tried to pound its way out of her chest.

She blinked, shifting her glance past his face. The other man hovered behind him. He was younger than she would have guessed an agent or an assassin to be— twenty, maybe. He was also bigger than she'd thought he was when she'd kicked him. Staring at a spot on the floor, he wiped his hands on the front of his jeans before shoving them in his front pockets.

A student.

"Uh, Father." The younger guy looked at the floor. "Should I call campus security?"

Father? Looking back at the first man again, she noticed the white square in the center of his collar. How had she missed that?

"Father?" A priest. She nearly laughed with relief.

"Yes, I'm Father Charles Kelly, a professor here at Notre Dame. Nick noticed you sneaking around after hours and called me."

"Father, can I talk with you?"

The priest raised his eyebrows. "You hid out in my office after hours to talk with me?"

"No, I..." Taylor blushed.

"Just thought of it now that you've been caught here after hours?"

Taylor nodded and the priest shook his head in resignation. "All right, child. We can talk, but it won't prevent disciplinary action for staying in the library past hours." He turned to Nick. "Thank you for sharing this with me, Nick. You may finish your rounds. I can take it from here."

The priest took a seat as Nick left.

"All right, young lady. You know who I am. Now, may I ask your name?"

"Taylor Wilson."

"All right, Taylor." He looked into her eyes as he folded his hands in his lap. "So, how did you end up in my office tonight?"

Taylor let loose a torrent of words. Father Kelly's mouth opened and closed several times as she talked, but he remained silent through her entire story—the bombs, the snowmobile, the call, the airport. Everything. She knew Phil had told her to trust no one, but this was a priest, for goodness sake.

"My God." Coming from him, it definitely sounded like a prayer for help. "So, you've been living in the library for two days?"

"This will be my second night, Father. I'm leaving in the morning."

Taylor watched him consider the options. His expressive face chronicled the inception and demise of each thought. After a couple of minutes, he frowned.

"Is this true?"

She nodded.

"Is your wedding ring engraved?"

She blinked at him. Her ring? "Uh...yes."

"May I see it, please?" He reached out his hand.

Taylor's heart lurched as she pulled it from her finger.

It was the only thing she had left of Phil.

He held the simple gold band beneath the light and read the inscription—her and Phil's initials and their wedding date. "When's your anniversary?"

She smiled. He was quizzing her. "September first."

He handed back the ring and began pacing.

"I know it's late and you have a ride to catch in the morning, but I'd like you to come with me to one of the women's dorms. You can call the FBI from there, and then I'm sure Sister Margaret can find a bed for you."

She frowned. "I thought you believed me."

He grinned. "I do. Your tale is too strange to be fiction. Still, working with young adults, I have learned it is generally best to trust, but verify."

"I see." There was no way she was going to call the FBI. They'd keep her from finding Phil.

His smile faded as he shook his head. "I don't think you do. I want you to call the FBI, not because I want to check your story, but because I'm afraid for you. And I'm afraid for the university while you are here."

"Oh." Her stomach dropped. "I'm sorry. I didn't think." She'd been worried about her family's safety but hadn't thought about the university. "I thought I'd be safe here. That the campus was big enough and I would be here a short enough time that no one would even know I'd ever been here." Now that he'd brought it up, it was easy to transpose memories of the bomb sites to the university campus. She swallowed, hard. Endangering others wasn't part of the plan. She might not know who the bad guys were, but she knew what they were capable of. That's why she had to find Phil. Together they would figure out what was going on. Together they'd make things right and get their lives back. "I didn't mean to put anyone else in danger."

He patted her hand. "I believe you, Taylor. I also believe you are still in danger. I'd say you need help from the FBI."

"I think, Father, I may just need a miracle."

Taylor sat in a chair and listened while Father Charlie

called Sister Margaret, the Rector and Staff in Residence of Farley Hall.

"Maggie?" He listened to the voice on the other end. "I know it's late, and I'm sorry. I'm bringing you a young lady. Do you think you could find her a bed tonight on the Q.T.?" He listened, smiling. "Not one of yours, no. I won't be able to tell you any more than that, I'm afraid."

Taylor could hear the female voice grumbling.

"Thanks, Maggie, you're a peach." He ended the call by closing his cell phone. "Sister Margaret is my twin sister. We've been a two-for-one deal since birth. We even got the call at the same time." He grinned. "Anyway, she'll take you in tonight and not bother you with questions."

Taylor blushed, uncomfortable that anyone else should be put out by her presence. "Thank you. I'd have happily slept here."

"I know." He nodded, smiling. "But I'll be more comfortable with you safely tucked in a bed. And so will you."

They walked through the Fieldhouse Mall with its partially snow-covered gardens and strategically placed benches.

"Once you're at Farley Hall, you can call the agent you mentioned." Father Charlie's directive was couched as a suggestion.

Taylor repressed a smile. Her parish priest used that technique as well. She shook her head. "Father, I don't have much faith in the FBI. I didn't even before I heard Phil's phone message. They haven't done a very good job of protecting me or finding who is really behind the explosions." Taylor purposely stepped on the white icy patches on the sidewalk for the pure joy of hearing them crunch, reminding her of a simpler time. She'd have that again soon. God willing.

"Perhaps they have evidence they haven't shared with you."

Taylor dismissed his comment with a shrug. "I still don't trust them. Besides, if I call at all, it shouldn't be from the university. They'll place me here. I shouldn't be connected to Notre Dame any more than I have to be. It isn't safe." Their breath made clouds in the cold air.

He stopped walking and looked at her as he rubbed his chin. "You think the FBI is behind your husband's disappearance and the bombings?" Even though there was no one else within sight, he spoke just above a whisper.

She shuffled her feet on the chill sidewalk. "Well, no. It's just that anyone monitoring the FBI's phone lines would know where I'm calling from."

"You think someone is bugging the FBI?"

Taylor winced. It sounded so foolish when he said it. So... paranoid. She looked across the mall at the miniature Stonehenge with a red granite ball in the middle. A floodlight on the far side of the circle made the stones cast long, dark shadows. Cold seeped through her jacket. "I don't know what I think." She frowned and looked back to the priest. "All I know is what Phil told me." She blinked back the sudden moisture from her eyes. "If I'd run when I'd gotten the text message, I might have a business to go home to."

"Hmmm," Father Charlie pondered aloud. "Perhaps, but I hardly think you can shoulder the blame. Unless there is something you've done that you haven't mentioned?" He raised his eyebrows in question.

She shook her head. "Nothing I can think of. Aside from these last few weeks, I've lived a fairly uneventful life." She gave a sad little smile. "Fulfilling, but unremarkable."

The moon slid from behind a cloud to light their path. It found the bald spot on the top of Father Charlie's head and highlighted it, making it look as if he wore a halo. The vision gave her comfort.

They started walking again, side by side.

"I still think you should call. It might appear you have something to hide, otherwise."

Taylor sighed. It was one of the reasons they suspected Phil.

"I think you would be safer in protective custody. The people around you would be safer as well."

"Maybe. Maybe not. I'm pretty sure everyone would be safer if no one knew where I was." They walked under the arched entry to Farley Hall.

"I'd like you to think about it. Pray about it."

Ah, pray about it. A good Catholic would agree with the priest, would call the FBI. She didn't feel like a good anything at the moment. She smiled. "I will, Father."

They walked the rest of the way in silence.

Wearing a bathrobe over her flannel nightgown, Sister Margaret Kelly pulled open the door. She was taller and thinner than her brother. Her curls were sleep-crushed on one side. She gave Taylor a brief assessing look before turning to Father Charlie. The look she gave him was clearly one of disgruntled affection.

Father Charlie smiled at her. "Why don't you show our guest where she can sleep? It's late."

She arched a brow. "Is it? Can't say I've noticed."

Chuckling, Father Charlie turned to Taylor. "I'm afraid you're seeing her at her worst. She's always cranky when awakened early."

Instead of ripping off her brother's head, something Taylor wouldn't have blamed her for, Sister Margaret laughed. "He's right, you know. It takes eight hours of sleep and a cup of coffee before I'm human."

"A cup?" Taylor asked with a smile. "Even with eight hours, I have to have at least two cups before I remember my name and why I got out of bed at all."

Margaret grinned. "I think I like you. Now, why don't you follow me, and we'll find our beds. Charles Michael can let himself out."

§

Miles away, on the twelfth floor of the Minton-Capehart Federal Building in downtown Indianapolis, Phil stared at the computer screen on his desk. He wrote a few more lines of code and ran the simulation program. Audio poured through his headphones while simultaneously appearing as text on the screen. Six down, four surveillance programs to go. The blast had taken more than his house and peace of mind. It had taken the project's dedicated server, but the technology remained undetected and continued to function flawlessly. Most importantly, the blast hadn't taken Taylor.

He glanced at the digital clock on the screen. She should be here by now.

Special-Agent-in-Charge Jackson rapped on the glass partition. "Kennedy, my office." It had been so long since he'd been an active agent it took Phil half a second to remember he was Kennedy. His boss had decided it was safer and cleaner to revert to his old name and rank while he was back inside the bureau. Separating the old from the new kept his new identity secure, but it chafed inside almost as if he were denying Taylor and the life they'd created together.

Taylor was here. Phil leapt from his desk, smiling. He was halfway out of the office before he remembered what he'd been working on. He spun back to the desk, encrypted the code, and logged off.

As he left the cubicle, the distinctive tones signaled the system shutting down.

He hurried after Jackson, weaving his way through the bullpen of occupied cubicles and down the hall to Jackson's office. It had taken far longer than he'd anticipated for Sean to get her, even with the standard recon and debriefing. But he trusted his buddy. Sean wouldn't take chances with Taylor.

Phil followed his former boss through the door. "Taylor." The word froze on his lips. She wasn't in the office. Sean was. Worry grabbed him by the throat as he turned to his old partner. "Where is she?"

Jackson sat behind his desk. "Close the door."

Sean reached around Phil and pulled the door shut.

"O'Hearn." Jackson's nod was cue enough for Sean to begin his report.

"We missed her."

"You what?" Phil grabbed the back of a chair. He only consented to stay in the office doing the tech stuff because Sean, the field expert, was getting Taylor. Sean, his best friend since college. They'd entered the training program at Quantico together. Sean was the one person Phil trusted with the tracking code. Not some rookie. He shook his head. "What the hell happened? You weren't supposed to come back without her."

"There's a leak. She's better off out there."

Phil's fingers dug into the chair's upholstery. "Dammit, Sean, we've suspected a leak for some time. She's supposed to be in protective custody."

"She was. She ran."

"I know that." He ground his teeth. One stupid decision heaped upon another. He'd told her to run early on with the text message. It was his mistake. She wasn't a trained agent. No matter how smart she was, this wasn't her background. She didn't think like a spy. Now, just when he relied on her lack of training to keep her safe and bring her in, she caught on and eluded everyone. Damn it!

It was his fault she wasn't safe. He never should have agreed to work on the project. He'd retired. He should have stayed retired.

"Sean, you should have her. You're the best." Phil shoved the chair aside. Taylor was in danger. "I gave you the damn code to find her. This should have been a cake walk. What the hell went wrong?" His fists were clenched as he stood nose to nose with O'Hearn.

O'Hearn took a step back. "Jesus Christ, Max, you know I've done my best to keep her safe. Get hold of yourself."

Before Phil could reply, Jackson butted in, "Calm down, both of you." As SAC, he didn't need to raise his voice to command silence. "Max, sit down."

Phil slumped into the unoccupied guest chair he'd previously manhandled. Sean sat in the second chair, out of swinging range.

"I don't have time for your bickering." Jackson eyed both men sternly. "What we really need to talk about is the operation. The Bedouin Ship is finally sitting in Consul-General Farah's conference room. Our intelligence says Accawi claimed the statue was dirty to keep it for himself. That didn't go over well with Farah. Three security firms eventually cleared it without reservation. The technology is sound."

Sean nodded. "We knew the technology was sound. Max created it. We probably put out the rumor questioning Accawi's motives." Discrediting sources of accurate secret intelligence was standard operating procedure. "When Accawi red-flagged the sculpture, we suspected he had inside information. When he threatened me and went after Max, we knew it. The man is known for his temper. He threatened underlings to keep his wife's drug problem a secret. He killed a DEA agent."

"Why is he after my wife? This wasn't supposed to touch her." The whole thing had been one huge mistake. "I should have never used her mug as the prototype. I should have followed my instincts and never—"

Jackson interrupted. "I was the one who insisted the connection with your art was secure—untraceable. It should have been. We still aren't sure it's not. Abernathy reported that the code for the standard chip in Taylor's mug was accidentally put in Shared Files."

Phil turned to Sean. This was precisely why he'd insisted on a separate dedicated server for this operation. "I gave it to you after the safe house SNAFU. You've had it what? Twenty-four hours? What the hell happened?"

Sean shook his head.

Jackson turned to Phil. "The originating signature is yours."

Phil looked the SAC in the eye and spoke softly through gritted teeth. "Like hell."

Jackson nodded. "Something is going on here we aren't seeing. O'Hearn, other than rumors, is there any sign the technology has been compromised?"

"No. No signals blocked. The codes Max recreated pick up the transmissions flawlessly."

"Great. What about Taylor? We have her location. Let's bring her in."

O'Hearn cleared his throat. "Max, I know how you feel, but you must realize the mission is more important than just Taylor. We aren't babysitters."

Phil held his clenched fists at his side. "We babysit all
the time. Informants, defectors... if Taylor doesn't qualify
for protective custody, I don't know who does."

"You have a good point, Max, but so does Sean."

Phil opened his mouth to protest, but Jackson silenced
him with the raised palm of his hand. "We've got a black
op mission with a security leak. That, along with Taylor's
safety, is top priority. But the point O'Hearn was trying to
make is that we tried to pick her up after the SNAFU at
the vacation house, but we lost her."

"Dead?" Oh, God. Phil sank back into his chair as if
someone had cut him off at the knees. "How?"

Jackson shook his head. "I simply meant lost. We
don't know where she is."

Phil was on his feet in an instant. "How can that be?
She's got a homing signal for Christ's sake." He rounded
the desk. "Let me at that computer."

Leaning over the desk, his hands flew across the
keyboard. In seconds Taylor's signal appeared in Indiana.
The weight on his shoulders lessened. He pointed to the
screen. "There she is. You must have screwed up the
code." He zoomed in on her location. "She's at South
Bend International Airport." He looked across the desk
at O'Hearn. "We need to find out where she's going." He
returned his focus to the computer. "I'll check ticketing."

"We already did." O'Hearn's words reclaimed Phil's
attention from the screen.

"What?"

O'Hearn tugged on his collar. "The signal hasn't
moved in twelve hours." He paused, looked down at his
hands, and then met Phil's eyes. "I'm sorry, pal, but those
coordinates are a bank of lockers. She stashed the mug.
We'll find her eventually. And... since she's apparently
gotten good enough to disappear, she'll be fine until we
do."

Phil raked his fingers across the keyboard. "Damn it."

Jackson nodded. "We checked the airlines and cab
companies. Nothing. Caught her on video at the ATM, but

no sign of her leaving."

Who else had followed her signal? Thousands of agents had access. They already suspected someone was dirty. Now, no one was excluded.

"Shit." Phil glared at O'Hearn. "Don't tell me someone grabbed her."

O'Hearn's demeanor instantly shifted from concerned friend to agent. "No signs of struggle. Looks like she ditched the mug, tried unsuccessfully to get money and then intentionally disappeared."

Phil returned to his chair and nodded slowly. He'd told her to run.

"Before this, we tracked her easily, even without the signal. So, in retrospect, we're pretty sure Accawi had her scent the entire time, too." Sean's blue eyes seemed calm.

"If it is Accawi." The first bomb had been detonated using a remote, but there wasn't enough left of the fuse to prove the phone Accawi ditched in Starbucks was the one used. The Bedouin Ship had ruined Accawi's career and put his entire family in jeopardy. Accawi might target the artist, but it was a stretch. Artists didn't install listening devices; governments, intelligence agencies, and law enforcement did. Killing the DEA agent made sense. And maybe targeting Sean. After all, Sean was the go-to guy. But Taylor? Why? No matter how he ran it through his head it didn't make sense. There wasn't enough of a motive. But he couldn't come up with anything else. Phil rubbed a rough hand through his hair.

Jackson picked up a file from his desk. "He's our main suspect at the moment. He lost face when the statue turned up in his garden. One of the first things we recorded after the statue was installed at the consul-general's office was Accawi going bat-shit, declaring his innocence, and swearing revenge against the infidels who framed him. He had some god-awful gravestone thing called a 'kerb set' delivered to his estate. The chief secretary claimed Accawi is being shunned and speculated it's for when he commits suicide to atone for his sins against Islam. Then, Accawi seems to have dropped out of sight."

"Great. A nutcase with nothing to lose targets the artist of the vehicle of his shame." It didn't make any more sense when Jackson presented it. "So why is he after my wife?"

Jackson shook his head. "We have no idea."

Phil scowled. How the hell could he have foreseen this? "You find him and stop him. I've got to find her."

Jackson nodded. "Your orders are in the top drawer."

§

At seven the next morning, Taylor's head was as cloudy as the overcast sky. Four hours of sleep tended to have that effect. Her jaw creaked in a yawn. She crawled out of bed. It would have been wonderful to have been able to sleep longer. She pulled up the sheet and smoothed the comforter before leaving Sister Margaret's spare bedroom. Her ride wasn't until nine-thirty, but her internal clock didn't care. It told her seven was late, and she should be moving. She would sleep later she promised herself as she stumbled down the hall to the bathroom.

"Coffee's ready," Sister Margaret called to Taylor from the apartment's small kitchen.

"Thanks." Taylor had already caught its scent and was headed that way. She was clean, but the warm shower had done little to revive her. She hung her duffle bag on the back of a chair and draped her coat over it.

Margaret handed her a steaming mug. "Milk?"

"Please."

The nun handed her a cow-shaped creamer before returning to her own mug on the tiny kitchen table.

Taylor slid onto the chair and took her first sip. "Thanks." The woven tablecloth was a cheery blue and yellow check. So normal.

"I hadn't noticed how long your hair was. It's beautiful down. Makes you look so young, like the newest freshman."

The coffee was thick and strong, Ethiopian if Taylor had to guess. "I don't feel young."

Sister Margaret nodded sympathetically. "I'm tired too, and I got more sleep than you or Charlie." She glanced at the clock, a black cat whose belly was the clock face and tail the pendulum. "I expect him here any moment. He promised donuts."

"Donuts." Sunday mornings after church, she and Phil would stop at the bakery on the way home for donuts and a newspaper. Every Sunday they'd contemplate the selection in the case and end up getting what they always ordered—two apple fritters for Phil and a chocolate croissant for Taylor. They weren't even donuts, and yet they called them donuts. Every Sunday.

"Don't you like donuts?" Sister Margaret's brow was wrinkled with concern. "I'm sure I have some cereal or fruit or something else you can have."

Taylor shook her head. "No, donuts are fine. Just coffee would have been fine. I haven't told you how much I appreciate your letting me stay the night like this. It was above and beyond."

"Nonsense." Sister Margaret waved it off with a bony hand. "It was nothing. Besides, Charlie bringing donuts is payment enough for any number of inconveniences. Not that you are one, mind."

Taylor smiled, wishing she'd met Sister Margaret and her brother under different circumstances.

They spotted Father Charlie through the window as he neared the front door. "Just look at that bakery box!" She hurried to the door and greeted her brother with a huge grin. "Oooh, you got a dozen!"

"Dozen and a half," he answered. "Our guest needs to take plenty with her when she goes. The three of us couldn't eat a dozen between us if we tried."

Margaret flipped open the box. "Yum! Not a bad one in the bunch." She offered it first to Taylor. "What'll you have?"

Thinking of Phil, she selected a fritter, damp with apples and sugar glaze.

"Our friend needs to make a private call this morning," Father Charlie said, selecting a Long John glistening with white frosting and multicolored sprinkles. He quirked an eyebrow at Taylor.

She shouldn't. It could be dangerous.

Sister Margaret nodded, a mouthful of raised-glazed donut keeping her from saying anything for several seconds. "You can use the extension in my bedroom. Take your coffee and donut with you."

Taylor didn't want to call, but she didn't want to argue with Father Charlie either. She stood reluctantly, coffee in hand. Sister Margaret's bedroom was at the end of the hall, past the bathroom. She was half way there when Margaret called after her, "Dial nine first to get out."

Taylor stood next to the bed and picked up the phone. Father Charlie still seemed to think calling Cochran was a good idea even after everything she told him. Or maybe because of it. Was her judgment flawed by her proximity? Did his distance allow him to see the situation more clearly? She dialed the number on the card Special Agent Mark Cochran had given her a lifetime ago. As she pressed the last number, everything shifted into focus. No. She hung up the phone. This was stupid. Father Charlie didn't understand. She needed to disappear, not call the FBI.

CHAPTER NINE

Taylor stared at the phone. Cochran couldn't protect her. Hadn't protected her. It would be foolhardy to call the FBI when she had no intention of going in. She picked up her mug and fritter, left Sister's bedroom and returned to the kitchen.

Father Charlie looked up from his Long John. "That was fast."

Taylor squared her shoulders, hating to disappoint the priest. "I decided not to call. Too risky." Taylor watched for some sign of disapproval or disappointment but couldn't sense any.

"Well then, best sit down and have your breakfast." He smiled as he spoke.

She sat and picked up her fritter. The sweet apple pastry glistened with moisture. She set it down untasted and glanced at the clock. The stubborn hands refused to move.

The shrill tone of the phone made her jump.

Sister Margaret rose and answered it. "No, I didn't, but perhaps my guest did." She turned to Taylor. "Did you call Special Agent Mark Cochran?"

Taylor gaped at the nun. "I...no...I hung up before the call went through."

Father Charlie nodded. "Divine intervention. Best take it in Maggie's room."

Back in Sister's room, Taylor looked out the window without seeing a thing. Her hand shook as she picked up the phone. "Hello."

She heard the click as Sister Margaret hung up the kitchen extension.

"Taylor?" Cochran's voice burned her ears.

"Y...yes." The word came out strangled and weak.

His voice buzzed in her ear. Something about the priest calling and her being lucky he had.

She gaped. Father Charlie had called Cochran.

"I want you to come in. I'm sending someone for you right now."

No way. She shook her head, not listening as Cochran described her contact. She was going to Lisa's by way of Atlanta. Phil would be there, or he'd arrange to meet her somewhere. Together they'd figure out how to untangle whatever the trouble was. Then they'd go home. Start over. A new art studio. New greenhouse. Phil loved her. That much she was sure of. Together she and Phil would face this and beat it.

"We'll put you in protective custody." This was where he'd yell at her for taking her truck and leaving the safe house and Agent Peterson, but he didn't.

"Protective custody?"

"Someone tried to get you at your brother's in-law's house."

Her voice shook. "You know about that?"

"We had agents there, watching you, protecting you."

"Protecting me?" It wasn't funny, but she laughed anyway. "You've got to be kidding. That was protection? Really? And now you want me to trust you again?"

"I want you to stay put. Jacobs is coming to get you."

"Yeah, right. I feel so safe now."

"Taylor, that's enough. You will hold your position. Understand?"

"Hold my position?" She slapped her hands over her mouth but couldn't prevent the giggle from bubbling up. This was insanity. She hung up the phone. He hadn't asked her where she was. She hadn't given him the address. Still, she had no doubt someone was coming to get her. Probably more than one someone, from more than one place. Goosebumps rose on her arms. Who else had Father Charlie's call alerted? Waiting for the agent wasn't safe for her or for Father Charlie and his sister.

The digital alarm clock said 8:43. Crap. It was nearly forty-five minutes before she was scheduled to meet Chaz. How long would it be until the Feds arrived? Who else knew where she was? She needed to get out of there. Now. She needed to get Father Charlie and Sister Margaret away as well.

§

In the dark quiet of a suburban home office, a laptop computer made a digital copy of the call to Cochran's office, just as it had for every phone call Cochran received since he'd been put on the Wilson case. Neither he nor the bureau had any idea it was there.

The laptop automatically sent a text message to a cell phone, alerting the owner. Long before the call ended, the location of where it initiated was known. And acted upon.

§

Taylor stood with her back against the hallway wall; her thoughts a tangled mess. She wanted to blame Father Charlie. She'd confessed everything, but it hadn't been Confession. He'd done what he thought was best.

Voices penetrated her misery. In the kitchen, the priest and the nun debated food, pitting the bad of fat and sugar calories against the pleasure derived from eating them. Such normal conversation. Different foods were faring differently. Good ice cream was apparently always worth eating while French fries were apparently almost never worth it—except sometimes when salt and grease were required.

She never should have put them in danger.

Tears filled her eyes as she watched the pair. How had this become her life? She had to warn them and get them out of here. Now. She blinked away the tears and pushed away from the wall.

They both looked her way. "How did it go?" Father Charlie's eyes searched her face for the answer behind the answer.

She looked into his eyes and then away before

answering. "It was a mistake. My being here puts you both in danger."

"Nonsense."

She shook her head. "Did you tell them where I was?"

"You need protecting, and I was afraid you wouldn't call. Please, don't be angry." He looked down at his hands.

"Did you tell them where I was?"

He looked confused. "No, I... I thought when he called you back everything would be straightened out. That you'd tell him."

"Well, I didn't. They're sending someone to meet me, but I didn't tell them where I was. They didn't even ask. They traced the call or something."

"Oh," his smile faded for a moment before returning at half strength. "I'm sure it's nothing to worry about."

"What makes you think the bad guys don't have the same technology?" Her stomach hurt. "What if something bad happens?"

"Then it's on my head because I made the call."

He had no idea what he was saying. A feeling of danger closed in on her, and she frantically began collecting her things. "I have to go. And you should, too. Both of you. Somewhere safe."

"We'll go with you. Just let us grab our coats." He got up from the table.

"No." She'd already endangered them enough. Besides she wasn't going to wait for the FBI. She was catching her ride. Soon. "You need to go somewhere I'm not. With a lot of people. So you'll be safe."

"You'll still take the donuts," Sister Margaret insisted, rising and closing the lid on the box. "To share with whomever you're meeting. Everyone likes donuts."

They didn't seem to understand this wasn't a game. Taylor's chest ached.

Sister Margaret set aside the box and pulled Taylor into her arms, holding her close. "It's going to be okay. You'll see."

Taylor prayed Sister was right, but her prayer lacked confidence. She glanced at the clock. There was still too much time until her ride. It didn't matter. She couldn't risk Father and Sister any longer. She stepped from Sister's embrace. "I'd better go."

Father Charlie handed his sister her coat. "Let's go, then."

Taylor shook her head. "You can't come with me." They still didn't understand. How could she make them realize the danger they were in?

Father Charlie snagged Taylor's jacket from the back of the chair and handed it to her. "You mustn't argue with a priest, Taylor. It doesn't work and there's no time for it."

Sister Margaret chuckled. "He's right, you know. The man's stubborn as they come. You'd best let him have his way."

Taylor knew they shouldn't go with her. It wasn't safe. But Father Charlie was right about one thing, she didn't have time to argue. She shoved her arms into the coat sleeves and slung her bag over her shoulder. "I beg you. Please, don't follow me. Go to the dining hall. Go to church. Go anywhere I'm not. Please."

Father Charlie opened the door and held it open. Chill autumn air billowed in. "Nice try. Maggie, you coming?"

"Just getting the donuts."

Short of tying them up, there was nothing she could do to stop them. They walked three abreast on the wide university sidewalks. She picked up her pace, trying to put some distance between them. Father Charlie took hold of her arm, probably trying to make certain she didn't bolt. She was trapped. The buildings cast long shadows. Students left the dorms in small groups. Some called out to her religious escort attracting too much attention to them. She flinched each time Father or Sister waved back. The hairs rose on Taylor's arms as more and more people jostled along the sidewalks.

It was still early when they reached the circle on Notre Dame Avenue. Her heart slammed in her chest. The ivy on the stately brick wall beside her hung brown, leafless and dormant, smelling dry and dusty like fall.

Sweat trickled down Taylor's back as she scoured the area for Chaz's blue Notre Dame minivan.

Father Charlie turned back to her. "He isn't going to see you if you hide in the shadows."

If only. Come on, Chaz, hurry up.

The blue minivan with the large Notre Dame logos decorating its hood, back and sides rolled into the circle. Her ride.

Chaz stopped the van and got out. He walked to the side door and tugged it open. Two other riders were already inside. A third person approached the van. She turned to Father Charlie.

"That's my ride." She walked toward the van.

Sister Margaret stopped. "That can't be your ride. Chaz Nicholson is a student."

Taylor stumbled to keep from running into the Sister. Two loud bangs sounded. Like a car backfiring. Sister Margaret slammed backwards into Taylor's arms.

Taylor caught her, staggering under her weight. The bakery box was crushed between them.

"Oh, no."

A man, quick as a football lineman, tackled her from the side, slamming both her and Sister to the pavement. Taylor's head hit the ground with a bright burst of pain. Red and silver stars exploded on a black field. Weight, hard and heavy, pressed her to the concrete, squashing her. Above her, the world erupted in screams, shouted directions and protests. As she struggled to breathe, Chaz's minivan roared off in a cloud of exhaust. Blood spewed from a hole in Sister Margaret's neck as someone wrenched her from Taylor's arms.

She twisted beneath her assailant's weight.

"Hold still."

Taylor used her elbows to jab at the man on top of her, wishing she'd taken a self defense class. She pushed herself to her hands and knees. "Sister!"

The man shifted above her, knocking her back to her belly. "Stay down."

Like hell she would. Someone shot Sister Margaret. She had to do something. Stop the blood. "Oh, God. Oh, God. Sister... Father..."

Father Charlie's face was pale as ash. His eyes wide and staring. His mouth gaped, but no sound escaped. He fell to his knees.

Sirens wailed. The police were coming. They'd help.

A masculine hand appeared next to her face. She tried to bite it.

"Taylor, I'm Jacobs with the FBI. Cochran told you I was coming. Were you hit?" He pawed at her.

"Not me, Sister." Dear God. Dear God. Why? She stared at her hands covered in Sister's blood.

A large black van pulled up beside them. Two men in dark suits scooped her up and put her inside even as she struggled to stay with Sister Margaret.

The door closed. "We're clear. Let's go."

Jacobs' hands skimmed over her body. "Were you hit?"

Hit? He'd slammed her to the ground. "Sister." The word choked her. Sister had been shot. The blood. Tears burned in Taylor's eyes. So much blood. Could someone lose that much blood and live?

"There's a lot of blood," Jacobs announced as the van began to move forward.

Hands pulled at her, prodded.

"Not me, Sister Margaret. We have to help her. Let me go!" She screamed and kicked and flailed, but she was pinned to the van's floor. The carpet was gritty and damp and smelled of wet pavement and spilled coffee.

"Hold still, you're safe."

He had her thoroughly pinned. Her muscles screamed with inaction. Breath burned her lungs.

"Taylor, I'm going to turn you over and look for injuries. You will remain calm."

When he loosened his grip, she spun in his arms and swung at him.

"Damn it, Taylor. I'm the good guy. FBI."

"If you were the good guys, you'd be helping Sister

Margaret."

A voice came from the front seat. "Having a little trouble back there, Jacobs?"

"Shut up." He lay on top of her, forcing out what air had managed to fill her lungs. "Now, Taylor." He spoke directly into her ear. "I need to find out where you were shot and how bad the wound is. Which means you are going to have to trust me."

"Where was she hit?" the voice from the front seat asked. "I need to call in and that's going to be the first thing Cochran will want to know."

"It wasn't me. It was Sister Margaret."

"We know Sister Margaret was shot, but there were two shots fired." Jacobs flipped her over and lifted her shirt to check for wounds.

"I wasn't hit. Sister Margaret was." She looked Jacobs in the eye and demanded. "Is she all right? Is she alive?"

He got off her and helped her up. "I need Sister Margaret's condition," he told the driver.

The driver turned his head and spoke over his shoulder. "Will do. What about our girl?"

Jacobs picked up her right arm, examining it as he spoke. "A bullet grazed her right arm. No stitches required." His blond curly head blocked her view. He ripped open a sanitized cleanser packet and cleaned the wound on her arm. She hissed in pain.

"Sorry." His blue eyes were serious. He raised his voice to talk to the driver. "Most of the blood on her shirt is not hers."

Her shirt stuck to her body like a bloody second skin. Taylor's head spun.

Jacobs talked into a mini recorder. "The victim was combative, until I indentified myself, and now appears to be in shock. I knocked the wind out of her when I tackled her. She's breathing okay. I don't think I broke any ribs. Gave her a big bump on the head, though."

He spoke as if she weren't there listening to every word. She was fine. Fine.

Taylor shook as if she were cold, but she really wasn't. It was just adrenalin leaving her body now that she didn't have to fight her way free.

From a growing distance, she watched Jacobs clean her arm, smear it with antiseptic ointment and bandage it. Just a scratch, really. Not like Sister Margaret. She tried not to think about the blood. But it was there when she closed her eyes. Red.

He was talking again, but she didn't pay attention. None of this made any sense. If Phil was involved in something this nasty, wouldn't they try to kill him and leave her alone? It didn't make sense.

Nothing made sense.

She looked up at the ceiling, her vision graying around the edges, her head spinning. Jacobs' voice came from farther and farther away.

Taylor found herself lying on her stomach with her left cheek pressed against the cold, rough concrete. A crumpled, discarded cigarette butt lay an inch from her nose making each breath smell like a dirty ashtray. But she was the one bleeding, not Sister Margaret. Blood pooled under and around her, hot and metallic at first and then cooling, freezing her.

She was dying, but it didn't hurt. Not physically, at least. It was hard, watching without moving, feeling without being able to express it.

Phil crouched over her. She could see it was him, though her eyes were closed. It was too late for him to save her, but that was okay. He was with her, and that's all that mattered. She'd been right. He hadn't abandoned her.

She ached for his touch. He reached out his hand. She willed him to pick her up, to cradle her in his arms. But he didn't touch her. Instead, he dipped his index finger in her blood. She watched, stunned as he traced her prostrate form with his finger, using her blood like a police chalk outline.

He muttered something she couldn't quite catch about art and design, "too much red." He left, rejecting her.

She woke with a jolt, unable to move. Oh, God, she was dead. Her heart thudded in panic as she again tried to move but couldn't. Her breath caught in her throat.

Wait a second. The dead don't breathe. Every muscle tensed. She opened her eyes. Several more seconds passed before her memory caught up to her. Cochran. FBI. She was in the back of a van wrapped in a silver space blanket. The bench seat was hard, and she was damp with cold sweat. This was real. Phil and his rejection weren't. She wasn't dead.

It wasn't her blood she'd seen. It was Sister Margaret's.

The blond agent was crouching at her knees, speaking into a cell phone, but she didn't wait for him to finish.

"Is Sister Margaret okay?"

"I'm sorry. She was pronounced dead at the scene."

There'd been so much blood. Too much blood. Taylor let the tears flow.

She took a shaky breath and dashed her tears with the back of her hand. Sorry wouldn't change anything. She wanted to blame Cochran and the FBI but couldn't. It was all her fault. She wanted to find Father Charlie. Apologize. Her fault. Instead of allowing them to walk with her, she should have run from Father Charlie and Sister Margaret. Run as fast and as far as her legs could carry her. She fisted her hands, letting her nails dig into her palms. She'd been stupid. So blasted stupid.

She needed to get smarter before someone else died.

The van began to slow. Gravel rattled loudly against the underpinnings as it pulled off the road. Now what? She sat up. Her entire body clenched as she watched a dark blue sedan come from the other direction. It made a u-turn and rumbled to a halt directly behind them. "Who?" Her voice came out as a whisper.

"Cochran." Agent Jacobs said in the same tone of voice her mother once used to announce her father was home when Taylor was naughty.

One look at Agent Cochran's expression as he yanked open the door let Taylor know she was indeed in trouble. His face was all angles, from his clenched jaw to the narrowed slits of his eyes. He focused those eyes on Taylor. "I told you to stay put."

Maybe it was seeing a familiar face for the first time in a long time. Maybe it was the giddiness of recently faded fear. Whatever it was, she felt safer than she had in weeks.

He continued to rant. "Of all the stupid, asinine moves... When I give you an order, you do it. Do you understand? You could have been killed."

"Sister Margaret was." Hated tears filled her eyes.

"Dammit, Taylor. Stop crying." He sounded more like an enraged parent than the agent in charge.

She shook her head, taking deep breaths, trying to get her emotions back under control. "But Sister Margaret..."

"Not your fault."

She wiped her face on her sleeve and shook her head. "It was my fault."

"Claiming fault doesn't change anything. We've got to get going."

Cochran offered her his hand and pulled her from the van. He looked her up and down, frowned and jerked her forward, away from the van. "Masters, Jacobs, get out of the van. Now. Taylor, get in the back of the sedan."

She hesitated, following his eye to the trickle of fluid winding its way through the gravel beneath the van. "It's leaking gas."

"Everyone in the sedan." He pushed Taylor in front of him. "Now."

The other agents reached the car the same moment Taylor and Cochran did. Taylor watched as they left, half expecting the van to explode, but it didn't. They drove a safe distance and stopped. Cochran said something to Jacobs, popped the trunk, and got out. Jacobs got out of the passenger side, leaving the door open. He rounded the front of the car and got in behind the wheel.

Taylor turned in her seat, but couldn't see Cochran behind the open trunk lid. She looked at the agent seated beside her. "What's going on? What's he doing?"

The agent didn't acknowledge he'd heard her.

Naturally. Taylor turned her back on him and looked out the window at the quiet stretch of highway. She felt the car shake as Cochran closed the trunk.

Caarraack!

Taylor jumped at the sudden noise. A red light streaked toward the van.

A concussive wave shook the car and would have knocked Taylor to the floor had she not been wearing her seatbelt.

Cochran was in the car in an instant. "Go." He pulled the door closed as Jacobs accelerated.

Taylor's jaw gaped. She stared at Cochran. "You... you..." She couldn't formulate the sentence.

"Blew up the van," Cochran completed the thought. "Yes. Now, you're officially dead."

CHAPTER TEN

Inside a small two-bedroom apartment off I-694, Taylor stared out the living room window at the sound barrier that lined the highway.

"I don't want to be dead."

"You're safer if people think you are."

Taylor shook her head, dislodging the curly brown wig they'd insisted she wear. Cochran had explained the plan several times on their way to St. Paul, Minnesota, but everything he said came down to one word—orders. Maybe he'd had orders to fake her death and had simply taken advantage of the leaky gas tank to make her body unrecognizable, but to her it all seemed so random. Why were they in Minnesota instead of Indiana? Weren't local departments territorial? She hadn't gotten a satisfying answer for that, either.

"My family must be going crazy." She remembered how her parents had been after Charlotte's death. They'd never expected to bury a child. A parent never does. Now they thought they were burying a second.

"We wouldn't have done it if it weren't necessary."

She turned to look at him. "Blowing up the van was necessary?" It seemed like such a waste.

He nodded. "They'd have wanted to see the body."

"Now, you'll just show them my ring instead." Two daughters. Two closed caskets. She fingered the pale groove where her wedding ring had been. Her hand felt naked and her heart sick. Had they ruined it to make it look as if it had been in a fire? Probably. They'd taken her belongings when she'd arrived in Indianapolis to clean up—her money, her watch, her wedding ring, the key from her shoe—everything. On top of everything else, it seemed unfair for the government to be constantly robbing her. She glared at Cochran. "What did you guys do with my key?"

"What?"

"The key from my shoe. Every time I have something, you rob me."

"We don't rob you."

His smile irritated her. "I never get a receipt."

"You want a receipt?"

"No. I want the key. And my money."

He shook his head. "It's evidence."

"Of what?" she snarled. "That I own stuff? That I have a bank account?"

He smiled, and she wanted to hit him upside the head. Instead, she plucked at the scratchy red and white striped sleeve of her new long-sleeved T-shirt. She hated stripes. Once again she was dressed from the skin out in new clothing hand-selected by someone else. She had a suitcase full of similar selections she'd yet to lay eyes on. Maybe she was paying her own expenses instead of being robbed. Not that it mattered anymore. She was dead.

She stared blindly out the window. Cochran's flip statement as they raced away from the burning van hadn't registered until she'd seen the national news at the airport.

Her death had headlined.

Wasn't it Andy Warhol who'd said everybody got fifteen minutes of fame? The bureau's official statement that the fatal attack happened just as she'd been about to go into protective custody wasn't the fifteen minutes she'd wanted. Neither was film of the burning van, the footage of her personal bomb craters, or the speculation on her culpability in Sister Margaret's death.

The news anchors seemed to let anyone voice an opinion. Old customers defended her. Good person. Hard worker. A maverick with a gentle soul. Made the most beautiful gardens. Others weren't quite as kind. Notre Dame students wondered aloud if she'd been involved with drugs? Been a spy? A victim of terrorists? A Mafia moll? They correctly blamed her for Sister Margaret's death.

There'd been no comments from the "undisclosed FBI survivors," Father Charlie, or her family. She ached for Father Charlie, her family, and Notre Dame. Now, she'd never be able to tell Father Charlie how sorry she was. Her own family would grieve unnecessarily. And once Phil saw this, he would believe she was dead. She needed to get to a phone as soon as she could and leave him a message.

§

Cochran watched Taylor disappear into her own world. Her eyes adopted a glassy, unfocused look and her normally expressive face stilled and became unreadable. It happened that way sometimes. He'd dealt with enough protective relocations to see a spectrum of reactions. Some wept with relief, some with grief. Some found moving and getting a new name an exciting game. Sometimes there was anger and the relocation team received the brunt. There was always stress. It took concentration to adopt a new identity.

He looked out the window at the wall that was supposed to block the noise from the highway. It was an acoustically textured affair painted an ugly goldish brown. Windblown refuse had come to rest tangled in the long, shaggy grass at its base. The shoddy mowing, barely visible from a speeding car, was glaring from the apartment window.

Knowing her profession, Cochran wondered what Taylor thought as she stared at the view. He glanced back at her to find her eyes closed and her lashes damp with tears. A single drop slid down her pale cheek, making his heart clench. Her deep breaths said she was fighting the tears, trying to be strong. He wanted to tell her it was okay to let go. That she'd feel better for the release.

If ever there was a woman who needed a shoulder to cry on, Taylor was the one. But he didn't offer. A hug, even a well-meant one, was ill-advised. She was too vulnerable. It would be too easy for her to bond inappropriately with the agents assigned to protect her. Normally, such thoughts wouldn't have occurred to him. He could have offered a supportive hug without worry. But Taylor was different. With her, he was at risk. Had she not been married, or if he'd met her under different circumstances, he might have made a play for her. As it was, he respected her, himself, and the job too much to allow himself to act on his attraction.

He had to try something else.

He took a step back and cleared his throat. "It's not that bad," he said, conversationally.

Taylor opened her eyes and turned to face him. "What isn't that bad? That Sister Margaret died because of me? That everyone I know and love thinks I'm dead? That, since nothing remains of my life, I might as well be dead?"

"No." He nodded out the window. "That wall outside the window—I'm thinking that once the snow falls it will look just fine."

She turned back to the window and looked outside. "You're crazy." The look she gave him underscored her words.

"Really." He continued to look out the window. "I've seen places like this in the winter. They're almost nice."

She looked at the view. "No." She shook her head. "Snow covers a multitude of sins, but not something as big and ugly as that. Some things are too horrible to be whitewashed."

"The wall or your situation?"

"Both.

He nodded. "I've seen situations like yours before, too. Time can be like snow. Covers the old ugliness and prepares everything for the new growth in spring."

"Pretty philosophical for a lawman."

He nodded. "The FBI has sensitivity training. We're trying to improve our image."

The tension in his shoulders eased as she smiled at his words.

§

The gunman brushed back a lock of black hair and focused his blue eyes on the newspaper report of the shootings. He sipped his triple-espresso in the crowded coffee shop on the Notre Dame campus and smiled. He'd killed a nun. Hmm. He'd done the world a favor with that one. Any woman who proclaimed she was so superior she'd only marry God deserved to die. Well, at least she'd been honest. Even whores thought they were above men but never proclaimed it aloud. Well, not without intense encouragement. But women would do anything; say anything, with the right encouragement. God, he missed that. But that was the past.

This was now. He controlled the itch. It didn't control him.

The air around him buzzed with different versions of the nun's murder and Taylor's supposed death. He loved the way the stories grew with each telling, becoming wilder and closer to the truth with each embellishment. It was interesting how everybody had a different theory of who Taylor had been and why someone wanted her dead. Seemed everyone believed the bitch was dead. Rave reviews from the critics. He wished he bought it, but you could never trust a woman. His mother had proved that, and Therese had confirmed it. Something about Taylor's death smelled off to him. A fatal explosion outside of town. Possible, yes, but far too convenient.

Where had she been going before the priest turned her in? He needed to know. Had she stumbled onto the truth? Been fed something? He fisted the newspaper.

No one knew.

It was dumb luck that she figured out how to disappear the same moment he decided to take her out himself. Dumb luck. Bad timing. If he believed in those things.

Accawi should have accomplished the job long ago. He'd underestimated the man's incompetence.

He smoothed the newspaper and scanned to the end

of the article. Funeral arrangements for both women were listed as they would be, real or not. Well, he'd find out the truth soon enough. Regardless, he'd be at Taylor's funeral in his official capacity, of course, watching for Accawi. If the man believed Taylor was dead, he might go too far and ruin everything. Accawi had become a liability.

CHAPTER ELEVEN

It was a good day for a funeral. Taylor sat at the kitchen table as wind spat hard snow pellets at the window. Her parents would be dressing for the funeral. There'd be a visitation beforehand like they'd had for her sister all those years ago. She remembered Charlotte's oak casket and how her mother sobbed in gratitude when the funeral director gave her a lock of Charlotte's hair. Her mom wouldn't even have that this time.

Taylor bit her lip and jumped up from her chair. She wasn't going to cry. She strode to the coffee maker with her cup. Well, not *her* cup.

The coffee here was nothing but hot, brown water. Taylor sighed. Lacey was incapable of making a decent pot. She poured the thin crap down the sink. What a waste.

Her mind turned to Sister Margaret. It was nearly time for her funeral, too. Except she was really dead.

Tears trickled down her cheeks.

§

The shooter stood in the balcony of Our Lady of Sorrows Church scanning the gathered mourners from behind the stolen news camera. He'd been assigned duties elsewhere, but they couldn't stop him from attending the funeral. Nor would they recognize him with long, pale hair bound in a femi ponytail.

So many people gathered to weep over Taylor. It was disgusting. The number of mourners was a testimony to how conniving and deceitful the woman was. A man wasn't to blame for falling under her spell. Taylor was a witch, and a lucky one at that.

She had to have wonderful luck to have missed being killed by bullets shot at such close range. He'd hit her, of course, but despite the bureau's official position, he suspected she wasn't dead. Call it instinct.

Information on her condition or location hadn't reached him yet, but it would. And when it did, he'd get her one way or another. He might even give Accawi one last chance to exact "revenge."

"Are you getting this?" The chirpy, blonde news slut looked at him but didn't see him. He'd introduced himself as her replacement cameraman. She never suspected a thing.

She was ordering him around like he was her peon— just like Therese. Just like his ninth grade phys-ed teacher. Only she didn't call him a sissy. A faggot. The reporter bitch would soon learn he was no one's flunky.

He looked forward to teaching her like he had taught Therese and Ms. Janson and the other whores. She'd learn to respect him. See him as a man. His lips curved in anticipation.

He scanned the crowd from behind the lens. He shouldn't be attending Taylor's funeral. Wouldn't be among the people attending the nun's. Killers attending funerals were predictable. Cliché. Every agent felt sure Accawi would be there. And he would, but not because he'd pulled the trigger. Accawi would be looking, as the shooter was, for some sign to prove Taylor really was dead.

His eyes shifted to the priest. Father Dennison stood at the pulpit beside the pall-draped cherry casket. "When I think of Taylor, I think of sowing and tending. She nurtured all she encountered, whether it was plants or relationships. Nothing she began was ever neglected. No little sister she mentored was abandoned. No friendship left to wither and die."

Even the priest had fallen under her spell. The shooter

nearly snorted in derision, glad to have the camera for camouflage. He knew women like Taylor. They might pretend to be a goody two shoes, but they were all lying whores who liked it rough and then cried rape.

"I remember Taylor as a young girl, little slip of a thing, all of eight, maybe. She came to me asking if she could plant and take care of the big garden in front of the rectory.

"What could I say, but yes?" He smiled at the congregation. "I remember the Ladies' Auxiliary saying how cute it was. They'd just sneak back and fix the garden after she left." He shook his head. "Imagine our surprise when the garden looked wonderful. When weeks became months, and she tended what she'd sown. The parish gardens have been her job ever since."

The priest rested his hand on the pall. "Planting and tending—her friends, flowers, and faith. How she became the target for terror and death is a question whose answer we cannot begin to fathom. Those were not her seeds. We trust that, as with Job and others whose persecution defy reason, God has a higher plan we have yet to realize.

"Taylor would want us to cling to our faith in this time of sorrow."

The shooter focused the camera on the priest's face. This man was either a practiced liar or thoroughly under Taylor's spell. He acted as if he believed his words. As if he believed the woman had been honorable. No woman was honorable. It was against their nature.

Behind the camera, he panned the crowd. Her family wept in the front row. Naturally, they bought the story of her death. Two rookie agents hid in plain sight, much as he did, though not even approaching his level of success. One stood in an alcove to the side of the congregation wearing glasses with a micro-camera in the lens to film the crowd. The other stood in the cry room off the altar. Next to him in the balcony, two other news stations filmed. They'd had their IDs checked on the way in, but that posed no difficulty. Professionals prepared. The regular agents were looking for Accawi and Taylor's grief-stricken husband, not a cameraman with his credentials in order.

He shifted his weight and continued to balance the camera. He wasn't supposed to be there. Had been told to "monitor the footage from a remote location." Him. Called "too recognizable." "A person of interest" to the know-nothing lower-level agents. Ridiculous. There was no worry he'd be seen as anything other than a cameraman. He was a chameleon.

§

Taylor's hand shook as she spread a thin layer of mayonnaise on a slice of bread and added several slices of deli roast beef. Behind her, one of the bedroom doors shushed open. Steps approached. She turned and watched Cochran walk down the hall.

Agent Lacey had taken her lunch into the surveillance room to spell Cochran.

"You want horseradish on your sandwich?"

Cochran nodded.

Two states away, her funeral Mass would be over. She imagined a line of cars following a black hearse that supposedly carried what was left of her body to the cemetery. The procession following Charlotte's funeral was engraved in her mind. Her mother's hands strangling a sodden handkerchief. The white line around her father's tightly clamped lips. How could she put them through that again?

Life as she knew it had ended, but here she stood making sandwiches. She had the sudden urge to chop the sandwich into bits and knock it to the floor. But she didn't. She finished with the horseradish and set the knife on the counter with deliberate calm.

She handed Cochran his sandwich and carried her plate to the table. "What are we doing sitting here? Shouldn't we be out there looking for clues to whoever is behind this?"

"We're keeping you safe."

Safe. What did that mean? Alive, but unconnected? A victim, rather than a participant? Her plate rattled as she placed it on the table and took a seat. "There has to be something we can do. Something I can do while we wait. Some way to find Phil and prove he's innocent."

Cochran shook his head. "And just how would you do that? The FBI has a lot of people looking for him. If they can't find him, what makes you think you can?"

She should have never told her story to Father Charlie. If she hadn't, she'd be in Florida with Phil. Or at least Lisa. Sister Margaret would be alive. She would be doing something.

She turned from Cochran and bit her tongue before she said something she was certain to regret. Outside, the sky spat ugly little snow pellets against the ugly sound barrier background. The wind picked up, making the scrubby soft maples shift and dance.

She took a deep breath and released it slowly trying to ease the tension from her body. "I meant, are we trying to get the people behind all of this? Do we even know who is really behind this?"

Cochran gave her a pointed look. "We aren't doing anything. We are keeping you safely under wraps. You are staying put. The Bureau is following leads, identifying and searching for suspects."

Suspects. He meant 'suspect.' They'd never looked any farther than Phil. "It's not Phil." She had no proof to back her up, but she knew Phil was innocent. Phil was trying to keep her safe.

"So you've said."

She wanted to lash out. "And I'll say it again, because it is true. It's not Phil. He loves me." She'd managed not to yell, but it had been tough.

He sighed. "There isn't a Phil. Philip Wilson didn't exist until six months before you married him."

"What?" Taylor stared at him. Her palms were damp and her hands quaking. "What do you mean he didn't exist until just before we got married?" Her voice grew more agitated with each word.

"Just that. Copies of databases are made every few years. So, when a record is inserted into a preexisting file it shows up if a search compares present files with the archived ones. Archived files are physically kept elsewhere to eliminate tampering, which is why it's taken this long. Everything we've found leads to the same conclusion. Your husband lied about who he is."

"I don't believe it." Her chest tightened. No way was that possible. He grew up in West Allis, Wisconsin. He studied metallurgy at the University of Minnesota and art in New York.

"There is no record that he, his sister or his parents existed prior to January first of that year. No birth records. No death certificates. No school records. Nothing. Then, after January first, Phil and his family appear. Their records were inserted in the appropriate files so that they appear in school records and county birth and death records. Someone created your husband's identity approximately six months before you met him."

She sat on the couch, staring unseeingly at the art deco painting on the wall. He hadn't existed. How could that be? They loved each other. They were married. Of course he existed. She was going to stay with his sister. Wasn't she?

Cochran had to be wrong. Why should she believe he'd be any better at getting intelligence on someone than he'd been at protecting her?

"Well, if there isn't a Phil, there isn't a me, either. And if you make me someone else, I'll be just like Phil, without a past."

Cochran shook his head. "Phil wasn't in protective custody."

"How do you know?"

"Intelligence."

His cocky assurance chafed her. "What? They give you a list of everyone they supply with a new identity? That doesn't sound very secure."

"He's not in the program, trust me." He eyed her sandwich. "You gonna eat that?"

She looked at the sandwich, surprised to find it still there. She shook her head and slid the plate across the table to him. "What other reason could there be?"

He picked up the sandwich. "Mob. Murder for hire."

"No way." She pictured Al Pacino in The Godfather. "No way. He didn't hang out with that kind of person. We didn't have that kind of money. He doesn't even own a handgun. He's an artist. Gentle. Nonviolent. Definitely not a mobster, definitely not a murderer." She shook her head. "There's a better chance of him being a spook."

"A spook?" He laughed.

"Covert agent. Deep cover FBI."

Cochran shook his head. "No way."

She wanted to knock the smug right out of him.

"How do you know he isn't covert? If everyone knew who the covert agents were, wouldn't that defeat the whole covert part?" She watched him make short work of her sandwich. "They wouldn't tell you, would they? That whole 'need to know' thing."

He stood and carried the plates to the sink. "He's not covert." He left her in the kitchen and walked the six feet into the living room area.

She followed him, still talking. "Why don't you just admit it? He could be, and you wouldn't know it. Just like he could have testified against some drug lord or terrorist and been given a new identity. You wouldn't know that either, would you?"

"He could be a spy against the US, maybe, but not one of us." Cochran put his gun on the table next to the recliner and sat facing the door.

In that moment, she hated Cochran. "Phil is not the enemy."

Cochran shrugged. "But Taylor, he's not innocent, either."

She sat on the couch and drew her knees to her chest. "You made your mind up about Phil's guilt from the beginning, and nothing I say will be able to change it. He's a good man—a good husband." Her voice broke. She looked to Cochran to give her something to hang on to, knowing he wouldn't. She took a shuddering breath. "I don't understand why you can't see some scenario where he could be the victim, too.

"Phil got a call and ran, leaving you with a bomb."

"Maybe he didn't know. Maybe... Maybe..." Her chest hurt with unshed tears. Maybe Phil hadn't been a good husband. There'd been a bomb, and he'd left her. Maybe Cochran gave voice to the words she couldn't say, to the thoughts she'd tried hard to keep at bay. Maybe that was why she fought him so hard. She shivered in the flimsy shelter of her own arms.

"Come here." Cochran's voice sounded grumpy as he bridged the expanse between them to pull her close. His arms were warm and safe, solid and real in a world where nothing else was. She clung to him, closed her eyes and wished he were Phil. If only Phil hadn't left...if he'd come home, they could have solved this together. She wouldn't be forced to play dead.

"You know what?" Cochran patted her back before setting her away from him. "I think there is something you can do. We don't normally ask this of clients because it's too hard on them, but if you really want to help, maybe you can identify funeral attendees.

§

The sky hung low over Oak View Cemetery. It pressed against the weeping family and the flock of friends. Suspended over the open grave, the cherry casket was covered with flowers as the infidel priest offered prayers.

Arriving in the news van moments before the burial, Accawi was unmolested as he scoured the area for the betrayer. Anger colored everything he saw through the lens of the News-22 camera. He kept back, out of respect for the family, unlike the tactless American reporters who roamed through the crowd asking stupid questions—"How did you know Taylor?" "Who do you think is responsible for her death?"—trying to get close enough to the family to ask the really stupid questions. "How do you feel?" "What role do you think her husband played in her death?" "Do you blame the FBI and local law enforcement for failing to protect her?" Such disrespect would not be tolerated in his country.

He spotted the man who called himself Kahil. Who called himself Philip. The foolish disguise did not conceal the man within.

Accawi smiled inside. No man could watch behind a camera when his beloved wife lay in a casket. The woman, Taylor, was not dead. Philip, the betrayer, had faked his wife's death in an effort to protect her. The foolish effort pleased Accawi.

Taylor would be his. And Philip knew it and feared it.

How fitting.

At the edge of the crowd, he stared at the betrayer until the weight of his eyes made Philip glance his way. Then, Accawi slashed his finger across his throat. They were too far apart to do more.

When the demon paled, he grinned and then climbed into the van.

Yes. Revenge was a dish best served cold.

§

Inside the apartment's command center, Taylor idly watched the monitor as she waited for Cochran to cue up the funeral photos for her to identify.

"Okay." He looked over his shoulder at her. "This is a compilation of photos of people attending the funeral and burial. I want you to look at the people to see if there's anyone you don't recognize or who shouldn't be there."

"Shouldn't be there...like everyone, since I'm not dead and shouldn't be having a funeral."

"Taylor." His expression reminded her of the one her piano teacher gave her when she hadn't practiced.

She moved closer to the monitor. "Will there be audio as well? Will I get to hear my eulogy?"

He shook his head. "No audio. Just video."

"Did an agent stand outside with a camera taking photos in the open, or was he hidden?"

"They use a van with a bubble camera on the roof. Most of the time people don't even know they're being photographed." Cochran's hand hovered over the keyboard. "Any more questions or are you ready?"

She braced herself and looked at the screen. People at her funeral. The entire concept was surreal. "Ready, I guess."

Her Sunday school teacher seemed on the verge of tears. Her best friend. Her neighbors. It hit her like a two-by-four. Reality. Dear God, they truly all thought she was dead.

Cochran stopped the slideshow. "Say their names and how they know you, please."

Her throat was thick with emotion. The desire to joke was gone. "Mrs. Kramer, my Sunday school teacher. Anne Fleishman, my best friend since grade school. Cliff and Joan Pierson, neighbors." Joan was the one that called 9-1-1 when the house blew. Tears blurred her vision and made it hard to recognize people. Everyone looked so sad. Customers. Friends. "Billy Mank." He'd taken her to prom.

Cochran handed her a tissue.

Tears coursed down her cheeks. Cousins she hadn't seen since she was a kid. Since her sister's funeral. Seeing them made her miss Charlotte all the more. Friends of her family. People she recognized but couldn't put a name to. Her stomach churned acid. Her breath came in sobs. She closed her eyes. She needed to do this but wasn't certain she could. Her parents were there, thinking she was dead. Hurting. She hadn't seen them yet. "I'm not going to see my parents, am I? I don't know if I could handle that."

"No. We're trying to identify unknowns. We know your family."

She nodded.

"Are you okay? We can stop."

She wanted to stop, but stopping wouldn't help. She shook her head. "I can do this." She took a deep breath. "Tracy and Jim LaBlanche, customers."

A lifetime later, Taylor watched the camera pan the crowd at the cemetery.

"There probably won't be anyone you haven't already

named here, but I want you to look anyway."

Her heart lurched as the camera captured her family from behind. Her rock-steady parents leaned together as if they were holding each other up. Her brother's family was a tiny knot with her small nephews tangled in their parents' arms. Too much pain. All of it unnecessary.

"No." The word emerged automatically. She covered her mouth to keep the hurt inside.

"Sorry."

Taylor ignored Cochran's apology. She wanted to make someone sorry. No matter what happened in her life, her parents shouldn't have to suffer. They'd already done this once. Her nephews shouldn't cry for her. She dashed her tears with an angry swipe. She'd find the bastards behind the bombing and the shooting and make them pay.

"We can stop."

She scowled at him. "No. I'm doing this." It didn't matter that the people at the cemetery were probably the same as the people at the funeral. It simply meant she had to look harder. She narrowed her eyes and named people in the crowd.

"Where's the other reporter?"

"Who?"

Taylor didn't take her eyes off the screen. "The reporter from Channel 22 was at the funeral. Sharon Tatro from Channel 15, the guy from TV-33, and what's-her-name from Channel 22 were all at the funeral." She pointed at the screen. "There's Sharon and the TV-33 guy, and the Channel 22 camera, but no reporter." She stared at the cameramen, but couldn't see their faces. There was something about the blonde Channel 15 cameraman that seemed vaguely familiar, but she couldn't put her finger on it. She watched him for another moment. No, she was wrong. She didn't know him. She was right about the reporter, though.

"Maybe you just missed her." He stopped the stream and replayed the last few minutes.

Taylor watched carefully. She hadn't missed anything.

There was Tatro and crew, TV-33's camera and anchor, the Channel 22 camera, but no reporter. "See."

"Humph, that is odd." He made note of it.

They watched the last few minutes of the video, but there was no one unexpected. Taylor blew her nose. Drained, she slouched in the chair. Her back ached. Her left leg tingled in pins and needles. The last thirty minutes had been an exercise in futility.

§

Lacey followed Taylor into the bedroom.

"I'd like to be alone, please." Taylor toed off her shoes and climbed into bed fully dressed. She was tired. So tired.

Lacey sat on the other bed.

Taylor turned her back on the female agent. What part of 'I want to be alone' didn't the woman get?

"I've been an agent for fourteen years. Worked on dozens of protective custody cases," Lacey said. "Doing what Cochran had you do this afternoon is...well, we don't usually have clients do it. It took a lot of strength. I don't think I could have done it."

Funny, Taylor didn't feel strong. She felt bruised. She'd been wrenched from her own search because of a gunman and was trapped in Minnesota, kept in bubble wrap, while they looked for somewhere safe to stash her. The one thing Cochran let her do to help had been exhausting and futile. It was so damn frustrating. Tears leaked out of her eyes, dampening her pillow.

The bed creaked under Lacey's weight. "I just wanted you to know I'm here to listen if you need to talk."

"Thank you." Taylor croaked, her throat tight with tears. Taylor didn't need to talk. Didn't want to. What she needed was for Lacey to go. Lacey didn't understand what she was going through at all. It was the loss, yes, but not just the loss. Of course she was sad, but she couldn't wallow in it. She had to do something. Find Phil. Then, she'd know if her faith in him was justified or as blind as Cochran believed. What she couldn't do was sit and wait, hoping someone else would find the truth someday. She needed to come up with a plan for what to do next.

"Lacey," Cochran called from the other room. "Jacobs is back. I need you to take the perimeter."

"Sorry, Taylor. We'll talk more later. I promise."

Taylor listened to the door close. Good. Whatever she did would have to be done without the FBI. Their focus, at least Lacey's and Cochran's, was protecting Taylor, not finding the solution. Whatever plan Taylor followed would have to be one she came up with on her own. Alone.

They hadn't left her with many resources. She was in an unfamiliar city, she couldn't enlist the help of family and friends, and she didn't have any money. There were clothes in the dresser, but she couldn't tip her hand by packing. She had access to food, but what she really needed was cash. Cochran had money. He'd taken hers, but Heaven only knows what he'd done with it. There certainly hadn't been any left lying around. And Lacey... even though they shared a room it wasn't as if the agent emptied her pockets onto the dresser at night.

This wasn't going to be easy. Still, they appeared to trust that she wasn't a flight risk. Somehow, she was going to have to take advantage of that.

CHAPTER TWELVE

"There were three television stations at the funeral and yet only one had footage?" Cochran frowned. Jacobs was back from Indiana with recordings of the local news coverage and more footage of the funeral. Nothing about this case was routine. "Are you sure you didn't just miss it?" He sat on the edge of his chair facing the bank of monitors that displayed the news programs out of Fort Wayne.

Jacobs nodded. "I'm sure. Stations 22, 33, and 15 were in the back of the church and at the cemetery, but only one has footage. See for yourself. I recorded the broadcasts." He fiddled with the remote for a couple of seconds. "Top left. Channel 33. It's their lead story."

They watched. It was the standard funeral footage shot from the back of the church with a voiceover telling the history of the case. They showed stills of the two bombing sites, a picture of Taylor's smiling face and a sound-bite from a witness of the shooting at Notre Dame. There was another sound-bite of the priest at the funeral extolling Taylor's virtues and a few seconds of mourners at the graveside.

"Friends, family and the authorities are baffled as to why Taylor Wilson was the target of these attacks. There's speculation that there may be a connection with her husband Philip. Officials are requesting help finding Philip Wilson, age thirty-three. If you have information, you are requested to call the local FBI at..."

Jacobs hit the pause button. "I hate it when they do

that. Clogs up the phones. Makes us look like idiots."

"Tip lines work." Cochran stared at the screen with its frozen copy of Phil's license photo. According to Taylor, it was a goofy shot with glasses he apparently didn't need, facial hair he no longer sported, and swelling that disguised his bone structure. She laughed when she learned it was the picture they distributed for identification purposes. Cochran shrugged. "Well, maybe not this time."

Jacobs hit play. "The Marten family is no stranger to tragedy. Fourteen years ago Taylor's older sister Charlotte was the victim of domestic violence when her husband, Brad, shot her in the head before turning the gun on himself." Jacobs hit pause again. "Did you know that?"

Cochran nodded. "It may be why Taylor is so obsessive in her belief that Phil would never harm her."

"I'd think it would have the opposite effect, making her suspect every man."

"Not according to her parents. Taylor was thirteen when Charlotte died. She became ultra-conservative in picking her friends and, later, her dates. She stayed away from football players, hockey players, wrestlers— anything violent." He turned back to the television. "What else have you got?"

Jacobs switched to Channel 22, WPTA. "There's really no need to watch this. It's just stock footage and info for the tip-line." He flipped to TV-15. "This one is odd. They should have had funeral footage and quotes. Sharon Tatro, their anchor, elbowed her way to the family. But here they have Tessa Schneider sitting in for her. Claims Sharon is sick."

Cochran frowned. The entire TV-15 broadcast seemed light, as if Sharon Tatro's illness had eliminated their ability to cover the news. The story was huge. It made the national news on several stations, but the only footage of the funeral itself came from Channel 33. "Did we confirm Tatro's illness?"

"I'm expecting a report any moment." The fax machine started printing. "This must be it."

He handed the report to Cochran.

Cochran's suspicions rose as he read. "Channel 22's reporter, Alison Davis, and cameraman, Cameron Craig, were found unconscious in the back of the van behind a mausoleum in the west corner of the cemetery." He looked up at Jacobs. "Taylor noticed that News-22 had a camera at the cemetery, but no reporter. We need to take a closer look at that footage." He looked back to the page. "Looks like Craig and Alison will be fine, but toxicology is running tests on both of them and their water bottles."

The news about Channel 15 was worse.

Feeling ill, Cochran summarized the report aloud. "Our guys located the Channel 15 van with cameraman Fredrick Hemerez's body inside. Sharon Tatro is still missing."

§

As Fuad Accawi drove away from Taylor Wilson's false resting place, Aisha's face shimmered in his mind's eye. He had gotten used to seeing her every time he closed his eyes, but this type of daytime vision was new.

She smiled and beckoned.

Ahh, she was lovely. Not as she'd been in the end, with the glassy glint in her eyes, but as she'd been before the blue-eyed monster poisoned her, lured her with expensive pieces of art, and fed her pretty little nose.

"My love," he whispered, reaching a hand to touch her face.

A horn blast shocked him from his reverie. He jerked the steering wheel right and swung his car back to the correct side of the yellow line.

Once again in control of his vehicle, he looked for his beloved wife. She was gone. His heart fell.

"Aisha, my love, I will avenge your death. I give you my word. The man who betrayed you will suffer, and you will find peace."

Kahil or Philip Wilson, it mattered not what the man called himself. He now knew what it was like to see his beloved wife terrified and on the run. Soon, he would see her broken and beaten, and know it was his actions that caused her death. His manhood would be ripped asunder, but he would live, denied an honorable death and tortured by his inability to protect the woman he loved more than life. Day after day, night after night, her death would haunt him. It was fitting that Philip Wilson suffer thus.

Taylor was not dead, but he would find her. Allah was on his side.

§

The gunman showered away the blood from his afternoon's excesses before leaving the hotel room. The taste of power clung to his lips. God, he had missed this. Sharon Tatro had been as beautiful naked as she'd been on television. As beautiful and as faithless. She was a married woman, but she'd opened herself to him. She'd cried and protested at first, like any woman, but in the end she'd begged, claimed to love him, made all sorts of crazy promises. Stupid bitch. As if he would be fooled again by the vows of a woman.

He thought of Therese on that last day. She'd met him at the door with a big bouquet of anthurium. She always bought him flowers every time she invited another man to join them. Anthurium and calla lilies. "Him" and "her" flowers. To thank him for playing along. To thank him. She thought their trios were her idea.

He was still sore from the night before. There'd been two studs and himself. They'd fought over her and taken each other. She loved it.

"I'm sorry about our special dinner last night. I didn't know Devon was going to come. It was just supposed to be Nick. You aren't mad at me, are you?" She set down the flowers and made the cute pouty face that said, 'game on'. She unzipped her shirt nearly to her navel. Her breath fanned his face smelling of gin.

Oddly enough, he didn't feel like playing. "I'm not in the mood, Therese. It's been a long day. I just want supper."

"But I was such a bad girl last night, Daddy. You are just going to have to whoop me good." She offered him her rump for a smack.

Normally, the promise of violence would stir him, but not tonight. Max had left this morning for a week in Hawaii. The first time in ten years they were taking separate vacations, and it was all because Therese wanted to go to Mexico.

She narrowed her eyes. "You wish you were going to Hawaii with him, don't you?" Her voice was sharper than normal.

"Therese, what is this about? I'd really like to eat. I'm starving."

She backed away from him a step. "You know what I did today? I found the key to that lockbox under your bed. And do you know what I found?"

Of course he knew. A fragment of ice traced his spine. The key had been taped to the bottom of a locked desk drawer. She had to have been searching for it for a while.

She reached in her bra and pulled out the photos. Max in the shower. Max dressing. Max asleep with a massive hard on. He reached for them.

She jerked back her hand. "Does Max know about these?" She laughed. "Of course not. Everyone thinks you're a real man, but you're not are you? You're a fag, aren't you?"

He lunged for the photos, but she danced out of reach.

"I called him to invite him to one of my special dinners, so he could meet the real you..."

He swallowed hard. "Are you nuts? I work with Max."

"...but he'd already left." She held the photo of Max sleeping, so he could see. She stroked the image of Max's penis with a manicured nail. "He's quite the man, isn't he? I'll bet he's dreaming of a woman." She turned her eyes to him. "Not like you."

"Therese," he warned.

"I wondered who you'd want to do if he came to dinner—Max or me." She ripped the picture in half. "Who you'd be jealous over if I did him. Who you loved the best. Then, I thought about last night with the boys. Every time we have a dinner, it's not me you watch, is it? It's the guy. It's not me you fantasize about? It's Max."

She jutted out her swollen lower lip. "You aren't really a man, are you? You're a fag."

His fist hit her jaw so hard she flew against the counter. Not really a man. He hurt Therese like he'd never hurt her before. But he showed her.

He was a man.

Faithless whore. He'd had a full week to perfect his story and dispose of the body. She was the first Foxy Lady, but no one knew because no one ever found her.

All women were alike. Taylor claimed eternal love and faithfulness, but he had no doubt she'd spread her legs for Cochran or whomever else she thought would help her. Why did otherwise smart men fall for women? The Spartans had it right. The warrior brotherhood was what mattered. Women were nothing but lying, scheming whores.

Still, he enjoyed them now and again. Sharon had been most satisfying. He'd been right about her fear— ambrosia, rich and sweet. It made him hard just thinking about it. About the others.

He closed the door and left her in the room he'd rented, sliding the "Do not disturb" card in the lock. The room was paid for through the end of the week. With luck, no one would find her until then.

Riding the elevator to the ground floor, he caressed the heart shaped locket in his pocket. The gold was warm beneath his thumb, soft and smooth. He shouldn't have taken the souvenir. Mementos like this were dangerous. Helped establish guilt. The Foxy Lady Murderer had collected hair. He smiled. He'd keep the locket until tomorrow and then mail it to Accawi.

He laughed at his own brilliance. Blaming Tatro's death on Accawi would put a nice bow on the package. He'd "solve" Taylor's murder and Sharon Tatro's all at once.

§

Later that evening, Accawi accessed his special Hotmail account from the computer in a popular coffee shop. He was not alone in his quest to destroy the evil one. A man in his position knew where to look for others likewise betrayed. He grinned in satisfaction as the message appeared. The enemy of my enemy is my friend.

"Playing hide-and-seek, the rooster ran with the chick. They like their mini-apples. I'll address the crowd when the cheers die down."

It read like the gibberish the "invest now" spammers sent to fool the filter, but the message was transparent. Taylor lived. She was with Agent Cochran in Minneapolis. Accawi's contact had lost their trail for the moment, but he would have their direction soon.

Accawi grinned and logged off his account.

American intelligence was like a sieve. Where mistakes were tolerated, more mistakes would happen. They would do well to follow his country's example.

Soon, the betrayer's wife would be in Accawi's hand, subject to his tender mercies. He had played with her like a cat did a mouse. She was frightened enough to play dead. But as any doomed mouse knew, it was only possible to stay still so long. One move. One twitch and he would take her. He'd hold her in his hands. Touch her. Destroy her innocence as Kahil/Philip had ravaged Aisha's. He would keep her alive until her husband came. When she knew the man her husband truly was, she would beg for death. And being merciful, Accawi would grant it. Philip would watch her faith in him die moments before the light faded from her eyes. Only then would he allow Philip to bestow upon him, Accawi, the greatest of gifts—an honorable death. He would reunite with his beloved while leaving Philip alive to see his beloved's death like a never-ending film loop in his mind. The perfect revenge.

§

Taylor awoke fully clothed in yesterday's jeans and

sweater. She stared at the darkness of the ceiling trying to convince herself to get up and flick on the light. The digital clock by Lacey's bed explained why she felt so sleep-drunk. She'd slept for twelve hours. That was enough to leave anyone with a fuzzy head. All the plans and conclusions she'd reached in those moments before sleep claimed her had tangled with her dreams until they seemed like nonsense this morning. She was back where she'd started, needing to escape from the FBI once again in order to follow Phil's instructions.

The sooner she got to Miami, the better. But how? She was a guest of an FBI protective relocation team. She'd been lucky to elude them once. It wasn't as if she could simply leave again. Or could she? They didn't watch her every second. Those times she cooked, she tended to have the kitchen to herself. Maybe...

Her bladder insisted she get up. She sighed. Never argue with a bladder. Bladders are opinionated, stubborn, self-centered and absolutely unwilling to listen to reason.

"I made coffee." Lacey called from the kitchen as Taylor left the bathroom.

Taylor stopped mid-step. She looked down the hall. Unlike yesterday, the kitchen table was in perfect alignment with the hall, and Lacey sat at the table facing the bathroom door apparently watching for Taylor.

Taylor walked into the kitchen trying to pretend everything was normal. That she wasn't hatching plots that didn't involve the FBI. That Lacey hadn't moved the table to watch the hallway. That Lacey didn't make the world's worst coffee.

Taylor poured herself a mug, wishing there was instant coffee to add to the thin liquid that came from the pot. It didn't even look like coffee, more like weak tea.

"Coffee okay?" Lacey asked.

The girl had no domestic skills, but she tried. Taylor glanced at her.

Lacey wasn't looking at her, though. Her head turned to look at the door, the hallway, and the window before returning to Taylor.

She was checking all the exits with a diligence Taylor hadn't witnessed before.

Taylor's heart beat faster.

"Lacey, has something new happened?"

Lacey said nothing. Her expression was the telltale FBI neutral.

Taylor's heart rate went up a notch. "What?" Her hand shook. She set down her cup before she sloshed coffee all over the table. "What happened?"

Lacey left the table and pulled a box of cereal out of the cupboard. "You want me to pour you some cereal? I'd make eggs, but you wouldn't want to eat them." She glanced at Taylor as part of her visual circuit. She wasn't obvious about it, but Taylor could see she was panning the area over and over like a stealthy automatic sprinkler head.

Taylor got out of her seat. "You're not going to tell me."

Lacey smiled. "Don't worry. You're safe."

Maybe. But when she woke up this morning, all she had to do was come up with a brilliant plan to slip away from the FBI and keep them from finding her while, without money or transportation, she located Phil. Hard, but not impossible. Now, with the way Lacey was acting, it seemed as if dead might not be safe enough. It seemed the bad guys were once again on her tail and her parents' pain, her nephews' tears, the loss of everything were worthless, pointless. Meaningless sacrifices on the altar of...of what? Stupidity? Mistaken identity? What could Phil possibly have done that would send wackos after her?

She paced to the counter and back to the table. The apartment was a cell she needed to escape from.

"Do you want cereal?" Lacey held up the cereal box.

"No. I'll make eggs." Taylor crossed to the refrigerator and opened it. The Thanksgiving turkey Jacobs had bought took up most of the top shelf. Taylor wanted to knock it to the floor and kick it until she couldn't kick anymore. Her mother should be coming over to her house to spend the day making pies, rolls, and salads. But she didn't have a house. And her mother didn't have her. Her hand shook as she got out the eggs.

She had to act normal but she couldn't. What the heck was normal, anyway? "Have you eaten? Have the guys?" Without waiting for an answer, she pulled a skillet out of a drawer, set it on the burner, and prepared a breakfast feast.

When she was done, Taylor set two loaded plates on the table in front of Lacey—eggs, bacon, toast, pancakes. "For whoever isn't on watch. You want to take it to the room, or should I?"

Lacey looked at her as if trying to read her thoughts.

Taylor turned back to the stove.

"Aren't you going to eat?"

Taylor shrugged. "Later."

Lacey nodded. When she took a plate to the control room, Taylor dumped the coffee down the sink and started a new pot.

A few minutes later, she was drinking real coffee. The caffeine helped, but it wasn't enough. Making breakfast and washing the dishes weren't enough either. She needed to dig up a tree or lug bags of fertilizer.

She opened the refrigerator to put the eggs away.

The stupid turkey still sat there. She had to have something to do to think. She had to have something to do to not think.

Thanksgiving pies, rolls, and salads.

She'd make them and think of her mom, like her mom was probably making them right now thinking of her. Then, maybe she could think of a plan rather than torturing herself with what she'd lost. And with Thanksgiving came leftovers—leftovers that would be perfect for a girl on the run without any money.

§

Cochran left the command center and walked into the kitchen. Taylor's back was to him as she rolled out pie dough on the kitchen table. According to Lacey, she'd stopped talking about the time she'd started cooking. The cooking could be normal—after all, Thanksgiving was tomorrow. But the silence wasn't. In his experience, Taylor made noise as she cooked. She hummed, chatted, sang and even occasionally grumbled as she worked, but she was rarely silent. Even her employees called her a plant whisperer because she talked to the plants and rocks.

He watched her, but her actions seemed normal, focused on the task at hand.

"We're going to have Thanksgiving, I see."

She froze at the sound of his voice. Not a good sign. He expected a smile. He placed his yolk-smeared plate in the sink. "Thanks for breakfast."

"You're welcome." Her shoulders looked stiff as she resumed rolling the dough.

He waited for her to say something else. Ask a question. But she didn't. Shit. Lacey was right. Taylor was up to something. "What kind of pie are you making?"

"Pumpkin and apple."

"I like pumpkin."

She nodded once.

He frowned. "But I'm sure you figured someone had to, since there were three cans of pumpkin in the cupboard."

Taylor said nothing. She shifted so her back was to him as she rolled the pie dough.

He watched as she picked up the pie pan and held it over the dough. The circle of dough was as big around as the pan. She put the pan to one side and started rolling again.

"Looks big enough to me. How big are you going to make it?" He didn't know squat about making a pie. His comments were meant to draw a response, but they didn't.

It was clear she didn't want to talk. That might mean she just didn't want to talk, or it might mean she was thinking something…planning something. Just standing beside her he could almost hear the wheels turning in her head. She was doing more than just making pies. He'd underestimated her in the past. He wasn't about to do it again.

"What's wrong, Taylor?"

She cut her eyes in his direction for a moment. The message in her narrowed glance was such a perfect combination of "aren't you supposed to be somewhere else?" and "don't ask stupid questions" he almost laughed. She could give his mother a run for the money.

Ignoring him, she gently folded the dough into quarters and placed it in the pan.

"Where were you going when we rescued you at Notre Dame?"

"Rescued me," she snorted. "If it weren't for you, there wouldn't have been a gunman... or funerals." Her hands were busy pressing the dough into the pan and fussing with the edges.

Maybe her silence was mourning.

He tilted his head to get a better look at her face. Her jaw was clenched, but her eyes were dry.

Maybe her silence meant something else.

"Atlanta wasn't just the easiest place to get a ride to that day, was it?" They'd glossed over this in previous questioning sessions. There was no doubt she was the victim here, but he also had no doubt her loyalty to her husband might cause her to keep secrets.

She shook her head and sighed. "I know you think I'm nuts to believe in him." She waved her hands as if erasing the air. "Let's not get into that again. Nothing's changed."

"Were you going to Atlanta because you thought he'd be there?"

She stirred and then poured the pie filling into the unbaked shell.

Crap. That's exactly what she thought. Why hadn't he figured it out before? "What made you think he'd be there? Did he contact you?" What if her movements hadn't been as random as they thought? What if all this time she'd been acting on information Phil had given her? Information she hadn't shared. Maybe she wasn't as innocent as they supposed. As soon as she set down the mixing bowl, he grabbed her upper arms and turned her to face him. He wanted to shake her, but kept his hands gentle. "What did he tell you?"

"He didn't tell me anything. He left a clue."

"A clue that told you to look for him in Atlanta?"

She shrugged.

"Where is it?"

She stepped back and he let her go. "You took it. The football schedule."

"Christ, Taylor."

She frowned at him. "Don't swear." She rubbed her arms, but he knew he hadn't hurt her.

"He's left you clues before." It wasn't a question. The football schedule wasn't in the safe deposit box. She'd gotten it somewhere else—either the Bachman's house or Notre Dame. She knew there would be another clue, and she knew where to look for one. "That's why you went to that cabin." He looked her in the eye. "You've been keeping information from the FBI. Do you know how much trouble that puts you in?"

She stuck out her jaw. "I didn't keep anything from you."

He scowled.

She looked away. "While we were together."

"From the top, Taylor. I want to know what you knew, from the beginning."

Her eyes met his again. "Do you really think I'm behind everything that's happened? Do you really think I blew up my house and my business and then arranged for someone to take shots at me?"

"No, but I think you've withheld crucial information that has resulted in murders."

"Murders." The color drained from her face. "You mean someone other than Sister Margaret is dead? Who? How?" She clutched the edge of the table.

He pulled out a kitchen chair. "Sit down before you fall down."

"No." She shook her head. "Who?"

He leaned against the table. "You start. From the beginning, Taylor. I want to know everything you've known, everything you've suspected from the start."

She looked him in the eye. "How can you turn this into some kind of power play? Who's dead? What aren't you telling me?"

"I'm telling you that you need to tell me everything because you're not the only victim here."

"I..." Taylor's jaw dropped. "You think I was selfishly putting others in danger? That I was treating this as some kind of game?" Her eyes looked bruised. "This is not my fault." She pointed her finger at him. "You're the pro who is supposed to be handling this. You're the one who made me fake my death. Who's dead, damn it? Tell me. I'll tell you everything, but not one word before I know who's dead."

"I can't tell you that."

She gaped at Cochran. "You arrogant S.O.B." She pushed against his chest hard enough to set him back a step. "You and your damned need-to-know attitude. I was going to tell you everything. Everything. But now..." Her hands fisted at her side. "If you think I'm going to just stand here wondering which member of my family was murdered just so you can pressure me into giving you some useless information, you're nuts." Tears streamed down her cheeks.

"It's not your family, Taylor. I'm sorry, I thought—"

She didn't let him finish. She shoved him again. "Jerk." And stormed from the room.

§

Later that afternoon in Fort Wayne, Indiana, Phil and Sean entered the Luxury Suites hotel lobby. To the untrained eye, everything appeared normal. Guests checked in, swimsuit-clad families headed to the pool, hotel staff poured pretzel mix in bowls for the complimentary Manager's Reception. Phil looked for Jackson, but the Special Agent in Charge wasn't in the lobby.

"Jackson's probably waiting for us upstairs." Phil pressed the elevator button. He hated murder scenes.

The elevator arrived. Sean smiled as the door closed. "Just like old times."

Phil bit his tongue. Of all the memories Sean could

have smilingly referred to, murder investigations weren't the ones Phil would have chosen. They had so many good times to remember. He'd just as soon forget about the murders he'd worked.

On the third floor, Jackson stood just inside the crime scene tape talking with a man in a cheap, dark suit that screamed 'police detective,' but his shield said 'captain.' "Right on time. I just got here myself." He greeted his agents and then turned to the police captain. "They're with me."

The captain nodded. "Gotta say this is one case I'm glad to be handing over. I'll leave a couple of my officers to watch the perimeter like we talked about. But, otherwise, this one's yours." He raised the yellow tape for Phil and Sean to duck under.

Agent Eider met them at a drop cloth spread outside room 378. A camera hung around his neck. He nodded in greeting. "Kennedy, you back?"

"Temporarily, at least. What have we got here?"

"It's a messy one."

Phil felt the weight of Sean's gaze. The unasked questions. He took a deep breath and held it. He didn't expect investigating this scene would be easy. No murder scene ever was. Not that they saw that many. Only the ones that crossed state lines or otherwise fell under their jurisdiction. They were at this one because it was tied into Taylor's case, somehow. It couldn't be as bad as the last murder scene he'd investigated. And no matter what had happened here, Taylor was safe in protective custody. He let go of his breath in a determined blast. "Let's get started."

Eider nodded. "We're pretty sure it's Sharon Tatro. Her press credentials are on the dresser where we found them." He pulled off his blue booties. Several clumps of dark hair clung to one side. "You can go in. We're finished here. We'll bag everything when you're done."

Jackson scowled as Eider tossed the booties into the trash instead of sliding them into an evidence bag. Phil was surprised. It wasn't like Eider to be so careless with evidence.

"Bag those," Jackson growled. "They're carrying evidence."

"Sir?"

He visibly bristled. "Do I need to tell you your job? Those booties are covered with hair."

"The entire room is, sir." Still, Eider plucked the booties out of the trash and put them in an evidence bag, as ordered.

Phil tugged scene-protection booties over his shoes and pulled on a pair of surgical gloves. The door to room 378 was propped open with a smooth plastic lab case. Phil steeled himself. It didn't matter that he'd signed on as the tech guy. Not now, not then. He'd seen too much death. Been responsible for too many bodies. The all too familiar chill numbed his soul. This was why he'd left active service. But this crime scene was directly related to his operation and Taylor's continued safety. They needed his eyes, his perceptions.

A stretcher with an open body bag waited against the opposite wall. He stepped closer to the room and wrinkled his nose at the ripe smell of death and blood. Crap. It even smelled like a messy one. Images of the Foxy Lady murders flashed through his mind. He'd hoped never to see anything like those brutalized prostitutes again. He entered the crime scene while O'Hearn and Jackson plucked booties from the open box.

The room was like every budget hotel room he'd ever stayed in. The door opened into a narrow hall. An open closet with its standard theft-proof-metal hangers and iron/ironing board combo were on the right. The door to the bathroom was on the left.

He poked his head in, noticing the blood and the hair first. "Dear God."

The perpetrator had sprinkled the entire scene with clippings of hair in a variety of colors and lengths in order to camouflage DNA evidence. No wonder Eider hadn't been concerned about the hair. The majority of the body was on the floor of the hot, bright closet of a bathroom. He stared at it trying to identify body parts. This lump of flesh didn't resemble the woman he'd watched on television. The perp had carved her up like a sick sculpture. He stepped into the bathroom. O'Hearn and SAC Jackson followed.

"It's like a fucking Picasso." Jackson stood at his elbow. "Thirty years in the bureau, and I've never seen anything like this."

Phil wished he could say the same. "Reminds me of the Foxy Lady killings."

"How does this remind you of the Foxy Lady killings?" Sean's tone and expression were both puzzled. "He tattooed the bodies I'm so Foxy. Hers isn't. And Dempsey didn't leave a trace of himself behind. This," he stood in the tiny entryway and pointed at the hair strewn everywhere. "Whoever did this didn't care what was left. Besides, Dempsey's dead. I shot him, remember?"

Phil nodded, as if he could forget. "It's the extremes that connect these cases—and the hair. The Foxy Lady killer took hair, this guy left it. It feels too extreme to be accidental."

Jackson shrugged. "I don't see it, but maybe this is a reverse copycat. Could be this guy read about Dempsey. It wasn't exactly a low profile case."

"Still, you might have a point, Max. He might not have signed his work, but he's not a one-timer either. Look at the mirror." Sean pointed into the bathroom.

Phil's throat was raw as he read the words written in blood. TAYLOR IS NEXT. "Dear God." Phil's eyes skimmed over his own reflection—haunted eyes, pale face. He should have stayed away. He looked down. A severed, manicured finger rested on the counter. His stomach tightened. Taylor's fingernails were never manicured like that. He slammed the door closed on that line of thought.

"You okay, Max?" Sean's hand was on his shoulder.

Phil cleared his throat, ignoring the question. "Looks like he used the victim's own finger to write with."

Sean nodded. "Accawi must have flipped."

Phil looked at Sean's reflection in the mirror. "Accawi

didn't do this." He pointed to the woman's hand balanced on the toilet seat. "The perpetrator used a blade to sever both the hand and the finger."

"So, Accawi could have done that."

"I don't think so. The level of destruction and desecration doesn't fit Accawi. He'd kill, but it would be ritualized. He'd slit her throat, stone her, maybe burn her alive, but he wouldn't mutilate the body like this. This was done by an animal."

"Unless he was trying to turn her into a sculpture. In retribution."

Phil shook his head. "That's not his culture. Besides, the motivation is missing. If he suspected there was something wrong with The Bedouin Ship, why not go after me? Why kill this woman? Why go after Taylor?"

Sean shrugged. "Because you disappeared?"

"I don't think so." Phil stepped around the remains. "Something else is going on here." He slid past Sean to follow Jackson into the bedroom. "Something that makes this personal. Makes Taylor the target. I just don't know what it is."

Sean followed him until he stopped at the dresser and looked at Sharon Tatro's identification.

Phil and the SAC walked farther into the room. There was more hair and blood here, especially on the bed. One of the pillows cushioned a length of blood-smeared rope and a scattering of broken plastic cutlery.

"Accawi didn't do this. It just feels wrong." Phil remembered John Michael Dempsey, the suspected serial killer Sean shot. There had been something about that case that felt wrong, too. Unresolved. Despite the baggies of hair Sean found in the lockbox in Dempsey's truck. Despite Dempsey being in the right city at the time of each murder. Maybe it was the lack of a trial and conviction that made it feel unfinished. Whatever it was, the "off" feeling permeated this scene as well, making it too damn familiar. He felt the weight of Sean's gaze on him. "There's just something about this that seems familiar. Do you feel it?"

Sean shook his head. "I think Taylor's name on the mirror's got you rattled."

"Maybe. Do we know who the room is rented to?"

Jackson pulled his notebook out of his pocket. "Juan Smith. Checked in the day before Taylor's funeral. The woman at the counter doesn't remember what he looked like. Medium build. Medium height. Dark hair. Sunglasses, maybe."

"Maybe?" Phil shook his head. "That description could be anyone, including the three of us. Don't they have security cameras in this place?"

Jackson shook his head. "Might be why our guy picked this hotel."

The blood soaked carpet squished beneath their feet as they walked back to the bathroom.

Phil looked at the mirror before turning to SAC Jackson. "I'm going to Minneapolis to get Taylor. Her death didn't fool anyone."

§

Thanksgiving afternoon the pressboard kitchen table nearly groaned under the weight of the turkey and all the trimmings, but Taylor and Cochran sat in the living room with their plates. Lacey and Jacobs were on watch, having already eaten in shifts.

"I really am sorry, Taylor. I thought you knew it wasn't your family."

"And just how was I to know that?" The weight on her shoulders was less than it had been but hadn't totally disappeared. Someone else had died because of whatever the heck was going on, and he still hadn't told her who it was.

"I wouldn't do that. I'm not that big of a jerk." He turned on the game. "Lacey said you spat on my pie."

"No, Lacey said if she'd been me she'd have pissed on your pie."

"So it's probably safe, right?" Cochran eyed the large piece of pumpkin pie on his dessert plate.

Taylor shrugged. "Probably."

They ate in silence for a few minutes watching the Packers play the Lions.

"You're going to have to tell me everything. You know that, right?"

"I should have pissed on your pie." If Phil's message and instructions saved one person and didn't risk Phil, how could she justify not telling him everything?

"Taylor."

"Fine. But I want you to help me find Phil."

"Of course. I'm all about finding Phil."

Except he was all about locking Phil up, and she was all about proving him innocent so they could be free to start their lives again. She was about to point out that fact when a newscaster interrupted the station break.

"Breaking news... Our Indiana affiliate W.A.N.E. reports that anchor woman Sharon Tatro's savagely dismembered body has been found in a Fort Wayne hotel room. Tatro disappeared Tuesday after Taylor Wilson's funeral. Authorities believe there may be a connection between Ms. Wilson's and Sharon Tatro's murders."

"Wha?" An invisible hand squeezed the air from Taylor lungs. Sharon Tatro's pretty face filled the screen.

"Tatro, who has long been known for her in-depth investigative reporting, may have stumbled onto the reason behind Wilson's shooting and the bombings that preceded it. Here we are with our national correspondent Bryant Hum..."

Savagely dismembered... Visions of horror films paraded through her mind. Taylor slapped a hand over her mouth and bolted from the room, barely making it to the toilet in time.

I don't want to die.

A phone rang once in the background.

She remembered Sharon Tatro from television—pretty and ambitious. Fort Wayne was too small for Sharon, but she was getting noticed. A couple more good stories, and she'd be called to a bigger town. She was probably looking for those stories, and now she was dead.

Maybe if Taylor had given the FBI everything she knew. She curled in a ball next to the toilet. Tremors wracked her body. Should have been me. Now was not the time to cower and hide. Someone was out there killing people. They had to do something. But what? Huddling next to the toilet didn't seem like such a bad idea. Taylor wiped her mouth with a wad of tissue and flushed the toilet.

Cochran knocked on the door. "You okay?"

She scrambled to her feet, lurching to the door. "Uh, yeah, fine."

He looked at her carefully, making his own assessment. "You need to get changed. We have to move you."

Taylor glanced at her clothing—red sweater, wool crepe slacks. "Changed?"

Cochran ushered her into her bedroom. "I got out some things. Put them on."

She looked at the black clothes—a hooded sweatshirt, jeans, two pairs of socks, and sneakers. There was a dull black ski jacket that looked as if it had started life another color, a black hat and thermal-lined gloves. She shivered. Hide in the night clothes. "Is this because of the TV?" That hardly seemed possible. A news report wouldn't send the FBI scrambling. There had to be something else. The phone call. "What else happened?"

He was already halfway out the door. "We got a tip. Get dressed. Fast." He closed the door behind him.

She dressed as quickly as her shaking hands would allow.

Lacey was in the darkened kitchen when Taylor tiptoed in, all in black. Lacey jabbed her finger toward the equally dim living room.

The breath caught in Taylor's throat, and her heart beat against her ribs. Please, God. She stumbled over her feet in her rush to obey. This wasn't her life. Her life was sunshine, nurturing plants, designing gardens. There were things she wanted to ask.

Near the window, Cochran opened the sash and

attached a portable fire ladder to the ledge.

"Come here. I'll go first. You wait five seconds and climb out the window."

She nodded. "Uh...what about Lacey?" The words barely squeaked through her constricted throat.

Cochran parted the curtains and looked out. "She has a different job." A blast of cold air announced the opening of the window. He backed out and then said, "Count. One Mississippi..."

"T...two Mississippi..." There was a sound at the apartment door—like firecrackers underwater. To heck with counting to five. Taylor backed her legs out the window. She could make out Lacey in the dark, crouched low. Something large slammed into the outside of the apartment door, once, twice. It gave way, taking the frame with it.

"Come on." Cochran urged from below.

Another pop. Not fireworks. No. Please. Just before Taylor's head dipped below the window sill she saw Lacey slam into the wall, limp.

Another fraction of a second and Taylor was on the ground. "Lacey..." her voice was more breath than whisper.

Cochran grabbed Taylor's hand, yanked her away from the building and into the scrubby trees. Soft maple. Poplar. She was forced to follow. Her mind raced in time with her heart. Was Lacey all right? Where was Jacobs?

Taylor's night vision stank. Every light they passed cast revealing shadows and made it harder to see in the dark. Thank God, Cochran didn't seem to have the trouble she did. He never stumbled as he pulled her over uneven ground to a parking lot. They ran past businesses closed for the holiday, yet still lit.

It was impossible to hide amidst all the light and shadows.

Cochran stopped so abruptly that Taylor slammed into him. He pressed her against the wall with the back of his arm. Her heart thundered so loudly she could hear nothing else. Lacey had been shot. "Lacey..."

In an instant, his hand covered her mouth. In another circumstance the motion would have angered her. Now it only made her gasp.

He released her, motioning for her to wait as he peered around a corner. She tried to become one with the block wall. The wait seemed interminable. Jagged breath after jagged breath. Then, all too soon, he tugged her around the corner. It was black in the shadow of the building. She couldn't see anything. She didn't know the area. Had it been day, she wouldn't have known where she was, but it was even worse at night. She stumbled on the uneven ground and bit her lips to keep from crying out.

There were sounds of other footsteps running. A voice she didn't recognize yelled her name into the darkness. She clutched Cochran's hand for dear life and swallowed a whimper.

They ducked into a doorway as flashlight beams crisscrossed the air. It was worse than a movie thriller. In movies you knew the main character was going to live. Here, she didn't.

Her throat ached with each breath of cold air. Her nose began to run, but she was afraid to sniff.

She followed Cochran around a group of stores on the top of a hill to the terraced levels below. He boosted her over a wrought-iron fence. Her hands shook. Her pants caught on a spire at the top. She felt the cold metal bite her skin as she wrenched free. They ran past dining tables, and then they were back at the cursed fence again. She scrambled awkwardly back over it. It wasn't until they were on the lower level, a quaint cobblestone street, that she noticed the huge highway overpass bridges looming. Beneath one, a barrel fire burned, revealing a cardboard city and its residents—a scene from a horror movie. Taylor panted as they ran further. Her lungs burned with cold air and exertion.

Voices called out. "Run, baby run." "You go, girl." "Stop thief." Hands grabbed at her. Someone caught her ankle. She stumbled and a weak scream squeaked out.

Cochran pulled out his gun and pointed it. "Let go."

His voice was low and more dangerous than Taylor had ever heard.

The hands around her ankle withdrew.

Cochran's hand closed around her wrist. He jerked her forward. Her eyes streamed as she followed where he pulled her. She had no idea where they were or where they were going. It was all she could do to keep up.

She thought she heard Phil call her name as Cochran pulled her from the road down a grass embankment. Shocked, she slipped and went sliding down the steep hill into the chain-link fence at the bottom. For several seconds she sat and breathed, drawing in lungful after lungful of cold, damp, fish-scented air. The thin fog rising off the Mississippi River glowed white where the streetlights hit it.

Cochran hurried to her side. "You hurt?" He was breathing heavily but not panting like she was.

She shook her head, not wanting to waste breath speaking.

"I think I saw a break in the fence about ten feet further." He grabbed her hand and tugged her to her feet.

They jogged along the fence to the loose, bent panel. Cochran ducked through it first and held it open for Taylor. Once through, he pushed the chain link flap back in place and grabbed Taylor's hand again. As he led her toward the trees and brush that lined the river's edge, Taylor heard voices from the road above. Men looking for them. Swearing.

"They went down there."

She ran, holding Cochran's hand as he veered around bushes and trees.

Without warning, he skidded to a halt in front of a large metal culvert, jerking Taylor to a stop.

"Wh—" not wanting to be discovered, she stopped mid-word. She panted next to Cochran, hands on her knees. Paper, weeds, and assorted trash were stuck in the fence that covered the mouth of the six foot diameter pipe. He let go of Taylor's hand to tug on the mesh. The lock that held the heavy mesh closed was broken, allowing him to open the gate. "In you go."

Taylor shook her head. "No."

"We don't have time to argue," he whispered between ragged breaths. He reached into his pocket and pulled out a six inch flashlight. "Take this. Go inside and wait for me."

"I can't, I'm..."

"You have to."

"...claustrophobic."

"Get in the damn culvert."

"What if..."

"Now." Cochran pushed her inside the storm sewer, closing the gate. "Taylor, security's been compromised. Nothing is adding up. You may be right about Phil. Once we're out of this, we'll go it alone to find Phil and the answers. Now, get inside."

"Okay." The joy his words should have brought was missing. She clung to the gate, unable to get her mind around anything but the men chasing them and the tunnel looming behind her.

"If I can't come back for you, I'll meet you at eight o'clock in the morning at the Perkins on Highway 88. Say it, eight o'clock, the Perkins on Highway 88."

Tears filled her eyes as she whispered the words.

"There's money in your coat pocket." He pried her fingers from the wire mesh. "And Kleenex."

She stared at him with eyes wide and pleading. She couldn't go in there.

The look in his eyes was somehow both reassuring and demanding. "Go!"

She could hear the sound of footsteps through long grass and leaves, the slide of gravel, the occasional word.

Squaring her shoulders, she let go of the fence, turned her back on the wide world and entered hell.

CHAPTER THIRTEEN

The tunnel was cold and damp and horrible with a stale metallic scent. The thin metal flashlight Cochran had given her illuminated the tunnel ahead but provided little comfort. Taylor hurried, like he'd told her to, all too aware of her vulnerability this close to the mouth of the storm sewer. Walking on the curved metal was a balancing act. Above, below and on both sides, the tube led her forward along a line of inch wide humps of metal separated by gullies two or three inches deep. She held her breath and walked with a wide stance, her gloved left hand skimming the wall for stability. Sometimes dirt, leaves and other debris matted the floor for a foot or two.

Concentrating on staying upright, she wasn't aware she'd been climbing a gentle grade until she looked back to see how far she'd gone. She expected to see the slightly lighter circle of the opening behind her, but there was nothing but the dull gray ceiling that sloped to meet the floor.

Trapped. Oh, God. There was less air than there'd been a moment ago. She swallowed heavily and tried to slow her racing heart. Stop it. It's an optical illusion, she told herself. The tunnel wasn't collapsing behind her. The ceiling didn't meet the floor. The tunnel merely sloped downhill to the river. She closed her eyes and concentrated on breathing.

"Tayyyylor!" The word came out of the darkness ahead of her, muffled and distorted by the passageway.

Her eyes sprang open and the flashlight leapt in her

hands. She fumbled with it and managed to hold on. Her heart thudded and her breath caught in her throat. Shaking, she flicked off the beam and stood listening in the dark.

"Tayyyylor." Like hearing a name shouted across a ball field the words were understandable but the voice unrecognizable. "Ohhhh, Tayyyylor."

She stood staring into the dark. Someone was at the other end of the tunnel. Someone who knew she was inside the sewer. Who? Cochran? Was the coast clear? She wanted to yell back but stopped herself.

"Readdeee or nnnnnot, heeeeere I commme."

She stumbled as the meaning of the words dawned on her. Like a childhood game gone horribly wrong, someone was coming for her. And it wasn't Phil or Cochran.

Heart pounding, she scrambled to turn herself around and head in the other direction. She didn't want to go deeper into the tunnel. The walls were too close. There wasn't enough air. But what other choice did she have? Gasping, she forced herself further into the storm sewer. She pushed herself, counting in a ridiculous attempt to keep her mind off where she was and who was behind her. "One, two, three. One two, three..." Ready or not, here I come.

Oh, God, please.

As if reality wasn't bad enough, every horror movie or reality show she'd ever seen involving sewers flashed through her head as she rushed deeper underground. She didn't see rats or derelicts with knives or sewage or gangs with guns, but like at a Halloween "fun" house she expected to see them at any moment. Oh, please, get me out of here.

Her side ached from running bent at the waist. She stopped and looked back. There seemed to be an easing of the darkness, almost like a glow.

Shit.

She pressed her flashlight into her abdomen to dim its light as she stared down the metal pipe. Someone was coming.

Clutching her side, she turned and nearly fell in her haste to be away. She ran with the flashlight in her right hand, her left hand still skimming the wall for stability. She ran as quickly and as quietly as she could, desperately praying. If she was quiet enough, if she was fast enough, if God was listening, whoever was following her would give up and go back. The guy couldn't know for certain she was in there. Surely she'd gone in long before he arrived.

Cochran could have taken her further along the river. That would be the normal thing to think—that she'd gone somewhere else. Had he gotten Cochran? God, please no.

This had to be a nightmare. Any moment now, she'd wake up tangled in her sheets with Lacey snoring across the room. She ran on.

Up ahead the sewer split into two smaller concrete pipes, maybe four or five feet in diameter. Smaller pipes. No. She hesitated. A part of her screamed, 'What does it matter which way you go? Choose one!' She crouched down, took a desperate breath, and forced herself into the one on the left.

The going was tougher. Using her left hand as a foot, she scrambled on like a three-legged dog or Tolkien's Gollum.

When she'd traveled long enough to be well outside the view from the opening, she stopped, flicked off the flashlight and listened. The silence was as thick as the darkness, heavy to the point of smothering. Her heartbeat, her breath, and the rush of blood through her veins were the only sounds.

Then she heard it. A soft, exotic, foreign-accented voice. "Taylor, my pet. You surprise me. Crawling through these narrow, airless tunnels with the weight of tons of earth pressing down. They are getting smaller, these tunnels. Every inch they get smaller."

Taylor sat in silence. How did he know about her claustrophobia?

"It's quiet down here. Like a tomb. Listen."

She inched away, moving noiselessly in the unremitting

darkness. She wanted to flick on the light, needed to, but fear kept her finger off the switch. She couldn't let the glow give her away.

"There are spiders too, have you noticed? Along the ceiling, spinning, waiting patiently? Skittering, sneaky, crawly little things. But patient. You can respect their patience."

She crept slowly, silently, blindly, keeping her hand extended. A spider web hit her face. It stuck to her. Clung. She froze for a heartbeat and then clawed at the web with gloved hands only to find them sticky with webs. A scream rose in her throat, but she choked it down, biting her lips to keep silent. Her rational mind knew the man behind her was more dangerous than the spiders, but phobias weren't rational. She wanted to curl into a little ball and whimper until Phil came for her. He knew how she was with spiders and cramped spaces.

But he wasn't here. She'd have to save herself. She would have to move.

Behind her, the voice continued—friendly, confidential.

"You'll find me a patient man, Taylor. A reliable man. I will wait here for you. I will wait here where the tunnel is wide—where there is air enough to breathe. I will not leave you to die alone crushed by the weight of the earth, rotting in this place, food for spiders and rats."

It was like the man could read her mind.

Move, damn it.

Taylor forced herself to inch forward, tentative foot by tentative foot. Images of collapsed tunnels and giant spiders filled the darkness around her. Her lips bled. Mucus was thick in her throat. She rotated her wrist around and around trying to collect the webs on the end of the flashlight so they wouldn't touch her. Just a little farther and she could turn the light on. Just a little farther and she would see there was plenty of room, plenty of air. Just a few more feet and the light would show the webs were empty. Just a few more feet.

Taylor moved on steadily. Her shoes shuffled quietly

against the concrete.

Phil, Cochran, where are you?

The sewer continued its slow winding ascent. The whisper of his voice followed her but grew steadily less distinct. She flicked on the light. The concrete tunnel was gray and surprisingly empty. The webs appeared pale and uninhabited in the blessed light.

She was able to breathe a little easier. It quickened her step and allowed her to concentrate on putting as much distance as she could between herself and the mad man.

The tunnel ended in a vertical shaft with a puddle of dirty water at the bottom. Taylor shined the light up the shaft. A metal ladder led past three smaller tunnels that branched off in different directions at different levels before reaching a dead-end at the top.

She climbed into the shaft. The sound of her pursuer's voice didn't reach in here.

It was a relief to hear nothing and to stand upright again. The air in this pipe was colder and fresher. She hurried up the ladder. The new tunnels were even narrower than the one she'd left, maybe two feet in diameter. They were all wide enough to belly-crawl through and crisscrossed with spider webs. Ick. At least she didn't see any spiders. She picked the top tunnel because up meant out to her.

Concentrating on the air movement and the possibility of escape instead of her dread of close spaces, or her fear of spiders, or her terror of the man who followed, Taylor headed in.

"Be glad it's November," she whispered to herself. "Too cold for spiders."

She spun the flashlight before her, cleaning the path of cobwebs as she dragged herself forward on bent forearms.

Visibility was limited in the slowly ascending tube. Taylor had no way to calculate distance. Her new wristwatch was useless. Was she crawling two yards per minute? Four? Six? There was no way to tell.

The tunnel ended abruptly in what looked like about a three-foot square room. A hand's breadth below the tunnel's mouth sat a square dirty puddle half filled with dirt and gravel. Above, moonlight angled through a side grate above another dirty little catch basin. Taylor recognized it instantly. Outside, this storm sewer was tucked into the curb. If someone looked into it, they'd see the catch basin with its discarded gum, stray coins, and scraps of wet paper.

There was no getting out here.

Combat crawling in reverse was painfully slow. Toes that had pushed were now required to pull. The light illuminated where she'd been instead of where she was going. Thinking it might be faster to roll over and use her buttocks and shoulder blades, Taylor turned herself until she was facing up. It was then she saw where the spiders were. Unpredictable surges of water had encouraged the spiders to make their homes out of harm's way at the top of the concrete cylinders.

Taylor could see them, long legs and plump pale bodies beside their round white egg sacs, inches from her face. Dozens of them. Hundreds of them.

The scream she'd held since she'd entered this concrete hell ripped out of her. It echoed through the tunnels and escaped into the night. She was paralyzed as panic seized her in a vise grip.

Spiders turned their multiple eyes hungrily toward her and licked their poisonous fangs. Your imagination. It's just your imagination.

Taylor forced herself to turn over, so she wouldn't see the hordes of blood thirsty predators waiting above her. She pressed her face against her hands and broke down. She hated spiders. Hated them.

How long she lay there paralyzed and sobbing, she had no idea. But when she finally opened her eyes, the beam of light from her flaslight seemed to have dimmed.

Oh, God.

She turned it off to save the battery.

Please, God.

The sound of her ragged breath filled every space in her head threatening to steal her sanity.

Stop it! There is air. Listen. Breathe. The tube was

tight, but it hadn't crushed her yet. There is air. Really.

She started wiggling back down the pipe, listening to the pep squad in her mind. It didn't matter that it was dark. There was nothing in front of her that she hadn't already seen and nothing behind her that she could see whether she had the light on or not.

Years later, by her reckoning, her feet encountered nothingness, and she realized she'd made it to the connecting shaft. She backed out further, until just the top half of her was in the tube. Bent at the waist, eyes closed in concentration, she found the ladder.

She pushed away images of her crazed stalker leaning back against the wall of the shaft, watching with amusement as she struggled out of the tube. Focus on the ladder. Careful. Don't forget the flashlight.

Clinging to the ladder, her eyes opened to the total darkness. Darkness and space. Air. Listen.

There was sound. Her heart, her breath, and maybe a faint irregular vibration in the air.

She felt her way down the ladder. How many rungs? She didn't know, but she selected her new route by straining her ears for that illusive sound, that vibration.

It came from the lowest of the three tubes, the one on the opposite side of the shaft from her previous path. It didn't make sense that this was the way out. Still, she took it. Collecting spider webs on the flashlight, she followed the dimming beam of light and urged herself to crawl faster.

The bulb's light was a mere glow when her hands ran out of tunnel. Another shaft.

Then, the light was gone.

She inched her upper body into the shaft, feeling with her hand for a ladder.

She barked her fingers hard against it and instinctively jerked her hand back. Stupid. Why hadn't she just grabbed it? Finding the ladder the second time was easier. She pulled herself onto it, holding tight with one hand while the other worked to cling to both ladder and dead flashlight.

Her feet bounced off the wall a few times before finding a rung to support them.

The sound she'd heard came from overhead. Now, in the shaft where it had originated, she could identify it as the rush of air from passing cars. She climbed up until the ladder ended and she smacked the top of her head. Backing up a step, she felt around, using the flashlight as an extension of her arm.

The concrete tube sounded different. She'd found a man-hole cover. Staring up at it, she noticed there were holes. As cars approached, light hit the holes and then disappeared again as the car rolled overhead with a whoosh of air.

She was under a street in the center of a lane where the tires didn't hit. Taylor watched and listened to the approach and departure of several vehicles. Random, yet steady. There was no way to predict when the next car would come. Taylor closed her eyes as tears of exhaustion washed her face. Too dangerous. It wasn't a dead-end, but it might as well have been one.

CHAPTER FOURTEEN

Cochran had stashed Taylor, led away a group of pursuers and then doubled back an hour later to find he'd fooled no one. The mesh gate that had protected the sewer entrance was bent and gaping. The padlock he'd repositioned was gone. Dammit. Fear for Taylor turned his stomach sour. He never should have left her. It was against protocol. It was stupid. No excuses.

He poked his head inside the metal gate to call to her, just in case she was still there waiting. A male voice rich with a Middle Eastern accent echoed softly in the darkness.

The bastard was still in there. If he hurt Taylor...

Cochran had neither night-vision goggles nor a flashlight, but still he hurried into the tunnel following the voice. He slid his left hand along the curved wall and held his gun ready with his right.

The oily voice grew louder and more distinct as Cochran neared the source. "...left you all alone in the dark, airless, tunnels beneath tons of dirt. It's so hard to breathe in here."

Cochran clenched his teeth. It was like the sicko knew Taylor's fear. He wasn't claustrophobic, but the voice still brought shivers. Stay strong, Taylor. I'm coming. He was going to have a hard time not shooting the man in the kneecap, on principle. Moving as quickly and stealthily as he could in the blackness, Cochran noticed the lessening of darkness in the distance. As he neared, the voice stopped. Cochran froze, crouching low. There was a brief whir and click before the voice started in again.

What the...? Cochran identified the sound and picked up his pace. There was a flashlight at the intersection, positioned so that its beam illuminated the first several feet of two smaller tunnels. Cochran imagined Taylor crawling deeper into the tunnels to escape the voice. Fear would keep her pinned underground while the man entered through a manhole and grabbed her.

He clicked off the recorder with gloved hands.

"It's safe, Taylor. You can come back, now." Cochran called into each tunnel pausing to listen. His voice echoed.

"Taylor!"

Nothing.

He picked up the flashlight. Which way had she gone? He visually scoured the entrance of each tunnel for signs of her passage. Neither looked disturbed in the dim light. He had a fifty/fifty chance of getting it right.

He chose the right hand tunnel and entered it, calling her name every thirty seconds or so.

Nothing.

The tunnel branched again. He crouched at the intersection and called her name. It was hard not to imagine her frozen in terror just beyond the sound of his voice. As the beam of the flashlight dimmed, he tried not to think of her batteries growing weaker.

He had to turn around. It would do her no good to have both of them lost in the sewer.

God, he hoped she'd somehow managed to find a way out.

§

The change in the noise above roused Taylor from her half-sleep at the foot of the ladder. A constant, dim light illuminated the holes in the manhole cover.

Taylor listened. The occasional whoosh was replaced by a steady rumble. She climbed the ladder and stretched to position her eye under the hole. Given her position under a road, it wasn't surprising that she identified the view above her as the underside of a car. What surprised her was that the car wasn't moving. She was under a traffic jam.

She shoved at the man-hole cover, jarring her shoulder but not moving the lid. Another shove, using her back and her legs, lifted the heavy circle out of its place for a moment. The thing had to weigh at least a hundred pounds.

But a hundred pounds of metal was not going to keep her from freedom. She'd moved bags of fertilizer that weighed nearly that much. Concrete ornaments could top a hundred pounds easily. She could move this one sewer cover. Her legs were strong. It was all about leverage, anyway. Her third effort pushed the cover high enough to clear the hole and catch one side on the road above. Taylor pushed and shoved the heavy metal lid until her arms ached, but still the hole wasn't clear.

Okay, so it had been a while since she'd moved garden supplies. She could still do this. After a rest. She retreated a couple of rungs down the shaft when the car above began to move. It didn't move much, though—not even an entire car-length.

Back at work, she managed to heave the cover entirely off the hole. Now she could see there was definitely not enough room to crawl out under a car. She waited impatiently for the traffic to move enough so that she was between cars. It didn't happen. Three cars, four. The SUVs and minivans had a little more space beneath them, but not quite enough. Seven vehicles later, an eighteen wheeler rolled to a stop overhead.

Without consciously deciding to move, she was out of the sewer and scrambling from under the truck. There were two lanes of traffic stopped. The occupants of a blue compact gaped and pointed at her as she popped up beside their vehicle. She skirted between it and a red four-door and raced to the side of the road.

A village of stores sat behind an over-flowing parking lot. More car-clogged streets led the way to one of the city's shopping malls. Newly freed from dark solitude,

Taylor found herself overwhelmed by the number of people. They'd all been above her, unknowing. There was a madman among them, yet they remained ignorant, blithely shopping the after-Thanksgiving sales. It was too normal.

She stumbled across the grassy divide into the parking lot. The cold air chilled her, sapping what remained of her strength. There were lines of people outside a large electronics store. She avoided it, searching instead for a gas station or some other place with fewer people and a restroom. The reflection in a plate glass window showed her to be a disreputable sight. Hatted and hooded, her formerly all-black attire was now concrete scuffed and gray-streaked with spider webs. She tried to brush off her jacket, but it was futile.

A restaurant promised the needed facilities. When the blast of warm sausage and syrup scented air hit her, the hunger she hadn't thought to acknowledge growled into life. With her mouth watering, she slipped around a group of women waiting at the hostess's stand and made her way to the ladies' room. One of the three stalls was occupied, but the sink area was empty. Glancing at the mirror, Taylor was startled by her red-rimmed eyes. She tugged off her cap and pulled down her hood. Even in its ponytail, her hair was a tangle. She washed her face. When she heard the toilet flush, she grabbed a wad of paper towels and escaped into the handicapped stall just in time to avoid being seen by the bathroom's other occupant.

Inside her stall, Taylor dried her face with the coarse gray paper. Seated, she inspected the contents of her coat pockets. She had five twenties and a package of tissues. Taylor sighed. What she really needed was a comb, food, and a plan.

Cochran had told her to go some place. Perkins and a number repeated. What number? She wracked her brain.

Eight. He said eight. Eight o'clock. Highway 88.

She shivered uncontrollably, her teeth chattering. Disjointed thoughts danced around in her brain.

She'd been lost down there. Lost and trapped. With spiders. Waiting to die while slippery voices played in her head and the tunnels collapsed and the air disappeared.

But she hadn't died. Tears filled her eyes.

She hadn't.

She was safe in a handicapped stall in a restaurant ladies' room. Safe.

Once outside the restroom, she ignored her stomach and headed toward the door to look for the brochure stand bearing the "Ride the Bus" sign. She plucked out a bus schedule. There was a stop near Highway 88. Nice, but only limited help since she didn't know where she was now. The crowd at the hostess stand had cleared, so she made her way back. Her stomach growled so loudly the hostess looked up from her computer screen. Taylor's face grew hot.

"Table for one?"

She held out the map. "Can you show me where we are on this map and where the nearest bus stop is?"

The hostess took the map and circled a stop. "We're here. The bus stops right outside the door every fifteen minutes."

"Thank you." Taylor looked at the map. It wasn't far. According to the schedule, it was ten minutes away. A clock above the counter showed it was seven. She pointed to the bus schedule again. "Do you know how far this stop is from Perkins?"

The woman shrugged. "Perkins is by the overpass, so...I'd say a block, maybe two."

Taylor's stomach growled. She smiled.

The hostess returned her smile. "Do you need a table?"

"I think so." There was time enough to get to Perkins after she'd eaten.

While the waitress poured coffee, Taylor opened the menu and pointed to the first photo she encountered—a skillet loaded with bacon, sausage, eggs, hash browns, and pancakes. Her mouth watered at the mere sight of the photo. It was too much food, but she ordered it anyway just to speed things along.

Alone, she shifted on the plush booth seat as if it were made of nails.

Cochran's words came back to her. Security's been compromised... we'll go it alone to find Phil and figure out what's going on.

He was FBI. Was it possible for him to go it alone? Maybe. Leaving her alone in the sewer had to be against FBI rules. Her hands clenched around her coffee cup.

She had to find Phil. Going to Cochran didn't guarantee anything. But he had a gun, and she needed help.

§

City bus schedule in hand, Taylor hurried out of the restaurant. She had minutes to catch the bus that would take her to her meeting with Cochran. The sun sparkling off the lightly falling snow was so dazzling Taylor was blinded for a moment. As she hurried to the stop, the snowflakes grew from large individual flakes to fluffy conglomerations, like miniature snowballs. The mood of the people she passed in the line outside the electronics store was excited and anticipatory. Joyful. The buzz of their voices and the smiles on their faces went well with the Christmas music coming from outdoor speakers, but clashed with the over-fast beat of Taylor's heart and made her stomach protest the food she'd just eaten. She felt like Jason Bourne in a Norman Rockwell painting. Someone wanted her dead and she didn't know why. But, unlike the main character in The Bourne Identity, she didn't have highly developed survival skills. She had nothing. And if she didn't hurry, she'd miss her bus.

The blue and white Metro-bus pulled up moments after she got to the stop. A group of five or six teenage girls chattered their way out the middle door while she climbed up the front steps. Noting the fare, she tossed her coins into the meter before sliding into the first empty seat she found. The route map was printed on the wall above the windows. Three more stops.

Hot air blasted from overhead. Seven minutes. More than enough time to triple think everything. Was she making the right decision?

She was the only person to get off at her stop.

The snow was beginning to accumulate on the ground. Heavy with water, it was cold and slushy beneath her feet. Crap. She'd leave clear tracks wherever she went.

Taylor checked the street signs as the bus roared off belching diesel exhaust. She was in a residential section—a subdivision full of split-level ranches and two-story colonials with double dormers. A subdivision like the one she'd lived in as a kid. If the map was correct, Perkins was across the street and down several blocks. She took a deep breath and then blazed a trail in the new fallen snow.

She stopped at the end of the second block. Across the street, houses gave way to businesses. A strip mall with a drycleaner/laundromat and a Subway sandwich shop sat on the other side of the divided street. Perkins stood a long block ahead under the snow-blown American flag. Beyond Perkins was an overpass with ramps on and off the highway below. A CITGO station sat across from Perkins on the same side of the street as the laundry. What if Cochran wasn't waiting for her? What if he'd been shot or captured and tortured to reveal their meeting place? What if this was a trap?

She looked back at the subdivision full of ordinary houses with ordinary people living wonderfully ordinary lives. Images of her and Phil's home as it used to be flashed through her mind. Her throat felt thick. On an ordinary year, they'd cut down a Christmas tree the Saturday after Thanksgiving. Tomorrow. In an ordinary year. But nothing was ordinary.

Phil told her to "call Phillip."

Cochran told her to go to Perkins.

The man in the sewer told her she would die.

Father Charlie told her everything would be all right.

Sister Margaret died.

Cochran told her Phil wasn't real.

Phil told her he loved her.

Someone shot Lacey.

Someone killed Sharon Tatro.

She had $89.25 in her pocket.

At the intersection, a car slowed. Taylor froze in her tracks, muscles bunched ready for flight. The driver was a man with dark hair. She stilled like a deer in headlights. Her breath caught in her throat, but her heart pounded against the wall of her chest. The car rounded the corner and accelerated down the street. He'd slowed for the intersection. That was all.

Perkins was a mere block down the street. She should move forward, cross the street and find Cochran, but it was as if she were glued to the spot. What if Cochran wasn't there? Could she survive alone? The questions chased each other through her mind. She stood, rooted to the spot.

§

The huge American flag waved in fits and starts beside the Perkins sign. Seated in the black SUV, Cochran glanced at his watch. He'd broken every damn regulation there was when he'd taken heed of his old mentor's warning and run with Taylor. How the hell had Kennedy known about the security breach or about the upcoming raid? How had he known how to contact him?

He thought Kennedy had left the agency, but he must have moved up the ladder instead. Running had been the right decision, as his boss's message later proved, but he hadn't known that when he'd dragged Taylor around town and shoved her in that sewer. A stupid move, but last night he'd been out of options. Their cover had been compromised. They were out manned and out gunned, on the run, and losing ground. Still, right became wrong if Taylor wasn't safe.

He had a good view of the restaurant's door and the CITGO across the street. He tried to keep his eyes off the clock and his thoughts positive. Taylor was bright, resourceful, and brave. The set-up the madman had left in the sewer suggested that he hadn't gotten her. Cochran had gone as far as he could go in the tunnel and still meet her here. She had to have gotten out on her own. If not, he'd go back and look again before calling in a team he couldn't trust.

At eight o'clock, he turned off the car. The chance she was already inside the building and had been waiting for hours was extremely slim. Still, he had to check. There was also the possibility that she was hiding somewhere waiting for him to walk into the restaurant before she showed herself.

A busboy hurried out of the restaurant door with a shovel. He wore an open coat over his requisite black pants and white shirt, but neither a hat nor gloves.

Cochran got out of his car and watched the kid put the blade in the snow and push it like a plow. He made a rapid path to the parking lot before turning on his heels and settling the shovel down for the return swipe. Remembering being sixteen and having a similar work ethic, Cochran shook his head. The kid was back inside before Cochran had the chance to wade through the parking lot. As he gained the semi-cleaned sidewalk, Cochran glanced down the street. Through the falling snow, he saw a small dark form standing at the corner.

Taylor? She'd made it out!

He raced back to his car.

She backed away from the corner when he pulled up beside her and leaned over the seat to open the passenger door. "Get in."

"Cochran?" Her voice sounded young and unsure.

He frowned. Her hat was covered in snow. "Taylor!" His voice was sharper than he'd intended. "Get in."

"Cochran!" She scrambled onto the seat and slammed the door behind her. "They didn't get you. Oh, thank God." She sat in the seat shivering as he put the car into gear.

"Buckle up."

She tore her eyes from his face long enough to find and latch the seatbelt. "Are you okay?"

He shot her a confused glance. "Am I okay? Are you okay?"

"They shot Lacey."

Cochran concentrated on turning the vehicle around

and heading toward the highway. "I know. We were compromised. Are you hurt?"

"I'm fine. Is Lacey okay?" Her voice was edgy, as if she were struggling not to spin out of control.

"I don't know. Our cover was blown. Possibly an inside job. We're going to disappear for a few days."

"So we really are going it alone."

"For a while." Until Rogers gave him the all clear. He and the boss had saved each other's ass too many times to start doubting now. He looked over at Taylor again. She was dry-eyed but very pale and shivering. He flipped up the heat and turned the blower on high. "Taylor, I went back to get you as planned. I heard the tape the guy who was chasing you left down there. I'm not claustrophobic or afraid of spiders and rats and yet... I'm glad you made it out."

"It was a tape? You mean I could have gotten out that way?" Her voice shook.

If he weren't driving, he'd give her a much needed hug and let her break down even though he hated tears. But he was driving. And they weren't out of danger yet.

They drove in silence for several minutes.

When she yawned, he suggested she recline her seat and take a nap.

"I'd rather talk with you to help keep you awake. I'll bet you didn't get any more sleep last night than I did." She sighed. "I know you probably won't answer me, but I have to ask. What makes you think the attack last night was an inside job?"

Instead of lying back and letting someone else take control, she needed to know the whys and hows of everything so she could set her mind working on the solution. This was the Taylor he'd come to know. His lips twitched as he suppressed a smile.

"Normally, I wouldn't answer that question. My job is to protect you, not keep you informed. But there's nothing normal about what's going on." He kept his eyes on the road. He didn't need to look at her to know there was a grin on her face and a sparkle in her eyes. "We suspect someone from the bureau is involved because last night local drug enforcement, acting on a tip from our office, broke down the door to our apartment and shot Lacey. Of course, when they discovered that they'd been misinformed and went back to confront the referring agent, they found that agent was in the hospital recovering from gallbladder surgery and had been for several days."

"Oh no."

He nodded. "So, we're playing things a little differently from here on out. You and I are going to share information. You'll tell me everything you know, and we'll work together to find out what the hell is going on here."

§

She told him everything from the text message to the football schedule on the table at the Bachman's and the message on the answering machine. And all the while, Phil's first message played in her mind. Trust no one.

Afterward, Cochran was silent for a long time.

She stared out the window. Her mind raced like the SUV's shadow on the pavement. Why had she and Phil been targeted? Why had Phil run? Who was the man in the tunnel? Why had the newswoman been murdered? If Phil and his sister were truly estranged, how could she help? Would she even want to? Why would someone in the FBI want her dead? The questions spun in her head repeating over and over in time with the white dashed lane marker...why...why...why?

She was exhausted, but sleep was impossible. Every time she closed her eyes she was in the sewer again or watching Lacey slam into the wall.

Taylor knew she wasn't to blame, but she still felt responsible. Lacey had been shot protecting her, and she didn't even know Lacey's full name.

"What's Lacey's last name?"

Cochran frowned. "I thought you were sleeping."

"I wasn't. What is Lacey's last name?"

"Johnson."

Lacey Johnson. Please, God, Taylor begged. Make Lacey Johnson be okay.

§

Phil nodded to the man repairing the ruined door frame in the Minneapolis apartment and frowned at the wall Agent Johnson had dented the previous evening. The blood spatters on the floor were hers. Thank God her injuries weren't life threatening.

If he hadn't accidentally heard the chatter on the radio and given Cochran the heads up last night, things would be different this morning. If he'd had another twenty minutes, maybe he could have prevented the entire confrontation. Maybe he could have gotten Taylor. Maybe.

In the living room, Sean and the local crime scene unit compared notes. Phil shared a glance with him as he passed. Once again, Sean had beaten him to the scene. He must have guessed Taylor would still be a target. Great agents had great instincts, and O'Hearn was one of the best. With Phil, it was just plain luck that he had stumbled onto their frequency and bad luck he'd been too far away to stop it. He walked into what had been Taylor's bedroom. A red sweater and slacks lay on the floor beside one of the beds. He picked up the sweater and sniffed it, hoping for a lingering trace of Taylor. It smelled of fabric sizing.

"Sniffing her clothes? That's damn pathetic, Max. How do you know it wasn't Agent Johnson's?"

Phil glanced back at his partner. "Size. Taylor is a six. Johnson's a twelve."

Sean tapped his PDA against his palm. "You about done here? I'd like to get lunch."

"Yeah." There'd been no reason to come here besides the desire to connect with Taylor. They both knew what happened, and Cochran wasn't likely to bring Taylor back here.

Phil dropped the sweater on the bed. "Was there any evidence Accawi was here? In Minneapolis?"

"No confirmed sightings. We have reports of a micro recorder with a middle eastern accented voice on it from the storm sewer we think Taylor hid in."

"Think she hid in? Whose reports?" Individual agents might use instinct, but the FBI dealt with evidence, not vague suppositions. Knowing her claustrophobia, he had a hard time imagining her entering a sewer pipe. "Do we have the tape? Did we get finger prints or a voice match?"

Sean shook his head. "No tape. The reports are Cochran took it, but we don't know for certain."

"Has Cochran checked in yet?"

"We have nothing from Rogers."

Phil bit his tongue. This damn operation was one stinking SNAFU after another. "I want to search Accawi's compound. Ask his wives where he's hiding. Take him in for questioning."

"No way a judge is going to give you a warrant for any of that. Not enough evidence and he has diplomatic immunity, thanks to his job. The best you can do is sit outside and listen. Off the record, of course."

"Of course." Dammit. He just wanted his wife. Wanted her safe. Was that so much to ask? He felt so blasted helpless. He couldn't even figure out why she was a target.

CHAPTER FIFTEEN

Several hours out of the cities, Taylor and Cochran stopped at a shopping mall for lunch, clothes and supplies. Cochran paid with gift cards. Later, he filled the car's gas tank using more gift cards. The day was endless. Mile after mile. They left the snow behind, but not the cold. The setting sun made her eyes burn, then headlights blurred before her eyes.

It was nine o'clock at night when Cochran dug yet another card from his seemingly inexhaustible pile to pay for a motel.

The room was a classic budget room with two full-size beds separated by a single nightstand. She hesitated to sit on the greasy nylon bedspreads, but she was so darn tired. Listless with fatigue, Taylor slumped on the first bed.

"You hungry?"

Taylor shrugged. "Where are we?"

"Champaign, Illinois."

He looked at the pizzeria advertisement on the room key. "I'm hungry. How does pizza sound?"

"Fine."

He picked up the telephone. "You want sausage or pepperoni?"

"Sausage."

Cochran ordered the pizza, hung up the phone, and looked at Taylor who hadn't moved a muscle. "You look done in. Why don't you take a hot bath? I'll get drinks and some of that popcorn from the lobby, but I'll be back in plenty of time to meet the pizza guy."

She nodded woodenly and picked up the shopping bag with her new clothes inside, taking it into the bathroom with her.

"Lock the door. I have a room key, so just take your time."

Alone in the bathroom, Taylor stripped for her bath without looking in the mirror. She'd seen how she looked earlier when they'd stopped at the mall to exchange the severely scuffed coat with something else. She'd looked tired and pale and her eyes had that red rimmed, sad, about-to-cry look to them. No need to see that again. She hung her coat on the hook on the door. This new one was brown—wide corduroy lined with the same faux wool that decorated the collar. It was warm and actually kind of cute in that commando shopping grab-the-first-one-that-catches-your-eye kind of way. In the last month, she'd gone through more coats than she cared to count—the blue work coat, the white one, navy, black and now brown. Once again, her jeans didn't really fit and tomorrow her socks and underwear would come straight out of the package.

The hotel tub was more of a deep sided shower than an actual bathtub. The sides were straight up and down and it was barely long enough for Taylor to sit in with her feet pressed firmly on either side of the faucet. There'd be no lingering soak. Giving up, she stood, pulled the vinyl curtain shut, lifted the shower lever, and stepped into the spray. The hot water was heaven. She shampooed twice to get the dirt and spider webs out and used the entire mini-bottle of cucumber-mint conditioner.

The hotel blow drier had two settings, hot and hotter, but she made do. She heard Cochran and the pizza guy as she put on her new pajamas.

Cochran knocked on the bathroom door. "Pizza's here."

As she left the bathroom, the sight of him hit her in a confusion of emotions. She felt shy and ill at ease. It was safer and more economical for her and Cochran to share a room, but she'd never been in a hotel room with a man other than Phil. Nothing untoward would happen, she knew. Still, the sense of discomfort remained.

He pulled a can of soda from the brown plastic ice bucket on the dresser. "I was surprised to hear the shower when I came back with the ice. I expected you to be soaking."

"Wrong kind of tub." Taylor skirted around him and climbed into the bed farthest away from the door.

"Have some pizza." He popped open a can of ginger ale.

"Thanks. Too tired to eat."

"Try." He pulled a root beer out of the ice and carried it to her. "Here."

She set the soda on the bedside table and was rearranging the pillows to form a backrest when he returned with the pizza.

As soon as she'd settled, he opened the box and handed her a slice.

Her stomach growled expectantly. Maybe she was hungry after all. Gooey cheese stretched from her mouth before she managed to get her first bite free.

He put the box on the edge of his bed, sat down and took a slice.

With all that had happened, sharing a hotel room should be nothing, but she was glad he sat on his bed, preserving the boundaries.

They ate their first piece in silence.

"You did good today," he said as she took a second piece.

She looked at him, wondering what he meant.

Her expression must have shown her confusion because he answered her unasked question. "I meant, opening up and telling me about Phil and the clues. I wish you'd done it earlier."

Taylor bristled. "Would it have made a difference?" She felt guilty enough over what happened without Cochran adding to it. "Would it have saved Sharon Tatro or kept Lacey from being shot?"

He shrugged. "Outside chance. If you'd told me the day we picked you up, I'd have had you call the number again and leave a message. But not after we declared you dead. The best we could've done then would have been sending someone to locate and question Lisa. Depending on what she knew and was willing to tell us, we may or may not have been able to do anything other than monitor her to see who she contacted."

The tension in her shoulders eased. "Is that what we're going to do? Call in the information and send someone to check out Lisa?"

Cochran shook his head. "Not with the mole. Your sister-in-law is off the radar at the moment. She's safer that way and so are we if we go to see her."

"Are we going to go to Miami?" She wanted to go to Miami. Needed to find Phil.

"I don't know. I plan to sleep on it."

"We should go. Once we find Phil, you'll see all this has more to do with your mole than anything else."

He looked her in the eye. "Think what you want, Taylor. Phil is up to his eyeballs in something. But I'll agree that, in light of this new information, there is reasonable doubt he isn't the one targeting you."

She smiled. "Well, I guess that's the best I can expect from you."

"While I don't think Phil placed the bombs or shot at you, I do think he did something that caused someone to target you. And, while it may be true he wants you safe, I don't share your opinion that he's got your best interests at heart. He still ran in the face of trouble, and he still hasn't turned himself in to the authorities in an effort to protect you."

"I think he's trying to lead me to safety."

"I know you do." Cochran looked Taylor in the eye. "You go right ahead and hold onto that if it makes you feel better."

She slapped her slice of pizza back into the box and glared at Cochran. "Don't pity me. I may not know everything that's going on, but I do know Phil loves me.

He's trying to keep me safe." She crossed her arms over her chest. "You'll see. When we find Phil, he'll explain everything."

"I hope you're right." He picked up her piece of pizza and extended it to her.

"I am."

Taylor set down the crust of her third piece of pizza and slid under the covers.

Cochran picked up the remote. A series of stations flicked across the screen before he settled on a college football game. "Mind if I watch the game?"

"No." She closed her eyes and let sleep claim her.

In an instant, she was back in the storm sewer standing thigh deep in frigid water at the junction of three tunnels. Black water poured from two of the tunnels funneling into the third, roaring like a thousand voices. She struggled to stay on her feet as the torrent shoved her backward. A dark figure stood in one of the upstream tunnels. With the sound of the water, she shouldn't have been able to hear his slippery foreign voice whispering promises of death, but the words played in her head as if he were speaking inches from her ear. There was an unspoken message woven amongst the threats. He knew things. Private things about her.

At the sound of her name, she turned to peer down the second upstream tunnel. Phil was ten yards inside the tube, running toward her, calling her name and shouting out instructions. The faster he ran toward her, the longer the tunnel grew, separating them. The louder he called, the more the water roared, garbling his words.

She lunged toward him, slipping and falling into the frothing stream. Freezing water sucked her down. She panicked, tried desperately to move, but she was frozen. Hands yanked her to her feet.

As her head cleared the water, she saw Cochran. "You okay, Taylor?"

She turned back in the deepening water to face the tunnel Phil had been in. It had grown so long she could barely make out a form at the end of it. She screamed his

name as he disappeared. The first tunnel merged with
the second and the evil-voiced man with a large knife
clenched in his fist ran after Phil.

"Phil!" She struggled against the cold current. She
had to help Phil. Had to rescue him. The water was now
waist deep and surging toward her chest.

"Taylor." Cochran's voice was insistent, but it didn't
matter. She turned back to the tunnel Phil and the
madman had been in only to see it begin to shrink, like
the pupil of an eye in bright light.

"No!"

Cochran grabbed her arms. "Taylor." His fingers
pressed gently into her biceps. "Taylor, wake up. You're
having a nightmare."

She opened her eyes to the plaster ceiling of the hotel
room instead of the corrugated metal of the storm sewer
tunnel. She was on the floor between the bed and the
wall. Her bedding was in a tangle around her legs.

"Taylor." Cochran looked into her eyes. "You awake?"

"Yes." She struggled to sit.

"Good." He helped her to her feet. "That must have
been quite the dream. Did you hurt yourself?"

She shook her head as she perched on the edge of the
mattress. Cochran picked up an armful of bedding and
tossed it onto the bed beside her.

Phil, the sewer, and the water had seemed so real. She
looked at Cochran. His brown eyes were full of concern.

"It was just a dream," he told her as if reading her
mind.

"I need to find Phil."

He nodded. "We'll try."

§

Taylor woke the next morning to the sound of a key
in the door's lock. She rolled over and looked at the
clock—9:23. Panic shot through her body. Where was
she? Where was Cochran?

She looked up just in time to see him enter the room.

"I got breakfast." Cochran balanced bowls, plates,

coffee cups and juice glasses like an experienced waiter.

Taylor scrambled from the bed to help him unload. She took the plate of pastries off the bowl of fruit and set them both on the dresser. "Why did you let me sleep so late?"

"It wasn't just you. We've both been running on empty. I decided not to set the alarm."

"Are we going to go to Miami?"

"I don't know yet. We're going to find a public library at some point today and do a little online detective work. We'll see if there really is a 1600 Pennsylvania Avenue in Miami and, if there is, who lives there." He handed her a covered Styrofoam cup with several creams balanced on top. "Have some coffee. It's pretty weak, but it's all they had. We can look for a Starbucks or something on our way out of town."

She took the coffee. "Is there a library in this town?"

"Probably, but it doesn't matter. We'll hit the road and find a library wherever we find ourselves right before the after school rush. We'll get in, do our search, get out and drive off. No one will notice us in the wave of kids."

She knew he was right, so she tapped down her desire to go now, search now. Hurry. Once they hit the road, there was nothing to do but sit. She stared out the window having pretend conversations with Phil's sister. "Hi, I'm Taylor Wilson. I married your brother Phil who told me to come here and say, 'Bob Smith sent me.' This is Mark Cochran, he's with the FBI..." or "Hi, you don't know me, but your brother told me to come here and say 'Bob Smith...'...my house blew up, can I stay with you?" She shook her head. It was ridiculous. She couldn't go there and say any of that. Lisa would think she was insane. Anyone would.

Taylor slumped in her seat.

Around two that afternoon, Taylor felt the car slow. She looked up from the atlas she'd been studying when Cochran pulled into the crowded parking lot of a small café. He squeezed between a rusty pickup truck and a slightly off-kilter power pole and shifted into park.

"Lunch time."

Taylor closed the atlas. No need to save the page, the road they were on was too small to be shown on the map. Ever since they'd taken the detour somewhere in Kentucky, she had no idea where they were. She had no doubt Cochran knew. The man had an innate sense of direction.

"Are we ever going to get back on the highway?" She sounded as irritable as she felt.

"Absolutely. After we visit the library. But first, lunch. I'm starved."

"Where are we, anyway?"

He pointed to the sign above the restaurant. "The Jewelbox Diner. Best barbecue in town," he read. "Actually, the best southern cooking around according to my brother Ken. He drives truck down this way. "

"So, you meant to come here."

He looked confused. "Of course. Did you think we were lost?"

She shook her head to hide her smile. Well, she'd been lost.

Cochran put his hands on his hips and arched his back so hard his spine cracked. "Ahhh, that felt good."

Phil used to crack his back like that. She wondered where he was.

"Come on," Cochran urged, breaking into her thoughts. "Let's eat. By the way, your name is Tammy. "

"Tammy, why Tammy?" She hurried to catch up.

"Because I can remember it."

"You can't remember Taylor?"

He grinned. "I can remember it just fine. But this is the kind of place that remembers strangers. On the off chance someone happened by looking for us, we wouldn't want to make it easy for them. So, you're Tammy."

She raised her brows. "And who will you be?"

"James."

"James?" The name tickled her. It was such a formal choice compared to Tammy.

"Yep."

"Anything else I need to know, Jimmy?"

"I said it was James."

"Right, Jimbo."

He shook his head. "Just follow my lead."

"No problem, Jim Bob."

Shaking his head, he opened the door. The moist, food-scented air enveloped her like a hug.

"How many?" The slender hostess looked from Taylor to Cochran. "Two?"

Taylor took a deep breath and sighed, "Of everything."

The hostess's chuckle was as warm and thick as gravy. "I hear ya." She led them to a booth.

Taylor slid onto the cracked, red vinyl seat, good mood firmly re-established. "How do you stay so slim working here?"

"Moderation." She handed out the menus. "I let my man order everything, and I just have me a bite or two, or three."

"Sounds like a plan. Order away, Jim. Anything you like and dessert." She handed back the menu unread. "What's best?"

"For dessert? Sweet potato pie. No doubt. The bread pudding is something special, but I'd go for the pie if I were to choose just one."

Cochran shrugged and handed his menu back to the hostess. "May as well pick something for dinner, too. Enough to share."

The woman's laughter rang out. Her mouth was open wide enough to show off her dental work. "You make it too easy." She turned and called to the waitress. "Di'monde, bring this table Mama Pearl's special." She turned back to the table. "Sweet tea?"

"Yes, please," Taylor said. "Are you Pearl?"

"No, miss. I'm Ruby. My mama's Pearl. We're all gems or jewels here. It'd be tiresome if we all weren't so cute. I'll go get you that sweet tea now, honey."

The level of energy dropped when Ruby walked away.

"Say, Coch...er...Jimmy crack corn, how did you know

there was a mole? Was that just a guess based on what happened, or did someone tell you?"

"I got a call from a guy I used to work with years ago. Real solid guy. I thought he left the agency, but I guess he went into covert operations. Anyway, he was in the area, overheard the locals planning a raid on the safe house and knew our location had been leaked. He suspected you were in danger."

"Me?"

He nodded. "I didn't ask questions, I just got us the hell out of there." He grinned. "And he was right. Max is a real solid guy."

A young man brought the tea.

Christmas music played overhead. Elvis singing Blue Christmas.

Taylor's smile faded.

"You okay?" Cochran asked. His eyes were soft with concern.

"I guess." Taylor stripped the paper from the straw, scrunching it into a wrinkled blob at the bottom before removing it. "It's just the Christmas music." She dripped tea from the end of the straw onto the paper wrapper, watching it grow and writhe like a worm. It was something her dad had taught her to do. Something she'd teach her kids someday, if she ever had kids.

Where was Phil?

Elvis kept crooning depressingly about having a blue Christmas.

"The music?"

She nodded, turning her focus to unwrapping the silverware from the paper napkin. She forced a smile, but it felt stiff. Maybe she'd get her good mood back if she tried to sound happy. "Usually this time of year, I'm scrambling around trying to find the perfect gift for everyone." It was no good. She missed Phil too much. She placed the fork on the left and the knife and spoon on the right of the imaginary plate. The napkin she meant to drape on her lap never left her hands. "Phil and I sit by the fireplace every year and compose our Christmas letter. When business slows down, I take time off and start baking." Her eyes burned with emotion at the memory. "Phil calls me Mrs. Claus and jokes that I supply half the town with cookies." She looked across the table at Cochran. "What's your favorite Christmas cookie?"

"I don't have one."

She shook her head. "Everyone has one."

"I like fudge, but it isn't a cookie is it?"

She lowered her head again and shrugged. "Close enough. My dad likes fudge. Mom likes coconut thumbprints with cherry preserves. I like Russian Tea cakes best, and Phil's favorite is cornflake wreathes." She always had to make two batches because he liked them so much. She cleared her throat. "My brother likes spritz, Marlene loves the deep-fried rosettes, and my nephews like frosted sugar cookies. And then, there's the crew. They each have their favorites. And Father Dennison likes peanut butter blossoms. I end up making twelve different kinds." She stared into space, trying not to remember the silly things Phil did to sneak one more cookie.

Tayor managed a smile for the young woman who delivered their food. Di'monde. How could a person fail to smile at a girl named after a diamond? It surprised her to find she had shredded her napkin. Her cheeks grew warm as she asked for a replacement.

An embarrassment of food sat before her.

"Wow, this looks wonderful." Cochran dug in.

Julie Andrews' voice filled the air with all her favorite things.

Taylor shoved her sorrow to the back of her mind and focused on the plate before her. The barbecue pork was moist, tender, and flavorful. A spoonful of lima beans swam in the thick bean liquor that mated with the hickory-flavored brown sugar glaze of the baked beans. A chunk of buttered cornbread glistened next to the fried chicken. Her mouth rejoiced.

She'd eaten maybe a quarter of the food on her plate when a cell phone rang on the other side of the room. Rachmaninoff—the exact series of notes that Gene Wilder played to open the musical lock in the movie Willie Wonka and the Chocolate Factory. The exact same ringtone as Phil. She paused with her laden fork in the air and leaned out of the booth to see whose phone it was.

"Tammy."

The phone rang louder, but Taylor couldn't spot anyone fumbling for their phone.

"Tammy."

Where was he? She set her fork on her plate. She'd called Phil's cell phone, but he hadn't answered. Cochran told her they were monitoring it, but no one had used it since the first bomb.

"Tammy." Cochran's hand on her arm reminded her that she was Tammy. The phone stopped ringing. She sank back into the booth.

"What is it? Are you all right?"

She looked his way but didn't make eye contact. She needed a moment to herself. "I need to visit the ladies' room."

He frowned but moved his hand.

Taylor felt his eyes on her as she crossed the dining room and headed for the hallway. She did her share of looking around the room as she crossed but didn't see Phil. Had she expected to? Had she really thought he'd been following them? Or had he arrived before them to have lunch? Of course not.

Safely tucked in the closet-sized ladies' room, the dawning realization kicked her in the stomach. How could he explain where he'd been? What reason could he give that would even come close to explaining what had happened? What excuse would she accept? That he'd been held hostage? That he was in a witness protection program? That he'd been drugged and unconscious until now? She discounted each idea as ridiculous. He'd left clues. Told her to go to his sister's. Why? Why leave clues instead of simply finding her? Everyone else seemed to be able to, so why not Phil? Where was he?

She thought she'd heard his voice call her name

Thanksgiving night, but it had probably been wishful thinking. She took a deep breath. When was the last time she was certain she'd heard from him? The Notre Dame Football schedule? The recorded message? Her throat ached. She should have left a message on the machine. Then, he'd have left one for her, and she'd have known he was all right. She leaned against the wall and closed her eyes. Worry grabbed her stomach and shook it. Her stomach cramped, rejecting its contents.

She huddled over the stool while bright Christmas music played overhead.

Shaky, she wiped her mouth and washed her face and hands. He had to be all right. All her dreams of happily-ever-after involved him. She could see them sitting together at the end of their lives, wrinkled hand in wrinkled hand, grown old but never growing out of love. Her eyes filled with tears she dashed away, berating herself. Don't be stupid. He's fine. She'd convince Cochran to let her leave a message, or they'd find Lisa and... Had he lied about Lisa? Her stomach rolled. Phil had a lot of explaining to do.

She glanced in the mirror. She was a little pale, but not enough to make her pinch her cheeks for color. She slapped a smile on her face. Everything was fine. Everything would be fine.

The walk back to the table seemed long, but she didn't bother to look at the other customers. Phil wasn't there. Out of the millions of people in the country there must be thousands with Phil's ring tone.

Cochran looked up from his plate as Taylor slid into the booth. "You look kind of pale. Are you feeling all right?"

She shook her head at the irony. She should have pinched her cheeks.

"I didn't think so. I'll have the waitress box your food."

Taylor watched Cochran wave down their waitress. He'd taken her head shake as an answer. Just as well. Despite the faded, pasted-on smile, she felt as wrung out as a damp dishrag. She'd been vomiting and too queasy

lately to blame it all on nerves. And if it wasn't nerves...
She closed her eyes. This wasn't the way they'd planned
it.

Cochran paid the bill and carried the pile of Styrofoam
boxes and plastic cutlery to the car.

She slid into her seat. "Do you think we could find
a drug store? There are a few things I'd like to get." She
looked at the clock. "After the library, that is."

They wound their way through town until they found
the public library. One look at the stately brick building
with the lamppost near the entrance stairs told Taylor
this was a Carnegie library. Inside, one corner had
been converted to a computer lab. Instead of making a
beeline to an open machine, Taylor grabbed Cochran's
arm. "Maybe we should call Phil and leave a message."
Her sudden reluctance to research Lisa was the direct
result of the "what ifs" running through her head. What
if Cochran was right and Phil was involved in something
horrible? What if this was a trap? What if Lisa wasn't
there, didn't know anything, or refused to help?

Cochran patted her hand and then brushed it from
his sleeve. "This first. We're here." Cochran went to the
desk. Taylor followed him to their assigned computer.
It seemed strange not to type 4gEt-me_kn*t. She hadn't
touched a computer since the FBI had taken hers. Hadn't
checked her email. Maybe she should... No. Whoever was
monitoring things was certainly monitoring that, as well.

She looked over Cochran's shoulder. He was in a
map program with street view. Lisa's house, or at least
the house at 1600 Pennsylvania Avenue in Miami, was
an unassuming two story with planters of deep purple
petunias out front. Cochran ran a reverse search using
the address. The owners were Glen Reid and Mary L.
Reid, each listed separately. Their phone number was
listed. Employers, listed. Mary L. was an accountant with
a large firm. It was frightening how much information
was available to anyone with a snippet of information to
start with and internet access. Taylor wondered if she

could find a picture. If they shared any social networks, she probably could.

Mary L. Was she Phil's sister, Lisa, or some random person? She blinked at the screen.

Cochran closed his pocket notepad with a snap. "Let's go."

A group of teens surged into the library as they were leaving. Outside, more kids poured out of an elementary school down the street. Crooked lines of little ones stood by the curb waiting to board the school bus. She swallowed the lump in her throat.

In a moment, she was in the car. Cochran pulled into traffic heading away from the school. "You okay?"

"Yeah." She wasn't, but she wasn't sure why.

They stopped at Walgreens.

Once inside, Taylor breathed a sigh of relief when Cochran headed up a different aisle. She hurried with her purchases. By the time he reached the checkout with a basket containing a fuzzy throw with a matching pillow, juice, snacks, and bottled water, she'd already bought a bottle of vitamins and a pregnancy test.

CHAPTER SIXTEEN

Cochran saw the letters E.P.T. through the plastic bag as Taylor tucked it by her feet. He did a double take, but the bag was no longer visible.

Good God, not that. She had enough to deal with in her life without adding pregnancy.

"We need gas." He started the engine. They really didn't. They had half a tank, but he wanted to give Taylor a chance to use the test, if she wanted.

She didn't head to the bathroom as he expected.

That's right, he reminded himself, watching her through the window. She'd just used the bathroom at the restaurant.

He went inside to pay.

When he returned, she'd reclined her seat and closed her eyes.

"Taylor, you want the pillow and blanket? I got it for you."

"That would be great. Thank you."

Her easy acquiescence surprised him. He'd been telling her what to do since he'd met her, and she'd fought him every step of the way. Now, she didn't tell him what she thought they should do next or ask if he had a plan.

§

Taylor woke with a crick in her neck. They were inching along a well-lit highway with a thousand other cars. The oncoming lane was a river of headlights. She moved her seat into the upright position. "Where are we?"

Cochran glanced at her. "Chattanooga. We'll be

stopping soon. How do you feel?"

"Fine." The answer was automatic and probably untrue. "Are we going to Miami?"

"Is Mary L., Lisa?"

Ah, yes, the question of the day. If Phil wasn't Phil... "I don't know."

"Me neither." He flipped on the turn signal and changed lanes.

She stared at the billboards. A woman in a hospital bed cradling a newborn. "Tennessee Medical—delivering more than the next generation". As a kid, she'd never noticed tampon ads on TV. Then, when she'd gotten her period, they were everywhere. Now...

Maybe her stomach issues were just nerves. But if she were pregnant, it would change everything. She closed her eyes and tried to remember when she'd had her last period.

§

Phil spoke into the satellite phone. "Cochran check in yet?"

There was a slight delay as Sean's words unscrambled. "No. Rogers suspects a mole. Probably ordered Cochran off grid, but he'll check in soon. You can count on it."

"What makes you think that?" If Cochran had been ordered out of sight, he'd wait for a predetermined signal before coming in. He was too smart and too well trained to rush things. He'd keep Taylor safe.

"He's standard issue. He could be holed up someplace, but he's the itchy type. My gut says he's driving around putting on as many miles as he can. Basic evasive maneuver."

"We got the vehicle?"

"No. He doesn't have one of ours, and he didn't use his own name to rent one. But don't worry, we'll find him."

Phil wished he shared Sean's confidence. "I'd rather we concentrate on nabbing Accawi and his informant."

"Don't worry, Max. We're better than they are."

Phil pressed the end button and looked through his

binoculars at the gate to Accawi's mansion. He wasn't surprised Sean hadn't asked for an update. No calls had come in or been made from the address. They both knew watching the estate was an exercise in futility, since Accawi was probably holed up some place awaiting word of Taylor's location. Still, with no other leads, Phil felt compelled to stake it out, just to be certain. In the race to get to Taylor, the starting location could mean everything.

He put aside the binoculars and looked at the time displayed on the cell phone. He checked for messages every day. Twice a day. Why didn't she call? It was a constant struggle to keep his desperation under control and to keep the picture of her face from filling his mind. If it was this hard for him, how was she holding up?

§

The next morning, in the silence of the hotel's bathroom, Taylor read the plus sign on the second test wand. Her heart beat a strange rhythm. The results hadn't changed. Not that she'd thought it would.

Two months ago the pink plus sign would have been reason for rejoicing, but now… Her breath came out as a ragged sigh.

She was not going to cry.

If there ever was a time for strength, this was it. As willing as she'd been to run around the country risking herself to find Phil, she was not willing to risk their child. This baby was the future. Their future. Her future. This baby was going to have family. Grandparents, uncles, aunts, cousins. A mother who loves it and a father. Hopefully, a father. That meant she needed to solve this now, before the pregnancy became noticeable and the baby became another pawn. The latitude she'd given Cochran to decide if they went to Miami or not disappeared. Phil told her to go to Lisa's and that's exactly what she was going to do.

She wrapped the tests in the plastic sleeves they'd come in and tucked them back inside the box before sliding the package into her bag. She couldn't explain, not even to herself, why she was keeping the tests.

"Ready to go?" Cochran asked as she entered the bedroom and dropped her bag on the floor.

"Yes." She made the mistake of looking at him. His eyes saw too much.

"What happened?" His eyes narrowed. "Did you throw up again?"

"I'm fine."

"Okay, then." He nodded, watching her with those too-observant eyes. "Grab your bag, and let's hit the road."

They swung through McDonald's for breakfast.

Without asking what she wanted, he ordered one full breakfast. "And a dry English muffin. No butter."

Her eyes met his. "You knew?"

"I suspected."

"I bought a test."

He nodded. "You take it yet?"

She nodded. "This morning." Her throat felt thick, but she refused to cry. "It's positive."

"You gonna be okay?"

Taylor had a momentary respite as he paid the woman at the window and took the bag of their food. She swallowed several times, but the lump remained firmly lodged in her throat. "Yes. This changes everything."

"I'd imagine so." He handed her the dry English muffin before shifting into drive.

The toasted muffin was warm and oddly comforting in her hand. She thought of Phil. Mental images of their dreams together blurred and melted. Her heart was lead and her stomach stone, but her mind was made up. "I have to go to Miami. I have to find Phil and solve this. Now."

"I agree. It's also time to make a move to catch the mole. I'll call headquarters and start the protective relocation process."

"What? Why?" Her jaw dropped. "I thought I didn't fit the criteria. I don't have information the bureau needs. I don't want to disappear permanently."

"You're right about the criteria. Most protective relocation clients are witnesses or families of witnesses who are given new identities to protect them, so they can testify in a trial and continue to live afterwards. But you aren't a witness, so we would expect your application to be denied. However, in this scenario, your application is not only accepted, but given high priority."

"Because things tend to blow up around me?"

He shook his head. "No. Because you have important information about the mole."

"But I don't."

"My guess is, you probably do but don't realize it." He held up a hand preempting her protest. "But whether you have actual information or not is beside the point. It's all about perception. We put it out that you have information. One phone call and you go from 'person of interest' to 'target.'"

"So, you use the leak to..."

He finished the statement for her. "...to make it look like you're coming in to give evidence about the mole. They'll set up a sting."

"If the mole believes it. He probably knows I don't have any information."

"That's the risk."

"But you and I will go to Miami?"

He nodded.

She took a bite of her muffin and chewed it thoughtfully. "You didn't come up with this idea because of the pregnancy, did you?"

"No. Just before you and I dropped out of sight, my boss and I discussed the option of using a sting to entrap the mole. It has always been a matter of timing."

The muffin lay like a brick in her belly. "I wish I really had information, but I don't. I don't know anything."

"Having information would make everything easier, but the bureau deals with things the way they are rather than the way we wish they were. I'll make the call. Then, we'll head south and see what, if anything, Mary knows."

§

"Cochran called." Bouncing off a satellite or two did nothing to dim the glee in Sean's voice. The man loved nothing more than being right. "Your girl wants to enter into the protective relocation program."

Phil's stomach flipped. "Why? What happened?" Taylor wasn't a candidate for a new identity. She was going back to her old life once they found the damned mole. Despite Sean's smug insistence that Cochran was regular issue, Phil knew better. Cochran was a terrier—smart, quick, tenacious. If he came back on the grid to make the request there had to be a compelling reason. "Was there another attack? Did something specific leak?"

"I don't know, but Rogers bumped her to the front of the Witness Relocation line, which makes me suspect they think she knows something or they want it to look like she does. They're going to bring her in. You need to get back here."

Damn it. He wanted her by his side, but he needed her safe. The safe houses weren't safe. Accawi and the mole were operating unhindered. He'd come out of retirement to stop them so Taylor would be safe. Bringing her in now made her a target. Holy shit. This was a damned sting.

§

From the passenger seat of the SUV, the Reid house looked just the way it had on the internet, minus the flowers. Taylor unwrapped her chicken sandwich and glanced at Cochran. "I think I should call the number Phil gave me and tell him I got the message."

Cochran took the SIM chip and battery out of his pocket and reassembled the phone. "If he answers, I want to talk to him."

The phone rang three times before the answering machine picked up. Once again, she heard Phil's voice repeating the same message, "Taylor, honey. Cochran can't protect you. You need to go see Lisa…."

She shook her head at Cochran. "It's the machine."

After leaving her message Cochran made sure the phone was in pieces again to prevent GPS tracing. Then they waited.

The sandwiches were long gone by the time a silver sedan pulled into the Reid's driveway and stopped beneath the carport. A tiny woman with frosted, dark hair and a stylish suit got out of the car.

Cochran slipped from the car. "Wait for my signal."

Taylor nodded, but her eyes never left the woman. She looked nothing like Taylor had imagined. Nothing like Phil. This woman was half Phil's height. Maybe five years older. She opened the back seat and reached inside. Her movements were short, gentle bursts like a chickadee's hop rather than Phil's catlike glide.

Cochran was in position. Taylor returned his nod and opened the car door.

She wiped her damp palms on her jeans and stepped into the yard. The thick grass felt different than the lawns in Indiana. Tough St. Augustine grass, instead of the softer, Kentucky bluegrass/ryegrass blend popular back home. She shuffled her feet. This wasn't how you met family.

The woman's arms were filled with grocery bags.

"Excuse me, Mrs. Reid." Taylor crossed the small front yard in several long strides. "My husband, Bob Smith, told me to tell his sister, Lisa, that he sent me."

The woman turned. Her eyes grew wide with what Taylor hoped was surprise but suspected was fear.

"Lisa, I'm Taylor Wilson."

The woman shook her head. "My name is Mary. You can't stay here."

The breath caught in her throat. She opened her mouth and closed it again.

The side door of the house opened and a pretty teenage girl emerged. "Mom, what's for supper? I've got practice in a half hour." She spotted Taylor and paused. "Oh, sorry."

"Here." Mary thrust the bags of groceries into the girl's arms. "Take these in."

"Okay."

Both Taylor and Mary watched the girl. When the screen door slammed behind her, Taylor turned to her sister-in-law. "You're right. I can't stay here." There was no way she would risk Mary and her family.

Mary's eyes softened. "He told me you might come.

There's another name you're supposed to use, so I know it's you."

Taylor nodded. "Tink."

"Jenny," she called through the screen door. "Bring me the manila envelope on the counter."

Mary smiled. "I was Lisa as a kid. Mary Lisa. No one calls me that now."

The girl came out of the house and handed the envelope to her mother. She glanced at Taylor with Phil's eyes. A lump formed in Taylor's throat.

"Thanks." She looked from her daughter to Taylor and then back. "There's one more bag in the car." She turned to Taylor. "This is my daughter, Jenny. My son, Mike, is at soccer practice."

Tears pricked Taylor's eyes. She blinked them back and smiled as Jenny closed the car door. "Nice to meet you, Jenny."

"Likewise." Jenny glided by on long legs, like Phil's. "Mom. Practice."

"Turn on the oven. I'll be right in."

Taylor's heart ached as she watched Jenny leave. Would her baby ever know Mary's kids? She turned back to Mary. "I should go. I'm sorry, I— do you know if he's okay?"

Mary's eyes swam with tears. She shook her head and handed the envelope to Taylor. "He sent a note for you. I can't let you stay, but there's a place. We just bought a house in Michigan. On the north shore. I put a key and a map in here. You can stay there as long as you need to. Lock the key inside when you go. I have a spare."

"I...thank you." Taylor's voice shook.

"Be safe. Maybe we'll see each other again."

Taylor nodded. Maybe.

Mary wrapped her in a tight hug.

Taylor ached to hold on forever. But she let go and stepped back. Tears ran down her cheeks. "Thank you."

Mary nodded. "God speed."

§

In suburban Indianapolis, five federal agents

surrounded the garage in anticipation of Taylor's arrival. Phil stood with those inside, waiting. Any minute now, the garage door would open and "Cochran" would drive in. He shifted his stance, depressingly confident Taylor was nowhere near Indianapolis.

He and Sean agreed. This smelled like a sting. And if they knew it within moments of hearing it, so would the mole. Of course, that also made this the perfect time to actually bring her in—if Cochran thought she'd be safer on the grid. Which was why he was there. Just in case... Trouble was, Taylor was safer hidden. Cochran knew that.

Phil glanced at his watch. Any time, now. His right hand brushed his leg holster. Sean's voice whispered over the ear bud. "Blue van license XZY 916. On my mark." Despite his certainty Taylor wasn't in it, Phil's heart picked up its pace. Sean's voice came again. "Now."

The garage door opened. The van pulled inside. The door stopped rising and began its descent. Perfect.

Before the garage door touched the ground, agents swarmed the van. The driver wasn't Cochran but another agent from Rogers' unit—Jacobs. Phil recognized the girl in the back as Special Agent Lacey Johnson.

bang their heads together. Instead, he melted into the shadows.

§

Taylor sat in the SUV clutching the envelope to her chest.

"What did she give you, Tink?" Cochran started the engine and pulled away from the curb. He'd heard everything from where he's been positioned.

Tink. Taylor looked at him. It was the one thing she hadn't told him. She thought of explaining but shook her head instead. He didn't need to know everything. She opened the five-by-seven envelope and drew out two computer generated maps, a page of driving directions, a house key, and a sealed envelope marked "Taylor."

She tucked the key and pages back inside and concentrated on the envelope with Phil's writing on it.

She traced his distinctive script with the tip of her finger. Tears she didn't bother to stem trickled down her cheeks.

"What are you waiting for? Open it."

She slid her finger beneath the flap.

"Read it out loud."

That hadn't been her plan, but she took a ragged breath and began.

"Taylor, stay with Lisa, she'll keep you safe. Keep your mug close. I'll come for you when it's safe. Never forget that I love you. ~Phil"

That was it? She flipped over the piece of paper and looked at the blank back. He'd never been much of a letter writer, but then they'd never been apart before. "So much for that. I can't stay with her, and I don't have the mug."

"When was it sent?"

Taylor looked at the white envelope and then the manila one. "I don't know. Does it matter? Lisa said the note was inside the one Phil sent her."

"The point is: she knows what's been going on. She knows the danger you're in."

"Which Phil probably told her and is why she offered her vacation home."

"I don't know."

"Why does everything have to mean something else? Why can't it just be what it is? Phil contacted his sister, told her I needed help and asked her if I could stay with her until he came to get me. She couldn't do what he asked because she has kids, so she's letting me stay at her cabin in Michigan."

"And it doesn't bother you that the sister he doesn't keep in touch with and doesn't know has kids would offer her house to you?"

"It's what family does." Taylor looked at the maps. "Lisa's cabin is on Lake Superior, twenty miles from Marquette, Michigan." She opened the atlas and laid it on her lap. Marquette, Michigan seemed a million miles from where they sat. "It's a big country." She was tired. Tired of sitting, tired of being homeless. Just tired. Her eyes burned with tears. "We just came from Minneapolis."

"We don't have to go to her cabin."

"Yes, we do. Phil will come for me there. Anyway, do we have the money to stay somewhere else?"

Cochran shrugged. "That depends. How long will it take to uncover the mole?"

She sighed. "How long until they do the sting?"

"I don't know."

Her head ached. Finding Lisa in Miami was supposed to solve her problems not create more. She slumped in her seat.

"Tell me about the mug. Why would Phil tell you to keep it close?"

"You've seen it. It's a really nice mug he made for me because I'm a coffee freak. But I have no idea why I'm supposed to keep it close."

"Do you think it could have anything to do with what's happened?"

She scoured her brain. "You had it. What do you think?"

"That it's a nice piece of contemporary art. You could probably sell if for several hundred dollars, but as far as it being a reason to blow up your house and your business and take shots at you... I have no idea."

"I think you're underestimating the price tag it could command, but you're right. If someone wanted it, why didn't they just steal it? It could have been blown up in either explosion."

"And yet, he told you to keep it with you."

"Too late. It's locked in an airport locker." She rubbed her tired eyes. "So, now what?"

"I'll tell you what. I'm beat. Let's check into a hotel with a guest computer in the lobby. Rogers will post an update on his daughter Libby's Facebook page. Maybe it's all over."

She wished.

§

Taylor stood over Cochran's shoulder as he checked Facebook. Tim Rogers' daughter's mood was frustrated and disappointed. The latest message. "Why doesn't anything ever go as planned?"

She sighed and massaged her forehead. "Is there any way we can fly to South Bend, nab the mug and hightail it to Michigan?" She groaned. "Never mind. We don't have the key."

Cochran looked over his shoulder at her. "I have the key."

Her eyes opened wide. "Really?"

He nodded. "I made a copy before turning in the original. I shouldn't have, but I know how personal property gets lost in cases like this."

Hope fluttered in her breast. She blinked at him like an idiot. "We can get my mug?"

"We can. I just don't know if we should. If it's worth the risk. Since Sister Margaret's death, you're a known quantity in South Bend. The last thing we need is for someone to recognize you and alert the authorities. We may not know why you are a target, but we know you are a target."

Thoughts bounced around her head like the ball in a pinball machine. "I don't know what to say. Phil told me to keep the mug close. I can only assume there's a reason."

"I agree." His eyes narrowed as he looked at her. "You look exhausted. It doesn't take both of us to figure out the best route to South Bend. Go to bed. I'll finish here and let myself in later."

§

Three hours later, Taylor was shaken from a deep sleep.

"Taylor, get up." Cochran gave her leg one last shake and then turned to the table.

She sprang out of bed, heart racing. Every light in the room was lit. She looked left and then right, searching for the source of the threat. "What's wrong?"

"Nothing. Here, put these on." Cochran shoved a curly brown wig and pair of red rimmed glasses into her hands.

Her mind raced, but her hands obeyed without question, twisting her long hair into a bun and pulling the wig over it. "What's happening?"

"I got airline tickets. You need an ID."

"Oh." She took a deep breath.

He yanked the top sheet off the bed and draped it over the curtain rod. "Stand here."

Her eyes were blurry and her face sleep-crushed and puffy as she pressed the glasses to her nose and stood before the white sheet. He took three pictures before handing the camera to Taylor and standing in front of the sheet himself.

"Take my picture."

She took two shots before returning the camera. He plugged the camera's memory card into a machine she'd never seen before, picked up the room phone and punched a series of numbers. "You get it?" He waited a fraction of a second before responding. "Good. Fifty minutes outside Wal-Mart with the money and the scanner. Okay." He hung up. "I guess there isn't time to sleep."

Taylor opened her mouth to ask what was happening, but realized he'd already answered. She closed her mouth and sank to the bed. "What time is it?"

"Eleven p.m. If you want a shower, you'd better get moving."

She'd been asleep for three hours. No wonder she was so tired. She stumbled to the bathroom. "When is the flight?"

"Two o'clock. Hurry up. You can sleep on the plane."

The night was colder than Taylor imagined it would be. She crawled around inside of the SUV collecting everything and tucking it into their athletic bags. Cochran followed behind her wiping everything but the front seat with wet wipes.

"What about hair?" Her own hair was hot beneath the wig.

"The rental company will vacuum. We don't have time. This is probably overkill anyway." He handed her the box of wet wipes. "Get in and buckle up. We'll wipe down the front seat at the airport."

The clock showed midnight as they pulled out of the

hotel parking lot. Cochran drove beneath the neon lights of the city as if he'd been there a thousand times before.

"How did you find someone to make fake IDs?"

"This is Miami. There's a large immigrant population. Illegals and fake IDs go hand-in-hand."

A block away a Wal-Mart sign glowed. "Now, you stay in the car, buckled in your seat, looking out the front window while I take care of this. These guys don't like an audience. Got it?"

She nodded. "What's my name going to be?"

"Tammy." He drove into the parking lot and parked just past a rusty black sedan. He looked Taylor in the eye. "Stay put."

"Don't forget the scanner." She pointed to the pocketsize machine in the cup holder.

"Right. Thanks." He rolled his eyes and shook his head as he closed the door behind him.

Taylor strained her ears, but besides the sound of the engine idling there was nothing. No voices. A minute passed. And another. What was taking so long? She'd expected a quick transaction. Here's the money. Here's the ID card. Don't forget the scanner. Adios. How long could it take? Another minute. Had something gone wrong? Maybe she should check. She craned her neck to see out the back window. Her hands itched to unlock her seatbelt. But what could she do? Scream? Run?

The driver's door opened.

If not for the seatbelt, Taylor would have jumped a foot. She smothered her gasp behind her palm and nearly got whiplash turning. Cochran.

"All set." He closed the door behind him and shifted into drive.

"What took you so long?"

He looked at Taylor and then at the dash. "Long? I was gone, what, five minutes?"

She felt her face heat. "Three."

Cochran laughed. "Everything went fine. How do you like your Florida license, Tammy?"

Taylor picked up her license. Tammy Wilcox. She

looked terrible in the photo.

They merged with traffic and followed the signs to the airport.

§

Phil woke at six and dialed the number to check his messages, expecting to hear the familiar "no message" recording. Instead, he had one message from yesterday late afternoon. How had he missed a call? The phony sting. He pressed his PIN and listened. His heart thrilled at the sound of Taylor's voice. "Where are you?"

Phil shook his head at the irony. Taylor called while he'd been standing in the garage waiting for her supposed arrival. The originating number was blocked, as it would be if she'd used Cochran's phone.

Forty minutes later, he keyed into the office. There, he logged on the computer, checked Cochran's phone log and triangulated the GPS signature on the unit during the minute they'd had it on. Taylor had called while driving in Miami.

Did that mean she was at Lisa's? He hoped so. His sister would accept and protect Taylor without reservation, just as she'd accepted his decision to enter the bureau years ago, swearing she'd always be there for him, no matter what. The FBI knew he had a sister, but her name had changed twice, and she'd moved several times since the last time they'd done a security background check on him. Easy work for any skilled agent, but who would think to look? Only Jackson and O'Hearn knew he was Philip Wilson.

The situation inside the bureau was at pre-explosion level. The software needed to monitor the intelligence collecting devices was operational once again, now with several redundancies to prevent future disruption. They didn't have the technology to create any more super bugs, but that was irrelevant. He still had no idea why Taylor was at risk. If Accawi had a personal vendetta against him as the artist for some reason, that shouldn't have touched Taylor at all. And why was the mole helping Accawi? It didn't make sense. Taylor knew nothing. Phil rubbed his eyes. None of this helped answer the questions at hand. How could he keep her safe? What instructions should he give her now?

He glanced at the clock. Sean wasn't due in for at least another hour. That gave him plenty of time to book two flights and a rental car in Miami. His buddy would want to go with him to pick up Taylor.

§

The remote alarm beeped on the gunman's watch. He leapt out of bed and logged onto his laptop.

This was no false alarm. The blip on the map tracked the beacon as it left the airport and turned west onto Highway 20.

The mug had moved.

A broad grin split his face.

"Gotcha."

CHAPTER SEVENTEEN

Taylor cupped the mug in her hands and looked out the window of their newly rented SUV. "That went well."

Cochran nodded as he turned north on Saint Joseph Valley Parkway toward Michigan.

The road hummed beneath the tires like a lullaby. The adrenalin that had kept her alert through the deplaning, mug retrieval, and vehicle rental process dissipated. She yawned. "I wish I could power sleep like you. As soon as we were in the air, you were out. You slept like the dead. How do you do it?"

"Training. When you work all hours you learn to sleep at a moment's notice." He spared her a glance. "Go ahead and nod off if you like. I'm fine. I don't need a navigator until we're closer to Marquette."

"What are we going to do once we get to Lisa's, er Mary's, cabin?"

"Secure the location and hold position."

She smiled at his choice of words. "Sit and wait."

He nodded. "The sting didn't work, but Rogers will come up with something else that will. With luck, the mole will be caught before we get to Marquette. If not, perhaps Phil will contact us and provide answers. Either way, I'll keep you safe."

§

Phil sat at an empty cubicle waiting for Sean. The flight was booked, the car arranged. To kill time, he logged onto the computer and automatically typed in the tracking code key for Taylor's mug. There was no reason, beyond habit, for him to do so. He knew where Taylor had left the mug. Knew she didn't have it.

Yesterday she had been in Miami, possibly on the way to Lisa's, but definitely under Cochran's eye. She wasn't likely to return to Indiana. So, Phil expected to see the blip static at the same coordinates. But it wasn't. It was heading north.

How was that possible? He ran a quick diagnostic. Everything was functioning correctly. Taylor should have been in Miami with Lisa. Had Lisa refused to help his wife? After all her promises? It didn't seem possible, yet the blip on the screen proclaimed something hadn't gone as planned.

Phil was still gaping at the computer when Sean sauntered in half a minute later. "Hey, Max, you're in early. Something up?"

"Looks like it." A few other agents were arriving, milling around in the familiar pre-morning briefing mode. He closed down the computer he'd been working on. "Let's go to your office."

Sean set his briefcase on the floor next to his desk as Phil closed the door. "What's up?"

He told Sean about the message from Taylor, the timing and location of her call, and the plans he put in place.

"You sent her to Lisa, huh? I'd never have guessed that. You trust Lisa that much?" Sean knew just where to poke, but after nearly fifteen years, the spot wasn't as tender.

"The inquest proved she didn't know her boyfriend was a mob enforcer." He hadn't had to defend her for a long time.

"Doesn't make your parents any less dead."

"I know. But she's family."

"Family you haven't seen nor spoken to since your parents' funeral."

"That has more to do with the bureau than with how I feel about her. You know that."

"I didn't know you'd been keeping an eye on her." He

leaned against the desk. "Makes you wonder. Smart girl like that." He shook his head. "I don't know if I could trust her again. You know, fool me once shame on you, fool me twice shame on me."

"You're a cynic. Lisa would never knowingly hurt family. Not then. Not now." Then why wasn't Taylor in Miami?

Sean shrugged. "Not my call." He pushed himself away from the desk. "So, we're going to Miami. Give me ten minutes to hand off some things."

"We aren't going to Miami." He pointed to Sean's PC. "Can I use your computer?"

Sean nodded. "Sure. Why?"

"Taylor's mug is moving."

A flicker of irritation passed across Sean's face. Sean liked to be the one on top of things and no matter how quickly he got the latest information, Sean always seemed to have it first. Except for the mug.

"You're kidding, right? I thought you said Lisa would help her." Sean rounded the desk and stood behind Phil. "There has to be a glitch. Why don't you head to Miami for Taylor, and I'll see what I can find out here."

"Not necessary." Phil turned back to the screen. "I requested the security camera footage. As soon as it gets here, we should be able to see who took the mug." He called up his email. "Here it is."

They watched the footage in fast motion. "There." Phil stopped the video and backed it up a few seconds. "Taylor and Cochran. The curly headed girl and heavy guy." There were no face shots. The couple kept their heads lowered, as if aware of the cameras. Still, he knew Taylor when he saw her.

"Could be someone else. Look at those mincing steps. Taylor doesn't walk that way."

"She's doing it on purpose to throw you off. It's her. I'd know that butt anywhere."

Sean snorted. "Well, you'd be the expert. Can't say as I've watched Taylor's ass enough to make a positive identification by butt alone."

"I'm canceling the Miami arrangements." He did that in a matter of seconds and then called up the blip that was Taylor's mug. "Where the hell do you think they're headed?"

§

Taylor didn't need the radio to tell her Michigan was under a winter storm advisory. The sky was white and large flakes of snow fell to the ground in increasing numbers as Cochran parked near a diner in Mackinaw City, population 856. Pretty little town. Shimmering Christmas lights lined the city streets, and carols played from outdoor speakers.

Lack of sleep made everything seem soft and muzzy. She paused to look through a bookstore window. Beyond her tired reflection there was a huge display of seasonal books and recommended reads. Christmas ornaments hung from the ceiling by shiny ribbons. Her mind kept tripping over thoughts of what she would be doing at this time of year under normal circumstances. She yawned and pressed the heel of her hand against her flat belly. She was officially dead, yet inside her a tiny life grew. It seemed more a concept than a reality. Truth be told, at this moment, nothing in her life seemed real.

She followed Cochran into the restaurant. Her stomach was ready for lunch, but the dull ache behind her eyes told her she was even more ready for bed.

"I'd have been happy with McDonald's in a hotel room."

"Mackinaw City doesn't have a McDonald's. Order soup with your meal. You're going to need crackers for morning."

Her eyelids felt like they were weighted with lead. She was tempted to lay her head on her arms and doze while they waited for the waitress. "Could we get this to go and eat it in the hotel?"

He shook his head. "Change of plans. I want to put a few more miles between us and South Bend."

"Why?" He'd promised her an early night, and she'd been clinging to that promise for hours. She wanted to get to the cabin as much as he did, but delaying their arrival several more hours in favor of an early bedtime wasn't going to hurt anything. They were already getting there faster than if they'd driven the whole way.

"Instinct. You can sleep in the car."

She sighed. "I didn't take you as an instinct kind of guy." Eyes closed, she put her elbows on the table and braced her head on her palms.

"Eyes open. Here comes the waitress."

Taylor forced herself to sit up straight. She ordered a BLT.

Cochran reminded her about the soup.

"With extra crackers," he told the waitress. "We both like a lot of crackers."

Did he really? She wondered. She'd spent days on end with Cochran, yet knew nothing about his life other than his job. "What is your life like when you aren't traveling around the country with me?"

The waitress arrived with the soup and a basket of soda crackers.

"Fill your pockets."

"Do you have family? A wife and kids? A girlfriend?" She absentmindedly filled her pockets.

"Yes, no, and no."

"Why don't you ever talk about yourself? I know more about Lacey than I do about you." She cringed as the words left her mouth. Lacey had been shot protecting her.

"I have parents and two younger brothers. My dad is an ex-cop, my mom taught home economics. Both are retired. One brother, Ken, is a truck driver. He's married with a two-year-old daughter. My other brother, John, teaches high school history. His wife, Kristy, is expecting their first."

"Geez, Cochran. You sound like you're reading a dossier. Do your sisters-in-law work?"

"Lexi's a nurse, and Kristy's a graphic designer."

"I have an older brother. Had an older sister."

"You never mentioned your sister before." The

gentleness in his voice waved the fog from her head.

"I'm sure I must have." A small part of her closed itself off to him.

He shook his head. "I've talked to your parents about her but never you."

"What difference does it make? I'm sure my parents told you she's been dead for fourteen years."

"Killed by her husband."

"Who is nothing like Phil. Don't even go there."

"I wasn't planning to. We're past that."

"Good. 'Cuz, she and I were nothing alike. She was young and easily led. He was the star quarterback. Years older than her and built like a bull. He was full of it, too. Big talker. Always threatening to bruise someone. My parents tried to warn her, but she didn't listen. She was only eighteen when she died. Young and foolish." Taylor shook her head. "Such a waste."

She turned to the window. Outside, the snow was falling in earnest. If it kept up like this they'd be in for some serious winter driving. "Are you certain you want to keep going? It's really starting to come down."

He spooned soup into his mouth. "We'll find someplace in another hour or two."

A swirl of white danced past the window. "Why not now? It's stupid to push on with as little sleep as we've had."

The waitress arrived with their sandwiches. He didn't answer her. Stubborn man.

She looked at her sandwich.

The silence stretched between them. Chin propped in her hand, she let her eyes drift shut.

"Taylor, wake up." He pushed her plate closer to her. "Eat."

§

The snow was falling steadily as they sat in line at the toll gate for the bridge across the Straits of Mackinac. Overhead, the message on the electronic sign flashed a "High Wind Warning" for the bridge and instructed all vehicles to "reduce speed to a maximum of twenty miles per hour, turn on four-way flashers, and utilize outside lane." It also recommended they turn their "AM radio to 530 or 1610" for updates.

Traffic across the bridge was slow but steady. At times, the wind shook the SUV, but Cochran and the other drivers seemed to compensate. The mechanical voice on the radio spoke of a winter snow warning and deteriorating conditions.

"The storm is getting worse. Don't you think we should stay in St. Ignace?" Taylor asked following a windy blast of snow that eliminated visibility for half a second.

"No. It won't be this bad once we're off the bridge." He drove another moment or two. "Could you turn off the radio? That voice bothers me."

Taylor turned off the radio and refrained from reiterating the forecast. She'd said her piece. Cochran had heard the report as well as she had. If he wanted to ignore it and drive longer in the storm, she'd let him. He wouldn't want to get stranded any more than she did. He'd stop before it got too bad.

Ten minutes later, they rolled into St. Ignace, passing signs directing them to Shepler's, Star Line, and Arnold ferry boats. As he predicted, the wind in town wasn't as bad as it had been on the bridge.

She closed her eyes as they left St. Ignace and headed for another tiny dot on the map.

§

He had them now. All of them. Accawi's body thrummed with anticipation. His source gave him the coordinates. "Follow the dot. It will lead you to the whore."

The woman was not a whore. He shook his head. Why did his source hate her so? No matter. He must focus, clear his mind of impure thoughts, and ready himself to sacrifice the woman to Allah. Aisha's blood cried for vengeance. He would not let the cries go unanswered.

CHAPTER EIGHTEEN

Taylor awoke to the sound of Cochran swearing. The clock on the dash said she'd been asleep for a mere half hour. The weather had slowed them to less than thirty miles-per-hour, but still the snow raced against the windshield like stars moving at warp speed.

Cochran muttered something under his breath and tapped the brake to slow them further. The anti-lock brakes engaged with a rhythmic groan.

Taylor watched the snow. Had she been driving, they'd be headed back to St. Ignace and a hotel room, but she wasn't the driver. Taylor stared at the ground ahead trying to determine if they were still on the highway or not.

A patch of blacktop appeared for an instant. The tension in her shoulders eased a fraction. She wanted to ask Cochran what his plans were now, but she didn't want to distract him from driving.

Minutes crept like hours. They were alone on the road. The plows weren't even clearing this stretch of highway. The SUV barreled through one drift after another. Taylor tore her eyes off the road to look at Cochran. His eyes were focused, unblinking at the windshield. Tension creased his brow. As if feeling the weight of her eyes, he shot her a quick glance.

"We should have stopped."

"Probably." She stared into the swirling white, resuming her search for some sign of the blacktop. There hadn't been any for quite some time. No signs, no road, no snow banks, just unending whiteness. "Do you think we should pull over and stop? It doesn't seem to be getting any better."

"Probably, but I'm going to keep going as long as I can. Maybe we'll hit a town."

Taylor picked up the map from her lap. "Have we passed Brevort yet? Epoufette?"

"I don't think so. I haven't seen a town or an exit since we started."

"Are we sure we're still on the road?"

"No."

According to the map, Lake Michigan was just to the left of the road. "Uh, you don't think we're driving on the lake, do you?"

Suddenly, Taylor saw a tree on their right. Close. She flinched. "Tree."

The SUV ground to a halt. Cochran swore. "We're not on the lake." He shifted into reverse. "But we're not on the road, either." The tires spun, shooting more snow into the air. He took his foot off the gas and shifted into low. The car didn't even rock forward.

"I don't suppose we have On-star?"

He shook his head.

Taylor sighed loudly. "Figures." She looked out the window. The car was running, the heater blasting, but the windshield wipers could barely keep up with the snow. The white stuff accumulated in thick, fluffy chunks that clung to the passenger side window for a long time before melting enough to slide down and join the growing pile at the bottom. At this rate, it wouldn't take long before the entire car was cocooned in a smothering blanket. "How about your cell phone? Could you dial 9-1-1?"

"I think we'll wait until the storm dies down a bit. Reception might be a bit iffy with the storm. Even if it's not, we want a wrecker, not anyone else."

She knew he meant the mole. She pressed her palm against her belly and wished Cochran's instinct had told them to stop earlier.

They sat there, unspeaking, listening to the engine and the heater fan.

The snow continued to fall.

It was pretty, really. The kind of snow that made a person think of Christmas carols. The melody of Let it Snow flitted through her mind. If only she were in her living room, all toasty warm, snuggled next to Phil while the fire blazed in the fireplace at their feet. Of course, there was no house, no fireplace, and no Phil. The thought made her colder than the draft seeping through the crack in the door. She shook her head.

Cochran cleared his throat. "You were right. We should have stopped earlier."

She nodded.

"So, now what do we do?" They couldn't just sit there. She couldn't just sit there. Didn't Cochran see how the snow was accumulating? They were right next to the lake. Taylor had heard of lake effect snow. It dumped enough snow to be measured in feet rather than inches. Feet. The SUV would be buried. She dried her palms on the legs of her jeans.

She felt him watching her. "What?"

"It's going to be okay."

"How is this going be to okay? I wasn't a girl scout. I don't know how to survive in a car in a blizzard. What if the exhaust pipe gets snowed in, and we don't know it? We could asphyxiate. What if the snow gets so deep it buries the car and crushes it with us inside?"

His smile infuriated her. "Relax, Taylor. I know you're claustrophobic but think about it logically. Cars have to pass all sorts of stress tests. There's no way a little snow is going to crush us. Now, if we were in the mountains in an avalanche, maybe, but we aren't. So, take a deep breath and relax."

She took a deep breath. He was right. She knew he was right. But her heart raced and there didn't seem to be enough air.

"What if we freeze to death, and no one finds us until spring? What if a snowplow comes by and buries us?"

He laughed. "All right, worst-case-scenario-girl. If we didn't have gas, there is an outside chance we'd freeze to death, but we have a full tank. Our body heat alone will keep the interior of the car above freezing. We might get cold, but we won't die. Now, as far as the plow goes, we are in a big SUV. If a plow comes along, the driver will see us, and we'll be rescued."

"But we aren't on the road."

He shook his head. "That's right, but I doubt we're more than a few yards from it." He patted her hand. "Now relax. Why don't you crawl under that blanket and get some sleep. I'll dig out the tailpipe so the exhaust will dissipate nicely. While I'm out, I'll see if I can't spot the road."

Taylor blinked at him. "You're going to take a walk?" She looked out the window at the storm. "Are you nuts? You're supposed to stay with the vehicle. Even I know that. Finding a vehicle is a heck of a lot easier than finding a frozen body. Didn't they give you survival training in agent school?"

He laughed. "Of course, they did."

She glared at him. "And you're just going to ignore it? It isn't funny. My grandma grew up on a farm. Her dad went to the barn in a blizzard to feed the cows. He almost walked right past it into the field where he'd have frozen to death. As it turned out, he hit the corner of the building and clung to the side of it all the way to the barn door. He tied himself to a length of rope for the return trip, just in case. Every October after that, he ran a line from the kitchen door to the barn door, just in case. So, if you think you're traveling blind, looking for a road in a blizzard, you are nuts." She shook her head. "You aren't doing it."

By the time she finished ranting his smile was gone.

He held her by her upper arms and looked into her eyes. "Taylor, I know what I'm doing. Even had I not been trained, I am not stupid. I'm not going for a walk. My guess is, we are all of five yards from the road. Once outside, I should be able to see some sign of it. If not, I'll look once the storm ends. But I promise to never leave sight of the vehicle."

"Oh." She felt stupid and sheepish. "I'm sorry. I...I don't know what's wrong with me."

"You're exhausted. You've had maybe four hours of sleep in the past twenty-four. There's a list as long as my arm of the things you've dealt with in the past month that no person should have to deal with. Cut yourself some slack. Crawl into the back, curl up under that blanket and go to sleep."

"But I...you..."

He handed her the blanket. "I'll only be a minute."

§

Accawi checked into the last available room at the motor lodge as a group entered the cramped lobby. According to the man at the desk, this was the last motel for fifty miles. It was a sign. Allah was with him. Outside, the storm still raged. Accawi pocketed his key and trudged back into the miserable cold to room 12. Only infidels would choose to live in a place so cold and so far from Mecca.

Once safely inside his room, he consulted his handheld monitor and grinned. The blip hadn't moved. Philip Wilson's woman was fifteen miles down the road and had been there for hours. If the attendant was correct that there were no motels for fifty miles, she was stuck in the snow in the middle of nowhere.

All was as it should be. He had only to trust and pray. Allah would deliver his enemies to him.

At the appointed time, Accawi washed his face, hands and feet, faced Mecca, spread his prayer rug and began to pray.

Afterwards, he slept lightly on top of the covers.

The alarm clock woke him. Outside, the snow was falling lightly on newly plowed roads. Though he could not see the horizon, he knew the sun was nearing it. Time for prayer and preparation. Again, Accawi washed his face, hands and feet. He checked the monitor before turning to face Mecca. The beacon had not moved. It seemed destined that today was the day he would avenge Aisha. "Allaha akbar." God is great.

Allah's eyes were upon him as he finished his prayers. Peace filled him as he strapped on his gun and knife and slid the garrote into his coat pocket. His path was one of righteousness. There was serenity in knowing he could not fail. He left his room and drove out of town.

Five minutes later, when the lights of the plow appeared in his rearview mirror, he smiled.

He left the car, waded through knee deep snow to the middle of the highway, and frantically waved his arms.

He praised Allah as the plow slowed to a stop and the driver poked his nose out of the cab. "You need help?"

Sunlight broke through the clouds and fell upon Accawi.

Allaha akbar.

§

Taylor left behind a dream of Phil and home to find she was alone, lying on her back, fully dressed in the back of the SUV. Muted sunlight made the windows glow white. She moved and her stomach protested. Ugh. At times like this her world became very narrow. Puke and pee.

She scrambled over the seat and fumbled with the door handle. The darn thing was stuck shut, pressed closed by restraining snow. She slammed her shoulder against the door. Snow slid from the window, but the door only shifted a couple of inches. Her stomach churned. Taylor slapped her hand against her mouth and hit the window control. The window opened. Thank God.

Her stomach felt better, but her bladder didn't. She kicked the door with both feet, shoving until it was wide enough to squeeze through. She exited the SUV into a marshmallow world.

Any other time, she'd have stopped to admire the surreal beauty. But this morning, as she sank thigh deep in the cold, damp snow, all she could do was swear. The cold and wet heightened her urgency. She had to pee. Bad.

The snow was heavy and densely packed. She climbed on the top and was able to take several steps before

sinking to her thighs again. Crap. Cochran was nowhere
to be seen. She was tempted to drop her jeans and just
squat in the snow, but she forced herself on. That cluster
of snow-laden pines wasn't too far. She could make it.

Inside the shelter of the trees, she skinned off the
damp jeans and sighed. Sweet relief. Goosebumps rose.
The denim clung as she shimmied her pants back up.
Who would have thought snow would be this wet?

Now that her brain wasn't preoccupied with other
matters, she acknowledged the unmistakable growl of a
snowplow. She found the best vantage point and crouched
in the trees, watching through the branches. The view
was a winter postcard scene. The sunlight reflected off
the snow in a million sparkles. When she brushed the
snow from a large branch, she could see the back end of
the SUV.

The snowplow driver had dark hair and a swarthy
complexion. He followed Cochran to the SUV, and said
something, talking with his hands as much as his voice.
Taylor was too far away and the ambient roar of the plow
was too loud for her to hear a word he said.

He walked out of sight. A few minutes later, the roar
of the plow changed. A wave of snow obscured her vision
of the car for a moment. Then, there was silence as the
sound of the plow died.

It seemed odd to her. Why turn off the engine?

When next she saw him, he was carrying a shovel and
a substantial looking chain with hooks on either end. He
handed the shovel to Cochran.

Cochran shrugged and bent out of sight behind the
SUV's back end.

As Taylor watched, the snowplow driver raised his
arm and swung the chain as if hitting something. Twice.

Taylor slapped a hand over her mouth to stifle her
scream.

She stumbled forward to help Cochran but stopped
before she cleared the tree line. This was the bad guy. He
hadn't seen her. Yet. Running toward him wouldn't help

Cochran. She had to go for help.

She looked at the dark haired man only to find him staring straight at her, smiling.

CHAPTER NINETEEN

There was nowhere to run. Nowhere to hide. Taylor knew it, but she was carrying a new life inside her now. No way would she roll over and play dead. She ducked behind the tree and, when she couldn't see the crazy guy anymore, she ran. Her heart was loud in her ears. Her breath came in gasps. This wasn't how it was supposed to end. She'd lost Phil, she'd never hold their baby, never...

She fell through the thin crust of snow again and again. The man who was after her would use her footprints to gain on her, but there was nothing she could do except keep going. A whining buzz filled her head. She stumbled, slamming headlong into the snow. The distinctive buzzing grew louder—snowmobiles. She was about to be murdered in this frozen hell and someone else was out enjoying a glorious day. The irony struck her. She struggled to her feet and lunged another step further. Two more steps and she'd be beyond the small copse of trees and into the sunlit open field.

Two snowmobiles roared out of another grove of trees and into the clearing. She screamed for them to stop, waving her arms as the snowplow driver slammed into her back, knocking her face first into the snow.

The man was heavy on her back. Snow stung her face. If the snowmobilers hadn't seen her before he knocked her down, they wouldn't stop. They'd roar off over a rise and disappear. Oh, please let them have seen her.

Plow guy was saying something in her ear, but the snowmobiles were so loud she couldn't hear him, so loud they must be almost on top of them. Thank God, the cavalry was here.

She could hear yelling as the snowmobile riders killed their engines.

The weight on her back eased when her captor stood, but her relief was short-lived. He grabbed her arms, yanking her up.

She struggled to her feet.

"Taylor, stay down."

Was that Phil's voice? She jerked herself free and dropped like a stone. Her heart skipped a beat. Small spits of noise sounded overhead. Gunshots through silencers. She'd heard it often enough by now to recognize the sound. Acrid bile rose in her throat. She tried to pray, but all that came out was a whispered, "Phil, Phil, Phil."

Time stretched. She crawled through the snow on her elbows, trying to stay low, trying to distance herself from the plow guy and his gun. He was on her again, smashing her deeper into the snow.

The mug in her pocket dug into her hipbone. She inched it from her pocket. A weapon.

Her face, pressed against the snow, burned with cold. Her ears and head ached as she listened hard and tried to interpret the sounds. Muffled thuds, curses. The beat of her heart was deafening. She held tight to the mug. She turned her head, but all she could see was snow.

The pressure left her back and once again someone grabbed the back of her jacket.

She lurched, crying out. "No."

"It's over. Get up." It was the voice in the sewer but without the accent.

She exploded out of the snow, swinging her arms and screaming. She hadn't gotten this far just to die. He wasn't going to kill her now. He wasn't. She swung her mug at his head and made contact. He dropped to his knees, grabbing his head and cursing.

Taylor sprang backwards.

The man she'd hit rose from the snow. Her racing heartbeat picked up speed as she recognized Sean

O'Hearn, Phil's art agent. Her jaw gaped. "Wh…?" But his voice…

"Taylor." Phil called her name.

She turned her head. His face was unshaven and haggard. "Phil?" She hadn't been hearing things. He was here. Her heart stuttered, leapt. She had the sudden impulse to laugh. "Phil." He'd finally come to save her.

The snowplow driver grabbed her from behind and pulled her against him. She gasped, inhaling the nauseating stench of diesel. Her eyes never left her husband.

Phil's expression was one she'd never seen before. Furious. Dangerous. He pulled a gun. She gasped.

The man pinned her arms to her sides and dragged her back, distancing them from Sean and Phil. Her mug was gone. She'd lost it when she'd fallen.

He held a knife to her throat.

She was frozen in place, unable to reach for Phil. It didn't matter that her upper arms were pinned. Phil's gun mattered. The coldness in his eyes mattered. She didn't know this Phil. Couldn't think beyond the gun.

The man behind her with the knife whispered doubt into her ear. His voice seemed too calm for the situation.

"The blade your Philip used to slay my Aisha will spill your blood." He jerked her tighter as he spoke. "The blood of his unborn children will be poor payment for my son. The cocaine he used to poison Aisha will not numb your fear. You will meet your God cursing the name Philip Wilson. He will find no rest for all his days, Inshallah."

She stared at Phil. Cochran's words circled in her brain. Not who you think he is…responsible somehow… didn't exist until you met him. She tried to shake her head and cry, "No," but it came out sounding choked.

"Blinded by love." The man behind her chuckled. The knife pressed tighter to her throat.

Taylor shivered as the blade pressed cold against her skin.

Her captor's ragged breath singed the hair at the back of her head. "He told my Aisha his name was Kahil. He brought her his art to display in my garden, tempting her, seducing her to betray me, her husband. He even poisoned the art, placing ears and eyes where none should be. Spying through art."

Taylor squeaked in protest. This wasn't her husband he was describing. Poisoning art. Ridiculous. The man was insane.

"Your Philip sold the statue to the Consul-General." He said Phil's name as if it were the vilest of curses. "He killed Aisha. Watched her blood stain the ground. Laughed at my sorrow. Foolishly believed he had killed me and my sons. But once again he is wrong. My sons will thrive. The only one the blue-eyed devil has killed is you, his beloved wife."

Taylor stared at the men before her. What did he mean Phil's eyes were blue?

She managed to speak the words out loud. "Phil's eyes are brown, not blue."

The arm around her waist flinched. She felt her captor's confusion. "No. You are wrong." She saw movement to her right as the man looked over her shoulder.

§

The bastard holding the knife to Taylor's throat poked his head from behind her. His eyes met Phil's. This was the moment Phil had been waiting for. His training kicked in. Target acquired. He sighted and fired in less than a breath. A second gunshot echoed in his ear. Three feet in front of him, two feet to the right, Sean's shooting stance was framed by two distant pines, taller than the rest, spearing the cerulean sky.

Phil's bullet, the first, hit Accawi a half inch above the bridge of the nose in a splatter of blood. Accawi's arm fell from around Taylor's neck.

His gun still at the ready, Phil's eyes followed the body down to the white snow. It was over. He drew a deep breath, felt the muscles in his neck and shoulders loosen as he turned to Taylor, a smile already forming on his lips. "Taylor."

They'd done it. They'd saved her.

Taylor stood frozen, her hazel eyes too large in her white, blood-spattered face. A crimson stream turned the collar of her brown coat black. Even from ten feet away, he reached out for her. Between one heartbeat and the next, her muscle tone disappeared. Her eyelids fluttered. Then, she crumpled into the bloodied snow beside Accawi. Crimson on white. Taylor. Her blood or Accawi's? Red blossomed on the snow. Taylor didn't move. He ran as in a dream. Legs frozen. A second later, he was at her side. On his knees. "Please." A million prayers in a single word.

Sean peered over his shoulder. "She okay?"

"I don't know. I don't know." The right side of her face was coated in blood. "Oh, God." Blood smeared beneath his gloved hand, oozing again as his fingers passed over her. Too much red. "Oh, God. Please." He pulled off his glove and stroked her cheek, the bright red, alien against her pale skin. Her cheek was cool. "Call an ambulance."

Sean's bullet, or maybe his, had grazed her right temple. He'd aimed at Accawi but so had Sean. And Sean was the better shot. He wiped away more blood. The wound didn't look too bad, but she didn't stir. An inch and a half long. Not deep.

The collars of both her coat and sweater, as well as the coat's zipper, were sliced through. But the cut on her neck wasn't bad. A thin red line. Not serious. Certainly not fatal. The hospital would close it with paper sutures. He ran his hands over her, frantically checking for other wounds. She'd lost weight. His fault. He stroked her cheek.

"Wake up, sweetheart." This wasn't supposed to happen. She was supposed to be safe.

The right side of her head and her neck appeared to be the only injuries. He kissed her left brow, willing her to wake up. This sure as hell wasn't the way he'd imagined their reunion.

"Taylor." He scooped her up in his arms. "Taylor, wake up."

Sean hovered. "They're sending an ambulance. And I called the crime scene unit. You okay here? I need to check on Cochran."

Her eyelids fluttered. "Thank God. She's coming to. Help me get her to the sled, first."

§

Taylor awakened slowly, reluctantly. Oblivion was safe. Nothing exploded in oblivion. Nothing burned. No one died. Taylor clung desperately to the void, but the distinct, sweet coppery scent of blood crept in.

She stiffened automatically, afraid to move. Strong arms held her close. A hand pressed against the side of her head. In a moment of blind panic, she struggled to be free.

"Hush, Taylor," Phil said. "It's me. It's okay. You're okay."

"Phil?" She opened her eyes.

"I'm here." He pressed a bloody handkerchief against the side of her head. "A bullet grazed your temple. The cut on your neck isn't deep. You're bleeding, but you'll be fine." His kiss tasted of desperation and worry. She stroked his arm, automatically.

"Phil." She felt... she felt... fragmented and confused. She wrapped her arms around him, crying in the familiar comfort of his arms. His embrace felt like home. She pressed her face into his neck, inhaling his scent. This was exactly where she'd dreamed of being since she'd awakened in her front yard on the stretcher. She wanted nothing more than to remain safely unthinking in his arms, in this moment, forever. But memories intruded. All the questions she had, all the feelings she'd felt hit her at once, and she couldn't get her mind around it. She raised her hand to the compress on the right side of her head.

"You're okay. It's just a scrape."

"Where have you been? Why didn't you come for me?" She searched his face for answers.

"I tried," he said. "Why did you take so long to call?"

"Call?" Like this was her fault. "I called. I followed every clue you left." She looked him in his dark brown eyes as her mind ricocheted from subject to subject.

His arms felt so darn good. She clung to him, needing to simply be in this moment, but once again her mind would not let her totally accept this comfort. Nothing made sense. The snowplow driver was dead. He'd hit Cochran. Phil had a gun. Taylor pushed out of his arms again. "Cochran." She was sick with guilt. How had she forgotten him, even for a moment? She struggled to stand, but Phil pulled her back down.

"He's fine. Sean went to check on him while you were out."

Taylor relaxed for a moment before tensing again. "How do you know he's fine?"

§

Cochran woke up with the urgent need to vomit. Unable to do anything else, he hoisted himself onto his hands and knees and retched into the snow. Finished, he struggled to his feet. The back of his head felt like a pick-ax speared it with each heartbeat. He pushed through the pain, forcing his mind to recent events. Taylor. The snowplow. Oh, God. He needed to get to her

"Better now?"

Cochran flinched at the voice behind him, automatically grabbing his gun from the holster. His world blurred and wobbled as he turned to face a deeply tanned, dark haired man with brilliant blue eyes.

"Holster your weapon, Agent Cochran. I'm one of the good guys."

Cochran spat into the snow, but didn't take his eyes off the man or lower his gun. "Put your hands on your head."

The man raised his arms. "This is ridiculous."

"Perhaps, but I'd like some identification, if you don't mind."

The man smiled condescendingly. "Should have asked Accawi for his identification. Maybe then, you wouldn't have been face down in the snow sucking exhaust while the woman you're supposed to protect was held at knife point."

Accawi? It took Cochran a second or two to equate the

name with the plow jockey. The pain in his head made it hard to see straight. Thought was agony. Still, Cochran managed to hold the gun steady. "Where's Taylor? Is she okay?"

"She's fine."

He hoped it was the truth. "Your identification, please. I want you to reach for it slowly using the thumb and index finger of your left hand."

"I know the drill," the man said, but didn't move a muscle to comply. "You can holster that gun. If I'd wanted you dead, I wouldn't have pulled you from under the SUV."

"Your identification. Now!" Raising his voice had been a bad idea. His head hurt so much the edges of his vision turned black.

Thank God the man finally reached to get his identification.

The man was Sean O'Hearn, according to driver's license and bureau identification. Philip Wilson's art agent.

Cochran sat in the SUV, put the battery in his phone and called headquarters.

"Yes," his boss confirmed. "Both Taylor's husband and his art agent are covert special agents."

Cochran's head swam. Taylor had been right. "Excuse me, Rogers, but what the hell is going on?"

"Until yesterday, when Special Agent in Charge Jackson briefed me, I knew what you knew."

Rogers' words stopped Cochran's rant before it began. His boss had been left out of the loop. It was like a crazy dream—all confusion and no logic. Cochran would be the first to admit he and his team had made mistakes. But his errors in judgment paled when compared to whoever decided to keep his boss out of the loop.

"So, now what?" His head hurt too much for thought.

"You're stuck with them. They lead, but you are on their Squad until further notice. Cochran, you stick to that girl like glue. There's shit everywhere, but I know you're clean."

Cochran snapped the phone closed. If his head hadn't

been throbbing when he made the call, it would be now. Taylor would be happy Phil wasn't the bad guy, but Cochran wasn't happy. Sure, one bad guy was dead, but he'd been shot down before he'd exposed his contact. This case wasn't over by a long shot.

He slid from the car and made his way to O'Hearn.

"Done checking me out?"

O'Hearn's smug grin made Cochran's hand itch. He hated cocky bastards like O'Hearn. "Yeah."

"Good. Let's go then." O'Hearn led, following his own tracks back to the trees.

Cold sweat covered Cochran. His snow-wet clothes clung to him. When he shivered, the pain in his head made him wish he were dead. He struggled to stay on his feet as he followed O'Hearn through the trees and into another clearing. The man they called Accawi lay crumpled in the snow, blood and brain splattered all around. A bloodstained Taylor was cradled in her husband's arms. Philip Wilson had his back to Cochran, but his body language said he adored Taylor.

"Hey partner, it's time we get out of here." O'Hearn interrupted the tender moment with no apparent remorse.

Wilson turned, and Cochran's jaw fell as he recognized the man who'd acted as his first bureau mentor. "You're Philip Wilson?" Cochran's head swam.

There's shit everywhere.

"Cochran, thanks for taking such good care of my wife."

Taylor looked from Cochran to her husband and back again. "You two know each other?"

She looked as dazed as Cochran felt.

The world wobbled. He needed to sit down.

O'Hearn continued talking as if nothing was wrong. "A cleanup crew will be out within the hour. I'll take Agent Cochran and meet you at the hotel. We can finish our reports, bug out, and be back at the office by morning."

Taylor gaped at Phil. Everyone was talking nonsense. "Office? What office? How do you know Cochran?" When Phil didn't answer right away, she turned to Cochran.

She was going to ask him how he knew Phil now, but as she opened her mouth, Cochran swayed on his feet. His face looked wet and green-tinged. "Are you okay?" In a heartbeat, she was out of Phil's arms, stumbling through the snow. She'd gone no more than a couple of yards when Cochran crumpled like a puppet without strings.

She knelt in the snow at Cochran's side. The breath caught in her throat. He looked dead. "Cochran," she whispered, touching his cheek. His eyes were closed and his skin was clammy beneath her fingers, but his chest rose and fell in a regular rhythm. Memories of a long-ago first aid class returned. Breathing, bleeding, broken bones. Treat for shock. His clothes were as sodden as hers were. She elevated his feet. "There's a blanket in the car. Somebody get it."

Phil touched her arm. "We need to go."

"We can't. He's hurt."

"Help will be here in a couple of minutes. We need to be gone when it arrives."

"But—"

"Taylor, this is messy enough already. There isn't anything we can do. Sean will handle it. It will be less complicated if we go."

Taylor looked into Phil's eyes. "Cochran is hurt."

Phil winced. "He would understand. He'd insist you go with me."

She shook her head. You don't leave an injured person until help arrives.

Sean's mouth hardened. "Damn it, Taylor. For once in your life, can you do what you're told without question? How many more lives do you need to risk?"

It was as if he'd slapped her.

"I..." Her mind didn't seem to work. Mouth gaping, she allowed Phil to pull her to her feet and guide her to the sled. He pressed a helmet on her head.

She heard the distant wail of sirens just before the sled roared to life. She held onto Phil. Sean's words pummeled her, though she knew they were lies. This wasn't her fault.

CHAPTER TWENTY

Taylor clung to Phil's waist as the sled flew over the snow. Phil was here. He was safe. She'd found him. Or he, her. The hows and whys could wait. He was real. She wished she could press her cheek against the back of his jacket and breathe him in, but the helmet made it impossible. She tried not to think. Phil would explain everything once they were safe. Sean would take care of Cochran.

He slowed the sled to a halt outside a motel.

She shivered and her hands shook as she pulled the helmet from her head. The newly formed scab came off with the helmet. Blood inched around her ear, but she ignored the pain. Phil stood before her. That's all that mattered.

"Are you all right?" He took the helmet from her and set it on the seat. "You're bleeding again."

"I'm fine." Her teeth chattered.

"My God, Taylor. You're freezing."

"I'm fine." She protested as he hustled her down the hall to his room. He unlocked the door and ushered her inside. "Get into the bathroom and out of those wet, bloody things."

The bathroom was small, but he followed her inside and took a quick series of pictures before turning on the hot water in the bathtub.

The cut on her neck hurt as she fumbled with her ruined coat zipper. "Will Cochran be all right? We shouldn't have left him." She was sure he wouldn't have left her.

Phil batted her clumsy fingers aside and undressed her with deft hands, peeling icy garments to reveal goose bumps. "We weren't leaving Agent Cochran; we were avoiding the questions that will start as soon as the paramedics see Accawi's body. The situation is complicated enough without two more people for local law enforcement to concern themselves with. Sean's a professional. He'll take care of everything and make certain Agent Cochran gets the best possible care." He pointed to her throat. "I've got some paper sutures I'd like to put on that as soon as you're out of the shower."

Before she knew it, she was in the shower with the curtain drawn and blessedly warm water raining down on her. The cut on her neck and the shallow furrow on the side of her head burned when the water hit them. The old Phil would have joined her in the shower. The old her would have expected him to. The new her felt oddly relieved to be alone. And even though she knew it was for the best, it frightened her.

"Phil?" She hadn't heard him leave the bathroom, but she couldn't be sure.

"Yes."

She could hear he was just on the other side of the shower curtain, but he felt so far away.

"How do you and Cochran know each other?"

"We met years ago. It's complicated."

"Complicated?" Complicated how? Cochran was FBI and Phil...She stuck her head outside the shower curtain. "Were you in trouble with the FBI?"

Phil shook his head and smiled. "No. Take your shower, Taylor."

She looked at Phil. He needed a haircut. He was so familiar and yet so different. "Our house blew up, and you left me."

His smiled evaporated. "I know, Taylor. I thought it would keep you safe, but it didn't."

She pulled her head back into the shower and let the curtain close. Easy tears blended with the cascading water. "How..." She had to clear her throat in order to continue. "How could you think leaving me would keep me safe?" Funny how she'd given the same answer to Cochran and thought it meant something.

"Finish your shower, Taylor."

Her chest ached. "But—"

"It'll keep, honey." His voice was gentle. "Take a few minutes to warm up and get clean. I'll get those sutures ready. We'll talk when you're done."

He hadn't really answered any of her questions. She felt as if he were leaving her all over again. She leaned against the shower wall, and let it support her. She knew he was right. She needed a few minutes to wash the blood from her hair and think about what had happened and what she needed to know. Still, it hurt to hear the bathroom door close.

By the time the conditioner had rinsed down the drain and her body was dried and moisturized, the flow of blood from the deep scratch on her neck and the graze at her temple had trailed off to a slow ooze. Taylor dabbed away the extra blood and looked down at the sodden pile of her discarded clothes. She had nothing dry to wear. It shouldn't have been an issue. Phil was her husband. She'd never felt shy around him before, but nothing was the same now. She wrapped a too-skimpy hotel towel around herself and took a deep breath. Her hand shook as she turned the knob.

Taylor felt Phil's eyes on her skin as soon as she left the bathroom. The towel wasn't enough protection. The sheet hanging from the first unmade bed caught her eye. Perfect. She focused on it as she hurried past him.

"I'm sorry. I forgot you didn't have anything to change into." She heard him rustling around behind her.

One hard yank and the sheet came free in her hand. She was wrapping it around herself as he held out a blue T-shirt.

"Here, put this on."

She shook her head. Even though she'd slept in his old T-shirts nearly every night of their married life, she didn't want to wear one now. She couldn't breathe in his scent without wanting him. And she refused to be lulled into the comfort of a past that might turn out to be a lie. "I'm fine."

She didn't know if her refusal hurt him, but he didn't argue and that was all that mattered.

The dresser wore a short fringe of medical tape. "Have a seat. I want to look at your wounds."

Wrapped in her modified toga with one end of the sheet crossed over her left shoulder and tucked beneath her right arm, she perched on the edge of the bed.

Phil glanced at the scabbed area on her right arm where the first bullet she'd encountered left its mark. He arched a brow as he looked in her eyes. She raised her chin and offered no explanation.

He picked up a tube of adhesive. "I'm going to paper suture your cut. It isn't all that deep, but it gapes in spots. You don't want a scar."

She wrapped her arms around herself and focused on the blinking light of the smoke detector on the ceiling as he knelt before her and worked on her. The warm, comfortable scent of Phil was too much. She blinked back tears she refused to shed.

He finished with her neck and turned to examine her temple.

"Did you know the house was going to blow up? Is that why you sent me into the back yard? Is that why you left?"

"Taylor, honey." Phil's hands stilled on the side of her face. "You can't possibly think I would purposely leave you in danger."

Her throat felt tight as she closed her eyes and pulled away. "I don't know what to think."

"I don't blame you. But you have to know I love you."

Her face was cold where his hands had been. Her heart wanted to melt at his words, but she shook her head.

"I do love you, Taylor. I believed leaving you would make you safe. I would never have left, had I any hint the house was about to explode. Never." He gently held her arms. "Sean said someone was gunning for me and to get the hell out of there. I left to draw off the attack, not leave you with it."

She opened her eyes and looked at her sheet-covered thighs. "But you didn't come back."

"Yes, I did. As soon as I heard the blast, I turned the car around. I parked a block away and cut through back yards. I found you in the back by the boulder and carried you to the front."

She looked at him, searching his face for some reason to believe him. The paramedics found her in the front yard. Cochran asked her how she'd gotten there. "But nobody saw you."

"There was a lot of smoke. Things were pretty chaotic. I made certain you were okay and left." His eyes pleaded with her. "It was one of the hardest things I've ever done, but I had to go. I couldn't risk the wrong person seeing me and spurring another attack. Still, I checked on you in the hospital."

"How is that possible? The FBI was watching my room."

"I was on the list as one of your night nurses."

"You didn't wake me? You let the FBI blame you. You let me think you'd abandoned me."

"To keep you safe. We determined that you'd be safe if whoever was after me thought I'd abandoned you. The perp would go looking for me, and we'd track him."

She shook her head. "But I wasn't safe. And who is 'we?'"

He sat on the bed in front of her. "I'll start at the beginning. But first..." He sat beside her on the bed. "Let me hold you."

She didn't move. It would be easier to judge his explanation on its own merits if she weren't in his arms as he gave it, but she ached to be held.

Phil smiled sadly. "Come here." He drew her into his arms. "I think I need this more than you do."

She wasn't as certain. His embrace felt like home.

"Six months before we met, I resigned from the FBI and became Philip Wilson."

Taylor's breath caught in her throat. Hadn't she suggested this exact scenario to Cochran? It hadn't felt like such a betrayal then. "So, everything you told me about your life before was a lie?" Did that make their marriage a lie, too?

Phil shook his head. "No. It's all true. My parents died in a car accident. My sister, Lisa, lives in Miami. I haven't seen her since I started with the FBI. I spent my childhood in West Allis. Everything I told you is true. I just omitted a few things. I was born Maxwell Kennedy. My family moved to California when I was thirteen. I was a covert agent in the FBI for ten years. But there was no need to tell you any of this. It was all over and done with before we met. I quit the bureau to become an artist."

"I don't understand. If you quit, why did our house blow up? How did Sean know to call?"

"Sean is FBI first, art agent second. He agents my art for the FBI."

"But I thought you didn't work for the FBI."

"I don't, but my art does." Phil sighed. "It's complicated."

Taylor heard the sound of the key in the lock. The door opened, hit the safety lock, and closed with a bang.

Phil groaned as Sean's voice came through the door. "Sorry to interrupt, Max, but I've got Taylor's clothes, and I needed an Advil an hour ago."

Her clothes. Thank God. She needed to hear more, but if Phil's words were going to continue to strip her of everything she thought she knew, she needed clothes on to hear it. She slid from Phil's arms and headed to the bathroom.

Phil followed her to the bathroom. "Taylor. I'll make it right." He took the chain off the door. "I'll tell you everything and answer all your questions. I promise."

"Might not want to make that promise." Sean entered the room as Taylor closed the bathroom door. "She's got zero clearance and the mission isn't finished."

Taylor froze on her side of the door. He hadn't told her everything, to this point. But she fully expected him to, now that they were back together. If they were going to stay together, that is.

"Stay out of it, Sean." Phil knocked on the door. "Honey, open up. I've got your bag."

Her hand shook as she opened the door.

Phil blocked the doorway with his body as he handed her the bag. "Are you okay?"

She nodded.

He eyed her as if he recognized her nod as a lie. "This meeting with O'Hearn is unavoidable, but I'll make it fast. You and I aren't done talking. And I will tell you everything."

Sean was in the room, talking in the background. "Sorry I got here so fast. The cleanup crew pulled Cochran's rental out of the snow for me. Guess you had enough time, though. What did you guys do to my bed?"

Taylor felt her face grow warm. She and Phil were married. What they did or didn't do together in private was none of Sean's business.

Phil shook his head. He'd always been better at filtering out Sean's crap than she had. "Take your time getting ready. We'll get something to eat when you're done. Okay?"

He waited for her nod before letting her close the door.

Even with the door closed, she could hear Sean's voice. "Don't let her distract you. We're a long way from finished, and I'm not just talking paperwork."

She opened the door a crack. "Sean, how's Cochran?"

"He's going to be okay. He's got a pretty bad concussion and carbon monoxide poisoning. The paramedics gave him oxygen on site. He'll keep getting it until his blood tests come up normal. He probably won't be released until tomorrow morning."

§

Phil looked at the latest version of the fatal shooting scene he'd keyed into the reconstruction software. This couldn't be right. He re-plotted the bullet's trajectory and ran the simulation again. It hadn't changed. He typed an email to the cleanup team. "Resend the coordinates of the 40 caliber bullet in quadrant G-11." He hit send.

The return email repeated the coordinates Phil already had. He checked the matrix. Shit. He'd keyed it in right. The software ran the same scene again in slow motion, just as he remembered it. Accawi poked his head out from behind Taylor on her right. Both he and Sean pulled the trigger. Taylor jerked her head left. His bullet hit Accawi a half inch above the bridge of the nose. Sean's skimmed Taylor's head.

Sean was framed between the two tallest pines. His stance was perfect. The image burned so deeply in Phil's mind's eye he could have added the colors—cerulean, crimson, forest green.

Phil ran the scenario again, this time assuming Taylor's head remained still. Sean's bullet impacted her eye. Phil's blood turned cold. He stopped the simulation before it could detail the extent of the damage.

A matter of inches. Her death would have been ruled an unfortunate accident.

He'd hit Accawi precisely where he'd meant to. But Sean was the better shot.

It had to be an accident. He wrote an email to SAC Jackson, including the raw data and his findings, asking that Jackson double check everything and compare it to the ballistics findings. But he didn't send it. Instead, he sent his computer into hibernation, filled Taylor's mug with coffee and brought it to her where she sat at the head of the bed. His wife. His child. He was going to be a daddy. He struggled to keep the smile off his face and wait for her to tell him.

She looked up from her Sudoku magazine and took the mug. "Thanks. Where did you get this?"

"Sean brought it back with him." Along with her bag, her purse, and the positive pregnancy tests. Sean had been out of line when he searched her things. She wasn't a suspect.

"Thanks, Sean." Taylor smiled at his partner, not suspecting a thing.

On the other side of the room, Sean looked up from his computer. "No problem. Hey, Phil, are you done?"

Phil shook his head. Every discharge of arms required an extensive amount of paperwork. Fatalities, even more. He hadn't even started filling in the standard forms. The bullet trajectory, the unwarranted search of Taylor's stuff, the eerie familiarity of the murder scene, the compromised mug code... each item taken individually meant nothing. Collectively, they raced around his brain forming a pattern he wished he could deny.

Sean stretched. "God, I hate this part of the job."

"Me, too." He knew he should send the email. The sooner Jackson had it, the sooner he'd know if he'd made the computational error.

His beautiful wife leaned against the headboard with her eyes closed as she breathed in the coffee steam. Her smile made his heart ache. That smile was the reason he got up early and made coffee. How was he going to keep her safe until this damned mission was over and they got their normal lives back?

Phil's phone vibrated, alerting him of a text. The plane tickets had arrived. He was returning his phone to its holster when he heard a knock on the door. The local guy must have texted from right outside the door. He exchanged automatic glances with Sean. "Plane tickets."

The local agent flashed his ID as he handed over an envelope with the tickets and a paper sleeve containing keycards for another hotel room. "If there's anything else..."

Phil nodded. "Thanks, Devon."

The door closed, and Phil glanced at the tickets before setting them on the dresser. "I see you got them changed for tomorrow, so we can take Cochran with us."

"Did Devon say anything about the second room?"

Phil held up a paper sleeve containing keycards. "Second floor. Should Taylor and I move, or do you want to?" He set the keycards next to the plane tickets and then made the mistake of looking at Taylor. Curiosity sparkled in her eyes.

Crap. He shook his head, wanting to postpone the questions until they were alone.

"Phil, how did you find us? How did the mad man? We were being so cautious. Cochran didn't keep the battery in the cell phone so there wouldn't be a GPS signal to trace. So, how did you find us?"

"We—"

Sean interrupted with, "Your mug."

What the hell? He glared at O'Hearn. After all the talk about clearance, why the hell would Sean say that? The man's lips were set in a shit-eating grin.

The color drained from Taylor's face. "My mug?"

"Is equipped with an information collection device, created and installed by your husband. The rest is classified." Sean was smiling like a proud papa. Phil wanted to knock his block off. Was he trying to make trouble?

And the idiot wouldn't shut up.

"With the creativity and intelligence this man has, the possibilities are endless. Endless."

Taylor sputtered for a second before glaring accusations at Phil. "You bugged my mug?"

Shit. Phil shook his head. "They aren't listening devices. They're just homing devices."

"You've been tracking me? Why?" Her face developed a slightly green tinge.

"Honey, are you okay?"

She narrowed her eyes at him. "For how long, Phil? How long have you been a spy? How long have you been spying on me?"

He wanted to strangle Sean. "It wasn't like that." He hurried to the side of the bed. "It was a test. There are two different types of technology. I was using the standard one as a constant to compare with the classified one. I monitored the signals for a month and then every now and again to make certain both devices were still working."

She got off the bed and stood to face him. "You knew where I was all the time? You knew where I was, and you didn't come get me?" Her voice grew in volume with each word until she was yelling. The frayed bond between husband and wife unraveled even further.

"Taylor, you left the mug for a while. I lost you."

She looked at her mug as if it were poisoned.

"When the blip didn't move, I thought I'd truly lost you for good." He'd undergone training to withstand interrogation, and here he was blithering like an idiot. But he couldn't stay silent and lose Taylor.

"I think you just did." She shoved the mug at him, sloshing hot coffee everywhere. "Take this. I don't want it." She pressed it into his chest for a second before letting go.

The coffee soaked his shirt. He let it drop and reached for her. The heavy mug bruised his left foot as it bounced off.

"Taylor, it's not like that. It wasn't like that." This wasn't the way he'd meant to tell her.

She batted away his hands. "What was it like, then? You made me run all around the country when you could have rescued me at any time. I don't understand."

"Taylor, listen to me." He reached for her.

She hit his hands away. "Go away. Get away from me." She shoved her way past him, and he let her go.

He was losing her. "Taylor, please."

She shook her head and refused to make eye contact. Her voice cracked. "Why couldn't you have stayed lost?" She grabbed the envelope with the door keys from the dresser top. "I'll take the new room. The two of you can share this one." Three steps later she was out the door.

He raced after her. "Taylor."

Before he reached the door, Sean clasped a hand on his shoulder. "Let her go."

He spun around, knocking Sean's hand free. It took every inch of will power not to slam his fist into Sean's face. "Are you fucking nuts? It's not safe. Someone is after her. Why did you tell her about the mug in the first place?" Another step and he was out the door. What was that room number? 212?

Sean's voice followed him down the hall. "At least give her a chance to cool off."

A partially burned out exit sign hung over the stairwell

door. He pounded up the stairs. He couldn't lose Taylor now.

He stood outside the door. What was he going to say to Taylor to make it right? His heart slammed in his chest. He took a deep breath and held it, willing himself calm. He loved her. She loved him. He exhaled slowly. She had to listen to him.

§

Taylor's back was still pressed against the door when Phil knocked.

She knew it was Phil, even without looking through the peephole, but she looked anyway. He looked worried, or maybe that was just image distortion.

His hand appeared large as he raised it to knock again. "Taylor, honey. Open the door, please. We need to talk."

He was right, they did, but she wasn't ready to let him in. He'd lied to her. He'd bugged her mug. She vibrated with the need to hit something. "Go away."

"Please, Taylor. It's not safe for you to be here alone."

"I don't care."

Phil's clothes were wet in front where she'd dumped the coffee. She should have thrown the mug at him instead. Should have bounced it off his head. She wished... she wished... she wished Cochran were well so they could leave, already.

"Taylor, please." The door rattled as he shook the knob. "Let me in."

"No."

She wanted to be gone, to never see the lying jack-ass again, to never hear his name—not that it was his real name—again. She stopped just short of wishing him dead, just short of wishing she weren't pregnant. It wasn't her baby's fault she'd chosen a bald-faced liar to be the father.

"I'll wait."

Shaking her head, she left the door and sat on the bed. The red numbers on the clock radio changed. Why hadn't he gone to get her if he knew where she was? Someone shot at her. Someone killed Sister. No, wait. She'd ditched the mug by then. Maybe when she left the mug, she'd also left his protection. Another minute passed. Two. Three. She expected more pounding, more demands to be let inside. Had he left? Her heart was a cold lump in her chest as she got off the bed and looked out the peephole. He was still there, leaning against the wall across the hall. She breathed a sigh of relief but didn't unlatch the door.

Instead, she walked into the bathroom, got a glass of water, and drank it one slow sip at a time before returning to the bedroom. Let him wait. The television remote sat on top of the set. She turned on the TV and thumbed through the stations. Nothing was on. Five minutes. Ten. She turned the television off and checked the peephole.

Phil still leaned against the wall in his wet clothes. He was probably cold. Well, she'd been cold. Stuck in a storm sewer with spiders. She paced the hotel room, pausing for a quick peek out the hole. Still there.

He looked settled. Patiently waiting like an old dog. He was like that. Predictable. Faithful.

She should let him in. After all, she needed answers. But he'd kept secrets. She wrapped her hurt around her like a cloak. Her throat was tight with unshed tears.

She turned her back on the door and watched the clock.

Five more minutes.

He didn't move.

Hand on the safety bar; she waited for the minutes to pass. She flipped off the bar, unlatched the deadbolt and opened the door. "Get in here."

§

He didn't smile, not even in relief. If he smiled, she would probably slam the door in his face. You only make that kind of mistake once. Instead, he followed her into the room and closed the door behind him, pausing only to secure every lock in place.

She said nothing, didn't even look at him as she sat on the bed.

"Thank you."

She shrugged. "Don't thank me. I don't know why I

let you in. I can't believe anything you say." Her voice cracked.

The physical distance was too great. He approached with hesitation and sat next to her on the bed. "I never lied to you."

She snorted. "Yeah, right, Phil, Max, or whatever your name is."

"It's Phil. It was Phil when we met. It became Phil when I left the bureau." He needed to touch her. He wished she'd look at him. It would be so much easier if she did.

"Which was when? Tomorrow?"

He plucked the damp shirt from his chest. "Six months before we met."

"Which is why you work with Sean, provided drugs to some poor woman, filled your art full of listening devices, lied to me, and bugged my mug? Did you need the thrill? Well, you sure wouldn't have found it listening to every conversation I had over coffee. It must have bored you to tears." He could tell by her voice she was trying to cling to her anger.

"You know it isn't a listening device." He reached for her hand.

She crossed her arms. "I know nothing. Actually, that's not true. I know I don't need excitement. I need love and stability. I need a business I care about, a husband I can trust who is as crazy about me as I am about him, and I need a safe and happy home for—" She shot him a panicked look and snapped her mouth closed.

The baby. He almost smiled then.

She looked away. "It doesn't matter. Why did you leave the FBI? And if you really left it, why did you go back?"

"I left because it got to be too much. Too many murders. Too many bad guys. I went back because of Sean."

Taylor narrowed her eyes. "If you aren't going to tell me..."

He shook his head and held up his hand to stop her from telling him to leave again. "To understand why I left and especially why I went back, you have to understand why I signed up in the first place."

"Okay." Taylor leaned back against the headboard.

"Sean and I were roommates in college."

Taylor's eyes widened. He'd never talked about Sean, except in the present tense as his art agent.

"You wouldn't recognize the Sean I met freshman year. He was scrawny and awkward. Neither of us knew anyone at school. I took him to lift weights with me. Pretty soon, we were best friends.

"Anyway, junior year, my sister, Lisa, fell in love with a smooth-talking gang enforcer. The finger-behind-the-trigger of a major kingpin—drugs, extortion, prostitution, trafficking. You name it. She worked for the firm that audited one of the gang's companies. He treated her like a princess. She had no idea who or what he was, but my parents heard rumors that he was grooming her to overlook things at work. They warned Lisa, but of course she didn't believe them. She told him. A couple of weeks later, on April 10th, he followed them on a scenic coast drive and ran them off the road."

"You never told me the car accident was murder." Taylor's voice sounded raw.

Phil nearly groaned. "I should have told you."

She shrugged, but wouldn't meet his eyes. "Doesn't matter."

But it did. He swallowed hard. "I'm sorry. I didn't think." He snagged one of her hands. "Taylor, when I left the FBI, I left my past behind. All of it. I didn't look back. I moved forward. You were forward. Our life together, forward. My parents, Lisa, and all that happened was in the past. I wanted to leave the past behind and make my future with you. Do you understand?"

She shook her head. "Not yet. Keep talking."

"Okay." He took a breath. She hadn't pulled her hand away from his. "Lisa blamed herself. I wasn't very sympathetic."

"Did they catch the boyfriend?"

"Yeah." Phil nodded. "The FBI caught him, he was convicted, and sent away. Sean was there for me through it all. I don't think I'd have made it without him."

He saw in her eyes shadows of the things she didn't say. He'd left his family in the past, but not Sean.

"Then that summer, his mom OD'd, and her lowlife husband disappeared."

"And you were there for Sean."

He nodded. "We were like brothers. Senior year, all Sean could talk about was being a cop. Federal cop. Keeping the country safe." He shrugged. "And before I knew it, it was all I could think about. National security. Keeping people like my parents and Lisa safe from gangs and spies and... As soon as we graduated, Sean and I headed to Quantico. It was FBI all the way."

They'd been so damn naïve. He'd been so naïve. Sean always handled the violence better.

"It was perfect for a while. Sean and I spent a lot of time undercover. We made a great team. Sean's gift for languages proved helpful. The man is a natural mimic. You've heard him use it in jokes, but it's even more effective in the field." He watched Taylor watching him and wondered what she was thinking.

"So what happened?"

"The Foxy Lady murders."

She looked puzzled for a moment and then her expression cleared. "The serial killer who cut up prostitutes?"

He stared at their joined hands and nodded. "Debby Sue Lindemeire. Pretty girl. Good family. A run-away that ended up being a kidnapping across state lines. I can still see her face—the before and after shots." He shook his head, remembering. "We didn't get the case until the third body, Jessica Jones. We chased leads and dead bodies all over the county after it became a federal case. Yolanda Johnson, Kim Vong, Chandra Hinsel, Jasmine French..."

Taylor touched his hand. "I'm sorry you had to go through that. It had to have been awful."

He looked at her. "It was worse for Sean. He'd just broken up with his fiancé." At first Phil thought the case kept Sean from thinking about Therese, but then it got obsessive. Sean kept copious notes, cut newspaper clippings...

Phil's stomach dropped. They hadn't gotten the case until Jessica Jones. Now, he couldn't remember if Sean had photos of the Lindemeire and Wild murders before or after they'd been assigned the case.

"The case really captured Sean's attention. He seemed to live and breathe the Foxy Lady murders. He seemed so much sharper than on any other case. So much sharper than any of the other agents on the scene. It was almost like he knew ahead of time what we'd find." Phil shook his head. What if he wasn't sharper? What if...

No.

Dempsey, the killer, was dead. And why would Sean kill Sharon Tatro? Why would he target Taylor?

"Phil?" Taylor's worried voice interrupted his thoughts. "Is something wrong?"

"What?" He looked at Taylor.

"You just stopped talking. Is something wrong?"

"No." He shook his head. "I don't know. I was thinking about the Foxy Lady murders. The killer was always one step ahead of us, taunting us. There were times it seemed Sean and I were as much the target as those poor girls. Things the murderer did. Messages he wrote. It seemed personal, somehow."

"Was it?"

"Jackson didn't agree. Neither did the profiler. Said I was the one taking it too personally. And maybe I was." But with Tatro's murder, there was no denying that this time it was personal. In his mind's eye, he saw the bloody words on the mirror.

"But you caught the Foxy Lady Killer." She touched his arm to call him back to the present. "I remember reading about it in the newspaper."

He turned to her. "John Michael Dempsey. Travelling salesman, recreational drug user, married, three daughters. We placed him in five of the cities, knew he had clients in the sixth, but the profile didn't fit. He wasn't a loner raised by a single mother, possibly a prostitute. He hadn't been abused as a child. Wasn't homosexual. Wasn't ex-police or ex-military. Didn't seem to hate women. He had opportunity, but no motive." Goosebumps covered his arms.

"But the killings stopped."

"Yeah, after Sean killed him, the murders ended."

"So, Dempsey did it." She sounded so sure.

"Yes." Except the more he compared the two cases, the more similar they felt. "That's what they say."

He shook his head, but the feeling of déjà vu remained. Something about Tatro's death reminded him of those serial murders.

Taylor prodded him on. "Okay, so the murders ended. Then, what?"

"I changed. Felt numb. Those women had been tortured. It was the worst I'd ever seen. I knew some important part of me was dying. I had to get out. So I did."

"Did you talk to Sean about what was happening? Surely it bothered him, as well."

He shook his head. "No. The case helped Sean recover from Therese's betrayal. He was more excited than disturbed by the brutality of the case."

At the time, Phil had passed it off as the thrill of the chase. Now, he wasn't so sure.

"Anyway, I needed a clean break. I was given a new identity because I'd been covert and would be starting a business where my name would be my brand. I needed to leave my old identity behind." He turned to Taylor and took her hands in his. "And then, six months later, I met you and began to feel again." He kissed her hand. "You saved me."

"Then why go back?"

"Vanity."

"I thought you said it was Sean."

"I know. He definitely played a major role. He offered the opportunity, played on my strengths and weaknesses. But in the end, it was vanity."

"I don't get it."

"The intelligence community monitors—"

"Spies on."

He grinned. She was right. "Spies on persons of interest. Sean challenged me to find a way to take the unique properties of metals I used in my art and combine it with intelligence gathering instruments..." He winced at the level of jargon. "I made that mug for you because I love you and thought you'd like it. I stuck in the homing devices as an afterthought. A harmless test. There are two kinds of devices in your mug; the standard, detectable type and the new one. It's part of what I did before— using computers to gather intelligence to solve and prevent crime at the national level. This project seemed tailor-made. Art, metallurgy, and computer intelligence gathering all rolled into one big puzzle."

"Ah..." She smiled for the first time in their conversation. "He pushed all your creative, problem-solving buttons. Probably told you that you were the only one who could do it." She nodded. "Vanity."

"Anyway," he continued. "The technology was ready for a trial run and, with your mug, I could see if it worked in real life situations. It was no more sinister than that.

"The technology worked perfectly and was undetectable. I incorporated it into key pieces that Sean sold to a specific market. But when you and I began talking about starting a family, I knew it was time to pull out completely. Then the Iraqi Consulate's head of security, Fuad Accawi, claimed there were bugs on the piece meant for the Consul-General's office. He blamed Sean, the art agent who brokered the deal. Somehow, the piece ended up on Accawi's estate. The statue was returned to the consulate and came out clean. Accawi was discredited and judged a thief. It should have ended there, but it didn't. Sean was attacked, and then there was the bomb at our house.

"After the second bomb and the attack on your safe house, I realized the trouble originated from inside the bureau. That's when I sent the message to you that you should go to Lisa's."

"And I did."

"Taylor, all along there were agents trying to protect you while someone else apparently leaked information that put you at risk. I still don't know why Accawi targeted you or why the mole still seems to be after you."

"I don't know about the mole, but Accawi blames you for the death of his wife."

"What makes you say that?" He'd expected questions from Taylor, not revelations.

"It's what he said."

Phil rested a hand on his wife's thigh. "Maybe you'd better tell me exactly what he said."

Her eyes lost their focus as she remembered. "I was so frightened. I don't remember it word for word. He said you poisoned your art with listening devices." She glanced at him. "And he was right about that." She looked away, her voice a whisper. "He said you poisoned his wife with cocaine."

He nodded. "We knew she had a drug problem, but I didn't supply her."

"He referred to you as 'my Philip' like he knew you by another name. He said you killed his wife. That you laughed as her blood soaked into the ground." She shook her head. "Something like that. He said his wife knew you by a different name, Kyle or something. He called you a blue-eyed Arab."

"That's when you said, 'Phil's eyes are brown.'"

She nodded. "And you shot him." It seemed as if there was a trace of accusation in her voice even though his shot saved her life.

He reached out and gently raised her chin until she looked into his eyes. "Taylor, I didn't kill his wife."

"How did his wife die?"

"Sean said drug overdose. She was a recovering addict."

"Drug overdoses don't bleed."

Phil frowned. "No."

"Why would Accawi say her blood soaked into the ground if she died of an overdose?"

More to the point, why would Sean say she died of an

overdose if she bled to death? "I don't know."

§

"Fucking Bitch!" He tore at his hair. Accawi died, but the whore hadn't.

He pounded a fist against the table. The lame dick Accawi had the knife pressed to her goddamn throat. All he had to do was cut. But did he? No. He moved his head and got his brains blown out. "Shit!" Why wouldn't the bitch just die?

It's not as if women were hard to kill. Hell, you gave them a bag and let them poison themselves, or you plunged in the knife as easy as you plunged in your dick. Easier.

Accawi should have cut her head off.

"Dammit!" His hands shook as he envisioned Taylor with her long brown hair and her positive pregnancy tests. She wasn't going to win. He and Max were Spartans, comrades in arms, blood brothers. Meant to fight oppression, serve freedom, right wrongs.

His father had explained it all years ago. He taught Sean what it meant to be Spartan—brother love, strength, service, the role of marriage. Women provided comfort and release. The perfect wife had closed lips as she waved goodbye and open arms when her man returned. But perfect women were rare.

Women like Taylor were like black widow spiders— poisonous and deadly. They spun webs luring unsuspecting males. Once bred, they devoured their mates.

His father had been a Spartan. His mother a spider. His father broke free of the web, just as Sean must help Max break free. Taylor had already begun eating Max's brain, making him think he needed her, needed to spend more time with her, quit the project. Max didn't even know he was being eaten. He had to save Max. The spider couldn't win.

He took a deep breath. Accawi had failed, but that didn't mean he would. He just needed to stay calm.

Think, dammit. He was smarter than she was. Better.

Stronger. More worthy.

It wouldn't be that hard to get her alone.

CHAPTER TWENTY-ONE

Phil and Taylor sat in a restaurant booth looking over the menu. Taylor's stomach growled loudly. Her eyes saw the words on the menu, but nothing registered in her mind. A yawn stretched her jaw. Their discussion left her exhausted. So many secrets.

"The beef stew looks good," Phil said over his menu. "What are you thinking of getting? They have shrimp."

The conversation was too normal. She lowered her menu. Could she pretend everything was normal?

"Look, honey, they have lava cake." Phil pointed to the corresponding entry on her menu.

The waitress came. She ordered a BLT. She'd be able to eat the toast, for certain.

After the waitress left, Phil reached across the table. She managed not to flinch as his thumbs caressed the backs of her hands.

Her heart felt raw, like a skinned knee. There hadn't been time to process everything. Despite his explanations, she didn't know if she trusted him. Still, she knew she loved him. One look in his eyes said he understood. It made her want to turn away. If he were thoughtless, she could wrap herself in anger and leave. But how do you deal with understanding?

"It's going to be okay. We're going to be okay."

She looked at the silverware. "We have a lot to work through."

He gently squeezed her hands. "I know we do. But we'll manage. I need you. We're a family."

A family. Tears welled in her eyes. She still hadn't told him about the baby. "I need you, too." Her voice was a hoarse whisper.

"I cannot tell you how sorry I am for all that's happened. I made decisions that put you at risk. The fact that I marginalized the risks in my mind and never thought this could happen is no excuse. I've worked in the business long enough to know not to take anything for granted. Like us."

Taylor nodded.

The waitress arrived with their food, and Taylor dug in her pocket for a tissue.

When the waitress had gone, Phil leaned over the table. "I love you, Taylor."

Sean appeared at the end of the table. "How very touching." He plunked Taylor's mug on the table. "You need to stop leaving this places." He slid into her side of the booth, crowding her.

She frowned as she scooted over.

"You've got the world's worst timing, O'Hearn. Why don't you get lost until tomorrow?"

"Can't." He took a French fry from Taylor's plate and popped it into his mouth. "We accomplished the objective. We have the girl, but we've still got that leak to find. Until we do, there's no way to know if our friend with the snowplow was acting alone."

He reached for another fry, but Phil knocked his hand aside. "Don't refer to Taylor as 'the girl' while she's sitting right here. And don't eat her food."

Sean shrugged. "Whatever. Tomorrow, we stash her somewhere. That's a good job for Cochran, since he's ours for the duration. He'll be released from the hospital tomorrow morning." He swiped another fry. "These need catsup." He reached over Taylor to snag the bottle from its holder.

Taylor moved her plate out of reach.

"O'Hearn," Phil growled.

"Sorry. You know how I am around fries." Sean turned

to wave down the waitress. "I'll have an order of fries and a hot roast beef sandwich with mashed potatoes and gravy. And bring me a Coke or whatever, oh, and some horseradish, too." He turned back to Phil. "The clean-up crew checked in. Calling the ambulance got the locals involved, but our team is pretty certain they got everything. They've plotted everything on a grid and are sending it to Jackson." He looked at his watch. "Man, I hate these delays. I want to get to the office. Accawi shouldn't have been able to pinpoint their location. The two of you can live happily ever after, if there is such a thing, once we find the leak." He shot a glance at Taylor's fries before looking Phil in the eyes. "You should stay active, Max. You're made for this job."

"No, you were made for the job. You're a chameleon with a dozen different personas. I'm just me." Phil shook his head. "I like the intellectual aspects of it, the problem solving, but not the violence or the danger." He looked into Taylor's eyes. "I won't risk my family. Once this is over, I'm going to focus on being a sculptor."

Her breath caught in her throat at the intensity of his gaze. She wished they were alone.

Sean snorted. "We'll see. Anyway, it's not over yet. And you've got to recreate the stuff we lost in the blast."

"I recreated the monitoring programs." Phil picked up his spoon and scooped up a steaming portion of meat and carrots swimming in the savory broth. The rich, beefy aroma made Taylor wish she'd ordered the stew. "Once we solve this, I'll be out for good. But it doesn't need to affect our friendship."

Taylor's heart flinched at that notion. She wouldn't mind if Phil's complete withdrawal from the spy program created distance between her husband and Sean. Sean was like a meddlesome younger sibling, always butting in uninvited. Like now, when she would like to finish the conversation she was having with her husband.

"Hell, Max, we're more than friends. We're a team. Indivisible. Your marriage could end, but I'll still be here."

Sean's words commanded Taylor's attention. "What?"

Phil shook his head. "Don't be an idiot, O'Hearn. Taylor and I will see our way through this." He reached across the table to hold Taylor's hand.

She met him halfway. It was one thing for her to have doubts but quite another for Sean to. She and Phil had always been solid. Their relationship would be solid again once they got through this. And they would get through this.

Phil squeezed her hand, and she squeezed back. They were more than a team. They were a family.

"I didn't mean..." Sean's neck turned a dull red. "Of course you will."

She nodded. They would. But she'd save the news about the baby until they'd bridged the distance between them. Their love and commitment would bind them, not a child.

The waitress arrived with Sean's food, saving them from further awkward conversation.

They ate in silence, with Phil and Taylor holding hands across the table and Sean's eyes on his food.

As the meal came to an end, Sean cleared his throat. "Jackson needs your reports, and we need to have a strategy session. Are you coming back to the room?"

"In a little bit." His gaze warmed Taylor. Her stomach gave a nervous flutter, a sure sign of how far they were from normal.

§

Phil unlocked their room. As soon as the door was closed, they were in each other's arms. Taylor wasn't sure who initiated what, but it didn't matter. She closed her eyes and pressed her face against his chest.

This was home. Her heart didn't know whether to melt or break, but she was home when Phil held her.

She looked into his eyes for a moment, and then their lips met. His were soft and firm, moist and warm. They caressed hers as he spoke. "I love you."

She slid her hands up the back of his shirt, reveling in the firm flesh, the feel of muscles beneath his skin.

This wouldn't solve anything, but it didn't matter. She needed to feel connected to him more than she needed anything.

His kiss claimed her, and she melted against him. Then, instead of sliding his hands beneath her clothes, he pulled back. "I want you." He gently squeezed her upper arms. "I really want you, but this isn't the time. Nothing has been solved. You aren't safe yet."

She wanted to protest that until this second she'd felt safe in his arms, but she didn't. He was right. They knew there was a mole. Accawi hadn't acted alone. She slid her hands out from under Phil's shirt.

He gave her a peck on the lips. "I swear to God, after this, I'm leaving the bureau for good." Releasing her, he stepped back, putting space between them. "Before we go to Sean's room, I need to know...you said Accawi knew me by another name."

"Actually, he said his wife knew you be another name. Kyle or something, only more foreign. The blue-eyed Arab."

"Could that name have been Kahil?"

"Kahil." An icy finger ran up her spine. "That sounds right. Why? Who's Kahil?"

Phil held her by her upper arms again. "Taylor, you can't say anything. You can't even look like you suspect anything."

"O...kay." Her voice shook. Who couldn't she look suspicious to?

"No one knew about the technology."

Taylor shook her head. "We've already been through this. I know it's top secret. I won't tell anyone."

"That's not what I meant. I meant no one knew about it. Accawi claimed something was wrong with the statue, but all the scans judged it clean. The technology is undetectable. He shouldn't have known."

"Unless the mole told him."

"Right." Phil frowned. "But we didn't know about the mole when the statue appeared in his garden. We didn't know about the mole, for sure, until your first safe house was compromised."

"Wait. The first safe house wasn't compromised."

"Taylor, you should have never gotten the truck back. Someone used a recording of Peterson's voice to order its delivery and then shot at Peterson as you drove off. Blew out your passenger-side rear taillight, as well."

The bottom dropped out of her stomach. She'd wondered why Peterson hadn't given chase.

"But someone had to know about the technology."

"The fact that your mug had a tracking device got out, but only the fact that it had a standard tracking device. The new technology wasn't divulged. Nobody knew. Honey, I don't think you realize how restricted intelligence about this operation is. Until today, there were only three people who knew Phil Wilson was Max Kennedy—the same three who knew about the new technology and the connection between the art and the information gathering."

She shook her head. "I don't believe it. There had to be more people involved. At the very least, the guys who put the art in place so it would transmit correctly and the guys monitoring the transmissions would have known about the technology. Who else?"

"The people monitoring the transmissions don't know where the transmission is coming from. Their job is to deal with the information they receive."

"So, who were the three—you, Sean and your superior?"

"Exactly."

"So who's Kahil? Is he your superior?"

Phil shook his head, and Taylor felt cold all over. "Kahil is one of Sean's undercover personas."

"Didn't you say he was Accawi's first target? Why would he leak something that would send someone after you? After me? Sean is your friend. He warned you to get out of the house." She started to shake. He told Phil to get out of the house. Told Phil she'd be safe if he left. Sean had no way of knowing she'd be outside. She was supposed to have been in the house when it blew. "I don't particularly like Sean, but there has to be someone else."

Phil enveloped her into his warm embrace. "I don't have any proof, yet. There are a few things I need to run past my superior. But I had to tell you. You can't trust Sean, and you can't act like you suspect him, either."

She closed her eyes and pressed her face into his shoulder. How was she supposed to do that?

§

After an afternoon spent on reports, Sean left to pick up supper. Phil had Taylor watch the hall through the peephole while he laid out his suspicions on the phone. He waited while SAC Jackson watched the simulations. "Tell me I'm wrong."

"I can't. I wish I could, but I can't." He paused. "Send me the simulation showing gun 'one' firing bullet 'B.'"

Phil located and sent the file showing the scenario where the bullet from his gun struck Taylor.

"The angle is wrong. She's dead whether she moves or not, and the bullet doesn't end up in the same place. Shit." SAC Jackson paused. "Have you asked Sean about it? Found out what he thinks happened?"

"No. What with the other things, I wanted to run everything past you first."

"Good. I'll have the lab run ballistics as soon as the team gets in." He paused. "Max, I know we need to get into Sean's house, but it's Saturday and Magistrate Judge Madison is on vacation. Everything is circumstantial at this point, even the part about Kahil. I don't know if I can convince anyone else to give us a search warrant until Monday." He paused and Phil could almost hear the thoughts churning in Jackson's head. "I'm going over my memories of the Tatro scene, and you're right. Sean saw things I hadn't, when I was in a better position to see it. But about the Foxy Lady case…it's been years, and I wasn't on the scene with the two of you." He cleared his throat. "Is there any chance your feelings about Taylor getting shot are tainting your thoughts?"

"No. Sean's like a brother. I'd rather that suspicion point almost anywhere else." He paced around the bathroom. If he were wrong, Sean would see this as the ultimate betrayal. But if he were right... "The shooting, the special knowledge of both cases, the similarities between the murders, Kahil the blue-eyed Arab... it's too much to be coincidence, and there's no such thing as coincidence."

"Max, we need more than coincidence. O'Hearn is too good an agent to go after without solid evidence."

"There has to be a way to get Sean to expose himself while keeping Taylor safe." His mind skipped from one ridiculous scenario to another.

"Don't forget you've got Cochran."

"That's right." Mark Cochran was a definite asset.

"Keep me posted."

Phil closed the phone and encrypted his data. He was powering down his laptop when Taylor hurried from the door into the bedroom. "He's coming." She flicked on the television and sat on the bed. He shook his head at her frenzied attempt to look casual. Her face was so expressive he regretted the necessity of sharing his suspicions, but it couldn't be helped. She had to know.

Sean knocked on the door just as Phil locked his computer case.

He squeezed Taylor's knee on the way to the door. Telling her to relax wouldn't help.

The scent of pepperoni pizza greeted his nose as he opened the door. "Smells good."

"No kidding. I ate a piece in the car." Sean handed him the large pizza box but carried a paper grocery sack to the dresser. "You send Jackson your report?"

"Just finished. Jackson should be calling any minute now to tell me what I missed."

Sean checked his watch. "Naw, he'll wait until morning. Monday morning, that is. We're officially off the clock." He opened the grocery bag and pulled out a bag of chips and a six pack of beer. "Or as off the clock as we get with an open case."

Taylor smiled. "Pizza, chips and beer. Health food."

Sean shrugged, popped a beer and offered it to Taylor. She shook her head. "I think I'll stick to root beer, if there's one in the machine."

"Come on, let's see what they have." Phil grabbed his wife's hand, unwilling to leave her alone with Sean even for a couple of minutes.

When they got in the hall, Taylor squeezed his hand. "What did Jackson say?"

"We need proof."

"He didn't believe you?"

"He acknowledged my suspicions, but we still need proof." Phil fed quarters into the machine. "Root beer?"

She nodded. "How are you going to get proof?" The machine rumbled, and her can of soda fell into the tray. "I don't know if I can do this. It was one thing to act normal when Sean was hovering over his laptop, but I don't know what to do without that distraction."

"Don't worry about it. Concentrate on eating and the television. We'll visit Cochran in a bit."

"How is that going to help?"

"Sean won't come." He handed her the cold can.

"What makes you say that?"

"He never liked Cochran. He won't waste his time on a visit."

Back inside the room, Phil helped himself to a slice of pizza. "Taylor wants to visit Cochran, make sure he's all right." He gave Sean his what-can-I-do look.

Sean's eyes flashed interest or excitement for a split second before he shook his head at Taylor. He turned to Phil. "If you want to go, go. Just don't expect me to go with you."

Phil nodded. He'd anticipated Sean's words, but that flash of excitement or anticipation... Did Sean want them out of his way? "Well, if you think it's unnecessary, we can stay."

"You could, but would Taylor get any sleep tonight?" Sean picked up another slice and took a bite. "Go or don't, it makes no difference to me."

But it did, somehow, and that tempted Phil to stay, as well.

CHAPTER TWENTY-TWO

Cochran lay in the hospital bed, breathing oxygen pumped through the flexible tube taped beneath his nose. Other than the fact the tube irritated his nose, he felt fine. He thought about Max—who was Phil. Max—who had trained him toward the end of the Foxy Lady murders. Max—who had retired, but hadn't. He felt like a damn fool.

Now that he knew Phil was Max, it all made sense. He wondered how Taylor was taking the news that her artist husband was a covert agent. A smile curved his lips. As crazy as it had sounded, she'd been right all along. Max's ears had probably been burning. She'd forgive Max once the case was closed and their lives got back to normal. She loved him too much to do anything else. And there was the baby to consider.

He stared at the blank television screen. The nurse had unplugged it and the room phone claiming he had a concussion and needed limited mental stimulation to speed the recovery process. If only limited mental stimulation had been the treatment in high school, he'd have used those football concussions to his advantage. Now, it was just frustrating and counterproductive. They'd given Sean his phone, so he couldn't even call headquarters.

Instead of inducing relaxation, having no distractions just left him plenty of time for speculation. He knew the snowplow jockey was after Taylor, but he also knew Accawi wasn't the mole. Had that been the situation, the case would be over. And Rogers had made it clear this was anything but over.

"Cochran, are you okay?" Taylor walked through the doorway drawing Max in her wake. She hurried to his bedside. "How's your head?"

"I'm good. Just a knot." It surprised him how much seeing Taylor relaxed him. His job was to make certain she was safe, and he sure as hell would. He watched Max close the door. "Have you come to spring me?"

"Sorry, you're stuck here until morning. They don't trust us to wake you every hour like they will. I'm here to pick what's left of your brain."

Cochran shifted on the bed until he was sitting rather than lounging. "If we're coming up with strategy, why isn't O'Hearn here?"

Taylor shrugged. "He didn't want to come."

Max cocked an eyebrow. "Yet he seemed most anxious for us to go."

"Really?" Cochran spoke at the same moment Taylor did.

Cochran looked into Max's eyes. Crap. Max suspected Sean. "What's going on, Max, or is it Phil?"

"I know, long story. I'm Max at the bureau for the duration." He waved his hand. "But once this is done, so is Max."

Taylor's eyes pinned her husband's. "You never did tell me how you and Cochran know each other."

"I trained Mark. He came on for the last of the Foxy Lady murders. He was there when Sean shot Dempsey."

"Oh." She turned her head from Phil. "One more secret down. A million to go."

Cochran understood her hurt. For weeks, he'd watched her faithfully cling to her belief in Phil. He wasn't going to watch her abandon that faith now. "Taylor, he was covert. You're never going to know it all. Even if he had a normal past, you wouldn't know it all. Nobody tells everything about their past. It isn't possible."

She nodded. "I know." She turned back to Phil and swallowed hard. "Okay, moving forward."

Phil patted her arm. "Moving forward." He looked at Cochran. "But first, I need you to go back to the Foxy Lady murders. Remember the last body?"

Cochran nodded. Leslie Cunningham had been left at Angelwood Park tied on a swing. It was a hard scene to forget. It was even harder to remember. "What about it?"

"How did we arrive on the scene?"

"Sean drove, you rode shotgun, Jill Engel and I were in back. You sent us ahead to make our first impressions while you and Sean talked to the uniforms on site."

"Right. And who found the tattoo?"

He was mentally at the scene, could smell the blood and bowel of the decimated body. The minimal amount of blood for the catastrophic nature of her wounds said she'd been killed elsewhere and moved. He had the camera; Jill, the tape measure and evidence bags. The place was clean. No footprints, no fingerprints. The sand had been raked.

"We didn't see it at first, and we said so afterwards. Sean told us where to look." He looked at Phil. "So?"

"So, how did Sean know where it was? You were with the body. He and I were just walking up."

Cochran shrugged. "The local cops, I guess. I never thought about it. It was my first big crime scene."

"They didn't see it. They only called us."

"So how did Sean know?" He stared into Phil's eyes.

"I don't know. At the time, I didn't think much of it. He has the uncanny ability to spot clues and guess motives, especially in murder cases. I can do that with computers—think intuitively, know things I should only suspect. But how did he spot something he was not in a position to see yet? He did it again with the Tatro murder. And I began to wonder. Is he really that much quicker than I am, or does he have inside information?"

"You think he was the Foxy Lady murderer, and you

think he's the mole." It wasn't a question.

"And I need you to help me prove it."

They spent the next hour comparing what they knew, what they suspected. Taylor listened quietly and then interrupted.

"You're starting to rehash things. We're going to need to catch him in the act. She looked at her husband. "And he's planning something."

Phil nodded. "He encouraged us to visit you when he has every reason to want to keep us apart."

Taylor leaned forward. "Unless, he doesn't know we suspect him."

Cochran thought for a moment. "I agree with Phil, we have to assume he suspects."

"Okay, so what do we do now?"

Cochran's first reaction, and he had to assume it was Phil's as well, was to tell Taylor she wasn't part of the 'we.' She wasn't trained. Taylor needed to be shielded and kept safe. But he knew better than to say that out loud.

Phil answered, "The way I see it, things will remain quiet until we get to Indianapolis. Sean and I will report to Jackson, but, without anything solid, you and Taylor will be on your own. That's when something is likely to happen. We have to figure out what he has planned and catch him in the act."

"Doesn't that give him too much control?" Taylor asked. "Shouldn't we set things up ourselves? Give him the opportunity, and see if he takes it?"

Cochran smiled indulgently. They'd set a trap for him earlier, but he hadn't taken the bait. "What would you suggest?"

Taylor shrugged. "I could repeat some of the things Accawi said and hint that there are more damning things I almost, but don't quite, remember."

"Like the name 'Kahil'?" Phil nodded, surprised by his wife's perceptiveness. "Perfect. Add a little urgency."

"So, Taylor hints she has incriminating evidence, and then you and Sean leave us where?"

"Hopefully, at the rental car office. But if Sean is wise

to us, probably a hotel. You'll ditch the mug somewhere in the hotel and drop out of sight until you get the 'All Clear.' If he's monitoring the beacon, we want him to think he knows where to find you." He looked Cochran in the eye. "Once Sean and I drive off, you're in charge, Mark. I'm counting on you to keep Taylor safe."

"So when do I hint I'm remembering things?"

Cochran glanced at Taylor, waiting for the protest. She didn't do damsel in distress well. He was surprised she didn't rise to the bait.

"Wait for my cue. I'll ask you if you remember anything else." Phil turned back to him. "Sean will need to either contact someone to arrange the hit or lose me to do it himself. Jackson will monitor his cell. I'll be prepared for the brush-off. Someone will trail him, either me or a team, or both. Hopefully, he'll show his hand. Either way, we need to search his house. Jackson is working on the warrant. I'd like to be in on that search."

"How long are Cochran and I supposed to hide?" The reluctance to passively hide was clear in her voice.

Phil took his wife's hand. "Not long, I hope. It depends on what Sean does and what we find in his house."

"And if you find nothing? If it isn't Sean?" asked Taylor.

Cochran waited for Phil's reply. He didn't answer at first. Phil and Sean had been partners a long time. He had to be torn between hoping Sean was the mole and hoping he wasn't. If Sean was, and they caught him, the danger to Taylor was over. If Sean wasn't, it would be the end of their friendship. Hell of a position to be in.

Phil finally responded in a flat voice. "Then, I was wrong, and we go back to the drawing board."

Cochran reviewed the plans and the reasoning behind them. "I think the suspicions are justified. Foxy Lady, Tatro's murder, Kahil, what Accawi said...it's pretty overwhelming circumstantial evidence. We just need something solid to go with it. Sean will think he knows where Taylor is. If he wants her out of the picture for some reason, he may take this opportunity." He nodded and then looked Phil in the eye. "Is SAC Jackson onboard for this? Should I call Rogers?"

"Jackson's waiting for my call. Rogers is a good idea, but we'll let Jackson contact him."

"I hope this works." Taylor gave voice to what they were all thinking.

§

Taylor looked out the car window as they drove from the hospital to the hotel. The full moon reflected on the snow making the world brighter than it should be at nine p.m. in early December. "I understand why you feel it's necessary, but I don't want to hide any more. We just found each other again. I don't want to be away from you."

"Taylor, I love you. We will be together, but we have to ferret him out." He squeezed her hand, but it wasn't enough.

Her eyes burned with exhaustion. She knew she was tired, and sometimes being tired made her overly emotional. "And if it's not Sean? How long, then?"

"We'll figure it out, Taylor. Don't worry."

"We have to, because I need it to be over before the end of July." She turned to look directly at him. "We're expecting a baby." She hadn't meant to tell him this way, but now was as good a time as any. And it might give him added incentive.

"A baby?" His smile warmed her. "We did it, huh? A baby." He drove into the lot, parked the car and pulled her into his arms.

His lips were warm and tender. His arms, home. She melted into him.

"Let's go inside before we fog the windows."

She laughed, feeling lighter than she had in months. It was okay with her if they fogged the windows.

§

The next morning, Taylor and Phil met Sean and Cochran at the airport. By the time the plane landed in Indianapolis, Taylor wanted to kiss the ground. She wasn't the only one who'd been sick on the flight. Nor was she the only one praying as turbulence turned the short hop into a seemingly interminable roller coaster ride. She'd distinctly heard Cochran's voice behind her saying the Lord's Prayer.

Once they deplaned, she ducked into the first available women's restroom and splashed cold water on her face. Ghastly, horrible flight. She cupped water in her hands and rinsed her mouth. So much for making it a day without being sick.

Phil waited outside the door with a concerned look on his face. "Feeling better?"

Taylor nodded. It would take a while for her stomach to settle, but she was doing much better.

"Good. Cochran and Sean went to get the rental car."

When they reached the rental counter, Sean was second in line. He opened a blue sports drink and handed it to Taylor. "To replace the electrolytes you lost."

She took the bottle. "Thanks." Over Sean's shoulder, Phil shook his head. She understood.

"Where's Cochran?" Phil asked.

"Men's room."

Sean stepped to the counter.

"We should get two cars. That way, Cochran and Taylor can go one way while we go another."

Sean shook his head. "They've tightened the reimbursement policy. We only got the okay for one car. We'll have to drop them off on the way. Besides, they're supposed to lay low, not run around."

As Phil and Sean talked, Taylor backed up to a potted plant and dumped a quarter of the liquid into the dirt. She had the bottle before her when Phil joined her.

He took one look at the bottle. "I told you not to drink that." He mouthed the words more than said them. "The bottle was open."

"I know. I'm not stupid." She nodded at the plant.

Sean left the counter with the key at the same time Cochran joined them. "About time. I thought you'd fallen in." Sean turned to Taylor. "How's the drink?"

"Just what I needed. Thanks."

As they got into the blue SUV, Sean looked pointedly at Cochran. "You're looking green around the gills."

"I'm good."

"Maybe Taylor should give you a sip or two of her drink."

Taylor felt Sean's eyes watching her in the rear view mirror. "You want some?' Taylor offered as she slid into the back seat next to Cochran.

Cochran looked from the partially full bottle to Taylor. Then, he reached for the bottle. "Thanks."

Sean started the car.

Taylor looked Cochran in the eye and gave a tiny shake of the head. He acknowledged with a slight nod and brought the bottle to his lips as Sean looked over the seat and backed the car out of the parking spot.

"Thanks." He capped the bottle and handed it back to Taylor.

She smiled as she tucked the bottle into Phil's bag.

As they drove out of the parking lot and away from the airport, Sean and Phil talked in hushed tones.

Phil turned to face the back seat. "Honey, did you remember that name?"

"What name?" Sean asked.

"When Accawi held me, he told me things. About his wife's death. About her pregnancy. He said Phil was her false friend, the blue-eyed Arab, and...and...something else. There was another name." She made a frustrated sound. "It's right there. I know it is. But I just can't remember."

"Don't worry, sweetheart. It'll come back to you."

"I hope so."

Sean turned the discussion to football, as if there was nothing more important. Cochran leaned forward and joined the conversation.

Taylor leaned back and relaxed. Her part was done.

She yawned. The back of the car was toasty warm. The conversation dull. Lack of sleep the night before combined with the stress of the plane ride and the normal tiredness that plagued her the last few days. Taylor's head bobbed, and her eyes closed. A split second later, the twenty minute ride from airport to hotel had passed. She opened her eyes as Phil opened her door. "Come on, sleepy head, let's get you a room."

"You're coming in?" She blinked owlishly at her husband. "I thought you and Sean were just going to drop us off."

"Sean thought it was a better idea that we know exactly where you are, just in case."

In case of what? She was instantly more alert. She'd played the memory card, and it looked like Sean had taken the bait. Shouldn't Sean want to get Phil away from her before she remembered the name? Why would he want to go into the hotel? She let Phil help her out of the car.

The sun was warm. Fluffy white clouds reflected on the tall buildings that made up the neighborhood. Near the top of one of the buildings, there appeared to be a ladder or a gate suspended horizontally. "What's that?"

Phil looked up. "Permanent window washing platform." He pointed to the side of the hotel. "This building has one, as well. Let's go. We're falling behind."

§

Sean was already at the door when Frankie, his latest protégé, hurried out, bumping into him so hard he staggered.

He felt Frankie's hand dip into his pocket. The kid was still too damned sloppy with the exchange. Not that it mattered. Frankie's payment was the last of the uncut coke Sean had procured for Aisha. Frankie wouldn't know what hit him. Another tragic overdose.

"Watch where you're going."

"Sorry man, sorry." Frankie grabbed Sean, as if to steady him. Sean caught the "mission accomplished" nod. He could only hope Frankie had handled the rest of the arrangements with a bit more finesse.

The kid apologized again and rushed into the parking lot to his waiting car. He'd had potential. Sean was going to miss him.

"Better check your wallet," Taylor said as she and Phil hurried forward. "That almost looked like a pickpocket move you'd see on television."

"Want me to stop him?" Cochran asked.

Sean checked his pockets. The mailbox key was gone and in its place was the paper sleeve with the hotel keys Frankie had slipped him. His other pocket held his wallet and the rental car keys. He pulled out the wallet and keys for show-and-tell. "We're good. Just an accident."

He walked into the lobby. There were no accidents. Just like there were no coincidences. Max used to know that, but now Taylor had him too pussy whipped to think.

The other three hung back as Sean approached the counter to register for the room no one would use.

§

Taylor yawned.

Phil eyed her critically. "You sure you didn't drink that stuff?"

She hissed at him. "I told you, I'm not stupid." She glanced at Cochran.

"Me neither."

Phil nodded. "I need to make certain it goes to the lab."

"I put it in your bag."

He turned to Cochran. "He's up to something. I want the two of you out of here as soon as possible."

Cochran nodded, and Phil headed back to the counter.

Sean had just gotten the keys. "Let's go." He looked at the number on the slip. "406."

It was an awkward elevator ride up. Taylor was nervous that Sean was so insistent on seeing their room. "Aren't you guys going to be late for your appointment?"

Sean looked at his watch. "We've got a few minutes. I know Max wants to check out the room before we go."

She looked nervously at Phil. Had he and Sean dropped them off like they were supposed to, they'd have dropped the mug in the trash somewhere and headed out the back door.

Sean keyed them into the room and handed both plastic cards to Cochran. The room was a suite. The sitting room had a wet bar and a fridge. A short hall with the bathroom on the left led into the bedroom.

Taylor yawned as she took off her coat. Cochran yawned right after.

"They keep you up last night, Cochran?"

Cochran yawned again. "Yep. It's one of the reasons I hate hospitals. I swear, they'd wake you up to take a sleeping pill."

Sean chuckled. "Well, you guys can nap while we're gone. Just make sure you set the dead bolt."

Taylor sat on the bed closest to the bathroom. "Sounds like a good idea." She kicked off her shoes.

"Yuck, don't sleep on the bedspread. You never know who did what on that." Sean tugged the covers down. "There. That's better." He looked at Cochran and jerked his head toward the door. "Come on, Cochran, let's give them a couple of minutes of privacy."

Phil sat down next to Taylor. "You're going to be all right. You know what to do. If things change, follow Cochran's lead."

She nodded once, nervous now that Phil was going to leave her again. "How long?"

"I'll call Cochran as soon as I know anything."

She licked her lips. "I don't want you to go."

His lips caressed hers. "I know. It won't be long, I promise." He covered her mouth with his. She clung to him, wanting him to tell her everything would be okay. Fearful of what might come, she memorized his taste, the scrape of his beard, the warmth of his cheeks... He branded her with his touch, silently promising to return.

Someone knocked on the door. Her lips clung while he slowly pulled away. The conversation was silent, lip against lip. Stay. I have to go. Let me go with you. You have to stay. She ended the kiss. "It's okay. You better go."

She followed him through the sitting room to the door. "We'll be fine. You and Sean figure out how to catch the mole, so we can get back to living."

Sean beamed at her. "Good girl." He looked at Cochran.

"Throw the deadbolt now. Max'll want to hear it before we go."

Taylor watched Phil give Cochran the nod.

Then, they were out the door.

"We're waiting." Sean's voice filtered back into the room.

Cochran turned the latch that set the deadbolt and then pressed his eye to the spy hole. "Okay, they're gone." He turned back into the room. "Get the mug out of the bag, and let's get going."

She unzipped her bag and set the mug on the couch. "If Sean comes back, shouldn't we at least make it look like we're here? Maybe stuff the beds with towels."

"Good idea."

She hurried into the bathroom and collected every towel. They each worked on a bed. Creating a realistic looking lump in the bed wasn't as easy as she thought.

Cochran finished first. "Good enough. Get your coat on. We're out of here."

She followed him to the door, shoving her arms into her sleeves as she went. "Do you know where we're going?"

"First, we call a cab from the restaurant down the street and take it to the nearest movie theater. Then we watch two shows and wait for Phil's call."

"Okay." She waited for him to open the door.

He fumbled with the deadbolt, first trying to turn it with one hand and then using both.

"What's wrong? Let's go."

"I can't turn the knob."

She smiled at him. "Got lotion on your hands? Here, let me try."

He stepped aside. "I'm not wearing lotion. It isn't turning. It's stuck."

She tried. The knob wouldn't budge. Not a centimeter. She looked at Cochran. "Call the desk to send maintenance."

He patted his pockets and swore. "Sean's got my cell. He took it in the hospital when they had me under observation, and he never gave it back."

"So use the room phone." She crossed the room and picked up the receiver. Silence. Tapping the phone hang-up button did nothing. "It's dead." She replaced the handset and looked at the back of the phone. The cord that should have connected the phone to the wall was gone. She picked up the entire phone to show Cochran.

"Shit." He ran to the bedroom with Taylor at his heels. Same story. "Double shit."

She nodded. "Now what?"

He checked the walls. "There isn't a connecting door."

They both looked out the window. Four floors wasn't that far up in a twelve-story building, but it was way too far from the ground to jump. And there wasn't a ledge, per se, outside the window. Still, Cochran opened the window—all three inches of it that would open. The hotel was clearly not risking jumpers or accidental falling deaths.

"We can make noise and irritate the neighbors," Cochran suggested.

"If there are neighbors. It's too early for someone to be trying to sleep."

"We might as well try it." Cochran flipped on the television and turned up the volume. "It may only take an hour for O'Hearn to get to headquarters, ditch Phil, and get back here."

"If that's his plan." Would Sean hurt Phil on his way to kill her and Cochran? She closed her eyes. Please, God. Please no. There had to be some way to save them all.

Taylor turned the clock radio up to full volume. Her mind was racing almost as fast as her heart. "What if he planted a bomb in one of our bags?" She had to shout to be heard over the competing media. They left the bedroom, closing the door behind them, muting the noise by a few precious decibels. There was a television in the sitting room, as well. Cochran turned it to blaring. The noise made it hard to think.

They emptied both bags, searching every item, every seam of the bags. Nothing.

Now what? She looked at Cochran and shouted, "What if he planted a bomb?"

He flipped off the television. "What?"

The relative silence was a balm to her ears. "What if he planted a bomb somewhere else in the room? Or in the hotel?"

"When would he have had a chance to do that?"

"When did he have a chance to take the phone cords and tamper with the deadbolt? It's clear he's not working alone."

Cochran acknowledged her comment with a nod. "Save the hows for later, we need to concentrate on getting out of here." He walked to the door and looked at the hinges.

Taylor looked around the room, searching for inspiration. She looked at the ceiling. It was solid, not ceiling tiles. The blinking light of the fire alarm caught her eye. She dragged a chair under it. Unlike the smoke detectors used in houses, this one didn't have a test button or a battery. It was hard wired.

"Cochran, what about the fire alarm? We could light a match beneath the fire alarm and set it off." If they could find a match. It was a non-smoking room. "Or maybe we could break a lamp and start an electrical fire."

"We don't need to start a fire to set off the alarm. If I break the red vial on the sprinkler head, it will go off. Every sprinkler in the building will go off and every alarm, as well." He had his pocket knife out and was using it to work the pin out of the top hinge of the door.

"There's a red vial?" She looked at the sprinkler head. Sure enough. "How do you know these things?"

He gave her his "I'm FBI" look. "When it gets too hot, the vial bursts and the sprinklers go on. They'll evacuate the building and call the fire department. Then, we'll have to hope the firemen are real firemen and not someone out to kill us."

She looked out the peephole. Nothing. No one. It was like they had the entire wing to themselves. She could turn the television back on and bang on the door all she wanted, but no one would hear.

"The door is our safest bet. We need to get out of here and soon." Cochran went to work on the door and got the first pin out. Then, he knelt to work on the second. "My guess, based on past actions and the blue drink he gave you, is he has something more personal planned than the bombings Accawi tried."

Her hands shook. Personal, as in Foxy Lady personal? Dear God. If ever there was a time to cry, this was it. But she didn't. Wouldn't. There had to be something they could do. There had to be. She looked at Cochran. "How would he plan to get in the room?"

"The window."

"And just how do you expect him to get up here? He can't fly."

"Remember the window washer platforms? They reach every window."

"Right." Her heart fell. If he came in through the window, they'd be trapped. "You have your gun, right?" She wanted out. Now. "Maybe you could shoot the door open."

He smiled. "Ah...the magical shoot-the-door-and-it-does-what-you-want technique that's so popular in fiction. One shot and the door opens, or locks, depending on what the characters need. Too bad it doesn't work that way in real life."

"You could try."

He set down the knife and unsnapped the holster strap. "We'd be better off if I shot out the window. Maybe someone would hear it." He drew his gun and checked the cartridge.

It looked empty. Her heart fell. She remembered that Sean had taken care of all the guns at the airport, handing them to the inspector and then distributing them again. The three guns looked identical to her. Apparently, they looked that way to everybody.

He looked at Taylor and shook his head.

They couldn't sit there waiting. No one was going to ride in to the rescue. The noise was making her head ache. She walked into the bedroom and flicked off the television and radio. "How can I help with the door?"

Cochran went back to work on the second pin.

Taylor vibrated with the need to help, but the hinges were a one person job. She grabbed the pad of paper and pen provided by the hotel, wrote page after page detailing their predicament and asking for help. Opening the window, she freed a half-dozen pages to the winter breeze. They fluttered and flew. Some landed in the parking lot below. Others were whisked out of sight. There was no one in the parking lot to call to, so she returned to the sitting room.

Both pins lay on the carpet beside the door. Cochran banged at the hinges with no perceptible results. "Damn fire door."

CHAPTER TWENTY-THREE

Phil sat in the passenger seat of the rental car, but his mind was in room 406 with Taylor. By now, they wouldn't be in that room. At least that was the plan. And it was a good plan. So why was he worried?

They rode in silence for several miles. Why had Sean insisted they all go to the room? Why had he insisted Cochran lock the deadbolt? If Sean were innocent, he'd want to know exactly where Taylor was. Of course he'd insist Cochran use every lock there was to protect her. But what if Sean was behind everything like he thought? Then, what did those things mean? What had Sean done while he and Taylor were talking to Cochran last night? He was the one who'd picked the hotel. What arrangements had he made?

It grated on his nerves to think that he made the mistake of letting Sean drive, of letting Sean pick the hotel. Even though Taylor and Cochran wouldn't actually stay in the hotel, it was a mistake to let Sean choose it. Pray to God it wasn't a fatal mistake.

"You're far away. What's on your mind?" Sean's question yanked him into the present moment.

"Wondering who the mole could be and how we can stop him."

Sean nodded. "Any ideas?"

"Of who? No." Phil shook his head. "I guess I counted on Accawi for that."

"Telling us who the mole was?" Sean nodded. "I figured he would, as well. Shame he pulled a knife on Taylor, and we had to shoot him."

"Yeah." Only one of them hadn't aimed for Accawi. Did that mean Accawi didn't know who the mole was, or did that mean Taylor was the more important target? And why Taylor? What did she know?

"You know what's bothering me?" Sean asked and continued without waiting for a response. "How Accawi knew where Taylor was. He had a cell phone, but no internet. If he was tracking the mug's signal, he should have had a smart phone or a GPS or something, but he didn't."

"Maybe he lost it in the fight."

"The team did a thorough search. It just strikes me as odd. You think Cochran could have tipped Accawi?"

Phil looked at Sean. "What possible reason would he have to do that, assuming he even knew about Accawi?"

"Just running theories. You mentored Cochran before you resigned, didn't you?"

"You know I did. We were both part of that detail. You had Jill Engel. She was supposed to be your new partner. Instead, you convinced me to return with this crazy art and intel idea."

"Which worked extremely well, until recently."

Phil nodded. It really had. Until something went wrong. Doubting Sean as he did, he still couldn't pin down motive. Even if Sean was the Foxy Lady killer, why would he want to kill Taylor? She wasn't some anonymous prostitute. Why her?

"Besides," Sean continued. "How could I get another partner? We're Batman and Robin."

"Jill could have been your Batgirl."

"Naw, she'd have been as big a mistake as the original Batgirl was. But that's not the point. When you left, Cochran lost both his mentor and his chance to join a covert team. He's been regular issue ever since. If it had been me, I might have blamed you for screwing my career."

"His career wasn't screwed. He's lead agent on his team."

"Just hear me out, will ya? Let's say he is disgruntled. Remember how obsessed he was with your early art work? Swore you were a prodigy."

Phil shrugged.

"Then, you go and ditch him..."

"I didn't ditch him."

"... and ruin his chance for rapid advancement. You change your name and hit it big in the art world while maintaining a high level, low profile presence at the bureau. But he's still stuck doing relocation detail. Then, he sees one of your new pieces and puts two-and-two together. Maxwell Kennedy is Philip Wilson. He watches you. Figures out where your art is ending up. Somehow, it clicks. He's pissed. He sees an opportunity to earn a little extra cash and punish you for real and imagined sins. He clues in Accawi. When neither you nor Taylor dies in the first blast, he manages to get assigned to Taylor."

Phil shook his head. This was crazy thinking. "No way."

"What better way to extract revenge than through your wife? He's seen you together, knows how disgustingly loving you are. But you don't surface because you don't know she's at risk. So he ups the ante. He plants a bomb at her greenhouse, takes a potshot at a pushy coworker and then lets her slip through his fingers. He had a team waiting at Bachman's house, but you didn't show. Everything that happened with Taylor is explained. Finally, he's in control. He knows where she is. He uses her to draw you out, and it works. He knows we're moving in, so he calls Accawi to take us out."

He didn't know how to respond. Sean's theory had enough fact to almost make it reasonable—if he hadn't run the shooting matrix, if Accawi hadn't thought Sean's alias was Phil, if the newscaster's murder scene hadn't been so familiar, and if there weren't questions about the

Foxy Lady murders.

"I've got a point, don't I?"

"I don't know, Sean. Is work-frustration enough of a motive? People died."

"It would be for someone like Cochran. Someone for whom the job is everything. Someone who maybe counted on you to be there for him for the long run. Best buds." His voice started out calm, but grew louder and angrier as he continued. "He saw how Taylor had shackled you already, stripped you of your freedom, and poisoned your mind. Rescuing you was the only option. Killing Taylor would be nothing. A blessing..."

Cold sweat trickled down Phil's back. He didn't know the man beside him. Sean, the man he'd known since college, was not only the mole but also the Foxy Lady killer. And he definitely wanted Taylor dead. Thank God, Sean was there with him, and Taylor was safe with Cochran.

"...for Cochran, you know?"

Phil nodded, hoping like hell Sean would hold it together until they could get to Jackson. However, he was ready to take him out sooner if it came to that. Sean was as armed as he was, but Sean was driving. If he pulled a gun on him now, Sean was plenty crazy enough to ram them into a utility pole and kill them both.

"Sorry. Wacky theory, I know. Guess I'm grasping at straws, like you are. We all are."

He drove in silence for a while, but Phil's mind didn't stop racing. Was that what Sean really thought? Not the Cochran bit. The Batman stuff. If Sean saw them as a team—the dynamic duo—that would explain Taylor being the target when he told Sean he wanted to quit. Maybe. But the Foxy Lady killings had come first. Would Sean's break-up with Therese have triggered that? He should look up Therese. He'd never thought of doing that before. Why would he? It wasn't until recently he suspected Sean.

Sean broke the silence. "I'm anxious to see what Jackson thinks. If he has any theories about who could have been feeding Accawi intel. We know someone did. The man wasn't smart enough to figure out the technology on his own. And then, of course, he couldn't prove it." He turned to Phil. "You think maybe he was a cokehead like his wife?"

"Maybe." Phil didn't believe it for a second. Accawi had been pointed at Taylor, at him and Taylor, from the start. His actions weren't those of an addict. Taylor's words held the likely reason behind his actions—revenge for the death of his wife. A wife for a wife rather than an eye for an eye. "I'm sure the lab is running a tox screen." They turned onto the road with the parking ramp. Once they were inside, he'd have back-up. There would be another agent to watch Sean while he updated Jackson alone, giving Sean a chance to make his move.

And if Sean didn't make his move?

Phil refused to think about that. He'd make his move. He had to.

Sean pulled into the parking ramp at the federal building. Just a few more minutes. Phil willed himself calm. He couldn't do anything until Sean made his move, or he had the search warrant.

They parked, got out of the car and took the elevator to the top of the public parking ramp where they would transfer to the elevator that serviced the federal building. Beside the elevator, Agent Peterson puffed on a cigarette.

Peterson. Perfect. The person Sean had made a fool of with the truck incident. Peterson had every reason to want Sean badly. Peterson would have Sean now. Phil hit the up button.

"Damn. I forgot my laptop in the car. I'm going to need that." Sean looked from his empty hands to Phil's computer. "You go on and get started. Jackson likes to do these reviews one at a time, anyway."

This was it.

Phil shot a quick look at Peterson. You have him? Peterson nodded. He had him.

Phil shrugged and got into the elevator. "See you

upstairs."

§

The clock started when the elevator door closed. Fifteen minutes. Jackson had never debriefed anyone in less than fifteen minutes. Sean ignored Peterson and headed back to the car.

"O'Hearn," Peterson followed him into the parking lot. "I overheard SAC Jackson say Kennedy was going inactive once this case is done and that you'll need a new partner."

"I don't have time right now. Jackson expects me upstairs."

"I'll walk with you then."

"I'm on the first floor." He'd rather shoot the incompetent rule-follower than talk to him. He would do it, if he had a different gun, but he had Cochran's and— he stopped midstride. Peterson and Cochran had worked Taylor-detail until the truck incident. Who better to suspect Cochran than Peterson? Who better to warn Max of Cochran's violent tendencies toward Taylor than Peterson himself? Then, he could back Peterson's claims, rather than assert them as his own.

His stopping must have given the schmuck hope.

"My car's just over there. It would be faster to drive to the first floor and back than it would be to take the elevator down. I'll drive you to get your computer, and we can talk."

He turned to Peterson. "Where's your car?"

Peterson pointed to the row of cars closest to the elevator.

"Okay. Lead on." The idiot had just sealed his fate. He waited until they were next to the car to shoot Peterson in the heart. No need to drag the body any further than necessary.

Peterson crumpled to the floor. Sean snapped on crime scene gloves before rifling through the man's pockets for car keys, cell phone, and ID card. Sean took them all, as well as the man's service revolver. He popped the trunk, grabbed Peterson under the shoulders and hoisted him into the trunk. God, the man weighed a ton. He'd done Peterson a favor really, shooting him. Smoked like a chimney. Too much fat around the middle. The man was a heart attack waiting to happen. At least he hadn't bled much.

Once he deposited Peterson in his own trunk and cleaned up the blood with a wad of tissue, Sean drove to his rental and left the keys under the mat. He'd tweak the original plan, leave a little corroborating evidence, and get back to the hotel. He opened his phone, scrolled to Max's old cell number, one he knew no one would answer, and hit dial. The automatic service picked up, and he left his message.

"Max, why the hell aren't you picking up? This is important. I know you don't believe me about Cochran, but Peterson has the same worries. We're going to go back to the hotel to make certain Taylor's okay. I think you should go there, as well. I left you the rental. We're taking Peterson's car. Bring backup."

It took talent of forethought and a phenomenal memory to set up an airtight alibi and do the crime. He had to think of everything. But he was more than up for it. Just a little tweaking.

Chuckling, he drove out of the ramp, pulling into traffic. He'd wait until he was at the hotel before he had "Peterson" call and request backup. He practiced the words aloud to check for Peterson's voice and inflection. Oh, yeah. He had it.

Once he was at the hotel, he'd take Peterson up the window washing platform with him. He didn't need to be so careful about the window, now. He wouldn't need to be careful how he removed it. Better yet, he didn't have to put it back. That had always been the tricky part. Now, it didn't matter. He'd get in, shoot Taylor with Cochran's gun and Cochran with Peterson's, and then push Peterson out the window. He'd take the platform down; breaking it so it looked like it'd slipped. Once on the ground, he'd call in "shots fired" and meet Max and the backup team outside the locked door. Man, he was good at this. He could probably teach a class. Too bad no one would ever know of his brilliance.

§

Phil called Jackson from the elevator. "Is my team ready? He's moving."

"They'll meet you on the fourth floor. Judge Madison's back in town. Lacey's got the search warrant. Nail him, Max."

"I will." Phil hung up as the elevator door slid open on the fourth floor.

Agent Lacey Johnson stepped in, followed by Agents Kittel and Jacobs. She barely waited for the door to close before briefing Phil. "Peterson hasn't called in, but he's leaving the ramp, turning south on Pennsylvania."

"Cochran's phone is off," Jacobs said. "No location available."

Phil nodded. Cochran and Taylor had most certainly left the hotel and picked up a cab at the Big Boy down the street. By now, they were long gone, probably having lunch at Gretchen's Good Grub. "He's off grid for another two hours, minimum. We want O'Hearn to think he's in the hotel." He hit the button to return to the ground floor.

Lacey watched the GPS. "Peterson's turning right on East Merrill."

It was as Phil suspected. "Sean's heading back to the hotel. Where's the car?"

"Level one, next to the door." Jacobs handed Phil the keys.

Phil had the car started before all four doors were closed.

"Left on Madison."

"Got it." Phil threw the car into reverse.

The sedan bottomed out on the speed bump as Phil left the garage. God, let Cochran have Taylor safely out of that hotel room. He swerved in and out of traffic, ignoring the honking horns. Damn downtown traffic. He was tempted to switch on the siren, but didn't want to alert Sean of their approach. Their tires squealed as they turned a corner and ran a red light.

§

Sean pulled Peterson's car into the hotel's empty overflow lot and parked. He'd wait until he got Peterson onto the washing platform before making the first call. No need to rush himself.

He was about to get out of the car when a man poked his head out of the hotel's back door and looked around suspiciously.

Cochran.

Sean didn't know whether to laugh or curse. How had Cochran managed to shake off the drug's effects, never mind get out of the room? Sean slouched in the seat. No need to make Cochran nervous. Now what? No need to go to the roof and get the window washer. Plan C. What the hell was plan C?

Cochran hurried out the door, drawing Taylor behind him.

Apparently, they didn't drink enough of the drug, or they were smarter than he thought.

Cochran's gun was in Sean's holster, so he picked Peterson's gun up off the floor. Peterson and Cochran would have a shoot out in the parking lot, that much was clear. But what about Taylor? Which gun should he shoot her with? He drew Cochran's piece and looked at the twin service revolvers. Cochran had the motive, but he'd have killed her in the hotel room, not the parking lot, and certainly not with Peterson watching. Sean couldn't come up with a solid motive for Peterson to kill her, not on the fly like this.

It seemed destined for him to take Taylor with him and make her disappear. Taylor didn't deserve an easy death like his mother or Aisha. She was a far bigger pain, deserving far more personalized attention. When he was done, he'd lay her beside Therese. That wasn't a problem. Peterson's car was.

But if Taylor took the car... Now there was a plan. Or at least the start of one.

He rolled down the driver's side window and shifted the car into drive.

§

Taylor shook as she waited in the cement stairwell while Cochran looked out the door. They should have been gone nearly an hour ago. Who knew it would take that long to wedge open a door? They'd broken the blade of Cochran's knife and probably his gun as well. Using the butt as a hammer couldn't be good for it. But they were out, and that's all that mattered.

"There's one car, but I think it was there before."

She didn't remember any cars in the lot outside their window. But after running down the hall and all the turning involved in going downstairs she had no idea if this was the same lot or not.

"Okay. Let's go."

She followed Cochran into the parking lot, skimming the building with one hand and clinging to his hand with the other. Her heart was in her throat. Her palms were wet. It was all too familiar. At least it wasn't night, and no one was shooting at them. She watched Cochran's back, wishing she could see the corner to know how far they needed to go. Were they at the back of the building or the side? How far from this corner was the road to the restaurant?

Was that car moving?

Crack.

Cochran stumbled. His hand wrenched from hers as he fell.

Taylor was on her knees. "Are you all right?" Her words were a frightened whisper. It was clear he wasn't all right. Red covered the right side of his chest, as if he'd been hit by a red paintball. Dear God. She had to help him. Staunch the blood. She had to get away. Dear God.

The car pulled up beside them. Sean got out of the car and opened the back door. "Get in. Lie on the floor. You'll be safe."

Taylor's brain stalled.

"Hurry."

Her eyes snagged on Sean's gun. She swallowed hard and knew she had to obey.

"On the floor, quick."

She shook so hard every movement was awkward.

"Stay down. I'll cover you with a blanket."

The blanket settled over her head. The door closed at her feet. Why hide her? It didn't make sense. She heard the trunk pop open.

The car shook violently. She crawled across the floor to the passenger side door. Peeking out of the blanket, she fumbled for the door handle. It slid through her hands without unlatching the door. Locked. She felt up the door, looking for the lock. She hit the toggle switch and tried the handle again. Nothing. Damn child safety locks. She lost the blanket on her way to the other door. It was locked, as well. Outside the window, there were now two bodies on the ground, Cochran and Agent Peterson.

Agent Peterson? Where had he come from?

From her vantage point, Peterson didn't look too lively. Sean seemed to be positioning Peterson's body. He placed a gun next to his hand. Cochran was still on the ground, slumped against the wall—only there was a gun next to his hand, as well.

Sean was setting things up to make it look like Cochran and Peterson had killed each other.

She needed to get out of there. Now.

She crawled over the seat into the front as fast as she could. There weren't keys in the ignition. Damn it! She unlocked the passenger door and crawled onto the blacktop. The parking lot was huge and empty. How was she supposed to cross it without Sean gunning her down like a scared rabbit?

Did it matter? Visions of tortured and slain murder victims danced in her mind's eye. She focused on the nearest light pole and ran like hell.

The slap of her tennis shoes against the ground trumpeted her retreat. Any second she'd hear the crack of gunfire, feel the burn of a bullet. She ran all out, but it seemed like she was moving in slow motion. Her side ached as she passed the light pole unscathed and angled off to the drainage ditch that separated the parking lot from a solitary oak.

Almost there.

Cold air burned her lungs. The wind whipped tears down her cheeks.

Almost there. Just twenty more yards. She heard the car and dug deep, pushing herself.

It wasn't going to be enough.

"Damn it, Taylor. Get in the car now, or I swear I'll shoot you where you stand."

§

Phil pulled into the hotel parking lot, but couldn't spot Peterson's sedan. "Where are they?"

Lacey looked from the GPS screen to the area around them. "Go right, around the building."

There was one car pulling to a stop at the far side of the lot. The door flew open, and Phil watched as Taylor stumbled forward and got into the car.

The car accelerated before she got the door closed.

Phil wanted to scream. You never get into your attacker's car. Never.

He accelerated after Sean, and they bounced over the speed bump on the way out of the parking lot.

Lacey clung to the side of the seat and the armrest.

Ahead of him, Sean sped through the curves of the frontage road like a race car driver. Taylor bounced around like a rag doll.

Phil focused all his attention on closing the gap between their car and Sean's. Come on, Sean, pull over.

Darting in and out of traffic like a weaver's shuttle, Sean had to know they were on to him. Had to realize he wasn't going to get away.

Phil pulled onto the main thoroughfare to a chorus of horns.

§

Sean looked in the rearview mirror at the tinted windows of the bureau sedan.

Damn it. He should have shot Taylor when he had the chance.

Beside him, Taylor braced herself against the dash and the door. The stupid girl hadn't buckled herself in. If he got up enough speed, he could slam on the brakes and launch her out the window.

Up ahead, the stoplight was red. Cars slowed. Stopped. Great.

The sedan was several cars behind, trapped in the far left lane. Sean veered right onto the shoulder, passing cars in the turn lane. He'd exit, lose the tail, and get rid of Taylor once and for all.

Cross traffic clogged the intersection. He slowed to turn into traffic.

In that instant, Taylor opened the car door and launched herself into the ditch.

"Shit." Sean slammed on the brakes and shifted into park. Fucking bitch. How could one woman be this much trouble?

He rushed out of the car.

Maybe she'd been injured jumping from a moving car. Maybe he could finish the job.

He should have run the bitch down when he had the chance.

"Sean!" He froze at the sound of Max's voice. Max was supposed to be reporting to Jackson. This wasn't the way it was supposed to happen. He was smarter than all of them combined.

Max slammed into his back. They crashed to the ground as one, rolling through dirty snow to the bottom of the ditch. Max ended up on top. For a fraction of a second Sean enjoyed the weight of Max on top of him. Then, Max punched the left side of his jaw, and he saw stars.

He was too stunned to return the blow. They'd wrestled. They'd sparred. But Max had never hit him in anger before.

Max was screaming at him, "Damn it, Sean. We were friends." Max drew back his fist to swing, but Cochran's flunkies dragged them apart.

Were friends? This couldn't be how it ended.

He didn't struggle as the female agent cuffed his hands behind him. "You have the right to remain silent..."

Sean spat gravel and blood from his mouth. "Max, it's not what you think."

Max shook himself free of Jacobs' grasp. "Do you think I'm that stupid? Did you really think you'd get away with it like you did the Foxy Lady murders?"

Why the hell shouldn't he get away with it? He'd already gotten away with it. There was no evidence. He looked into Max's deep brown eyes. "What are you talking about? Everyone, from God on down, knows Dempsey killed those prostitutes."

"He didn't, Sean. You did."

Sean reeled at the look of hatred in Max's eyes.

"Why did you do it, Sean?"

Why did he do it? Why would anyone? "They were whores, Max. Anyone will tell you killing them is almost a public service. Nothing is sacred to a whore. Most of them would sell their own sons."

"You're wrong, Sean. And not all of them were prostitutes. Accawi's wife and the newscaster weren't."

Sean shook his head. "All women are whores." Max was soft hearted where women were concerned, but Sean didn't hold that against him. Many men were. Women were to blame. The duplicitous, greedy, self-serving bitches.

Somehow, he managed not to smile at the memory of the reporter. "The news bitch was supposed to be happily married, but she begged me to fuck her. Begged me on her hands and knees. What kind of man says no to that?" He looked at Max. "All women are faithless whores," Sean repeated. "Most men don't see it, though." He looked at Taylor. "You don't."

He saw Taylor standing on the far side of the ditch with her arms wrapped around herself, shaking like a bitch in heat. It was clear that Max had caught her scent by the way he turned to look at her. She was dirty, disheveled. The sleeve of her jacket was torn. Sticks and old leaves stuck out from her hair. Her nose ran and tears streamed down her cheeks. Disgusting piece of rubbish. Still, one look at Max and he knew that any second now Max would break his leash and scramble out of the ditch to take her.

Sean shook his head and turned to Max. "Accawi thought his Aisha was perfect, too. Blameless. But she was weak, like my mother. Even her hair and soul were like Mommy's, black as sin. Her pretty black eyes sparkled with desire for my bags of white powder. Taylor lusts for things, too. Equally nasty things." He looked at her. It wouldn't have surprised him to see maggots crawling on her. Rotten to the core.

"You supplied Aisha with drugs?"

Sean was shocked by Max's naiveté. He'd only given her the means to do it herself. Like his mother. Like Frankie. "Women like that should not be mothers. They will trade their children for a line or two. Of course, Accawi was blind to her." He shook his head. He'd done Accawi a favor. "Accawi should have thanked me."

"And yet, he tried to kill you instead."

Of course not. That would be crazy. Sean laughed. "He didn't try to kill me, Max old boy. Not me."

"Why Taylor?"

"Why did Accawi target Taylor?" Sean shrugged. "An eye for an eye. A wife for a wife. Accawi's an old fashioned type of guy."

"No. Why did you target Taylor?"

Sean laughed again, the truth pushed at his teeth to be free, but he wouldn't let it out. He would keep Max. When all was said and done, he and Max would be together. "You know, Max. I believe I have the right to remain silent."

CHAPTER TWENTY-FOUR

Phil parked in front of Sean's white two-story house. The crew was already inside. He held Taylor's hand. It had been a mistake to linger at headquarters to watch Sean's questioning even though it had given Taylor a chance to shower and change. Sean had treated the arrest and interrogation as a joke, handing over his house keys with a laugh.

"Look all you want. There's nothing to see. No proof of any crime. It's like I told you before. I'm innocent. Peterson and Cochran shot each other. I was checking Peterson when an unmarked car pulled up and started shooting at us. I saved Taylor. I was chasing after her to see if she was okay after jumping out of my car when Max slugged me. I think she needs psychiatric evaluation, jumping out of a moving car like that.

"All your suspicions are based on conjecture and inaccurate supposition. Whatever evidence you think you have is circumstantial at best. I'll be back to work by midweek, and you'll be bowing and scraping to avoid a defamation suit."

It looked like Sean had slipped over some invisible line. Phil didn't think he'd ever confess to the killings or tell anyone why he'd targeted Taylor. With any luck, there would be some answers in Sean's house.

Phil turned to his beautiful, bruised wife. "Are you sure you're okay waiting here? This could take a couple of hours. It's not like television, you know."

"I'm fine." She pointed to her coffee and lifted her

book. "I'm set."

They needed time alone together. Time he couldn't give her just yet. "It's almost over, I swear. We need to find some solid evidence."

"I know." She kissed his cheek, but he wanted more. "Go. Finish this. We've still got my resurrection to deal with."

Phil got out of the car and walked up the neatly shoveled walk and opened the familiar door.

Sean's living room looked just as it had the last time Phil had been in it in September, not significantly different than it had when he'd stayed there the week of Sean's mother's funeral. He scanned the room, as if for the first time, and forced himself to be analytical. Knowing what pictures hung on the walls didn't mean he knew if one of them concealed a safe. Just because he'd glanced at the books on the shelf beside Sean's television didn't mean one of those books didn't hide something. Evidence could be anywhere. But with Sean's confidence, it didn't feel likely.

He took a deep breath as they started on the ground floor and worked their way up. He kept hoping every picture they turned over would be concealing something. Anything. But so far, they had nothing.

Phil left the team scouring the attic and focused on the yard. He'd never been behind Sean's house before. Roaming around, Phil stumbled upon the snow covered trap door to a storm cellar he hadn't known existed.

Phil called for the photographer, picking the padlock while he waited. The door looked thick enough to withstand an F-5 tornado. Wooden steps led into the darkness. The center of each board was worn smooth from countless feet.

The place smelled like potatoes gone bad. Phil breathed through his nose as he led the way down. Instead of shelf-lined walls full of ancient canned goods and rotten bags of potatoes, there was an army cot and a wooden beer case.

Phil found the light switch on the wall. A naked bulb

hanging by a cord at the bottom of the stairs illuminated the dirt floor and plaster walls. His stomach fell.

The walls were covered in childish scrawl. The words "Be Nice for Mommy" written over and over. Hundreds of times. Seeping water had washed one section of a wall clean. The photographer snapped pictures.

An adjacent wall contained a stick figure drawing of a man with an overlarge penis sodomizing a small boy. Tear drops fell from the stick boy's eyes. The words below read, "Being Nice for Mommy."

Phil felt as if he'd fallen down the rabbit hole with Alice. Up was down. Left was right.

Be nice for Mommy.

"God."

He wasn't certain if he spoke or the photographer had. They exchanged sickened glances and quickly turned away from each other.

He hadn't known. Holy shit. He should have known, shouldn't he? Sean was his best friend.

This explained everything. Sean fit the psychologist's profile perfectly. Abused child. Possibly homosexual. Member of law enforcement. Misogynist. If his mother really put him through this, who could blame Sean for hating her? Lashing out?

The wooden case sat next to Phil's feet. Expecting something worse than empty beer bottles, he reluctantly opened the lid. Photos of the Foxy Lady victims. Debby Sue Lindemeire, Naomi Wild, Jessica Jones, Jasmine French... They were all there. From the first victim to the last.

He looked at the next photo. Therese. Beaten and bloody as the rest.

Dear God.

The photographer snapped away, chronicling what Phil found. Phil's hand shook as he lifted newspaper clippings from the box. Envelopes filled with hair. The evidence couldn't get more solid.

Then, Phil saw a picture of himself and Sean. He sank to the cot. There shouldn't be a picture of him in a box of evidence. The picture had been taken in college by the look of it. They each wore a suit and had an arm around the other.

Phil lifted the photo. It was a jigsaw puzzle. Two photos cut and merged to make one. Old date photos, minus the dates. Phil set the picture aside and wiped his hand on his pant leg.

The next photo was of him, as well, taken unaware as he studied. The next, as he slept in the nude. He stared at the normal army surplus cot with its normal green wool blanket before turning back to the pictures. The next showed him in the shower.

He wiped the sweat from his brow. There were more. A lot more. He thumbed through the remaining photos. God, how could I not have known?

Acid rose thick in his throat, choking him. He dropped the pictures. Shoving the photographer aside he scrambled up the stairs, barely making it to the top before vomiting.

He heard the photographer stumble and hit the wall. A spout of profanity rose from the hell hole.

The photographer swore again. "Kennedy, get down here. There's something else."

Phil groaned. Photos of murdered women, nude pictures of him, sodomizing stick figures on the wall, words proclaiming the mother's guilt... What else could their possibly be down there?

"I think I found his fiancé."

Phil climbed down the stairs. Not rotten potatoes after all. The photographer had knocked a hole in the plaster wall, revealing the broken bones of a lower arm. Therese was buried in pieces behind the blank wall.

Dear God. He hated this job.

§

Taylor closed the book and set it on her lap. She'd read the first page twenty times and still didn't know what it said. She picked up the too light to-go cup and set it down again. Empty.

Afternoon sun angled through the window making the

car toasty warm. Yawning, she looked at the dash clock. Phil had been inside an hour and a half. Searching would probably take longer than that. Cochran's surgery would probably take that long.

Please, God, let him be all right. He didn't deserve getting hurt any more than Sister Margaret and Sharon Tatro had. In her mind's eye she watched Cochran flinch and fall. Saw Sister Margaret. There'd been so much blood with Sister it was hard to remember anything else. Cochran hadn't bled as much. Did that mean he had a better chance? Please, God.

She turned from her thoughts and searched the windows of Sean's house for signs of life. Had they found anything? The house looked so ordinary. White two-story. Black shutters. Ubiquitous arborvitae flanking the front step. Normal. Boring. Not like the house of a monster. But looks were deceiving. Sean didn't look like a monster, either. She hoped they'd find something solid. Something that proved, beyond a doubt, that he was the mole and killer. Something to give closure to Father Charlie, Sharon Tatro's family, and Phil.

As she watched, the front door opened, and Phil came out carrying a box. They had found something. But Phil wasn't smiling. His face was grim and pale. She opened the door and climbed out, meeting him on the sidewalk.

"Something's wrong. Is Cochran okay?

"What?" Phil looked confused. "No. No call." He preceded her to the car, opened the back door, and placed the box on the seat.

Taylor looked at him closely. Neither Phil's color nor his expression improved. "And you found evidence, right?"

"Yeah." He closed the door. "We found evidence."

"Solid evidence?"

He turned to her and sighed. "Yes, Taylor. Solid evidence."

Cold invaded Taylor's bones. He was shutting her out. "What's wrong? Is it the evidence? What did you find?"

He got into the driver's seat, leaving her to get into the

passenger seat.

She took a deep breath and held it.

"We found Sean's ex-fiancé, Therese."

"Dear God. I'm sorry." She let go her breath. Finding a body was good reason for shock and distance.

"And these." He reached in his coat and drew several photographs from his chest pocket.

She flipped through them. The first were nice, unposed shots of a younger, unaware Phil—studying, standing on a bridge, walking down the street. Next, came the puzzle-piece photo—two photos trimmed to become one. Odd, but nothing too weird.

The next photo showed Phil in the shower. His face covered in soap as he rinsed his hair, his lithe body turned slightly away from the camera. His sculpted butt in full display. Her hands began to shake. She turned to look at Phil. His face was green-tinged. His bruised eyes stared helplessly into hers.

Certain she didn't want to look at the last photo, she reassembled the stack.

Phil nodded at the stack, silently insisting she turn to the last photo.

She blindly opened the pile to look at the last photo before lowering her eyes.

She'd seen Phil sleeping in the nude often during their married life. But the fact that Sean took a picture of him like this... Her stomach flipped.

She opened her mouth and closed it again. Words failed her.

He stared at her, expectantly. His eyes pleaded with her to help him understand. To make this better, somehow.

She didn't know how to do that. "Sean is in love with you."

"God, help me." He slumped in his seat.

She handed the pictures back to her husband face down. "It clears up the question of why he was targeting me, though."

"Jealousy."

She nodded. "I had what he wanted. He probably

hated every second you spent with me."

"I told him I was withdrawing from the project because you and I were going to try to have a baby. I told him how hands-on I wanted to be—diapers, feedings...I probably pushed him into action."

"You can't take the blame for any of this. He was twisted. You had no way of knowing."

He winced.

"You aren't responsible for his obsession any more than you are for those murders." She took him in her arms and held him as he cried.

EPILOGUE

Cochran double checked the address before pulling his car into the driveway. Phil said the new house had shaped up nicely. No shit. Brick and glass with a spacious front porch and lush garden. Talk about curb appeal. Cochran didn't know much about architecture or landscaping, but Phil and Taylor's new house looked like it should be on a magazine cover with the headline "A House to Come Home To."

He carried the six-pack of beer up the stone walk.

Phil opened the door. "Come in, Cochran. Glad to see Jackson finally gave you a day off."

He stepped inside and looked around. It was just as nice inside. Slate tiled entry, deacon's bench with a coat rack, family photos. Made him want to kick off his shoes and yell, "Honey, I'm home."

He handed Phil the beer.

"Thanks."

Taylor joined them in the family room. "Welcome." The hard ball of her stomach made her lean in to hug him. "Congratulations on the promotion. Now that you're a covert agent, do I need to call you something else? Mr. Smith, maybe?"

He grinned. "Cochran will do. If I told you my code name, I'd have to kill you."

She smiled back at him.

She looked so damned good. Healthy. Glowing. Hugely pregnant, but without the tired look his sisters-in-law got. He looked at her closely. There was something different about her. Something he wanted for himself. He knew he was staring. "You look…"

"Huge?" She blushed and caressed her belly. "Yeah, I know."

"No." He shook his head. The shadow that lived in her eyes when Phil had been gone was missing, but it was more than that.

Phil draped his arm around her shoulders, and she

settled against him. It hit Cochran. It wasn't her. It was them. "You look...you both look...happy."

She beamed at him and turned to Phil. The look that passed between husband and wife was so intimate, so loving, Cochran felt like he was intruding.

They answered as one. "We are."

THE END

ABOUT THE AUTHOR

Laurel Bradley believes prayers really do get answered. After eleven years of writing, Bradley has finally achieved her dream of seeing her stories in print. Crème Brûlée Upset, her contemporary romance novel, was released in early 2008. A Wish in Time, her time-travel romance novel, was a 2010 Foreword Magazine's Book of the Year Award Winner. Bradley, who lives in Wisconsin, graduated from the University of Wisconsin-Eau Claire with a Bachelors of Arts in English. When she isn't reading, writing, or painting with watercolors, she's cross-country skiing or decorating Ukrainian Eggs.

Please, visit Laurel online at www.laurelbradley.com.

www.ingramcontent.com/pod-product-compliance
Lightning Source LLC
Chambersburg PA
CBHW070304260626
47160CB00003B/707